Salt & Pepper Man

Charles Puccia

Salt & Pepper Man
Copyright © 2020 Charles Puccia
www.charlespuccia.com
Published by Carduna Publications

Paperback ISBN: 978-1-7345948-0-5
Audiobook ISBN: 978-1-7345948-1-2

Edited by Ben Way (benjaminway.co.uk)
Copy edit and proofreading by Ian Howe
Developmental mentoring by Caitlin Hensel, Dorrance Publishing
Cover design by Emiliano Molina
Typesetting by FormattingExperts.com

* * *

If you enjoyed reading *Salt & Pepper Man*, please rate this book or leave a review for other readers. It means a lot to me—and to Vinnie, who is busy investigating crimes at BIG with Blanca, and complicating his relationship with Ben.

Other books in the Vinnie Briggs series:

Chapter 1

No tourist expects the Mafia to greet them on arrival in Sicily for their Italian vacation, including Vinnie Briggs. But that's what happened, and much more.

It began with his arrival by taxi at Hotel Mezzogiorno in Giardini Naxos, a coastal resort two hundred and fifty feet below the Taormina, Sicily's most famous tourist destination. Vinnie was meeting up with his husband Ben Hausen, who'd arrived the week before to help co-chair a body-building and fitness expo. Vinnie spent the previous week sightseeing in Rome.

He looked forward to the Sicilian vacation and the extra time Ben had promised him. *We'll repair our deteriorating relationship, I'm sure*, thought Vinnie, having faith in the power of pasta, vino, and hot sex as a magical panacea. He also knew this wasn't just about their marriage but Ben's declining mental health. His own depression too, if he was honest.

Everyone said Vinnie was cheerful, funny, kind, highly intelligent, and a generous person, but his work as a private investigator on corporate espionage and embezzlement cases had jaded him. The few murders he had worked on nearly destroyed him.

And if not for Ben's support in those horrendous times, Vinnie couldn't have coped, and he acknowledged his debt to his husband's generosity with money and advice. He did the same for others. And yet he was smart and cultured, not an attribute usually associated with a person of his insanely huge size and ripped muscles.

After a week touring Rome, Vinnie arrived ready for action, assuming Ben had completed his committee organizing. He imagined Ben had put the polishing touches to his guest posing routine. *He's done at least twenty shows over the last few years, so this has to be a piece of cake.*

Vinnie stared out the cabin window as the Rome flight came into land at Catania Fontanarossa Airport. The glistening Mediterranean blue water below intoxicated him. He beamed watching the airplane's tiny shadow skip along the arid Sicilian landscape. He was smiling for no apparent reason. He disembarked, skipping to baggage claim, and wore his million-dollar grin all the way in the taxi until reaching the Hotel Mezzogiorno entrance. He beamed widely, throwing his arms out as if hugging the air.

A minute later his broad smile dropped onto the hot pavement. Two men moseyed toward him, which he took to be an illusion brought on by the bright sun. But a yelling voice dispelled that hypothesis.

"Can't be. Is that Vinnie-fucking-Briggs? Fucking unbelievable. Hows ya' doin'?" shouted a bulky, lumbering figure from thirty feet away. The big man was dressed as if returning from a carefree shopping spree at a gangster clothing store. He wore an oversized, garish, light-green T-shirt over brown baggy joggers. An old pair of dirty sneakers were on his feet. A silver chain encircled his seventeen-inch neck and garishly clashed with his gold wristwatch.

Holy shit, thought Vinnie, *it's Al Renato*. Vinnie's heart pounded like he was running a marathon yet he wasn't moving. "Howsabout yourself?" replied Vinnie, demonstrating his fluency in Brooklynese. He added with a wide smile, "Nice chain. Suits your outfit," knowing Al wouldn't pick up on the sarcasm.

The second man waited to speak until within four feet of Vinnie. His elegant dress suggested he'd just come from an Italian fashion magazine photo shoot. His light pink knit shirt fitted perfectly over black jeans. A white straw fedora sat on his head. He removed his designer sunglasses exposing long eyelashes that framed smoke-green eyes. Eight years since their high school graduation and Vinnie never forgot the gorgeous Paul LoBianco.

"Hi, Vinnie. What a pleasant surprise," he said, tuning up for a melody. "Wonderful to see you, and in Sicily of all places. It's been a while." His eyes roamed over Vinnie. "Wow, you're looking good."

"Hey, Paul, you too. Put on some weight... I mean in a good way. Been working out?" Vinnie asked.

Paul nodded. "Started lifting in college but I couldn't compete with these guys." He pointed to a large banner hanging outside the hotel entrance, which read:

MEDITERRANEAN INTERNATIONAL
FITNESS AND BODYBUILDING EXPO
IFBB Pro-qualification Contest
Guest Poser: Former Mr. Olympia, Ben Hausen

"Ben Hausen? Isn't that your husband?" asked Paul.

Vinnie smiled. "Going on three-and-a-half years. This is a delayed honeymoon of sorts, combined with Ben's work."

"Belated congratulations," said Paul.

"And where is he?" asked Al, looking over Vinnie's shoulder at the departing taxi. "I've heard a lot about him…"

I'll bet you did back at mob HQ, Vinnie thought. "He's co-chair of the expo."

Al nodded his head as if he understood, which Vinnie knew would be a first. His mind flashed back to their St. Mary's Elementary School days. Al mumbled stupid answers to the nuns' questions. "How should I fucking know New York ain't the capital of New York?" resulting in a boxing lesson from the pugilistic Sister Mary Alice. The day he was expelled, Sister Mary pronounced, "Dumbest kid I'd ever taught." Vinnie thought Al had the last laugh as brawling with the sisterhood introduced him to the mob enforcement profession.

"We leave in a few days, so I'm afraid we won't get to see your husband's performance. I would have enjoyed that. Maybe we can meet for drinks before we go," Paul said.

"He's pretty busy," answered Vinnie, lips straining to smile. "Take a raincheck for New York?"

For all Vinnie's dislike of the mob it didn't extend to Paul LoBianco. In his mind, Paul was a default mob guy by being Carmine Aquafreddo's nephew, the head of the Brooklyn mob. But Paul wasn't Al. He didn't hurt people. Vinnie accepted this rationalization to square the past, what with him and Paul being best high school buddies. Paul wasn't a bad man. *He saved my adolescence from going down the toilet, but drinks with Ben isn't on the cards.*

As if on cue, Ben walked out of the hotel's front door. He hugged Vinnie and kissed him on the lips. "Good, you've arrived in time for me to catch you. I left a note for you in the room which—"

"Uh, Ben," said Vinnie interrupting, "these are... uh, old classmates." Vinnie half-turned to face Al and Paul with no intention to make introductions. Too late. Ben turned and stuck out his hand.

"I'm Ben Hausen. Pleased to meet old friends of Vinnie."

Paul shook hands and introduced himself. Al latched on to Ben's hand, tensing his forearms. Al's nostrils flared. *Yeah,* thought Vinnie, *typical macho bullshit trying to prove yourself equal to Mr. Olympia.*

Al relaxed his grip but Ben squeezed harder and Al's lips twisted. Ben released, shooting a grimacing toothy smile.

"*Youse* pretty damn strong. I crush most guys," said Al, staring at his hand as if expecting to see bruises.

Ben half-turned to Vinnie and tilted his chin toward his extended palm transmitting the message, *what the fuck?*

Vinnie mouthed, "Later."

A ringing tone brought a phone from Al's pocket. "It's my cell," he explained and no one commented. He walked toward the parking lot holding the cell phone to his ear.

"About later," said Ben, looking directly into Vinnie's eyes, "it's a note I left you in the room. But you're here so I'll tell you. One of the expo organizers, Mario Volpe, owns a gym in a local village. On my first day he invited me to visit. Mario has a regional reputation and is a pretty decent bodybuilder. Anyway, I did the usual drill talking to his club members, taking selfies, and gave them a little show.

Gym-boosting stuff. Mario's fitness center is well equipped and I've been using it every day. He's invited me to stay for dinner with his family after my workout. I'll be back around ten or eleven. I'm sure you understand."

"But you promised we'd have dinner together on my arrival," said Vinnie, his eyes narrowing.

"I'm know and I'm sorry but this is important," Ben said.

Paul backed away to inspect the expo poster font up close.

Vinnie's fists clenched. Ben was reneging, not just on dinner but on his promise to spend more time with him in Sicily. He wasn't meant to be doing grueling gym workouts. This wasn't supposed to happen. This was the time to improve their relationship as well as Ben's mental state.

Ben looked over Vinnie's shoulder to the circular drive. "Here's my ride."

The driver stepped out, elbows on the Mercedes' roof, shouting, "No rush, we've plenty time."

"Thanks, Victor, I'll be over in a sec."

Vinnie glared at Ben. "You texted me to get an airport taxi because the limo driver—Victor—was occupied. And yet there he is. I stood twenty-five minutes in a line." Vinnie's skin prickled.

"Not Victor's fault. He's the only way I can get to Mario's. You know what? Forget it. I'm going to be late."

"I'm on my way," he said to Victor then called out to Al and Paul at the end of the path. "Nice meeting friends of Vinnie."

Al and Paul came over to Vinnie, who was still dazed by Ben's departure. Paul flashed a smile. "Looks like I'm alone tonight too. Al just got a call saying he's needed in Catania on business."

"Yeah," blurted Al, "so I thought to myself, why don't the two of *youse* go to the concert?" Al's ridiculous grin suggesting the novelty of his first and only original idea.

Paul's eyes and eyebrows rose together. "What Al means is that we have a pair of tickets tonight for a concert in Taormina and it appears you're free." Paul's eyes and head shifted to the limo pulling away. "I'd be more than pleased if you would join me."

"I've got a last-minute work thing. A change in shipment," piped up Al, his forehead lines bunching up as he searched for another idea.

Paul's lips stretched thin and he turned to Al. "Wait. What did you just say? You told me loading details, not a shipment change. If that's the case I'll need to come and do a shipping addendum." Paul's voice rose.

"Nah," grunted Al, "it's more in my area."

Paul pulled Al aside and Vinnie entered the hotel entrance to let them get on with their bickering.

"Fuckin' mob talk," he said under his breath entering the lobby. "And fuck Ben."

Chapter 2

Waiting in line behind two couples at the hotel check-in desk, Vinnie tried to forget about running into his old childhood friends, a blink in history. He tried but couldn't, especially not Paul. They'd been inseparable in high school. Even after Vinnie came out as gay they stayed good friends. And he had secretly desired Paul. Their time together diminished as high school girls hounded the gorgeous Paul LoBianco, and his teenage hormones willingly obliged. His weekends were reserved for dates, leaving Vinnie solo to cheer the school sports teams or finish projects. But they always had their weeknights for gaming sessions. *At least he never went steady until his senior year or I'd never have seen him.*

Yet Paul stood up for Vinnie against the gay-bashing school bullies. *He could have dropped me but didn't. And I really wanted to date him like one of his girlfriends. I was so naive.*

The hotel clerk called out, "Signore, per favore. Signore? Your turn. I am ready to help you."

The words broke Vinnie's reverie. It took a long two minutes of frustrating garbled conversation in half-English and half-Italian before the clerk understood Vinnie wanted to be in Signor Hausen's room and not the suite next door.

While the clerk went to the office to retrieve a magnetic keycard, Vinnie took a copy of *La Sicilia* from the counter. A single large photo took up the entire front page, and it showed two women's corpses in a refugee camp outside Caltanissetta. Vinnie was nauseous seeing the drab brutality of twisted, blood-soaked clothes. The women's arms splayed out to their sides as if pleading. He wanted to wretch. Tears filled his eyes. He empathized with the loneliness of refugees in unfamiliar place. *Just like me when I hid in San Francisco from the mob.*

The clerk handed Vinnie his keycard and asked him about his dinner selection that was included in the *pensione completa* meal plan.

"Signor Hausen did not give us his choice. And of course you have just arrived. You can choose both now."

Vinnie swallowed hard. "Just me. Signor Hausen will not be dining here tonight. Can I tell you later?"

"*Certo*, but before seventeen hundred," said the clerk, pointing to five on the wall clock. "Someone will bring your luggage to your room in a few minutes."

Vinnie didn't answer, disheartened by his own words. His first meal in Sicily would be alone. *Great.*

He felt dizzy. He wiped sweat from his brow. Was it from the suffocating sirocco heat, the dry African desert air descending on Sicily like another migrant crossing the water seeking refuge? The taxi driver had told him during the journey from the airport that not even Sicilians get used to the sirocco but they expected it like they did invasions, beginning with the Greeks and now the boat people.

He gave *La Sicilia* one more look, a farewell to the women who the day before were alive and had hopes of a new beginning. *Don't we all,* Vinnie thought.

Vinnie's thumb jabbed the elevator button. "This vacation's a fuckin' disaster already," he mumbled. On his fifth jab of the button a hand wrapped around Vinnie's wrist. He turned to a beaming face.

"I'm sorry about leaving so abruptly," said Paul, gesturing to Al standing outside smoking. He released Vinnie's wrist and his thumb rubbed Vinnie's with a protruding bump, the kind sustained after a break.

Vinnie massaged his wrist.

"I'm truly sorry about what happened to you," said Paul looking down and releasing Vinnie's wrist.

What happened? thought Vinnie. *Does he mean the airport taxi fiasco? Or Ben leaving me to dine alone?*

Paul continued, "It had nothing to do with me. I didn't know until I read about it in the papers."

Vinnie's head jerked and he gaped at Paul's sorrowful eyes. All the New York dailies and online media had reported Vinnie's near-death beating by the mob that Paul and Al worked for. *I'm getting an apology from Carmine Aquafreddo's nephew. I wonder if Uncle Carmine approves?*

"As you heard," continued Paul, not noticing Vinnie's blank stare, "Al has an unscheduled meeting in Catania tonight," he said, shaking his head with lips puckered to distort his handsome features.

An unplanned, sudden meeting that Paul didn't know about alerted Vinnie's PI antennae, adding to his witnessing Al shove Paul. He'd been wary from the first moment he saw Al, and to some degree Paul—old friend or not. He couldn't just dismiss their affiliation with the Aquafreddo mob, the one that had wanted him dead. Was the phone call to renew the contract on him? Murder on an installment plan?

In Vinnie's line of work, sudden changes were a bad omen. In several of his corporate cases the suspect's abrupt change revealed important clues. Vinnie's best friend and former boss had teased him saying, "You don't trust people, do you?" And Vinnie responded, "That's right. I've met them."

Paul continued, "Al was explaining that... well, it doesn't really matter. The point is we have tickets for this evening's concert in Taormina's Teatro Greco and he can't make it." Paul's voice cracked, his face stiff. "So I'm left with a spare."

Vinnie watched Paul's hand comb his thick hair and tilt his head. *Something's wrong,* he thought, then he mentally slapped his own face. *I'm on a fuckin' vacation. Stop analyzing.*

"Vinnie," said Paul, his face relaxed, the gentle smile returned, "what do you say? The performer is a popular Sicilian singer and songwriter."

"Carmen Consoli?"

"Yes! How'd you..." Paul lightly punched Vinnie's arm. "Of course, you'd have planned your itinerary and researched local events like a good PI."

Vinnie's lips parted as if awaiting words from his brain.

"You're surprised I know about the Briggs Investigative Group? BIG's the acronym, right?" asked Paul, tapping his nose. "I love it. A homage to your husband?"

Vinnie nodded. "Easy to guess once you meet Ben." His eyes narrowed. "But why have you been following my company? What were you looking for?" Vinnie asked, eyes blinking.

Paul's smile broadened. "Are you always this suspicious? There's nothing sinister going on. I read a *Wall Street Journal* article on you and BIG along with a couple of million other readers. You were always the smartest among us." Paul stopped grinning. "So want to come with me or do you already have tickets?"

"I tried. Sold out," said Vinnie. "I searched online for scalpers but a friend warned me that in Sicily nothing is real even if you buy from the box office. Too much fuckin' Mafia control... I'm sorry, I shouldn't have said that."

"No, it's fine."

"I'm tired," said Vinnie, breathing hard. *Maybe a concert's just what I need to take my mind off Ben.* "I don't know. Frankly, Paul..." Vinnie bit his lower lip and thought that going out with someone associated with the Aquafreddo mob was a bad idea.

"Paul, after what happened... your uncle... I'm not really over it if you know what I mean. And you're one of them. Sorry, I'm fuckin' stupid. That didn't come out right. Seeing you and Al, well... it's all coming back. That was a tough time for me."

Paul patted Vinnie's arm then put a finger to Vinnie's lips. "I understand and I only wish..." He paused, taking a deep inhale through his nostrils. "Wishing can't change the past. It's just another form of regret."

With a glance over Vinnie's shoulder, Paul's head tilted to

the large glass window and Al puffing on a cigarette. He and Vinnie stepped back from the elevator as the door opened. A man twice their combined size came out with a woman clutching his arm. Vinnie recognized the bodybuilder from a previous competition.

"Is there any way you might make an exception… uh," said Paul giving a quick glance at Al. "Join me for dinner and the best seats in the amphitheater." Paul handed Vinnie his business card. "My private cell is on the back. Call if you change your mind. There's something I want to share that I think will surprise you."

Vinnie tilted his head, a questioning look on his face.

"Only if you come tonight," said Paul laughing. "You forget I'm a lawyer, I know how to negotiate." Paul put a finger to his lips.

He heard Al calling, "You ready? I've got to get going if I'm to be in Catania by five."

Paul lost his smile and exhaled hard through his nose. "Meet me, please. There's something else… I can't talk here, not now with…" Paul's head nodded at Al as he approached. "It's something that might shock you… no, that sounds trivial but it's very serious. You'll understand more than anyone."

Paul said goodbye with hands pleading. Al shouted, "See ya' around, Vinnie."

By the next morning, one of them would be dead.

Chapter 3

Vinnie found Ben's note in their room. He read the same litany of excuses Ben had recited outside. Why should he be alone while Ben dined out with gym chums? Paul was an old friend. Technically in the mob, but was he really?

He never thought of Paul in that way. He'd known him since childhood. The Paul LoBianco he had known would never have harmed anyone. Could he have changed that much since high school?

Vinnie unpacked his luggage but before he finished he pulled Paul's card from his wallet. A partnership business specializing in international import/export. Paul didn't do contracts on people but legit legal work. *He had said he knew nothing about the attempt to murder me and I believe him.*

Paul answered his cell on the second ring.

"What time is the restaurant reservation?" Vinnie asked.

"Vinnie, this makes me very happy. I'm sure you'll enjoy the evening with me—it'll be just like old times."

Vinnie sat on the bed's edge and rubbed his forehead. *What did Paul whisper? Something about if I joined him he'd tell me a secret that would surprise me? Or did he say shock?*

Vinnie embraced the delusion that this was a night out

with an old friend and not a Mafia kingpin. And nothing close to betraying Ben. *How could it be? Paul is the proverbial straight arrow as I'm sure many women would testify.*

* * *

Al Renato walked up the metal steps to a small warehouse mezzanine office with an indoor window overlooking a loading area below. Overhead fluorescent lamps flickered. Six men circled a small desk cluttered with papers, an ashtray filled with cigarette butts, a desk lamp, and an empty pencil holder. The last time the walls were painted was around the time Archimedes was taking a bath in Syracuse.

Al stood behind the single seat in front of an old wooden desk, his hands resting on the chair back. Nino Ferro, Al's Sicilian contact, stood behind the desk. His upright stance, shoulders back, and neat button-down long-sleeve shirt tucked into dark trousers made him seem taller than Al despite being an inch shorter.

Behind the desk sat an old man who looked older than his sixty-odd years. His thin, gray mustache appeared to crawl out of his nostrils, struggling to reach the ends of his upper lip. Al had never met the head of the Catania mob but he knew the man behind the desk was without doubt Don Mimi Ragno. This wasn't protocol and Al's palms sweated like when Sister Mary Alice was in close proximity. Don Mimi inhaled air by sucking through his gaping mouth to reveal a row of crooked teeth with uneven gaps. Weather-beaten lines checkered his face like a veil. He placed his hands flat on the desk as if to keep himself upright, exposing liver spots on top of a dark complexion from too much sun.

15

Flanking the desk on opposite walls were two cattle-stock men with grimy, stern faces, their bodies perpendicular to Al while their heads twisted to face Don Ragno. Their baggy jeans overlaid with loose-fitting shirts didn't fool Al. They were packing.

A portly man wearing a suit that made him look like a lawyer was, in fact, a lawyer, *Avvocato* Sandro Grattinato. He didn't smile or acknowledge anyone but stood directly behind Don Ragno. Al was in this grubby, dank room because of Nino Ferro's instructions. "Come to the Catania warehouse alone, not with Paul. Get here after the siesta. Action is need on the cargo and there's no time to waste."

Al knew this was not a routine shipment change, because as Paul had noted if it were then he should be here. He arrived puzzled by two phrases during the phone conversation. "Action is needed" and "There's no time to waste."

What action? Why the urgency? The scheduled shipping date wasn't for another three days. What gnawed at Al's brain the most was that all meetings were arranged before leaving New York. The routine never varied: meet the distributors; check on the product; confirm delivery method. Paul prepared the international and governmental transport documents to meet regulations. The same regimen they had followed for two years. Never a change, never a problem.

"Is something wrong with the product?" asked Al, looking at the portly *Avvocato* who was the Sicilian legal counterpart to Paul, except that he undertook illegal work as well.

Al pulled the chair from the desk and started to sit.

"Stay standing," said Nino in a stern but not unfriendly way.

"What?"

"*Per piacere*," said the old man. He inhaled, then repeated Nino's words. "Stand up." His English had a strong Italian accent. The old man lifted his hands off the desk, turning the palms over, and slowly moved them upward to the ceiling as if levitating Al.

"We need to check you're not wearing a wire," Nino said.

Al snorted his disapproval. "You fucking with me? I've been here before. You know me."

"*Per piacere*," repeated the old man with a soothing inflection that did not hide an implicit threat.

"It's necessary. I'll explain once our man confirms," said Nino.

The beefier of the two guards moved behind Al and patted him down. Unlike Americans with a sense of decorum, the man had a long, hard grope of Al's genitals, causing him to jolt.

"Hey, you a fucking queer?"

The guard nodded to Nino and said, "*Va bene.*" He smiled and added, "*piccolo*," wiggling his pinky. The other guard laughed but Don Ragno's stern look quickly wiped away his smirk.

"You can sit now," said Nino. "Don Ragno doesn't speak English very well so I'll explain for him."

"Just tell me what the fuck is going on," Al said as he leaned back folding his arms across his chest.

"Don Ragno received some disturbing news from Don Aquafreddo," Nino said using the formal honorific for Carmine Aquafreddo that was never used in New York outside the *Godfather* movies.

Al unfolded his arms and leaned slightly forward.

Nino continued. "There's, what's the word, *traditore*..."

"Traitor," offered Al.

"No... *pentito*... uh, informant," said Nino, who smiled as if he had passed a high school English exam. "You have an informant in your organization and we needed to check you for a *microfono*."

Nino Ferro's finger ran along his breast pocket. "They can be very small these days and hidden in many places." He tapped his crotch.

"Wire. I get it," said Al. "And now you know I'm not fucking wired. So who's the informant?"

"Ah, the big question. Your companion, Mr. LoBianco."

Al threw out his arms and yelled, "No fucking way. He's Carmine's nephew. Have you all gone mad?!"

Nino jiggled his index finger and clucked his tongue. "Not us. The very uncle you mention called Don Ragno," said Nino, tilting his head to the old man sitting behind the desk.

"Paul LoBianco informs the FBI and they inform our Commissione Antimafia."

Al stood up, placing his hands on the desk and screaming, "Fuck! Fuck! Fuck!"

The two guards stepped forward but the old man waved them off. Al sat again, shaking his head.

"We must eliminate this threat. Your boss says we should do it before he leaves Sicily and you must help."

For a half-hour the men discussed possible scenarios. Al added an occasional sentence that drew no comment. With a nod from Don Ragno, Nino explained the plan.

18

The assassination would take place in the early hours of tomorrow morning. This kept the FBI from noticing Paul was missing until he failed to board the New York flight. Al would be out of Italy by tomorrow night, before the Commissione Antimafia found the missing *pentito*'s body.

Al folded his arms, unfolded them, and tapped the desk with one finger. He was to shoot Paul. He stared at his hands.

"Want to test out the merchandise before you return?" said a cheerful Nino, pointing to a small Ziploc bag containing a white powder.

It took Al several seconds to understand the conversation was no longer about the assassination of Paul but routine business.

"Nah, I prefer your local Sicilian pieces of ass. You know who I mean, right? Serafina and a good bottle of wine might calm me down."

"We anticipated this," said a beaming Nino. "Serafina was advised in advance and primed to provide you with extra pleasure."

Al stood but didn't move far. He liked Paul. They'd known each other since kindergarten. They played street ball. He was fun, easy going, and smart as fuck. What a waste. He'd miss him.

Nino escorted Al out of the warehouse and one of the bodyguards handed him a Glock. Before they reached the exit a voice called out.

"Wait!" yelled *Avvocato* Sandro Grattinato.

"Don Ragno asked me to pass along to you *un consiglio*— a piece of advice," said Grattinato, his eyes straining with a look of constipation.

"Yeah, what? I know what to do," said Al.

"This is something else," said Grattinato. "Don't expect Don Aquafreddo to thank you. Stay out of his sight for a month or two. And don't attend the funeral. Send flowers but nothing too big or showy."

"Yeah, sure."

"And one more thing. Go back to Giardini Naxos tonight."

"But what about Serafina?"

"I'll let her know about the change of plan."

Driving back he thought this had worked out well. *Paul's with Vinnie so he'll not see Serafina arrive.* Al slammed the heel of his palm into his forehead. *I fucking forgot to tell Nino about Vinnie!* He shrugged while taking the autostrada entry ramp.

* * *

Serafina Melloni arrived in all her glory at Hotel Girasole an hour after Al. She had a sexy vibrance and a wiggle of her pinky or her fluttering eyelids created havoc in men's loins. In Al's opinion, her only fault was incessant and unintelligible chatter and not understanding English except for a few words.

"Who doesn't speak English nowsadays?" he asked her. She replied with a shrug, a smile, and threw out her chest. Al forgot his question. His eyes surveyed every inch of Serafina as she sprawled nude across the bed. When he reached her toes she stood to uncork a bottle from her family's vineyard. Al passed the time finger flicking her nipples.

"*Salute,*" they said in synchrony. Al's large swigs emptied his glass in two and Serafina refilled it. He thought it odd she stirred his wine with a spoon. *A crazy Sicilian bullshit tradition or something?*

She wrapped her legs around his waist like cling wrap. He couldn't pull away, not that he wanted to. He finished the rest of the wine. She squeezed him like she was testing melons in the market. Al's eyes dimmed as his bladder informed his brain that he needed a toilet break.

He returned from the bathroom somewhat morose, realizing this was his last time with Serafina. He couldn't come back to Sicily. *Fucking snitch. Fuck Paul LoBianco.* He swigged the rest of his wine and Serafina poured him yet another. He didn't need more drink, he needed her. He nuzzled every area of her naked body. After a few minutes, he said he needed to lie still. The room was spinning.

"How strong is that stuff?" asked Al, slurring his words.

"Shh... *non ti preoccupare,*" said Serafina, watching Al's eyes slowly close. "Don't be concerned," she said in perfect English. When he awoke from his drugged stupor he'd notice her gone, making him very concerned until he was dead.

Chapter 4

Vinnie said the concert was exhilarating and Paul agreed. "Could you believe that setting? Magnificent, like being back in ancient times," said Vinnie, showcasing all his teeth with a smile that ached. "The ancient Greek/Roman theater and a full moon high in the dark sky."

"And what about Etna's red firestorm? It was like fireworks, only better," added Paul.

The exiting, intoxicated crowd filed out of the amphitheater to choke the narrow ancient street singing their favorite songs. Paul held Vinnie's hand as they walked, supposedly to prevent separation along the clogged, one-way pedestrian path. Vinnie thought the touch more than friendly but he didn't pull his hand away.

Entering the piazza in front of a massive Roman gate of the ancient walled city of Taormina, the crowd dispersed. Paul had arranged a car to take him and Vinnie back to Giardini Naxos. Inside the car, Paul directed the driver to Vinnie's hotel.

Both men turned their cells on during the descent that was slowed by the late-night concert traffic. Paul read his messages quickly without comment. Vinnie cursed reading his single text.

Staying out with local BBs from the gym.
Back late. Don't wait up.

"Everything okay?" asked Paul.

Vinnie didn't know what answer to give. A "no" wasn't enough. He leaned toward Paul. "Can I come to your place for a nightcap?"

"Ah... you sure? I asked during the concert and you declined. What's changed your mind?"

Vinnie muttered, his eyes briefly closed. "I'd like to talk. I could use... a friend. Get things off my chest. Are you a friend?"

"Vinnie, how can you ask that? We've been friends since grade school. Even after all this time I feel like it was only yesterday." Paul hesitated and lowered his eyes. "I know, there's my family connection. I'm not... fuck it, Vinnie. I'm not them, I—"

Paul broke off. The palm of his hand covered his lips as if he was about to cry. He closed his eyes for a few seconds, lips slightly upturned, then his eyes opened and he grinned.

"Actually, this is a good time to tell you. The concert wasn't the right place. I'm gay."

Vinnie laughed and clapped. "I knew it all along! I was right in high school!"

"How?" Paul asked.

"Back then? I don't know. Probably wishful thinking. Now? At the concert you looked at people taking their seats, but not the women, only the men, the good-looking ones. And you touched my thigh at least once... nothing more than tap but it was... uhm..."

"Strange?"

"Unusual. And you could have gone to the concert alone or found a 'date.'" Vinnie made little air quotes with his fingers.

Paul lightly punched Vinnie's arm. "And I've dated some men that... uh..."

"No, I don't want details," said Vinnie, holding up his hand, then chuckled, "Unless you want sex with me."

Paul's mouth dropped open.

"I'm just fuckin' with you! We missed that chance by about eight years." Vinnie's attempted laugh didn't make it past his lips.

Paul went quiet, his eyes narrowed, and he moved his mouth nervously. "There's something else, the second thing I said I'd tell you."

"It's okay if you'd rather not," Vinnie said.

"No, I want to." Paul stretched his arm across to hold Vinnie's hand. "It's, er... serious. Look, let's have a few drinks first." Paul looked out of the side window.

"What? Now you have to tell me."

"I will but this isn't the place," said Paul nodding toward the driver. "And I thought I knew how to tell you but now I'm not sure where to begin. It's complicated."

Vinnie looked away. He knew from his clients that if they said something was complicated, that meant something bad had happened and they were choosing which lie to tell. He rubbed Paul's arm.

"Let's start with you," Paul said, turning in his seat to face Vinnie square. "Tell me why you agreed to drinks. Something urgent to talk about, wasn't it? Clearly not sex but I'm open if you've changed your mind."

Vinnie didn't even smile at Paul's silly innuendo. His sucked in his cheeks and twirled his wristwatch.

"Take your time. Mine isn't so easy to explain either. Let's get at least one drink down before we begin."

Vinnie pulled out his cell phone and texted Ben.

I'm having a nightcap after the concert. Don't wait up.

The sedate hotel bar played low-volume background music. The entrance led first to the bar then across a wooden dance floor large enough for six or seven couples and on the other side a dozen tables and booths. The room echoed with conversations, interrupted occasionally by a burst of raucous laughter. No one worried about their conversations being overheard because no one cared.

Vinnie and Paul took a vacant table in the far corner. Paul ordered a bottle of wine, a local Sicilian, one of his export client's vineyards. They talked about the concert, which was followed by chit chat. With the second glass poured, Vinnie leaned back.

"So, you want to go first or should I? It seems like yours is more urgent," Vinnie said.

"And yours isn't?" asked Paul, his lips hinting they'd blossom into a beautiful full-blown smile.

"Yeah, you've got me. So do we flip a coin?" asked Vinnie.

"No, you go first. I need more time to think and drink this." Paul pointed to his glass of wine.

Vinnie took a short gulp of his then took the glass with both hands.

"He's ignored me for months. Not exactly ignored but, well, to be open, our sex has been like doing laundry." Vinnie paused. "And he's returned to bodybuilding—full immersion."

Paul nodded then said, "But wasn't he a bodybuilder when you first met?"

"Yes, but he was at the end of his career. He entered a few contests, mostly while I was in California, so it didn't really affect me."

Vinnie stopped seeing Paul's frown and wished he hadn't mentioned California, dredging up the memory of being beaten into a coma called on by Paul's uncle. "I'm sorry, I shouldn't have—"

"No, please don't be. It happened and it was wrong and I..." Paul stopped. "Well, I already told you I didn't know, so go on about Ben."

"Yeah, okay. You saw it. The fuckin' day I arrive and he's out for dinner. Isn't that a goddamn fuckin' kick in the teeth?"

On his third glass of wine, Vinnie ordered another bottle as he embarked on a full-blown rant about Ben's obsession with his posing for the expo. "He's treating it like he's a contestant," Vinnie said, swishing his glass. "Do you know what it means?"

"Uh-uh, I guess not," muttered Paul.

Vinnie droned on with details, including his suspicion Ben was heavily into steroids. Paul's eyelids drooped and his index finger traced imaginary figures on the tabletop.

"He's using chemicals too, I'm sure of it. He'll have health problems and not just physical but mental," Vinnie said, with two fingers tapping hard on the table as he continued to talk loud and fast. In the middle of his sentence the room went quiet.

Vinnie and Paul's heads turned to the bar. A woman in a tight, strapless dress and black high heels headed across the dance floor—Serafina. As she neared their table, Vinnie saw her dress was a composite of skin-toned fabric and translucent material in strategic areas that left nothing to the imagination... or everything. Her lemur eyes siphoned all the colors out of the dark room.

She bent over Paul and said, "*Ciao, bello*," in a voice that guaranteed eternal damnation that was probably worth it. She turned to Vinnie and gave him a nod. "*Salve*, pretty boy."

She draped an arm over Paul's shoulder and leaned into him while her eyes rested on Vinnie. She drank from Paul's wine glass, then whispered words in his ear.

Vinnie coughed and the woman turned to him.

"*Caro*, I must take Paul with me for a minute."

"What? Can't it wait?" asked Paul.

Serafina shook her head and spoke softly, with Vinnie catching only a few words. "Need... time... contract... come now."

"I approved and signed all of it. This is—" Paul didn't finish as Serafina tugged his arm.

"Now, and don't argue," she said, loud enough for Vinnie to hear every word as if she'd used a megaphone.

She walked over to Vinnie, sweeping her fingers up and down his neck until they rested around his throat. She leaned forward and in her sibilant voice said, "*Grazie*," and

Vinnie would bet a year's salary nothing about her met Vatican II standards.

The woman looped her arm through Paul's and steered him outside.

"What the fuck?" Vinnie muttered to himself. His thoughts turned inward. All night he'd been trashing Ben to Paul, exposing his husband's personal tragedies. *I'm being unfair to Ben? Once this expo's over he'll listen and get professional help. I just need to be more patient, more tolerant.*

After five minutes, Vinnie thought, *Where the fuck is Paul?*

Chapter 5

"Serafina, *che cosa*?" asked Paul as she tugged him along. "What's wrong?"

"Shh," she said and placed a finger to his lips.

This was not protocol. She never showed herself to him in public. She pulled him along until they stood before the closed hotel kitchen doorway.

"Everything's changed," Serafina said, her brown eyes growing bigger as she spoke.

"I'm with Al," she said, pointing a finger to the ceiling. "I put a Valium and half pill of Rohypnol in his wine. He'll dream for a few hours, giving you enough time to get far away."

"You drugged Al? Serafina, this is crazy. You'll blow my cover," Paul said while frantically gesticulating with his hands.

Serafina gave a long exhale. "Too late. They know," she said, looking over Paul's shoulder down the empty corridor.

"That can't be right. I've been careful."

"It's true. I heard Al on the speaker phone. You know he thinks I don't understand English except a few words. *Cazzo*, fucker. Do you know what he does to me? He—"

Serafina stopped talking to wipe her mouth with the back of her hand. "He's what you call a dumb fuck. And a bad fuck too."

Paul stopped her. He didn't want to hear this. He disapproved of her method of gaining inside information but neither he nor anyone else could stop her. She chose the call-girl role, learning more in the bedroom with mob heads, prominent judges, and politicians than any recording device.

"Just tell me what happened. What's changed?" Paul said, his face twisted.

"Al's orders came directly from Brooklyn. Your uncle Carmine Aquafreddo told him to *eliminate* you tonight." She sneered at the euphemism.

Paul gaped. He knew Al would follow orders; that's why Carmine gave him the Sicily assignment. Yet he found it hard to believe. They had known each other since elementary school. Even if not best friends they still had a bond. And he couldn't imagine his uncle would cause his beloved younger sister grief over the murder of her only child. Paul couldn't square the reality of the cruel mob world with his of love, friendship, and protecting real family—not the fabricated pseudo families of thieves and murderers.

Serafina snapped her fingers in front of Paul's eyes.

"Hey! You hear me? You need to hide—now. Don't waste time, get gone. And who is the man with you? Does he know?"

"Leave him out of this."

"I can entertain him while you leave. Show him something… different."

"No!" said Paul louder than he intended. "And anyway he's gay, like me."

"And you don't think I've managed a few gays? You did it with my sister and she said you liked it."

"Once."

Serafina grinned and lightly slapped Paul's face. "I think more."

"Okay, twice. But that's not the point. Vinnie is… fuck!" Paul didn't mean to say his name.

"Don't worry, your friend Vinnie is safe. I like him and I'll protect him too. How much does he know? Who knows he's with you? Are you lovers?"

"Lovers? I wish," said Paul, and knew he had spoken too freely. He avoided solecism as a lawyer as well as in his personal life.

"Vinnie knows nothing and let's keep it that way."

Paul stopped and took a breath. "Wait, Al knows about Vinnie. He knows we went to the Taormina concert together."

He looked at his shoes like a boy being admonished. "I was going to tell Vinnie about what I'm doing." Paul wiped his face. "Al will guess I told Vinnie, especially if I go into hiding."

In a calm voice, Serafina said, "Get rid of Vinnie and do it quickly. Tell him to avoid security cameras. You both leave separately and in different directions. Be smart if you want to protect your friend."

A sheen of sweat formed on Paul's lip. "Vinnie won't be safe once Al tells them about me and him."

"I'll keep him safe, and don't worry about Al," she said with a peck on his forehead. "He won't be telling anyone."

How can she be so sure? Paul asked himself. In seeking an

answer he felt Serafina put ceramic salt and pepper shakers into his hand.

"What's this?"

"I don't know, but Al had them in his pocket when he undressed to show me his overcooked pasta belly," Serafina said with a shudder.

"A souvenir?"

"He said Nino gave them to him."

Serafina rode the elevator to Al Renato's room for the last time. Paul didn't want to go back to the bar. He wanted to rewind the evening. Make a different decision. Wish he had taken Vinnie to his room. Made love to him. Now he had to say goodbye and not reveal that this was their last time together.

Vinnie was pouring his fourth glass of wine when Paul returned. He refilled Paul's and held it out to him as he placed the hand-painted ceramic salt and pepper shakers on the table.

"I've got to go."

"What? But—"

"Sorry. Business," said Paul.

"Now? At this hour? I'm not stupid."

"I know. But it's important and can't be helped." Paul took the salt shaker, wrapped it in the hotel's monogrammed cloth napkin, and handed it to Vinnie. "Take this as a remembrance."

Vinnie looked at the napkin, the evening turning surreal. Why a gift? What business could he be conducting at this late hour? Had he misjudged Paul?

Vinnie was about to raise his questions when Paul held

out a hotel keycard. "Use this to exit through the guest pool gate."

"Why? Won't you need it to get back into your room?"

Paul gave a joyless smile. "I have a spare card for special companions. It's important you do as I say. Please."

"Her. She's the reason, right? Is she going to your room?"

"No to both your questions, or at least not as you think."

"What does that mean? Is she Mafia?"

This time Paul's smile was genuine. "Absolutely not."

"Then who is she?"

"Serafina. A sister to my associate here. Strictly legitimate business."

"Dressed that way! Every dick in the room stood at attention when she moved her ass across the dance floor."

"That's a bit crude, isn't it?" Paul didn't hide his irritation. "Sorry, I didn't mean to snap—"

Vinnie interrupted. "You're right. It was crude even if it is true. She, I mean Serafina, is… just… well, when a gay man notices that means something."

Paul gave a wry smile, thinking of Serafina's offer. Vinnie might have enjoyed the experience. "Yes… well, Serafina's a long story for another time."

Vinnie stared across the room. "You said you had something to tell me. Something serious that might shock me, isn't that what you said?"

"It'll have to wait, there's no time now. I have to go and so do you."

"Is this about contracts you have to sign? I think that's what I heard your friend Serafina say."

"Vinnie—"

"Just say something," implored Vinnie.

"Okay. It's about my uncle Aquafreddo and something I've done. Now you have to go. Tell no one we met, and that includes Ben. It's important you do everything I've asked."

Vinnie gave Paul a fleeting glance as he turned to stare into his drink. He didn't understand. They were having a good conversation even if it was mostly about his problems with Ben. Paul proved to be an excellent listener, saying all the right things in all the right places. And this dismissal, which is what it amounted to, didn't seem right. What had Paul done?

Chapter 6

"What fuckin' happened?" Vinnie asked himself at the Gira-sole's private pool. He followed a path around the perimeter to the parking lot onto via Lungomare. He glanced toward his hotel then turned away to follow a line of cars crawling past in a midnight traffic jam. He walked a few blocks, hearing the din of raucous laugher ahead. He merged into the milling crowd, aged early twenties to mid-thirties. They smoked, cried out, shouted, shuffled, and laughed. Music blared from the nightclub every time the door opened.

Vinnie downed two Peroni sitting at the bar, his feelings bruised by Paul's dismissal. Bodies swayed to Italian pop music he didn't recognize. Two bodybuilders in tight-knit shirts pretended to dance. Two women attached to the men's arms rubbed their hairless chests and made an occasional grope below the belt. These men weren't here to win a contest and they wouldn't even if they tried. Their goal was to get laid using muscles as their Siren song. They lacked Ben's dedication.

And what about Paul? Was he a pretend gay? Was Ben a pretend husband? Several more beers caused Vinnie to stagger out of the club at three-thirty.

To avoid the road, he walked along the beach carrying his shoes in one hand. The cool sand between his toes brought a sensual pleasure. The sky was getting lighter but it was still hours away from sunrise. He trudged slowly across the beach in deep contemplation as he reviewed the night's events. He'd been bothered by Ben's message—clearly he intended to flirt with young bodybuilders. *Should I have told Paul about me and Ben? Was it just talk among friends? Is Paul even a friend?*

He thought of Paul's beautiful face, mesmerizing eyes, and well-tailored clothes that outlined his taut body. He recalled his furtive glances in the boys' high school locker room just to stare at Paul's naked body.

Vinnie's free hand fondled the wrapped ceramic salt shaker in his pocket. He advanced to the tune of lapping waves, an atomistic melding of past and present, Paul and Ben, serenity and turmoil. His surprise at learning that Paul secretly exhibited himself to Vinnie in high school with languorous disrobing, bending to expose his manhood, and stretching to showcase his teenage sinew. In hindsight, Paul should have known it meant as much for him as Vinnie. *If only he had admitted his true nature to himself it'd all be so different now*, Vinnie thought.

And Serafina's intrusion dissolved their serious talk.

And what of Paul's unspoken secret? Vinnie had guessed the subject—the Brooklyn mob and his uncle Carmine.

Vinnie was too drunk to think through the details and turned to morose self-pity. Yet it was he that had ring-fenced the conversation to center on him and Ben. He gave Paul no leeway. And now he wanted to know Paul's secret.

"Damn you, Paul. Why not stay and explain?" Vinnie said out loud.

Halfway across the Hotel Girasole private beach, Vinnie turned to look at the sunflower umbrellas and lounge chairs stacked in a corner hut that were hours away from perfect alignment on the beach by the hotel staff.

He gazed across the sand to the neighboring hotel, Albergo Rosa. Behind it loomed the Hotel Mezzogiorno. He moved from the waterline toward Albergo Rosa and its public footpath to the street. Before he reached the path he came upon a craggy old man with sinewy forearms sitting on a small stool untangling a fishing net. A swirl of police car's blue lights flashed along the alley.

"*Cosa successa*?" Vinnie asked, slurring his Italian.

The old man's eyes drifted up to Vinnie and he placed two fingers to his lips and kissed them, the Sicilian sign for dead. He whispered, "*Assassinato*," and his eyes went back to the net. Vinnie knew the word could only mean a Mafia killing.

"Who?"

The old man shrugged, then looked at Vinnie staring toward the police barrier.

"Polizia di Stato," the old man said, rolling his eyes while letting go of the net with one hand to wave it in a small circle. Vinnie smiled, sharing the same sentiment about the NYPD.

Vinnie knew he should turn around and continue across the beach to his hotel, but it was not in his PI DNA. He walked closer to the barricade, intent on blending into the small crowd that had formed. No one would notice him.

Why would they? He was just another curiosity seeker among a dozen or so others.

He stood behind two men speaking in rapid Italian, too rapid for him to comprehend until he understood one unmistakable word. "*Americano.*"

Sweat formed on Vinnie's brow even though it was still cool and a light breeze blew across the sand. His eyes moistened. *No, no, please God not Paul,* he implored despite having no belief in a deity nor any evidence the body would be Paul. He knew his conclusion was irrational.

Moving closer to the police cordon, Vinnie saw a straw fedora in the sand. He picked it up. It was Paul's, something that he confirmed by reading the Fifth Avenue label inside the rim. Vinnie fell to his knees.

"*Signore, ha bisogno di aiuto?*" asked a man in a white shirt and black trousers.

"Uh... uh, no, I'm fine."

"You're an American," said the man with a voice of authority. "I'm Commissario Delgrado. Do you know the man on the beach?"

"I... maybe... I..." Vinnie said as he stood up clutching the white fedora.

"There's no identification on the body. Are you willing to look and confirm?" asked the Commissario, nodding his head as if giving the answer. "And what is your name?"

"Uh... uh... I'm Vinnie Briggs."

"Then, Signor Briggs, please come with me." The Commissario waved to one of the policemen to lift the yellow tape that surrounded the crime scene. Commissario Delgrado turned to Vinnie. "Is not a pretty sight. Can you manage?"

Vinnie nodded and on the Commissario's signal the medical examiner lifted the white plastic sheet from the body. Vinnie stared at the small hole in the middle of the man's forehead and the pool of blood behind. He exhaled as if he'd been holding his breath for hours. Al wasn't going back to Brooklyn.

Commissario Delgrado grabbed Vinnie's arm as he stumbled forward. Vinnie's hand tightened on the white fedora.

"And?" asked Delgrado.

"That's Al Renato," answered Vinnie, his voice cracking.

The Commissario walked around, fidgeting like a man looking for a cigarette. He moved closer to Vinnie. "Did you know him?"

Vinnie nodded.

"How?"

"We were in grade school together in Brooklyn."

Delgrado gave a short laugh and then returned to his more stoic composure. "And were you traveling together?"

"No, just a chance meeting with him yesterday," Vinnie said, moving the fedora behind his back. Was Paul dead too? Where was his body? Did the Commissario already know about Paul? Would he have to reveal to the Commissario about his meeting with him? Why didn't he just go straight to his hotel as Paul suggested?

After a few minutes, Commissario Delgrado called the same police officer, who opened the barrier and asked him to take Vinnie's details. Commissario Delgrado walked away a few steps then stopped and turned.

"One more question, Mr. Briggs. How long are you staying in Sicily?"

"Another two weeks. I'm here for the Bodybuilding Expo."

This time Delgrado gave a barking laugh. "I'm sorry to say, Mr. Briggs, but I don't think you have a chance of winning."

Vinnie looked puzzled then smiled back. "No, I'm not a contestant."

"You are a… *tifoso*… what do you say?"

"A fan. No, not really. My husband is the chairman and the guest poser. His name is on the hotel poster." Vinnie saw the blank stare and continued, "The former Mr. Universe. Ben Hausen."

The Commissario puckered his lips and bobbed his head as if giving his approval. "Very good. But to be sure, please, I ask you to stay around."

"I have tours planned."

"Where?"

Vinnie rattled them off with the longest a day's outing on Mount Etna. The Commissario nodded approval. Vinnie walked up the Albergo Rosa's path to via Lungomare. Along the way he saw a pack of discarded Marlboro Reds: Al's brand. He picked them up—nearly full and with the health warning printed in English.

Vinnie dropped his clothes in the middle of the bedroom. With his adrenaline rush gone, exhaustion ushered in sleep as he nuzzled into Ben.

Chapter 7

Ben rose early. He gave Vinnie ice-cold looks as he dressed. He decided to skip the shower as he headed to the gym for a two-hour workout. Allowing an hour round trip meant he'd be back at eleven in time to catch up with the lazy committee members just finishing their breakfast or a few leaving their rooms after a night becoming acquainted with a contestant. Ben hated this fraternizing but understood it. Ambitious young men willing to do anything to gain an extra scorecard point. It happened, but under his watch no one won if they didn't deserve it.

Preparing his gear in the next room, he stumbled over Vinnie's clothes discarded on the floor in front of the doorway. He picked them up to place them next to Vinnie's dresser. Amongst the clothing pile was a ceramic salt shaker on top of a Hotel Girasole monogrammed cloth napkin. On the dresser lay two keycards, one from Hotel Mezzogiorno and the other from Hotel Girasole. Ben turned over the Girasole keycard, finding no clue to the room number or owner. His jaw tightened thinking of Vinnie's text about going out for drinks. With that guy Paul? What else did they do?

In the second bedroom Ben gathered his gym bag and added a syringe and three vials. He swallowed two pills of different colors, washing them down with bottled water from the room's minibar. The buzz would take fifteen minutes to come on. He'd inject at the gym to gain full advantage of the steroid.

In the main bedroom he stood a few seconds to stare at Vinnie's face buried into the pillow and a lightweight summer duvet pulled up around his neck. Ben walked to the door and stopped. He grabbed the Hotel Girasole keycard from Vinnie's dresser and went to the waiting limo.

Victor rolled down the Mercedes' driver window in the pickup area outside the hotel and said heartily, *"Buon giorno."*

Ben answered with forced cheerfulness.

"Another beautiful Sicilian day until the afternoon *scirocco* dries us to prunes," Victor said with a happy lilt in his voice.

Flashing blue police domes illuminated the neighboring Hotel Girasole entry.

"What happened?" Ben asked.

"Carabinieri. There's been a murder."

"Who?"

Victor shrugged, one hand off the steering wheel pinching his fingers together and moving them with a gentle wrist wiggle. Ben knew the motion could either mean "Who knows?" or "Who cares?"

Outside the gym and before exiting the car, Ben said, "I have a favor to ask," and handed Victor the keycard he took from Vinnie. "Can you find out who's registered in this room?" Before stepping out he took hold of Victor's headrest. "And any info on the dead body would be useful. Thanks, I appreciate it."

Victor nodded and drove to Hotel Girasole.

* * *

Vinnie awoke with a massive headache, his face blanched, and he decided not to turn on the bathroom's bright lights. He wasn't emotionally upset over Al because they were not close, never were. And he'd seen corpses. Yet a murdered grade school classmate made real an abstract truth. Kids grow up, live, then die. He was mourning in the anticipation of the future deaths of his childhood companions, Al being the first.

His head pounded, joining forces with an unabated fatigue despite seven hours of sleep. Too late for breakfast, which didn't matter as his stomach couldn't take it anyway. His tiredness unabated, he went to the hotel pool, dumped himself into a lounger, and attempted more sleep. But it didn't come. His mind buzzed with thoughts of Al's body and the she-wolf Serafina orchestrating Paul's hasty goodbye.

The most baffling thing was Paul's admonishment to keep their friendship secret, especially from Ben. Why? They did nothing wrong. Did he think Ben might beat the crap out of him as an enraged cuckolded husband? For all his muscles Ben didn't get into fights. Nor was he so stupid as to pummel a mob boss's nephew.

Did Paul kill Al? Vinnie's mind mulled it over. What did he really know about Paul, the adult version, not his teenage friend? *He's gay, but so what?* Lots of guys come out in their twenties or even later. Ben didn't acknowledge himself until after a few years in an unhappy heterosexual marriage. He had a child, for fuck's sake. So no, not uncommon. Is Paul inherently deceptive, a throwback to the family genes? Or using him? A setup? For what? *And where is he now?*

Vinnie dialed Paul's hotel room. No answer. He then dialed his cell phone, which went straight to voicemail.

Returning to his room to change for lunch, Vinnie opened the door connected to the adjoining bedroom to find Ben pushing the two twin beds together to make room for him to pose.

"I asked you to remind the hotel to take out these beds," Ben said while he paced the room. "Where's the special treatment I get as an expo co-chairman?"

"I did," replied Vinnie, aware that Ben's buzzing hornet attitude was a prelude to an argument. He'd seen it before, not just in Ben but with other bodybuilders. A latent side effect of too many growth-enhancement drugs. But Ben didn't do that, not anymore. He wasn't competing. He had promised it was over. Was this a breakdown?

With a sweeping arm, Ben demanded, "What do you call this?"

"Why didn't you take care of it yourself? You've been here a week. You only just noticed?"

Vinnie knew this wasn't about the bed. This petulant, simulated outrage disproportionate to the offense of beds not being moved out. Vinnie reconsidered this as a stoked-up drug-cycle rage. He returned to the main bedroom.

"I didn't need the goddamn space when you weren't here," Ben called out after him.

Vinnie's face flushed red. He'd been through the emotional ringer the last twelve hours. "You wanted to come ahead to prepare. Get everything fuckin' ready is what you said. In my book that includes the room," he snapped back.

"And where are the fucking floor mirrors!" yelled Ben, his voice rebounding off the ceramic floor tiles.

"How should I fuckin' know? You wanted to stay at a fuckin' three-star hotel rather than a fuckin' four-star in Taormina." Vinnie bit his tongue. It was the onset of a cursing match, like their last big one in New York a month before the trip.

"This *is* fucking four stars," Ben said with a TV wrestler's mocking gruffness, his arms folded.

Vinnie returned to the spare room, arms swinging in an arc. "This look like a fuckin' four-star hotel? They get the extra star because of the fuckin' private beach, not for the room amenities." He took deep breaths and tried to remember his yoga mantra. This pre-fight temper tantrum outpaced the quarrels of the last few months.

With hands clasped behind his back Vinnie turned and said, "I'm going to lunch. We're on the *pensione completa* if you hadn't noticed, or do you take all your meals with Mario?" He took some deep breaths and a few steps then turned around. "This has gotten out of hand. Let's start over. I'll get the beds moved and the mirrors brought up."

Ben unfolded his arms, tilting his head to one side, but didn't speak.

"What if we go to a local restaurant and avoid the dining room?" Vinnie asked.

"Can't," replied Ben, his breathing slowed as he kneaded a bicep. "I have an organizing committee luncheon."

45

"Of course you do," Vinnie said. He walked over to the desk stacked with boxes of protein supplements, creatine, nut bars, and vitamin packs. "Got enough?" he said sneering and then he walked out.

Vinnie sat alone at the table reserved for him and Ben, snapping the table napkin open. *I've ignored his edginess for months. I excused his sleepless nights as a sign of grieving for Rita and Gunter. I accepted his cramps, showering two or three times a day, and lack of enthusiasm for sex as part of grieving. And I overlooked the times he'd rush home looking for a quickie.* He had known all along these were signs of drug cycling, even if brought on by grief.

He cut into the rare *bistecca alla fiorentina,* red juices flowing. *What happened to Al? Should I tell Ben? Explain the drinks at the bar with Paul?* No, he couldn't. Before he finished the steak Vinnie's focus turned back to Al. *Why was he killed? And what made Paul leave abruptly after talking to Serafina?*

Returning to his hotel room, Vinnie found Ben pacing in the second bedroom with his shirt removed and walking in circles. Every few steps he stopped to stare at himself in front of a free-standing tailor's mirror. Ben lifted his arm straight out to the side. "No separation. Second rate."

"I see you have the mirror," Vinnie said, interrupting Ben's monologue. "I spoke to the hotel staff before lunch. They'll bring three out of storage and set them up tomorrow. What happened to your committee meeting after lunch?"

"Pathetic. Not enough food so I've just taken two protein shakes." He flexed his sixty-eight-inch chest spilling into the next town. "Cancelled. Too many wanted an afternoon siesta." Ben mumbled several unflattering remarks about the committee members.

Vinnie's hand covered his snort.

"Cut it out."

Ben stopped and did a double-bicep pose. "I look like shit."

"Ben, stop. You look fantastic, bigger than ever."

"Don't patronize me. See this?" Ben held up one arm and with the other hand dug a finger between the layers of muscle nestled between the two medial heads of the shoulder and his trapezoid. "This isn't right. Pitiful."

Vinnie shook his head. "Pitiful is right. You have the best physique in all of bodybuilding. You won the fuckin' Mr. O."

Crumpling on the bed, Vinnie trembled, his chin on his chest. This was an emotional overload. He was sure his cerebral artery was about to burst with the onset of a cluster-fuck headache. The last twenty-four hours had been a roller coaster of emotions. Tears soaked his cheeks.

Ben stopped admiring his armature of gaudy muscle on hearing Vinnie's soft weeping. He stood over him as he lay prone on the bed.

"Hey, what's up?"

Vinnie sniffled his answer. "I so much wanted us to have a good time while we're here."

Ben handed him a tissue. "Stop. You're tired and you worry too much about us. You'll get over it."

The words intended to console caused Vinnie to snap his head back to stare into Ben's eyes. He swiped a tear from his cheek.

"Me? I think it's you," Vinnie said, taking another swipe at his cheek. "There's something we need to talk about. Actually, a few things."

The room phone rang. Ben answered. "Uh-huh. I'll be right down." He hung up and looked at Vinnie. "That was Victor. He's waiting to take me to the gym."

Ben rushed to put on his shirt, picked up his gym bag, and started to leave when he turned to Vinnie.

"Go relax at the pool, have a wine cooler. You'll feel better by the time I return in a few hours."

Vinnie curled into a fetal position for an afternoon siesta. His mind churned during a semiconscious slumber. *What is Paul's shocking second secret?*

Chapter 8

If not for his cell phone's blasting music Vinnie would have slept until nightfall. The illuminated faceplate showed *17:00* on the 24-hour-clock setting.

He raised *la tenda*, the wooden slatted blinds that darkened the room to keep out the afternoon sunlight and heat. Sliding open the veranda door, he stepped into the baking heat of the patio. He returned to the nominally air-conditioned room. He read and replied to emails. Ben entered with a face flushed red and bloodworm veins crawling over swollen arms. "Helluva workout. Did you get to the pool?"

Vinnie looked toward the veranda.

"The gym shower has no pressure," Ben said, sniffing his shirt. "It'd serve them right for me to show up stinking like a goat." Ben burped a laugh. "You okay dining alone?"

Vinnie jutted out his lower lip, his hands clammy, thinking Ben had unpacked six months' indifference from his luggage. He was behaving like this was the good old competition days. Life's purpose was to become bigger and more sculpted than Michelangelo's David. No matter the monotony of life: *food—workout—injections—sleep—*

supplements—more food—more injections—a late workout— food—sleep.

And the cycles. The bulking phase produced an avalanche of muscle; the cutting phase lowered body fat percentage. To go beyond the results of only lifting heavy weights required drugs. The off-season bulking meant testosterone supplements like Cypionate and Deca, among others. The three months' cutting used Trenbolone Acetate, Masteron, and Winstrol, as well as the occasional Clenbuterol. After the contest began the testosterone Halotestin, T-3, and growth hormones.

Vinnie complained to Ben. "All I see is a blend of massive. Each with sequoia legs and *latissimus dorsi* like condor wings." Vinnie nearly laughed out loud at the time he attended his first contest with Ben, thinking it a Fellini circus muscle big tent scene. After the third time he developed a blasé unawareness, like New Yorkers with the Statue of Liberty—it's there, it's the same, it'll be there tomorrow. But he'd learned to see the differences. And cared only enough to cheer Ben to victory.

Retirement meant guest posing, seminars, interviews, and magazine photo shoots, as well as an opportunity to promote his UltraFit gym. The Sicilian Expo was an entrée into organizing.

But Vinnie saw that idea fall apart. Ben had yet to come to grips with the death of Rita and his protege Gunter abandoning bodybuilding.

Always the past haunts us, he thought. With that he realized the same applied to him. He had a past. Paul dredged that up along with Al's death. *Are my days avoiding the Mafia finished? Who's in greater denial, Ben or me?*

"I'm taking a shower," Ben called out, breaking Vinnie's daydream.

"Me too," Vinnie said coyly, building on Ben's good mood. "Should I join you?" he asked, pointing to the shower stall grinning as his hand lowered to below the waist to jiggle his crotch.

"Wish I could but there's no time. I've got to dress and review my notes for the after-dinner meeting."

Ben crossed the room nude into the spare bedroom to flex in front of the mirror with his member stiffening.

"Yeah, looking better," and he turned for a size pose with his dick swinging wide. He continued to speak. "I'll use the spare bedroom's shower to save time and you can use ours."

Vinnie was furious. Ben had a visible libido but no time for sex. Vinnie soaked under the hot water without palliative relief. He bent to pick up the soap bar he dropped and remembered Paul doing the same in the high school boys' shower room. Last night he and Paul had dubbed it the "soap event." The joy of immature high school silliness and seduction. Paul had regretted not following through on the tease but he couldn't, not then. The memory excited Vinnie until the shower turned cold. He'd skip the hotel meal and eat at a local restaurant. Why sit at the honorary table without the honoree?

Vinnie toweled himself dry in the bedroom as Ben walked in.

"You're seeing your old high school buddy for dinner tonight, right? What's his name?"

"Paul." Vinnie bit his tongue. Why had he reminded Ben of Paul's name?

"Yeah, Paul—that's him."

"He invited both of us, not just me. And no, he has other plans tonight," Vinnie said, returning the wet towel to the bathroom rail.

Ben shrugged and pulled clothes from his wardrobe at random. "You're welcome to join me at the committee dinner. There'll be other spouses, all women. I'm sure we can squeeze another setting in."

Vinnie imagined the dinner conversation focused on bodybuilding and war stories of past contests. And what would he do? Mingle with the wives? He wanted to scream "boring." His dignity was affronted.

"No thanks," he replied, not knowing why he responded with civility. "I'll go to a restaurant. I'll be back early to recuperate from last night."

At least he launched one retort. No need to mention the restaurant was a club that served snacks.

"Suit yourself—you do anyway," Ben said, concentrating on filling a briefcase with folders.

Vinnie shook his head and continued to arrange clothing on the bed. He decided on a dark pink, silk long-sleeve shirt—long sleeves being the standard Italian evening attire and certainly not short sleeves and shorts regardless of the summer heat. This wasn't Florida. The white trim collar and white cuffs added flair. *La bella figura*, thought Vinnie. He put on black trousers, black loafers, and slipped his bare feet into his dress shoes.

Ben pulled a short-sleeve knitted shirt over his head.

The 3X size didn't prevent the seams stretching with every arm twitch. Vinnie had often joked that Ben disproved the axiom that all gay men had inherent fashion sense. Ben's off-the-rack look had never bothered him until now.

Vinnie applied more low-grade hair pomade, the kind that didn't resemble 1980s grease but shaped hair to suggest "ungroomed" to belie the hundred fifty bucks spent at a New York hairstylist.

During the elevator's descent, Vinnie studied himself in the polished chrome doors. He adjusted his collar but not his frown. His mother's Italian genes sprang into action in the scorched Sicilian sun to give him a melted butter-brown tan. But under the elevator's artificial lighting his skin had a drab tone.

In the lobby, a redhead blocked Vinnie's passage. She was his height except for heels pushing her upward another five inches. She wore tight black denim capris shredded at the knee to reveal karate-kicking calves. A thin blouse accentuated a bosom that would paralyze a room full of prepubescent boys. Vinnie wondered if he was turning straight. *Nah, it's their wardrobes.*

"I'm Maria Alba Vitale," the woman said to him with a fresh-off-the-vine fruity voice. "Meet me outside. Look for a white Fiat Cinquecento on the street beyond the hotel parking lot." Her swirl befitted a place on the Ice Capades.

Vinnie detested getting orders, especially from cops and strangers. How did she know him? Who was she? After Al's body and Paul's warning Vinnie thought he was hallucinating. Had he been slipped bad drugs? The woman's directness and her swift exit didn't give him time to ask questions or refuse her offer. *I should just ignore her*, he thought, but that wasn't in his nature.

He walked across the hotel parking lot and saw a car's flashing headlights.

Chapter 9

Vinnie rested his forearms on the roof of an ancient Fiat Cinquecento that looked like it might have been in the original *Roman Holiday* movie. He bent at the waist to look down at the redhead who had addressed him in the hotel. She had her hands firmly on the steering wheel. He tapped the glass and she cranked open the window.

"Who are you and why am I fuckin' talking to you?" Vinnie attempted his toughest interrogative tone but the woman's hearty laugh disarmed him.

"I'm Maria Alba Vitale, like I told you. Now *basta* with the questions. Get in."

"No, I will not shut up."

"*Cavolo! Non fai cazzo.* Don't be a fucking jerk. Do as I say and get in. Paul is waiting for you."

Vinnie was surprised at the Cinquecento's front-seat acreage, unlike the rear that would cramp a three-year-old.

"What do you and Paul do together?" he asked, deciding to be blunt.

Silence.

"It's a simple fuckin' question."

Maria Alba wagged her index finger and matched it with

a gritty laugh. "Are you asking if we have sex? What's that movie where Jack Nicholson says, 'Can you handle the truth?'" Her laugh singed Vinnie's ears and he restrained himself from correcting her misquote.

"No, it's not about sex, although I'd be surprised given Paul's gay. I'm asking what connects you?" Vinnie said to avoid being sidelined by Maria Alba.

Vinnie learned that the woman was a lawyer, Paul's Sicilian counterpart. She handled the paperwork to satisfy the Italian import/export regulations.

The Cinquecento squirreled through a small village onto a narrow street with a steep angle that ended at a sheer precipice that looked suitable for hang glider launches. With a single sidewalk on the narrowest street and San Francisco steep, cars mounted the curb to park on the diagonal in case of handbrake failure. The alternative was the municipal lot at the top, but no Sicilian parked their car more than fifty feet from their destination if possible. Maria Alba found an opening a few steps from a small trattoria.

Vinnie saw Paul one step inside the door, his rigid stance suggesting wariness. His head turned from side to side. He'd dressed carefully in a long-sleeved white shirt accented by a darker gray collar and matching cuffs. He beamed a wide smile of pleasure but offset by a clamped jaw that alluded to his concern.

"Thank you for coming. If anyone could convince you to come I knew it would be Maria Alba," Paul said calmly.

Vinnie wondered if Paul intentionally disguised his worry.

"*Grazie mille*, Maria Alba," Paul said, bending forward

as Maria Alba pecked both his cheeks.

Paul took another step back from the entrance. "C'mon in. Food here's excellent. We'll eat then talk."

Maria Alba walked past Paul and Vinnie. "I'll leave you two alone. When you're ready, find me in the big dining room. *Divertivi giovanotti.*"

"What did she mean by calling us boys? And what good time are we going to have? I'm married."

Paul smiled and pulled Vinnie's arm.

"Why are we in this fuckin' one-donkey village, Paul? Are you attempting to seduce me?"

With an arm wrapped over Vinnie's shoulder, Paul said, "Shh... don't listen to Maria Alba. There are many ways to enjoy ourselves. Food is but one."

He ushered Vinnie down the long hallway. On the left side was the "big" dining area with eight tables, one occupied by Maria Alba. Continuing along the hallway was a unisex toilet on the left across from the kitchen. The corridor ended at a small room containing a two-seater table and a credenza against the rear wall.

A waiter at least three inches taller than Paul stood inside. He closed a sliding glass panel then drew a cobalt blue chintz curtain across. Vinnie gave the waiter an owl-like stare.

"What up? Why the secrecy?"

"It's okay," said Paul, pointing to one of two chairs. Vinnie sat down. "We're safe here but I prefer privacy for what I'm going to tell you. Relax and stop worrying."

Vinnie's eyebrows dipped. "Safe? What does that mean? It's not exactly a word to help me relax. The last time you ran away with no explanation and by morning Al was dead. What's going on, Paul?"

"I'll explain everything. Please, let's enjoy a few minutes together. For the antipasto try the *pepata di cozze*," Paul said, smacking his lips, "and for the main course I recommend *branzino al forno alla siciliana*. The fish is fresh and the simple preparation makes it melt in your mouth."

Paul gave him his glistening white-toothed smile and paid him compliments, and despite himself Vinnie returned them.

The waiter took a bottle of sparkling water from an ice cooler on the credenza and filled their glasses. Vinnie waited until he left with their orders then blurted, "What happened the other night? I mean Al. And what about you running out on me?"

Paul squeezed Vinnie's hand. "Good questions and I'll answer them. First, we eat."

"But—"

"Patience, Vinnie, patience." Paul stopped speaking as the waiter entered and opened a bottle of Carricante from a nearby vineyard. Vinnie brought the glass to his nose for a deep inhale. The smell reminded him of a herb garden.

"Good, isn't it?" Paul said. "We'll switch to a special local white called Etna Bianco when the main course arrives. It dances in your mouth."

A seductive aroma floated from the kitchen, breaking Vinnie's questioning mind. He savored each course. The waiter removed the empty bottle, leaving Vinnie and Paul's wine glasses to finish the delicious Etna Bianco, and then brought them their dessert. And for all Vinnie's questions and concerns, he realized he trusted Paul while knowing it was irrational and naive to do so. Lust and desire permeated the room.

"About Al, that ties into what I'm about to say."

Vinnie felt like cold water had been thrown on him. He came out of his reverie, his gut coiled, and he blurted out, "Paul, what are we doing here? I won't be seduced, and believe me it's a strain, but—"

"Me too. We missed our chance back in high school. Under other circumstances I might have tried. But not now, not with what I'm about to tell you."

Intrigue clouded Vinnie's mind. He couldn't come up with a single thought. The waiter brought two shot-glasses of grappa.

Vinnie waved him away. *"No, grazie."*

The waiter thought Vinnie didn't understand and said, *"Digestivo,"* then pinched his fingers together, tilted his head back and slid his hand from gullet to stomach imitating the swallowing of the liquid. Grappa was clearly considered to be medicinal.

Paul downed his in one go. Vinnie followed and thought his entire gastrointestinal tract was on fire. Paul gave a gentle, amused laugh then halted. His face darkened. He reached across the table to hold Vinnie's hands.

"I'm a traitor," he said.

Vinnie drew back his hand from Paul's. His mouth opened to draw bigger breaths. "What!"

"I'm getting out of the organized crime business," Paul said, tugging at his earlobe. "For your own safety, I can't tell you the details, just an outline."

Vinnie picked up his empty grappa glass and stared into it like it was a crystal ball. *Leaving the Aquafreddo mob? Was that even possible?*

"I brought you here, in this clandestine manner... a little too James Bond-ish, I know, but this keeps us both safe. I'm being watched and you will be too if they know of our association." Paul leaned back in his chair.

"They? You mean the Mafia, right? Your uncle and his henchmen?"

Paul nodded.

"And we're safe here?" Vinnie asked with eyes narrowing. "Then why didn't you come to get me? Or stand outside to meet me?"

"I guarantee this is safe for now, but possibly not in another day or two."

"Paul, why am I here?"

"I need your help. You don't owe me anything, but I think of you as a friend. And I regret not being able to stop what was done to you. I tried... no, I'm not going to ingratiate myself to you because anything I did on your behalf had not one iota of influence."

"Now you tell me. You didn't think to call or write me at the time? Not a goddamn fuckin' word. A little late to show remorse, isn't it?"

"You're right. I was a coward, intimidated by my uncle's authority and reputation. I believed if I contacted you it would make matters worse. My uncle is vicious and vindictive. An unscrupulous man, to say the least."

"And you didn't know this before?" Vinnie blurted out. "My life didn't matter. You'd have continued to work for your uncle knowing he kills innocent people or harms them like he did me? That didn't bother you?"

Vinnie crossed his arms, jaw clenched.

Paul sat back. His face sunk, his forehead furrowed, eyebrows lowered forcing his eyes into a squint, and he bowed like a guilty man.

With voice cracking, Paul said, "You're right. I am so sorry. I shouldn't have asked you to come here. I'm just as bad as them. I..." Paul's voice choked.

"You want me to forgive you, is that it?" Vinnie asked.

"Yes, and you know why? Regret is forgettable, heartbreak is not."

"What?"

"I wanted you in high school but denied myself. And when I heard what happened to you..." Paul's voice cracked again.

What the fuck? thought Vinnie. *I can't help Paul, but if I don't try then I'll be the one with a lifetime of atonement for failing an old friend.* Get angry and then forgive was advice given to him once by a very wise person—Ben.

Blood drained from Paul's face and his lips pursed.

"Yes, but... well, what I've uncovered in the last few months is..." Paul stopped and sighed. "My uncle's worse than I ever thought or even imagined. I have to get out."

"Did Al want to do the same?"

"No."

Vinnie stretched his neck and jutted his chin, his eyes red from barely suppressed anger. "I need to know more."

"I'll talk about Al later," Paul said while nodding. "Please, hear me out," he said, staring through Vinnie's eyes and into his head. "I have to finish something before I can make the break and I can't do it the way I'd hoped. I need help from someone I can trust."

"Uh-uh, don't even go there," Vinnie said, calmer than he felt.

Paul's two index fingers tapped nervously against each other before he spoke.

"Hear me out."

"Not going to happen."

"Please," Paul said and he rested his elbows on the table with both hands holding his forehead. "At least let me explain?"

"Be quick," Vinnie said, knowing it was a mistake to listen. He had made this same error several times throughout his career—he'd listen as a courtesy then find himself suckered into something he really didn't want to do. *I should get up and walk out now.*

"I need help from three people, and you're one—"

Vinnie began to speak and Paul held up his hand. "Let me finish please," he said, drawing air in through his nose. "Maria Alba is the second person and the third is Commissario Delgrado. I hesitate with Delgrado because corruption is ubiquitous in Sicily and the Questura's no exception."

"Me? How can I help? I know nothing about your business, not the details—zilch. I'd be out of my depth," Vinnie said. In his mind he knew he'd been right: he should have walked out after dinner. But now he couldn't control his PI curiosity. It's what drew him into the profession.

"You'll be guided. Maria Alba will be the go-between to avoid compromising you and me."

Vinnie glared, his eyes unfocused as if spinning like the balls on a roulette wheel. This isn't the way he worked. He followed Paul's orders at Hotel Girasole and look where that got him.

"Isn't it time to spell it out? What are we talking about exactly?" Vinnie asked with exasperation.

Paul put down his water glass and looked at the table-cloth.

"Look, you're going to have to speak frankly and stop beating around the bush. What is it you're doing or hoped to do?" Vinnie demanded.

Paul closed his eyes. "I'm an FBI informant."

Chapter 10

"Fuckin' hell!" Vinnie yelled. *He's going into the Witness Protection Program to keep his uncle from killing him,* he thought. Vinnie knew what the WPP meant because he'd been offered the same opportunity once. It erased one's life. Friends and family gone forever. He had refused, not wanting to lose Ben or his mother.

"Yes," sighed Paul, "literally a fucking hell." A penitent's relief enveloped his face. "I need help from someone I can trust." He paused for another sip of water. "I did have someone but I had to send him away. He's in hiding. I need you to take his place."

"Who?"

"My former lover and current business partner."

Vinnie leaned back shaking his head. "And that is...?"

"John Margate, Kathy Margate's brother."

Vinnie's eyes drooped. "Didn't you date her once? And later you dated her brother?"

Paul gave a smile. "What can I say? Kathy was from a time before I switched." His smile disappeared.

Get to the point, Vinnie thought. "John Margate's also in the mob?"

"Not like that, no. Er... John kept the Aquafreddo Enterprise, Inc. accounts. My uncle will assume he's helping me. John's gone into the WPP program. They'll not find him."

Paul's tongue moistened his lips. "John and I were going to work together to get all the details the FBI and anti-Mafia teams needed. Neither of us can do that now."

"Do what? I don't get it," Vinnie said, bunching his napkin between his fingers. "Don't you have enough already? If not, why would the FBI consider you for the WPP? I'm guessing you have the financial details, invoices, shipping information, and bank accounts."

"Yes, for the drugs and money laundering, but that's not what I want."

"Huh? I'm lost. What are you talking about?"

"I want to put my uncle and the people that hurt you in prison f-f-for life," Paul stuttered. "And... uh... if revenge isn't enough to motivate you, there are the young girls and boys who have already suffered too much for the crime of being born into poverty or the wrong color on the wrong continent." Paul dragged his palm across his lips.

"Are you talking about the trafficking of African immigrants into Sicily?" Vinnie asked.

Paul nodded, his eyelids shut tight and his lips pressed together.

"In and out. And do you know what people like my uncle and the other mob bosses say?" Paul asked, opening his eyes and not waiting for Vinnie's response. "I'll tell you, and this is straight from an FBI wiretap recording. They boast that they make more profit by exploiting immigrants than from dealing drugs."

Vinnie went into quick freeze. His body and hands ceased moving.

"I won't go into the WPP until I can get the evidence I need to send them down. I can't do it now," Paul said.

Vinnie brushed his hair back, his arm resting on the top of his head. *What is it that Paul needs?*

"Stop beating around the bush. Spit it out."

"You want the elevator pitch? Fine," Paul said, red in the face, picking up the tempo, his voice agitated. "I want to stop the Brooklyn mob from trafficking in Sicilian camps. I want to break the infrastructure so bad it won't be possible to resurrect it. Is that good enough for you?" Paul's voice was angry, his eyes narrowed into snake-like slits.

Vinnie looked away, slouching in his chair. *He's going to melt down. He was always calm and unflustered in high school, never like this.*

"I understand," Paul continued, speaking slower, his voice less edgy. "You think me a bad person because I didn't do anything about the drugs or violence. Maybe I am."

Vinnie's chin rose and now he looked directly into Paul's moistened eyes.

He sat up straight, returning Vinnie's stare. "It's like this. When I learned about my uncle's disregard for human life, I knew what I had to do. In the past I justified my work because I wasn't directly involved with any of it—my hands were relatively clean. I only handled the legitimate international trade."

Vinnie coughed.

"Yeah, yeah. I knew my work supported the other side of my uncle's business. And what about corporate lawyers that attend church on Sunday knowing their clients pollute the environment, run dangerously unsafe plants, or exploit child labor overseas?"

"So that's your excuse?" Vinnie said with a sneer. "Everyone does it?"

Paul gave a short bark of a laugh. "I did, arrogant fool that I am," he said and continued in a voice so soft it was nearly inaudible. "But when I learned of this..." He choked up, tears filling his eyelids that he wiped away with the edge of his napkin.

Vinnie didn't get it. He found the trafficking reprehensible and upsetting but Paul was in anguish.

"What's up, Paul? Really?"

Paul wiped a lingering tear away with a finger.

"I knew a girl in college who'd been a refugee and sold into the sex trade. She got out by luck and the help of one person who cared. We became good friends and have remained close ever since. She's a pediatric doctor specializing in children with trauma now." Paul's eyes watered again.

"What is done to these young girls," he continued, "is unforgivable, and yet I helped to make it possible. I need to make amends. That's what's up." Paul finished with fists resting on the table.

"You must have evidence already," Vinnie said, realizing that Paul had become too emotional and unable to give cold hard facts. "Can't you give what you have to the FBI? Testify at a grand jury?"

"It's not enough to make a legal case if that's what you mean. I don't have solid evidence, just circumstantial bundled up as conjecture. Everything's based on shipping manifestos and hearsay from Maria Alba. This trip was my chance to get irrefutable evidence. I was going to give the FBI and Italian anti-Mafia division the exact staging location and embarkation date. They'd make arrests at the time of loading."

Vinnie nodded, noticing Paul's face was a little less gray.

Paul explained that the change of staging from the Catania warehouse ruined any hope the authorities could get direct evidence of trafficking. "And to make matters worse," Paul said morosely, "they won't bundle the hostages with a wine shipment but with a commodity." He mumbled, shaking his head, that he had no idea what that might be.

"Where?" asked Vinnie.

"I don't know. Has to be outside Catania and large enough to hold thirty to forty refugees for quick loading into containers all at the same time," Paul said, scrunching up his face, his eyes becoming vacant. "That's it."

Vinnie threw his napkin at Paul and his stomach growled despite the *grappa* digestive.

"Where do I come in?" Vinnie asked, quickly adding, "I mean, if I were to help."

"You will, I know it. I love ya!" Color returned to Paul's cheeks and a smile reemerged.

"Hmm," Vinnie muttered.

"Maria Alba and I are going through all the upcoming shipments to narrow down the possible new staging sites. She'll let you know."

Vinnie nodded as if he understood but he had doubts. Sicily was a huge island and lots of places could hold a bunch of refugees before loading into containers.

"I'll need to have the shipment date or at least an estimate," Vinnie said, realizing he was suckered.

"Probably a week, two at a push. The changes have delayed them. It's not easy to move that many people to a new area without someone noticing."

"You'll have to narrow that to within two or three days tops." Vinnie smacked his lips and shook his head slightly as if in meditative reflection. "How is moving people to a new location more difficult than before?"

Paul gave a short-lived smile, explaining that Catania—a Sicilian regional province—issues permits to transport companies to take refugees on day excursions as that reduces tension in the overcrowded camps. With the Catania warehouse exposed, the mob would need to go elsewhere, most likely the Province of Messina that included Taormina, Giardini Naxos, and the northern range of Mount Etna.

"Even the Mafia can't circumvent bureaucratic paperwork," Paul said, grinning.

Vinnie hissed, cupped his two hands, and motioned as if guiding a driver into a tight parking spot.

"Again I ask, what does it all mean for you and me?" he asked.

"For starters, tell no one of our friendship past or present. This isn't going to be dangerous if you stick to that advice," Paul admonished.

"I got it the first time. And let me guess, Serafina is the source about Al murdering you."

A smile crossed Paul's face.

"Hmm," Vinnie murmured. "If Serafina knows so much why can't she find the new location and date?"

"She might have, given more time, but not in her current, er, line of work. Someone would have to ask for her as an escort and be involved with the trafficking. But most of all they would have to be as stupid as Al and use his speaker phone with her in the room." Paul stopped, the color draining from his face. "She saved my life."

"And you're okay that she prostitutes herself for the information?" Vinnie asked, sounding reproachful.

"No, I'm not," Paul said, his tone defensive, "but it's her choice. Believe me, I and others—including Maria Alba—have begged her to stop. She won't until she destroys them. Maybe this will be enough."

"Destroy? Who? Why?"

"A long story. Put it down to revenge for what was done to her family."

How much is revenge here? How much is omertà? *What a strange place*, Vinnie thought. "I'm guessing you were involved in Al's murder?"

Paul looked upward. "You're asking if I shot him?"

Vinnie's eyes narrowed.

"I didn't," Paul said, louder than he meant. He lowered his voice. "The Catania meeting brought on Al's death."

Vinnie's cupped hands invited Paul to spill the beans. He was shocked to learn it was Serafina holding the smoking gun.

"You're kidding me? Fuckin' unbelievable."

"Why? Because she's a woman?" Paul scoffed. "She was taught to shoot by our waiter," Paul said, nodding toward the sliding door. "He took Olympic gold for the Italian marksmen team ten years ago."

Paul's voice lowered as he swirled his water glass. A perfume of rosemary soaked in heated olive oil wafted from the kitchen. Vinnie stared at Paul's doleful slump and thought of what might have been.

As they reached the sliding door, Maria Alba startled them, standing on the other side. "Is everything alright, *tesoro mio*?" she said as she gently pinched Paul's cheeks.

Vinnie's head snapped around to look directly at Paul. "Her! Really?"

Paul's face reddened. "We worked closely for many hours on legal paperwork. It can get boring. It'd be different if you were here," he said with his biggest smile of the last hour.

"Uh-huh. And what happens now? Where do you go?" Vinnie asked.

"Maria Alba has a safe hiding place for me." With those words, Paul hugged Vinnie and gave him a typical Sicilian parting kiss on each cheek.

The Cinquecento sped downhill, headlights parting the darkness, and Vinnie ruminated over the evening's revelations. He'd forgotten to ask Paul about the ceramic salt shaker so turned to Maria Alba.

"First I've heard of it," she answered with a shrug.

Entering the Hotel Mezzogiorno, Vinnie focused on talking to Ben about their relationship in the morning, given the late hour. He had an idea for a different approach to persuade him to seek counseling.

The elevator lurched on startup, causing Vinnie to reach out and support himself against the wall. He wasn't feeling well. As he opened the bedroom door he caught a glimpse of a flickering wall shadow.

Chapter 11

Vinnie stumbled across the bedroom threshold. A dim forty-watt lamp cast a faint shadow over Ben propped upright against the headboard reading his iPad.

"You still up? Pretty late if you're keeping a routine, isn't it?" Vinnie asked with a slight slur.

Once in the bathroom, his gurgling pee and the yellow stream reminded him of the headlights of oncoming cars piercing the Cinquecento's windshield. *Trafficking of refugees! Was it real? Don't tell Ben.*

"The hotel management finally got off their ass and had two more mirrors brought up," Ben bellowed.

"Uh-huh. I had a great supper at a small trattoria," Vinnie said, knowing it wasn't true. He regretted going. He'd just gotten himself into deep fuckin' shit no matter how "safe" Paul claimed it to be.

Ben peered over the top of his iPad to watch Vinnie come out of the bathroom. "I'm not happy with my routine and to be honest my percentage is too high," he said while Vinnie returned to the bathroom to cover up his retching. Ben spoke louder. "I'm at ten when I should be at six or seven."

Again with the body fat, Vinnie thought. He knew Ben's BF percentage by heart but just in case he forgot Ben reminded him at least once a week.

"I need more gym time," Ben said as Vinnie exited the bathroom.

Vinnie picked up his shoes and tossed them next to his nightstand. "I thought this ended in New York?" Vinnie knew this was not the way to start the conversation or the right time, but he couldn't stop himself. He was too wound up. "No one is judging you," he added pointedly.

"The fuck they are. They'll be looking at a former Mr. Olympia and notice all the flaws." Ben's nostrils flared, and his grimace dismissed Vinnie's comment.

There was no arguing with irrationality. That thought triggered the memory of dinner and the trafficking. *Fuckin' Mafia! And I agreed to help Paul. Talk about irrational.*

"I'm exhausted," said Vinnie. "You're Mr. O. They can't take it back. And your publicist will use Photoshop to remove any imperfections." Vinnie regretted his last words. "But of course they won't need to. You're perfect and I love you just the way you are now."

Ben put down his iPad, went to the mirrors in the adjacent room and did a double-bi pose, Schwarzenegger-style.

"Look at these shoulders. They lump up. No separation."

"Don't be so fuckin' stupid. They look great," Vinnie said, knowing he just blew his cool attitude. He went to Ben and rubbed his arms and shoulders. He attempted a kiss and received a push as Ben sprung a side pose, inflating his chest into a slab of squared-off pectorals. "No fucking definition."

"Hey, c'mon. Let's go to bed and let me enjoy those muscles. I'll show you how much they separate," Vinnie said, regaining his composure but hoping he'd say no. He really was exhausted.

"Not funny, Vinnie." Ben went to the spare bathroom and Vinnie finished brushing his teeth in the master bathroom. At least his acid reflux had stopped but not his eyes pulsing in their sockets.

Ben lay on his back staring at the ceiling. Vinnie scooched across into him. He rubbed Ben's massive granite legs then moved to massage his genitals, hard and oversized because of implants to satisfy his former boyfriend's fetish, long before Vinnie.

"I'm not in the mood," Ben croaked.

"I know. I'm just getting your attention. To tell the truth I'm pretty bushed too." Vinnie stifled the urge to say that the "not in the mood" had been the case for a few months. Yet he snuggled up against Ben.

"Not now," Ben said, rolling on his side, his legs tight and ass clenched so that not even a jackhammer could get through.

Vinnie struggled to sleep and awoke after a brief slumber. He couldn't stop thinking of the refugees, the pictures of them drowned and their bloated bodies washing up on the otherwise beautiful beach. And then there was Paul intent on giving everything up to help them.

On the third awakening he moved to the spare bedroom so as not to disturb Ben. He tried to read but found himself going over the same sentences two or three times. He peed in the spare bathroom.

Washing his hands, Vinnie stared into the mirror, leaning over the basin to get a close-up look. An unhappy face stared back. He wiped away tears using toilet tissue and discarded it in the waste basket. A rolled-up newspaper sealed with tape lay inside. Vinnie had no doubt what it was—Ben protecting the maids from getting an accidental prick from a discarded needle.

He unraveled the newspaper. This wasn't supposed to happen. "I'm off the juice," Ben had promised after his final competition, hand on heart.

Vinnie had been relieved. He knew as well as Ben the consequences of continuous drug cycles. They'd attended the funeral of bodybuilders killed prematurely by organ failure. And they knew strongmen turned invalids before they reached the age of forty-five.

Ben promised he had stopped. He devoted himself to training a nineteen-year-old wunderkind called Gunter Hoffman. He'd made him into a colossus in seven years.

Vinnie's mind reflected on the timing. *When did I first notice a change? Maybe nine months after Gunter quit bodybuilding? I should have seen it sooner. Ben was getting bigger than our living room, but he was always enormous so I didn't notice the incremental increase.*

He chalked Ben's mood swings down to depression over losing Rita, her noble death saving the lives of others from a powerful terrorist bomb. Yet Ben was never wild, just full of innocuous unpleasantry or disdain. A few pimples sprouting along his back was nothing much. Or had he covered them with liquid foundation and a colored concealer? His ass wasn't the usual minefield of sores brought on by multiple injections, like before, but again he might have hidden them with another cosmetic formula. He ignored his unabated semi-hard dick and the sudden urge for sex without warning, then a week of more erectile dysfunction. *He denied he was on a doping cycle and I believed him. Fuckin' stupid.*

But the syringe in his hand couldn't be denied. Vinnie opened the spare room desk drawers to find a drugstore of pills, needle boxes, and vials.

Vinnie's body shuddered, the rage rising in him followed by contempt for his false hope that Ben would seek counseling. He skulked back to bed. This wasn't going to work. They'd grown apart, separated by steroids and growth hormones and depression.

Vinnie awoke at nine to find Ben and his gym gear gone. *I should go back to New York, leave him with his fuckin' iron buddies. Would he even miss me? Would he even notice?* Vinnie looked at the ceramic salt shaker on the desk. Paul would miss him. *Could I abandon him? Why not? The Mafia and trafficking isn't my problem.*

Vinnie fumed at himself. He'd yet to renege on a promise and he'd never abandoned a friend. But was Paul really a friend?

He dressed in a boxer-style bathing suit covered by a white Henley three-button short-sleeve top, the bottom two buttons undone. It was acceptable attire for the hotel's *prima colazione* buffet breakfast.

He entered an empty room and his stomach growled with displeasure. He checked his watch. Nine-forty. Serving stopped at nine-thirty.

"Signor Briggs," the *cameriere* said, interrupting Vinnie's stupor. "*Al caffè-bar abbiamo cornetti, brioche, caffè, cappuccino, succo di frutta.*" In other words, "Get lost and go to the terrace café at the pool."

The terrace counter was a din of clanking china plates and cups and a fuzzy fugue of voices. Vinnie put a hand to cover one ear and asked the barista to have his food served on the pool deck. He had a choice of tables and picked one close to the fountain for the serenity of the sound of cascading water, the splashing covering the noise of the café.

Vinnie dipped his brioche into his lukewarm cappuccino and looked beyond the pool to the sandy beach, a reminder of Al. Serafina as the assassin was ridiculous yet true. He tried to picture the scene. Serafina tripping in her high heels, pushing into Al who somehow accidentally shot himself in the back of the head—like a farcical TV sitcom which brought Vinnie a brief smile.

He wondered about Paul being a valuable FBI asset. Wouldn't they know about Al and stop him? And the CIA were notorious for "eliminating" threats, so why the need for Serafina? Not a damn thing made sense.

Vinnie sipped the remains of the cappuccino, wistfully eyeing the crumbs on his pastry plate. Who blew Paul's cover? The leaking Questura? And why didn't Paul go straight to an FBI safe house, given the mob had identified him as the informant? Did safe houses even exist like in the spy movies? Or was the CIA daily rate too much for the FBI budget? Vinnie smiled at his ridiculous ideas but the humor calmed him.

But tranquility didn't last long with thoughts of Paul's very dangerous decisions—screwing with the Mafia was never a good idea even if they were family. And if he helped Paul, then wasn't he breaking a promise he made to Ben about never getting involved with the mob again?

Vinnie squinted, noticing somebody on the other side of the pool moving chairs. Not a body but a Greek Adonis in a postage-size bathing suit. Vinnie's pulse increased as the bronze patinaed torso sauntered across the pool deck on muscular legs, moving with a Lipizzaner's elegance. When the Greek warrior was within ten feet Vinnie saw a tuft of silky chest hair.

The man was hotter than the noon sun. Vinnie removed his sunglasses, which Signor Gorgeous mirrored to reveal chestnut-brown eyes. He flashed Vinnie a widescreen smile.

"*Scusa, ha bisogno di altro?*"

Vinnie smiled at the question. Did he need anything else? He answered, "Yeah, comfort and trust."

"For that I'll need to send out," the beautiful young man said, tilting his head to increase the size of his smile.

"I'm sorry, I didn't realize you spoke English. Forgive me."

"For what? I'd gladly give you what you want if it were in my power."

"And who are you?" Vinnie asked suspiciously.

"Technically, I'm the lifeguard, but we're... how do you say... not too many."

"Short-staffed."

"*Si*, short-staffed so I also help serve from the bar."

"*Grazie mille*," Vinnie said. He wanted to order something extra just to have the handsome lifeguard return.

"You're very welcome."

The man stepped closer to take Vinnie's empty plates away. The proximity of his tight skimpy speedo gave no doubt of his ample package. On turning around, he showcased his smooth ass in case Vinnie missed it the first time. *In the US he'd be charged with indecent exposure*, Vinnie thought.

"And what's your name?" Vinnie asked.

The lifeguard/waiter pirouetted, holding the tray high in one hand, his free arm swinging for balance.

"*Scusa*, Signor Briggs. I'm Gianni Vaccaro. I normally don't interact with the patrons unless they are drowning and then they don't ask for an introduction." Gianni pretended to gasp for air but nothing could hide the mirth in his eyes.

"You know my name?"

"We must. We are told to learn the names of special guests and you are with Signor Hausen, so you are special."

"Well, I'm Vinnie, so you can cut the Signor Briggs bullshit. I'm not an old man."

Gianni's brows bunched into a frown. "*Scusatemi. Mi dispiace.*" The smile vanished. "I didn't mean to suggest you are old. I can see you are a young man. We are told to address all guest in a formal way."

"Yeah, well tell your boss to go suck his thumb. How old are you?"

"Twenty-two, but in *Agosto* I turn twenty-three."

"And that makes me only six years older, actually five-and-a-half. I think you can call me Vinnie. Deal?"

"*Cosa?*"

"It means do we have a deal. *Un d'accordo. Va bene?*"

"*Si*, of course. And I'm available for anything you might need," Gianni said, winking as he placed his aviator sunglasses back over his eyes and walking away.

Did he see me blush?

A large cloud passing overhead dimmed the morning glow. Vinnie pulled out his cell phone and dialed Ben. "The recipient is unavailable at this time. Please try again later." He hung up without leaving a message. *Better to wait until I can see his face to let him know what I think of his needles and drugs.*

Chapter 12

Ben answered his cell, stopping to talk before he entered the hotel's dining room for the midday *pranzo*.

"Hello, this is Ben Hausen."

"Hi, this is Victor. About the Hotel Girasole keycard, it belongs to a guy called Paul LoBianco."

Ben muttered, "I fucking knew it."

"And the dead guy is Al Renato."

"How did you get the name so quickly? Usually the victim's ID isn't released until next-of-kin are notified."

"Simple, it's on the front page of *La Sicilia*. We don't get many dead Americans on the beach round here, especially not one associated with the Mafia."

Cursing didn't satisfy Ben's rage. He pushed open the dining room door so hard it slammed against the wall, bringing the room to a brief silence. He yanked a chair from Vinnie's table while churning out sentences. "Where did you go after the concert? What time did you come to bed? I never heard you. How late was it?" He waved off the waiter about to pour him a glass of wine. "You were out like a light this morning."

Vinnie turned from Ben to get the waiter's attention.

"Do you have Etna Bianco?"

The waiter gave a thumbs-up to Vinnie, who rested his elbows on the table and rubbed his jaw. He'd have a glass of wine before starting his own enquiry on Ben's drugs use.

"Well? I'm waiting," Ben said.

"I sent you a text saying I was going to a bar for a night-cap. As I recall, you also stayed out late, so don't get all sanctimonious with me."

"And your clothes just strewn across the floor? You never do that."

He's controlling the conversation, Vinnie thought while he scraped the tablecloth with his knife.

"Yeah… I, uh… didn't want to disturb you by fussing over my clothes… and you left early," Vinnie said as he moved his knife in a circle.

The food arrived and as if someone had flicked a switch, Ben changed the subject.

"I had a great session at the gym today," he said and gave an arm flex.

"Looks good. You'll give a great performance," Vinnie said as he crunched on a breadstick and poked at his fish. He put his cell phone on the table while giving it a glance.

"Expecting a call?" Ben asked.

Vinnie spooned more food into his mouth.

"Heard from your high school friend, Paul? Couldn't be waiting on Al, because he's dead," Ben said, breathing hard.

Vinnie choked on his fish and coughed. "How do you know that?"

"He made headlines, what with being in the Mafia and all."

The goddamn La Sicilia, Vinnie thought. *Do they have super reporters?*

"I would have told you but you're not around much. And I was never friends with Al."

"And Paul, are you good friends with him?"

Vinnie put his cell in his pocket. "In high school yes, but I haven't seen him since." He hesitated. How much to reveal? "Don't tell Ben," Paul had instructed. "Uh, we talked about touring Mount Etna together while you're busy with the committee and the competition."

Ben gave a twisted smile and tilted his head. "I'm sure you'll enjoy hiking the Etna trail."

"Fuck you, Ben. We're..." Vinnie stopped. He and Paul were not planning on touring Etna and to carry on with this lie risked revealing too much.

Ben used Vinnie's pause to say, "I'm skipping the gym this afternoon to work on changes in my routine. My sponsor sent new posing suits. I thought you might help me choose."

The waiter arrived and held out a bottle of the delicious Etna Bianco to Vinnie who said, "*Bravo.*" The waiter filled Vinnie's glass and started to do the same for Ben, but was shooed away. "No alcohol for me, I'm on a strict diet."

Now, thought Vinnie, *ask about his doping and the needles.* But he hesitated—something told him this wasn't the right time or place. The privacy of their room would be better in case it all unraveled into a shouting match.

"I guess you won't have time to help me if you're going out with Paul," Ben said sarcastically.

"No, actually he's here on business and is pretty busy. I don't think I'll see him again."

"Really?" asked Ben, his voice lilting.

And that was when Vinnie understood. Ben had skipped the gym to keep him away from Paul. Why was he suspicious? And the crack about "hiking Etna" was a thinly veiled code for sex. He should have said Paul had returned to New York to keep Ben from snooping. It was already bad that Ben knew Al Renato was in the Mafia and he'd assume, correctly, that Paul was too.

After eating they walked to the hotel elevator without speaking. In the lobby a man in a lightweight suit approached them with a uniformed Polizia di Stato trooper. The suited man walked up to Ben.

"Finally I get to meet the famous Mr. Olympia. Look at the size of you." Without warning he wrapped his hand around Ben's upper arm. *"Porca miseria,* like a lava rock."

Darkness cloaked Ben's face.

"Sorry, I forgot to introduce myself," the man said with a slight bow at the waist. "I guess Signor Briggs didn't tell you about me. I'm Commissario Delgrado. As you can tell, we Italians like titles. It's a sign of respect, but maybe you Americans are not used to this formality."

Ben's eyebrows knitted, his expanding torso stretching his T-shirt to reveal an underlying labyrinth of sinew. "What we Americans are not used to is people touching someone without asking permission."

The Commissario's barking laugh surprised Ben and Vinnie. "Again, you must forgive. We Sicilians are surely related to Tommaso Apostolo, who I think you call Doubting Thomas. He may have been from Palestine but somewhere he had Sicilian blood running through him." Another laugh.

"We may be worse than him. Sicilians don't even trust our own eyes or fingers. Nothing in Sicily is what it seems, which is how the dramatist Pirandello got the idea for his play. But I digress."

Ben cocked his head and turned to Vinnie.

"I think the Commissario is here for me about..." Vinnie hesitated. "Al Renato."

Ben grumbled, "No fucking surprise there. Your Brooklyn school chum connections coming out of the woodwork."

Vinnie's lips puckered as if about to blow bubbles.

Commissario Delgrado surveyed the hotel lobby as if seeking a stalker, then looked at Ben.

"Did you know Al Renato, Signor Hausen?"

"Like I just said, I met him the day Vinnie arrived. What's this about?"

Delgrado's nod accompanied his holding up an index finger. "We are investigating the murder of Mr. Renato, and Signor Briggs may have information to help."

Ben stared. "And how does this involve Signor Briggs?"

The Commissario gave a hearty laugh. "You not only have big muscles but a big brain. Very good. I like that. Well, Signor Briggs—"

Vinnie broke in. "Cut the Signor Briggs bullshit. I told you before, call me Vinnie. Got it, Commissario?"

Delgrado gave the universal stop signal and said, "*Va bene.*" He puffed and continued with greater solemnity. "As I was explaining, I learned that Signor... I mean Vinnie knew the victim. He identified the body at the beach."

Ben bulleted rage at Vinnie, who suddenly became fascinated with the straps on his sandals.

"Is there a problem?" asked Delgrado. He waited a second.

"*Va bene,*" he continued, his chin angled toward Vinnie's bowed head. "I believe Vinnie can help our investigation. I'd like him to come to the Questura to identify possible suspects."

Ben objected, saying Vinnie didn't know anyone in Sicily. Vinnie's eyes moved from his footwear to face the Commissario.

"Sure." Then he turned to Ben, saying, "This is my fuckin' business, okay?"

Ben's face turned warpaint red. He knew Vinnie had an aversion to police stations and he never volunteered to speak with the cops if he could help it, which made this an intentional dig at him. Ben stood up and marched off with no apparent destination in mind.

Commissario Delgrado offered Vinnie a ride in the Polizia di Stato car.

"No thanks. I get fuckin' hives riding around in cop cars."

Commissario Delgrado barked a hardy laugh and shook a finger at Vinnie. "I like you. I'll see you in a half-hour."

Before Vinnie could take out his phone to call Victor, Ben returned. "What the hell is going on?"

"You heard, I'm helping the police with their murder investigation."

"Bullshit. And the trip to Mount Etna with Paul? That's not true, is it?" Ben's eyes bored into Vinnie. "I'm not fucking stupid." Ben's arm swelled as he banged his fists on both sides of his head.

Vinnie retreated to the pool but stopped when Ben's hand grasped his shoulder.

"Is there something you want to tell me about Paul?"

"Like what?"

Ben gestured to a lobby sofa and sat on the cushions. Vinnie perched on the edge.

"I want to know," Ben said.

"There's nothing to tell." Vinnie's eyelids closed, wishing Ben would disappear. When he opened them he saw Ben hunched, his elbows resting on his knees.

"Vinnie, please don't get involved with him. Look what happened to your friend Al. Keep out of this, I'm begging you. These people are ruthless. Someone innocent always gets hurt."

"Al isn't... wasn't my friend. We went to St. Mary's Elementary School. Nothing more."

"And Paul? Is he more than a friend?"

The question staggered Vinnie. Why would Ben think that? Accuse him of infidelity? If anything, it was the other way around. Vinnie left Ben sitting on the bench alone and phoned Victor. He didn't want to be anywhere in his husband's vicinity so he waited outside in the midday heat. After fifteen minutes Victor drove up to the hotel entrance and got out of the car.

"Hello Vinnie, beautiful day," said Victor. He was far too cheery for Vinnie but even "hello" would have been overly enthusiastic. "Let's get you to the Questura. Don't expect much." During the ride Victor amused Vinnie with police jokes, emphasizing their feeble-mindedness. "Do you know why a Carabiniere was afraid to take a blood test?

Because he hadn't studied." Victor offered a smile but then sank into silence.

Victor parked the car in a shady location near the Questura building. No sooner had he turned off the engine than Victor's phone rang.

"I'm going to the gym. Come get me," Ben growled through the speaker like he was chewing a bag of nails.

"I'm waiting for Vinnie at the Questura."

Ben's growl turned into a roar. "No you're not! He'll find his own way back, or better yet maybe they'll put him in jail."

"No, no, that—" answered Victor.

"You don't know Vinnie. He can get arrested over a parking ticket. Now get your ass back here now."

Victor started the car, his hand lingering on the ignition key after the engine had turned over. Would the Commissario be hard on Vinnie? He would have to check on him later.

Chapter 13

A color-blind designer could not have done worse in choosing the paint scheme for the Questura's interview room. Vinnie smirked. Here's one area where the NYPD has more class than the Italians. He noticed cameras mounted in the corners and a two-way glass opposite him.

The door swung wide open and Commissario Delgrado entered, clicking his tongue. "No, no, no. This won't do. You are our guest and here to help. Please, signore... uh, Vinnie—come with me."

Vinnie followed the Commissario down the dimly lit corridor through the waiting area to the exit. The Commissario looked up at the blue sky as if he'd never seen it before, then descended five steps and walked half a block to Bar Luna with Vinnie in tow.

The café had five round tables outside, each with an umbrella and four chairs. The furniture crowded the sidewalk with two abutting the curb. The Commissario turned to Vinnie. "This is illegal," he said, waving at the tables, "they should not be here, but who is going to issue a penalty to the bar with the best *cornetti* in all of Messina?"

A handful of patrons stood at the counter talking to

a young female barista, her charming smile making her ordinary serving uniform into a fashion statement.

"That's Angela. A beauty, isn't she? The owner's daughter so no one fools around with her. Anyone that tries will answer to him and then me. I am her godfather." Delgrado deepened his voice to add, "I'll make them an offer they can't refuse," and finished the sentence with his now familiar hearty laugh.

"*Ciao, cara. Due granita limone, per piacere,*" Delgrado called out. He turned to Vinnie. "Like the *cornetti*, this is the best *granita* in all of Sicilia. Is lemon okay or do you prefer an ice coffee with whipped cream, *granita cafe con panna?*"

Vinnie stared ahead and Delgrado pointed to a corner table toward the back. "Let's sit there."

"I don't understand," Vinnie said. "I thought you wanted to interview me about Al's murder?"

"*Hai pazienza.* Wait. I'll explain soon enough."

Angela brought the drinks and gave Delgrado a peck on his forehead and began to prattle in Sicilian. Vinnie spooned the lemon ice and took a bite of his brioche. He tapped the side of his glass.

"Yes, you're right. Time for business," Delgrado said.

His voice lowered slightly but not much. He explained that the change in venue was for security. Vinnie shrugged.

"The Questura interview rooms are recorded and the tapes insecure," he said, as if this clarified everything.

Vinnie slurped the remains of his granita.

"I'll come clean. Is that the right expression?"

"Could be. Say more," said Vinnie.

The Commissario explained that his official assignment to the Questura of the Polizia di Stato ran concurrent with his position as Direzione Distrettuale Antimafia da Messina, the Italian Commission for anti-Mafia in the province that included Taormina and Giardini Naxos. The explanation painted a quagmire of interdepartmental issues. Vinnie learned later that in Sicily even a two-person office could stir up workplace politics.

"But I think you know this. *Si?*"

With a nod, Vinnie agreed. "Yeah. So get on with it," Vinnie said loudly and irritated. Heads turned.

"*Niente. Tutto a posto. Non preoccuparvi,*" Delgrado said, waving the back of his hands to the nosy patrons as if shooing a dog away. He turned to Vinnie. "More discretion, please."

Vinnie raised a finger to his lips, bringing a brief smile to the Commissario.

"I know you and Paul LoBianco were together the night of the murder. You went to the Teatro Greco theater. Magnificent, isn't she? A Sicilian treasure." He paused for a reaction but Vinnie remained silent. "And after, you returned to LoBianco's hotel—"

Vinnie's jaw dropped as he gasped air. "How do—"

"Because the hotel barman remembered the impressive couple that ordered two bottles of wine. Don't worry, we have said nothing to your... do you say husband or partner? I'm still confused on the proper words. We don't grass... no, that's English... *rat* is what you say, yes? Anyway, we don't talk about family matters."

Delgrado's belly laugh was louder than Vinnie's previous outburst and heads turned to the Commissario, who repeated his swinging hand and all heads snapped forward.

He knew Vinnie and Paul were at the bar, yet no security videos showed them leaving.

"Either you are ghosts or clever to use the pool exit." Delgrado gave a short hiccup laugh and continued. "Because you knew the pool cameras are... uh... *guasto*..."

"Broken," offered Vinnie, who didn't think a translation violated his personal code of silence when speaking with police.

"Yes, broken. The hotel manager has waited five weeks for management to approve the camera replacement." Delgrado paused, giving an anticipatory smile. "Another Sicilian treasure—the infinite wait before something is done. *La burocrazia.* We have this problem at the Questura. Months waiting for part replacements." This time his lips went to full stretch. "Do you want to know my solution to getting parts replaced quickly?"

Vinnie shrugged.

"Amazon Prime." Delgrado burst out laughing and despite himself Vinnie cracked a smile.

"Good. You are finally relaxing. Now I get to the interesting part, at least for me. I've learned you've been on the wrong side of the Aquafreddo Mafia. You have agreed to help your friend LoBianco." Delgrado paused a second for Vinnie to contradict and when nothing came he continued, "*Ho ragione?*"

Vinnie couldn't deny Delgrado was right on all scores. "Look, I, uh—" said Vinnie stumbling to explain.

Delgrado lost his smile. "We are here," he said swinging his arm around, "because we have at least one person leaking information to the Mafia. That is why your friend LoBianco had to run. A week ago he left a message for me on my office *segreteria telefonica*—"

Vinnie suggested answering machine.

"Yes, that's it. He thought it was private. I had warned him many times to only call my personal telephone. He had tried but I had no cell service. He called my office number and decided to leave a message as it was unimportant nonsense. Except leaving the message was enough to connect him to me. A clever Mafioso—and yes, there are some who are very clever—deduced that Paul LoBianco had no reason to know the direct number of the Commissario of the Anti-Mafia commission," said Delgrado, pointing to himself, "and he would only have it if I gave it to him."

The Commissario's jaw jutted, his eyebrows dropped, his speech somber. "I'm going to tell you the same as I told LoBianco, you only talk directly to me and only call my private cell number. No exceptions. *Capisce!*"

For a moment Vinnie thought he was having a bizarre dream and he'd soon wake up. But he was staring straight into the eyes of a tiger. "Fine, or, as you say, *va bene*. Now, what do you really want from me?"

"To help keep your friend Paul LoBianco alive, unlike Signore Renato."

Vinnie remained quiet.

"And for you to help us find the new trafficking location and date, as Paul explained to you."

"How... I mean you knew I met Paul?"

"Of course. We are his lifeline to the FBI and his ticket out of Sicily to safety."

"Okay," said Vinnie with one hand tapping the other, "but to be honest I'm having second thoughts." He was thinking of Ben's comment, "These people are ruthless. Someone innocent gets hurt." Vinnie stopped and scraped the inside of his empty granita glass with the spoon. "I'm not sure I can help. I don't know Sicily or anyone here."

"But you are a good investigator. I heard this from the New York PD," Delgrado said, rocking his head slightly as Vinnie's mouth hung open once more. "I did what you call a background check on you. I'm sure you understand?"

"Leave out the NYPD. Fuckin' bozos."

Delgrado gave one of his biggest laughs yet. "They told me you might say something like that! I like you very much."

"Yeah, yeah, so what's that got to do with my helping you? You may have noticed I barely speak Italian, let alone Sicilian," Vinnie said without disguising the irritation in his voice.

"You'll get help from me and Maria Alba. Just wait for our instructions."

Vinnie gritted his teeth. No one told him how to conduct an investigation. He decided on strategy. He was a good PI. Even the fuckin' NYPD said as much. Sure, he made a few big blunders now and then but in the end he fixed them to vindicate himself or others. He pushed his chair away from the table and stood.

Delgrado leaned forward, his fingers curling under one hand as if scratching the table and motioned Vinnie to return. "I trust you and so does Paul. If he survives it will be because of you. I believe you want Paul to live."

94

Vinnie wasn't sure if he liked that Delgrado had correctly assessed his feelings toward Paul to reach the spot-on conclusion. He cursed in English and added in a few Italian phrases.

"I'll help, but if anyone innocent gets hurt you'll be sorry you tangled with me."

The Commissario made the sign of the cross. "I know. I've also heard how you managed to get the New York police commissioner to apologize to you."

"Up yours," Vinnie said, and Delgrado smiled while lightly slapping Vinnie's cheek to provoke a begrudged partial smile in return. "You know, I still can't believe Carmine Aquafreddo would put a contract on his nephew. Do you know Paul is the only child of Carmine's sister?" Vinnie asked.

"No, I didn't. But you also don't understand that *omertà*—the Mafia code of honor—is stronger than blood among the Sicilian mob. Didn't you watch *The Godfather*? Pacino kills his brother in *Godfather II*. A good scene. They never should have made *Godfather III*."

Vinnie groaned and raised both arms high as if surrendering.

"The FBI had a wiretap on Renato's phone. He should have changed to an Italian cell. *Babbu. Stupido.*" Delgrado shook his head with his last words to confirm Al Renato was careless. "We know the assassination order came from Paul's uncle."

"Did you order Al's killing?"

"No. This isn't America. We don't shoot first and ask questions later. We aren't looking to give the undertaker more business. God and the devil do that." Commissario Delgrado shoulders drooped. The mirth was gone and his eyes narrowed. "Death is final."

Vinnie searched for Victor's limo and called his number to reach a recorded message. He rubbed his forehead and cursed to himself. He'd have to ask the cop for a favor.

"Looks like I need a ride unless you have Uber?"

Delgrado winked, saying, "Uber in Sicily is the next-door neighbor's daughter's eighteen-year-old boyfriend who has a part-time job at the family restaurant. I'll drive you in my personal car so you won't break out with police *automobile* rash."

During the ride, Delgrado regaled Vinnie with self-deprecating jokes about the police, the Carabinieri, the anti-Mafia division, and the government. He was in good spirits and Vinnie nearly as much by the time they arrived at Hotel Mezzogiorno.

Vinnie's good mood didn't last long. He entered the bedroom and walked through the connecting door to the adjacent bedroom. Ben was in a posing suit and running through his routine. A young bodybuilder sat on a small side chair, too mesmerized to notice Vinnie.

"Oh, hi Vinnie. This is Ciccio. He's Mario's nephew, you know—the gym owner? He gave me a ride back and I asked him if he wanted to see me practice my routine. He's only twenty-four and wants to earn a pro card. I think he's has potential."

No he doesn't, thought Vinnie, who had been to enough contests and visited Ben's UltraFit X-room with its exclusive "serious bodybuilder only" policy. Vinnie knew potential when he saw it and Ciccio didn't have it. He was no replacement for Gunter, who outsized him by the age of nineteen.

Ben flexed then did a half-turn. "This is new. I'm showing Ciccio tips and he's providing critique."

More bullshit, thought Vinnie. Ben wouldn't take advice from a novice.

"Come on in unless you're preparing to meet Paul later? Or writing a report for the Commissario?" The sarcasm dripped onto the tiled floor. Worse, Ben used Paul's name in front of a stranger and connected him to the Commissario. Vinnie left the room and slammed the door shut behind him.

"That kid's as queer as me and his posing has Ben on all fours. Fuck Ben and his fuckin' newbie," mumbled Vinnie to himself.

With a change of clothes, Vinnie went to the hotel's lounge to wait for dinner. He grumbled, his foot tapping an incessant beat against the floor. "Fuckin' stupid sitting here wasting time for a lousy fuckin' hotel meal."

He found a local trattoria that the clerk recommended. He smacked his lips after a three-part antipasto: *insalata di pomodoro, calamaretti fritti*, and *caponata siciliana*. He was waiting for *il secondo*, the main course, when the *cameriere* arrived with a glass of Etna Rosso.

"*Scusa*," said Vinnie, "but I didn't order this."

The waiter placed a wineglass on the table with an envelope. "*Un regalo*—a gift."

Vinnie asked who sent it. The waiter said he didn't know but said in Sicilian, "*che bedda*," while his index finger pulled down the lower lid of one eye, meaning a very good-looking woman.

The envelope contained a ticket for the Museo Regionale Interdisciplinare di Messina and a typed note. "Meet in two days @ 11:30 am in the Caravaggio room. Come alone. Tell no one."

Chapter 14

Nino Ferro had been the one at the Catania warehouse to give that stupid *cazzo* Al Renato the order to kill Paul, not get himself killed. Nino listened to his counterpart in Brooklyn, not sure he understood everything that was said in garbled slang.

"Always knew he was a *chump* but *woulda* thought he knew how to whack someone without getting himself killed. He was a no-class *cugine*. Don't get me wrong, I got no beef with you," said the ranting man.

"Yes, thanks. And we'll handle the next one," Nino said. "We've confirmed his reservation at Hotel Girasole—the same hotel used by LoBianco."

Nino stood guard outside Hotel Girasole with a picture of John Margate texted from New York. Along with Nino was a short, square block of a man with no neck, the one who had searched Al Renato at the warehouse. "Renzo, check the flight again."

Square-block Renzo confirmed the Alitalia flight from Rome to Catania had landed on schedule ninety minutes earlier. The midday sun beat down on the two men and they moved into the shade of a fruit stand with a large overhanging awning.

"*Che cazzo*, Nino," said Renzo. "Where the fuck is he?" He took two puffs of his cigarette. "Call them for god's sake. *Porco miseria.*"

"*Calmati*, Renzo. We'll wait another ten minutes," Nino said. "It's been set up. Al Renato confirmed it with Brooklyn just before he took the hit."

"We get Margate and take him for a ride," Nino said.

"Yeah, great plan by the *cacasodo* shit lawyer, *Avvocato* Sandro. Gives orders as if he's the *capo* and not Don Mimi."

Ten minutes passed and Renzo's bitching and moaning increased. He looked at the photo of Margate. They couldn't have missed him, but they had a backup plan. He went to the hotel receptionist to find out if John Margate had checked in. She said he hadn't arrived.

Seeing Renzo's shaking head, Nino called the lawyer, *Avvocato* Sandro Grattinato. "*Niente.* He's not here. We've been waiting nearly two hours," Nino said.

"*Un incidente sull'autostrada*—a highway accident delay?" asked the lawyer.

"No, I checked."

"Okay, come back. We'll do this another way," Sandro said.

Nino signaled to Renzo to bring the car around.

"That *cacasenno* Sandro shits us more wisdom. I told him we should wait at the airport," fumed Nino.

* * *

Ristorante Roma, halfway along Stillwell Avenue in Gravesend, Brooklyn, was closed until the eleven o'clock opening for lunch. It was a restaurant known to Vinnie and the entire Briggs family, not that they'd been since Vinnie's incident.

The proprietor, Carmine Aquafreddo, sat at a table in the rear of the restaurant, his back against the wall. Beside him was his thirty-five-year-old son Frank Aquafreddo. A thin man, under five foot seven inches, he sat with a vacant, sheep-like gaze that had earned him a childhood moniker of "Pecora." Neighborhood kids soon learned that only the family got away with using that nickname.

On the other side of the table sat Sal Friscollo, a six-foot, two-hundred-and-thirty-pound hulk with reptilian eyes and a circular face as if drawn by a pre-school child with a blunt crayon. His short shirt was unbuttoned to below his sternum to reveal more hair on his chest than on his head, and the sleeves bunched around his shoulder and stretched every time he moved.

"What happened?" Carmine asked. He gulped the remains of his espresso.

"Got a call ten minutes ago from Renzo. Margate never showed up," Frank replied.

Carmine nodded his head. "Smart move. I always knew my nephew to be bright. Got rid of the accountant once he heard we were on to him."

"He's a fucking traitor. We'll see how smart he is when I open up his neck," Frank said, and those words explained his nickname, Gola, from the Italian *tagliare la gola* or to "cut somebody's throat." He took pride in his nickname.

"Hmm..." muttered Carmine, shoving crumbs off his now finished pastry plate. "He's using someone else then.

He can't do it alone. Who?"

"My guess," Friscollo said in his baritone voice, "is it's that scumbag Vinnie Briggs. We messed up not finishing him off years ago." The commentary was a direct stab at Carmine's decision to rescind the contract on Vinnie.

"Why?" asked Carmine.

"I googled events at Giardini Naxos to, you know, cover our bases and it came up with a Bodybuilding Expo. I checked it out. The co-chair and guest poser is Ben Hausen, so if he's there I figure the fag Briggs is too," answered Sal, who tilted his head one degree either side, which was about the full range of motion. "Briggs will be there. He probably gets fucked by the showoff queers just for being with Mr. Olympia," Sal said, straining to smile, but his lips wouldn't oblige.

"Let's be sure," Carmine said, waving a hand at his son Frank the same way he had pushed the crumbs off his plates. "Find out if Briggs is there. He may well be involved."

Carmine remained rooted at his table nursing tea and checking the race forms. Two hours later Frank and Sal returned. They didn't sit.

Frank nodded. "Yeah, it's him."

Carmine looked at Sal for confirmation as if he didn't trust his own son.

"Yeah," Sal echoed, "no doubt. Our guy in the Questura says it was Vinnie-fuckin'-Briggs who identified Al's body."

That clinched it for Carmine. Frank would go to Sicily.

"Kill them both. No, wait. It'd be better to take Paul alive. Find out how much he's revealed and who he's working with. Briggs is of no use to us. Get rid of that piece of garbage."

102

Sal raised his hand as if in school.

"No," said Carmine, anticipating the question. "Not you. Better if we don't have too many of us over there. Frank can identify Vinnie. And nobody will notice Frank, unlike you."

Frank turned on his heels and walked out of the restaurant faster than normal.

"He's eager to start," excused Carmine to Sal.

"Yeah. I suppose Pecora's got to pack quickly to catch the Alitalia flight tonight," Sal said, but he didn't think that at all.

* * *

The Ionian Sea rolled into Giardini Naxos with gentle waves below a full moon and a dark evening sky. The perfect romantic setting, except Vinnie sat alone in bed and was thinking about Maria Alba's instruction for him to go to Messina in the morning. Why set it up for a forty-five-minute drive? Why not Taormina? Should he turn up or do a no-show? He pulled his knees up to his face, stared between his legs into the room and listened to an audiobook through noise-cancelling headphones. He didn't hear Ben come into the room but the glare from the bedside lamp caught his attention.

Removing his headset, Vinnie said, "You're back. Did Ciccio learn anything worthwhile?"

Ben rolled his eyes.

"Good-looking young man and he's developing. Do you really think he has pro potential?"

"Cut the crap, Vinnie. You couldn't care less if Ciccio is the next Mr. Olympia."

Ben undressed to his boxer shorts. He moved to the adjoining room, closing the passage doorway behind him. He returned twenty-five minutes later wiping himself with a towel, his hair wet from the shower he took in the spare bathroom. "I think light exercise at night helps. What do you think?" he asked, doing a side-chest pose then a single-bicep pose. He wrapped a towel around his waist.

"Yeah, looks good," said Vinnie with petulance until he spied Ben's erect penis punching through an opening in the towel. Vinnie put aside his headset.

"Ben… uh… look, I'm sorry I've been acting weird and stuff. Can we try to start again? Make your performance as good as it's ever been and do some fun stuff for us after?" Vinnie nodded to Ben's erection. "Is that a yes?"

Ben's grin wasn't as long as his stiffy. Vinnie had no doubt steroid injections had caused the unusual sexual arousal. Ben tugged at his penis and said, "Just a reaction to the workout. It'll pass."

Bullshit, thought Vinnie. *He's jacked from whatever dope is circulating around his bloodstream.* Yet Vinnie thought coitus with Ben in an overdrive sex state could be a solution. And he was horny so this might be good.

Leaping out of the bed, Vinnie stood swinging his dick, then bent to give Ben a choice view.

Nothing.

In days gone by this behavior would have them tearing at each other. They'd engage in no-holds barred sex. Vinnie became ecstatic every time Ben turned hard, his dick going from pink to red and then pounding him unabated. Then came the day Ben continued after he'd climaxed. It wasn't normal but Vinnie went along with the pretense that this was caused by a new protein supplement or whatever. Absolutely fuckin' bullshit. And by the next week the sex had stopped. He couldn't get hard.

And now Ben feigned no interest and tossed his iPad on the bed. He put on his boxer shorts, tented as if stuffed with a rolling pin. Vinnie recognized the intentional sublimation. In the past, a fully juiced Ben in this state would have fucked their front door keyhole. And five minutes later Ben went to the bathroom with his shorts untented.

Vinnie understood. He had just witnessed a roid-induced surge in libido. "What's up on the stage tomorrow?" he asked.

Ben grabbed the schedule from his night table and passed it to Vinnie without a word or even looking at him.

"Preliminary trials for Woman's Fitness," Vinnie read out loud, which he already knew having memorized the schedule.

"A free day for me then. I'll be at Gino's gym early then stay for lunch to fit in an afternoon workout too. I'll be back for supper then practice my new routine, something different," Ben said with indifference and flexing his pectorals.

"What?! You've got a fuckin' free day and you're not spending it with me?" Vinnie stopped himself abruptly. If Ben agreed to stay with him then he couldn't go to Messina.

"I figured you'll be with your old school chum Paul. Maybe screw him later while discussing the murder of your other buddy Al?"

The accusation burned Vinnie. It was true, the screwing part, in a hypothetical sense, because the way he felt now he would enthusiastically have had sex with Paul until his balls fell off. But Paul was in hiding and sex wasn't on the table.

Vinnie scoffed. "And Ciccio's a nice piece of young ass and he *adores* your muscles?"

"Fuck you, Vinnie. Just fuck off."

"Likewise."

Ben moved to the spare room and pulled open the sleeper sofa now that the twin beds had been removed. Vinnie heard him jerking off. *Yup, strung out on fuckin' growth-enhancing drugs.*

Chapter 15

Vinnie stood outside the hotel waiting for his ride, pacing in front of the doorman. He had seen the same man pass him twice. The guy was big, which wasn't suspicious given the Bodybuilding Expo at the hotel. But the guy's weight was like it would be at the bulking stage, not the lean, contest-ready shape. *Could be a trainer*, he thought.

Across the street at a crosswalk he noticed another stocky man in a bright white short-sleeve shirt watching the traffic passing in front of him, only he never crossed the road when there was a break. Vinnie also thought it odd the man stopped a stranger as if asking directions, but when a woman paused and pointed up the street the man remained rooted in position. He walked away a few minutes later in the opposite direction to where the stranger had pointed. In New York he'd be just one weirdo among many. Was that the case here as well?

Vinnie answered his cell on the third ring.

"Hi Vinnie, it's Victor. I've just dropped Ben at the Torre Rocce gym. I'll pick you up in twenty or twenty-five minutes."

"Is that enough time to get me to Messina by eleven-thirty?" Vinnie asked. "Maybe I should call a cab."

"No, *tutto* okay," replied Victor. "It's only a forty-five-minute drive, fifty tops."

Staring out of the limo window Vinnie gazed across the deep blue Ionian Sea to Reggio Calabria. He then turned over Maria Alba's instructions and read them again. "Go to the Museo di Messina and wait inside the Caravaggio room."

Vinnie thought this absurd yet here he was in a car to Messina. And with a dumb objective—to retrieve documents prepared by Paul and Maria Alba.

"Drop them off at my hotel or scan and send them by email," Vinnie had said to Maria Alba. She negated all possibilities. Email was out since Paul had no internet and she had appointments she couldn't avoid. Sending a courier to the hotel didn't work either as the hotel clerk or chambermaid could easily be bought off. Vinnie begrudgingly accepted her reasons as valid but still thought an alternative would have been possible. That's what he'd have done.

The limo pulled up to the museum with time to spare, just as Victor had promised. Vinnie roamed the museum until a few minutes before the appointed time and entered the Caravaggio room, awestruck by the painter's skill, as he had been in Rome. He focused on the second of the two Caravaggio paintings, *The Raising of Lazarus*. Was this an allegory for Paul? But unlike Lazarus, there was no resurrection from the Witness Protection Program. *Hmm*, thought Vinnie, *maybe this is an allegory of Ben and his drug use.*

Around noon Vinnie decided his contact was a no-show. He stepped out of the Caravaggio room into Commissario Delgrado.

"Magnificent, aren't they?" Delgrado said.

"What the hell? How did you know I was here?"

"Vinnie, please. We are not so backward. I had you followed. I knew you wouldn't contact me, which means you are working independently with Paul."

"You mean that big guy?" Vinnie asked and waited for an answer that didn't come. "Or the one in the white shirt? I'll bet it's both, right?"

Delgrado looked back to the painting. "Do you know there is a story behind this?" he said, pointing to Lazarus.

Vinnie shook his head.

"I'm sure you know that Caravaggio used ordinary people to match the role of the figures in his painting—a real carpenter or fisherman to represent a carpenter or fisherman, not models. For Lazarus he needed a dead body and paid gravediggers to unearth a corpse in early decomposition. The legend is that a local priest uncovered this sacrilege and brought Caravaggio to church. He offered him a drink of holy water reputed to cleanse venial sins. Caravaggio tossed it aside, telling the priests not to waste it on him as all his sins were mortal." Delgrado released a hearty laugh on his punchline and slapped Vinnie on the back.

"Come with me, Vinnie, your contact isn't coming. He must have spotted my team—just like you. *Figuraccia! Minchione!* I work with fools. Idiots."

Taking Vinnie's elbow, Delgrado steered him out of the museum and into the bright sunlight. He suggested they have lunch before driving back to Giardini Naxos. Vinnie said he'd call Victor and Delgrado chortled. "No, my friend. We eat and I drive. We have a lot to talk about. *Va bene?*"

Delgrado parked in an illegal shaded spot twenty feet from the restaurant entrance. The street was empty, with little traffic and no pedestrians, most people sitting for their midday *pranzo*.

The Commissario took hold of Vinnie's elbow and stopped him walking. "Now tell me about the person you were to meet."

Vinnie said Maria Alba didn't tell him, which was true.

"Please, Vinnie, don't play games," Delgrado said.

Vinnie smiled and the Commissario's eyebrows rose. "Then how would you know who you were meeting?"

"My thoughts exactly, but I was told I'd recognize the person."

"How?"

This time Vinnie lied. "From my work."

The Commissario shook his head. "*Va bene*, so don't tell me. I'll learn soon enough."

Fiddling with his fob to lock his car he heard screeching brakes. Delgrado looked up to see a white van abruptly stop across the street. Two men jumped out of the rear sliding panel door while the driver checked the side mirrors. The two men walked into the middle of the street. The shorter man nodded to the other, retrieved a pistol from his waistband and took aim.

The bullet exited the chamber with a barely visible smoke puff from the barrel. But the cracking sound was unmissable. Pieces of stone flew off the restaurant's masonry wall. A second shot, not nearly as loud, smashed the van's rear glass window. The two men scurried back to their vehicle, which drove away with tires squealing, leaving a burning rubber smell in the air.

Whether reflex or training, on hearing the gunshot Commissario Delgrado dove to the ground, taking Vinnie by his arm to pull him along. One of the stone fragments hit his car then ricocheted to hit Vinnie's foot but without force. After the second shot and hearing the van's squealing tires, the Commissario peered from behind the car, then ran into the street to try to see the van's license plate or other distinguishing features. All he saw was that it was white. This was one of those times he wished he carried a weapon.

Vinnie brushed himself off as he stood. He shook his foot and examined his scraped hand. He was shaking, the color drained from his face. "What happened?" he said, but Delgrado didn't hear him.

Across the road Vinnie caught sight of a tall person moving behind trees, probably a man but he was too far to tell for sure. He thought the person familiar but it was too far to see the face, which a wide-brimmed hat partially concealed. The man, if it was a man, had a bag slung over his right shoulder. The figure quickly moved behind a small knoll and out of sight.

"You okay?" Delgrado asked, returning from the road.

Vinnie leaned against the car for support and the Commissario braced him to prevent him from falling.

"Let me see," said the Commissario, pulling Vinnie's hand and also examining his clothing for blood.

"It's nothing," Vinnie said with his hand still shaking. "Just a scratch from you dragging me down. Nothing I haven't had before." Vinnie looked into Delgrado's eyes. "That was for me, right?"

Delgrado nodded.

"That means they know I'm helping Paul, yet I've told no one, not even Ben. He knows I've been with Paul but nothing about what I'm doing. And he wouldn't tell anyone because no one would be interested in me and Paul, only Ben's bodybuilding advice."

"I doubt that," said Delgrado. "People talk when they're angry or upset. Is Ben angry or upset?"

Vinnie didn't answer and forgot to mention the person he saw running away. The Commissario drove him back to Giardini Naxos.

Pulling up outside the hotel he decided he would tell Ben what had happened if for no other reason than to get a hug, if not sex. He needed comforting.

Upon opening the spare bedroom door, he found Ben posing for Ciccio.

Chapter 16

Avvocato Sandro Grattinato listened to the failed assassination of Vinnie Briggs while sitting in a tent in Cara Mineo, a former US military housing base outside Catania. If not for the armed guards patrolling the perimeter, the camp looked like a decaying 1950s American suburb. Rutted roadways brought 4x4 vehicles to a crawl to prevent damage to mechanical parts and internal organs alike.

Grattinato's sour-looking face turned rancid. "How the fuck did it fail? Frank Aquafreddo was there to point out Vinnie Briggs to the goddamn gunman."

The assassin explained he had Vinnie in his sights, an easy hit. "A rare fluke..." *So rare it had never happened before,* thought the gunman.

"I was bumped as I squeezed the trigger, otherwise Vinnie Briggs would be dead." He lit a cigarette thinking, *all because of this dumbass Frank Aquafreddo.* He kept this thought to himself, knowing Frank didn't take criticism well. He'd tell Sandro later. "And before I got off a second shot a bullet shattered the van's window. We were under fire and had to get the fuck out of there."

"You know, this might prove to be better," Grattinato

said cheerlessly and stroked his chin, "because both our moles at the Questura confirm Briggs has Commissario Delgrado's confidence."

Frank was confused. "How is this good?"

"Our guys will keep close tabs on the Commissario, listen to his recorded messages, official notes, and logs. They'll follow him when he travels with Briggs and that'll lead us to LoBianco."

Grattinato peered out of the tent flap. Hundreds of refugees with skin ranging from coal black to light brown ambled past. Their sweat gave their bodies a sheen that glistened in the hot sun. Regardless of skin tone, every man, woman, child, feral dog, or pigeon was exhausted, hungry, and lethargic. They shuffled around guided by the smell of vegetables and lamb cooking on propane grills at the designated *mensa*, the canteen.

Grattinato went outside to think but was confronted by children's shouts as they kicked a football on a makeshift pitch that the Romans once used for a similar sport. Laughter permeated the dirt pile meant to be a playground but the rubble, weeds, trash, and broken glass were more reminiscent of a dump. Cara Mineo camp was for those that left their homes as people and arrived as ghosts in a strange and hostile land.

He scratched his nose, fending off the stink of urine, dog feces, and decay. Grattinato wanted to be back in Catania in his clean office with his good-looking female secretary bringing him an espresso from the local bar. He stared at men, women, girls, and boys boarding a truck for an outing to Catania. Some would be processed out of the camp but most would return at night loaded with food they'd purchased at the local market using their EU refugee stipend or takings from begging.

Grattinato's thoughts were interrupted by a worker showing him a hand-painted ceramic vase ready for shipment.

"How many?" he asked, placing it on a small table.

The worker answered in Sicilian, "*Setti*," and pointed to a stack of seven crates.

"Not the crates, fool. The special cargo," Grattinato said.

"Eleven. We had twelve but lost one."

Grattinato took out his phone and searched for a signal.

"Ciao Nino, we're short one. As far as the other thing is concerned, Frank has an idea. He wants to pressure the bleeding heart LoBianco and force him out or make a mistake. It means losing two more. What do you and Don Mimi think?" asked Grattinato, but his hesitation and clucking made it clear he didn't agree with Aquafreddo, who was listening over Sandro's shoulder.

Neither Don Mimi nor Nino Ferro thought much of Frank's idea. Not on moral grounds, but killing refugees brought a flood of public sympathy—tears for the *poveracci*. And that brought political pressure, which meant a slow-down and temporary income loss.

"Sandro, you wouldn't burn a kilo of heroin to make a point and certainly not in public," Nino said. "Tell that *cazzo* fucker Frank to go home."

Sandro gave the handset to Frank.

"Nino, I know this will work," said Aquafreddo with schoolboy glee.

"Frank, it's a bad idea," Nino said, pleading. "We're already short." Nino wanted to remind Frank he had also warned against using the *stronzo* Al Renato to kill LoBianco predicting the asshole would make a mess of it. But Frank Aquafreddo had overruled that too.

Frank said he liked his idea despite Nino's objection. And Grattinato and Nino had the same thought even if neither knew the other's. Frank Aquafreddo was as fucking stupid as Al Renato. And because of Al's fuck-up they had a major problem—moving forty refugees to a village without attracting immigration's attention. The EU Commission was already on alert. The Questura and anti-Mafia division were watching too. They'd have to spread it out, sending reduced numbers to small locations. Then bring them to a staging area at the same time to quickly load the containers. What a mess, and now there was Aquafreddo's bullshit nonsense to deal with as well.

"We'll have to wait at least five days afterward," said Sandro, again talking to Nino on his cell. "You arrange for a site and I'll modify the shipping paperwork." He picked up the ceramic vase on the table. "The transport papers are ready courtesy of LoBianco, who was efficient at what he did."

"You understand that LoBianco might guess the new shipping location."

"Not if he understands Frank's message because he knows his cousin better than us. Frank won't stop at two." Frank was nodding his approval on hearing Grattinato's words.

"*Cazzo!* Fuck!" yelled Nino, flapping his hand. There wasn't much more for him to say. He plainly disagreed with the plan.

116

"One more thing. Frank says if Paul doesn't crumble, Vinnie Briggs will—a real crybaby pussy."

"If that's true, maybe he's already on a flight back to New York. Let's keep an eye on him."

Chapter 17

Vinnie was still shaking a day after the attempted assassination on him. *Seeing Ben and Ciccio together didn't fuckin' help. At least I didn't catch them fucking.* Vinnie mulled over his last thought. *But they may have been going at it before I arrived...*

He looked at his hand and removed a small bandage covering his scrape. He didn't like violence but especially when it was against him. *This is too much,* he thought, *but Delgrado tells me he thinks nothing more will happen. Since when do I trust cops?*

Passing through the lobby, Vinnie saw the free copies of *La Sicilia* on the table in front of the hotel check-in counter. Plastered on the front page was another grim photo of two dead African woman refugees in Catania's *Zona Industriale*. They huddled together, each holding the other's hand, their bodies riddled with bullets. The article identified them as a mother and her teenage daughter.

Vinnie read his copy of the paper at the hotel front desk as did other guests and employees. The chatter was not dissimilar to zoo noises. He couldn't read more than a few lines, not because of the language but due to the photo. The graphic scene, an image that no American newspaper would print or TV news organization would show, was etched on his cornea. Tears filled his eyes. Wiping his nose he retreated to the pool.

Reclining in a lounger, he looked at his iPad. Every so often he took small sips of his cappuccino. There was scant new information on the murders in English or Italian. Alternate photos appeared on the British and American websites but he didn't linger. Twitter messages declared the murders to be trademark Mafia killings, yet no one could explain the reason behind it. A few speculated that these women were trafficked, which contradicted the obvious assassination-style murders. There were many alternative and better ways to dispose of women enslaved in the sex trade than shooting them. And who kills the commodity? And even worse, makes sure everyone knows?

Commissario Delgrado's shadow crossed Vinnie's face. Tilting his head back, Vinnie saw the darkness in the Commissario's eyes, his face cheerless. "Come with me," he said in a monotone, as if talking was a hardship. He sat with Vinnie in a recess of the empty café bar.

"You know what happened?" the Commissario asked in an official tone. He didn't wait for an answer. "This is your friend Paul LoBianco's fault."

Delgrado bent over and lowered his voice. "The two young women's deaths were a message for Paul. 'Come out or more will die.'"

Vinnie sucked air through his mouth and didn't expel it for several seconds. His heartbeat was at a sprinter's speed. He didn't want to believe such cruelty existed but he knew it did.

"Here's what happens next," Delgrado said as if in a rush to get the discussion over. "You are going to contact who-ever is giving you instructions, and I'm sure it's Maria Alba, but whoever, and set up another meeting. This time Lo-Bianco comes along and we'll make a show of arresting him. Use the papers and media like the Mafia. With LoBianco in our custody the mob won't kill more refugees. There's noth-ing LoBianco can offer them. More killing will only bring disorder in the camps. More killing gains them nothing and possibly loses everything."

The Commissario's words had an opposite effect on Vin-nie, who thought the plan short-term. Yes, he saw this could save a few innocents but it wouldn't stop the human traf-ficking and deaths—the ones that didn't make front-page headlines. Just a temporary pause, nothing permanent. In two or three months, boys and girls would again get shipped in containers to America, Europe, and other destinations. Their fate doomed. Fresh "recruits" arrived on overloaded boats every day. The one in thirty-eight that survived the crossing didn't have much life expectancy improvement on dry land.

Vinnie thought about his agreement with Paul. They would stop this atrocious enslavement into sex trafficking with direct evidence. With a taut face, eyes staring directly into Delgrado's, Vinnie said, "Yes, I agree." He had just told one of the biggest lies of his life.

After the Commissario left, Vinnie thought about his investigative process. At his Briggs Investigative detective agency he relied on his New York team to bounce ideas around with. He and his staff brainstormed a case. He relied on Blanca's cool-headedness and skill to ferret out information online and through her inside contacts at the NYPD. His college roommate with a degree in IT provided expertise on computers and occasional hacking.

In Sicily, other than Ben, he had no one to talk to about his ideas. He had to risk telling him his thoughts. Forget Ciccio. He needed feedback. And he'd have to stop obsessing on the shooting that nearly killed him. He resumed his detached private investigator persona.

And his first investigative step was to learn more about the refugees.

Chapter 18

Although still shaken by the shooting, it didn't deter Vinnie from going forward with a visit to a refugee camp. The only way he knew how to understand the people and their conditions was to see it himself. Newspaper and online photos showed overcrowded boats, bodies washed up on the beach, and the gruesome image of the dead woman and her daughter gunned down in the Catania yard. In his experience, nothing compensated for the visceral understanding gained from being in a place. He decided against calling Victor to take him, worried he'd tell Ben.

Vinnie stood outside the barbed wire fence. The taxi driver tried to dissuade him from going but a fifty-euro advance tip changed his tune. Vinnie asked the driver if he thought the Mafia controlled the camps and the man put a hand over his lips. He asked the cabbie to wait and the driver pinched his lips and lowered his eyebrows.

"*Niente immorale*," the driver said with his hands held together in prayer.

"*Certo*, guaranteed," Vinnie said with a ten-euro note in his hand.

Vinnie crossed the road to the barbed wire fence. He

walked the verge of dusty cornstarch ground mottled with grass burnt a mustard yellow. Police toting machine guns patrolled the entrance but let him pass, possibly recognizing him as an *Americano*. Inside he faced trolling human remnants.

The camp, one of the smaller ones with under a thousand people, had a horror movie setting. Vinnie walked among the motley mass with garments arranged either to cover scabs or torn away to prevent chafing. He stopped a man to ask directions to the main tent and was confronted by an incongruously happy face and extended hand. He fished from his pocket a two-euro coin and placed it into his palm, and the man's face beamed.

"How old are you?" asked Vinnie, expecting to hear forty but was told twenty-five.

He stopped a woman with a small child, a girl. She called ahead and told Vinnie the man was her husband. They were Nigerians, which explained their good English spoken with a strong British-African accent.

He asked about their journey to the camp.

They'd been at sea for over a week before reaching Lampedusa, then transferred to this camp on the outskirts of Catania. The man told of a harrowing crossing on an overcrowded vessel. His wife almost went overboard in one swell in the unseaworthy boat.

"I'm sorry, I should have introduced myself. I'm Vinnie Briggs."

"Pleased to meet you. I'm Joseph Adebayo. This is my wife Ezine and my four-year old joy, my daughter Ibironke."

Joseph explained they were the lucky ones. He spoke of

below-deck passengers emerging with fuel-soaked clothes that burned their skin. Those on the deck were battered by the wind.

"And what do you do now?" Vinnie asked.

Joseph hesitated then asked Vinnie if he was with an organization.

"You mean the Red Cross or Greenpeace? No, I'm on my own."

The man gave an enigmatic smile. "Not that kind of organization, Mr. Briggs."

"Ah," Vinnie said understanding the man's intent. "To the contrary, I'm on their bad list."

The man laughed and told his wife, who covered her mouth to hide her missing teeth.

"You know what they say here?" asked Joseph, and he answered without waiting. "How can you tell if someone is not collaborating with the Mafia?" He waited but smiled in anticipation of revealing the punchline. "They're in the ground."

Ezine poked her husband. "Hush, Joseph, don't go saying things like that."

"Okay, woman, don't get mad at me," he said and bowed his head.

"This camp is run by bad people," Joseph said. "We receive little support from the Italian government or the EU while we wait for our asylum papers. Some find work in the fields at harvest time where no papers are required. We go to Catania or Agrigento to beg but we are kept out of the tourist locations."

Joseph's friendly, open manner made Vinnie like him

the more he spoke. The sun was hot and Ezine pointed ahead to large boulders in the shade.

Joseph talked as they walked over to them. "They teach us Italian for two hours a day, enough so we can beg," and he smiled a hearty smile.

He stopped talking as if he'd run out of words. Vinnie stood as Joseph sat in the shade.

"Let me tell you something," said Joseph, pointing to a rock for Vinnie to rest. "Every three days we get a pack of free cigarettes. Not everyone smokes... I don't. We turn them over to the Bangladeshi men. They sell them to tobacco shops and we earn three euros for each pack sold. For two packs, I can join a carpool to Catania. Larger camps have official trucks or mini-vans."

With the word official he turned to look around. "The money I get from the cigarettes and begging allows me to shop in the markets to get decent African food. What they serve here is horrible. Pasta every day."

"Is it enough?" asked Vinnie.

"We do okay, but some women sell themselves," he said, lowering his head. "And some are forced to do so by the bad men here." He leaned forward and whispered, "Police, other Africans—all controlled by the Mafia."

Vinnie nodded and closed his eyes for a second.

Joseph told him of young girls, as young as twelve, forced into the trade. Mostly they'd already been trafficked in Africa by their parents, even their own mothers. "These poor girls are deceived into going to Europe. Everything is arranged before their arrival."

All the blood drained from Vinnie. His stomach tightened and his throat constricted. Tears clouded his vision as he looked at the couple's young daughter playing in the dirt with a stick.

"How long will you be here?" he asked.

Joseph shrugged. "We've been here four months, I think we have a good chance to get our asylum papers sorted out in another six."

"That fu... fudgin' long?"

"That's pretty fast. Some take eighteen months. But we speak English, and I have a degree—not that I'll use it. I also know how to bake bread, very good too. And Ezine has a pediatric nursing certificate. A good one from a British college in Nigeria." Joseph leaned into Vinnie, speaking softly. "It's what caused our problem. Boko Haram..."

Vinnie shook his head, indicating it meant nothing to him.

"They're a militant Islamic group in West Africa that want to institute Sharia law. They learned Ezine was treating the children of their enemy. They killed her family and were looking for us when we escaped into Cameroon."

Vinnie left despondent. He gave Joseph fifty euros, figuring he deserved it more than the taxi driver. The wife kissed Vinnie's hand, which embarrassed him. He said nothing the entire return trip. The driver reminded Vinnie he had warned him against the visit but said no more.

Despite his distress, or maybe because of it, Vinnie knew he had a mission. He'd help Paul to stop the exploiting of the refugees by the Mafia. He sequestered himself on the room's balcony to avoid people. He went out to eat to avoid the main dining room and chats with the friendly waiters.

He called Ben, giving him an honest excuse. "I'm sorry but I need to be alone. This has nothing to do with you or us. I'll explain later but I'm not feeling well."

"Vinnie, what is it? Let me join you?"

"Thanks, but this is one time I would like some solitude. I'll try not to wake you when I come back." Vinnie stayed out past midnight, not at a club but sitting on the beach looking out to sea.

He had another rough night, tossing and turning. It had been two days since someone shot at him. He thought about Joseph, Ezine, and little Ibironke being trafficked by despicable men.

Mixed in with these thoughts came questions on the events at the museum. Who had saved him and the Commissario? The guy behind the trees? It had to be the waiter-marksman at Paul's restaurant. He didn't have a clear shot of the assassins from his position so he did the next best thing and fired at the van, thereby scaring them off. Vinnie mentally awarded him another gold medal.

Dreams and reality mixed in his semi-sleep state. He conjured Ben with Ciccio performing fellatio then having sex. He saw the hordes of bodybuilders fucking in every corner of the hotel and selling each other human growth hormones and other drugs. Men hawking their muscles that morphed into young girls being mauled by grown men. In his semiconscious mind, young refugee girls and boys were paraded on a stage in front of a cheering crowd. He turned over three times and awoke thinking, *If only I had one lead, one hint of where to begin.*

The last thought brought sleep but not for long. He

awoke early in the room that he thought had shrunk overnight. His heard his stomach growl. Food might be a temporary answer to his abject misery.

Chapter 19

This was Vinnie's earliest breakfast so far. Not true for the others. The lobby looked like the Ninth Fleet had come ashore. Battleship troops trawled the corridors and mobilized to attack the breakfast buffet. The staff doubled in numbers to placate the invaders. Vinnie stared at men in posers walking to the pool—an entirely different species. Their costumes unfit for swimming but perfect to maximize tanning.

He stood in line at the *prima colazione* buffet bar behind a man so wide it was impossible to see the selections ahead. At the hot-food counter the man scooped scrambled eggs from the serving dish until it covered his entire plate. He sheepishly turned to Vinnie, speaking in a South African accent. "Don't worry, mate, they'll bring some more. I'm starved. I arrived at four this morning after a fourteen-hour flight."

He returned a smile but felt like telling him he was choosing the wrong food before a contest. *He doesn't stand a chance,* he thought.

After breakfast, Vinnie changed into a bathing costume. Unlike the previous days with the pool near empty of patrons, today massive men took half the lounge chairs in what appeared to be a bake-off. The "normal" tourists slotted in like lime slices between the He-men. Vinnie was amused at the hotel guests trying to avoid staring at bodybuilders sporting tiny poser suits. Many of the "normal" male clientele appeared skeletal next to the bulls. After an hour reading, Vinnie took a few laps in the pool, then dozed amongst the stanchions of men browned to grade A maple syrup. He awoke to the sound of, "Signore... signore... Vinnie?"

"Huh, what?" he asked with Gianni's chest inches from his nose.

"The hotel concierge has a delivery for you. Should I get it?"

Vinnie shook his head and retrieved the envelope on his way to his room to change for *pranzo*.

"Do you know who left this?" he asked the concierge.

"*Boh.*"

Yeah, sure you don't, pal, thought Vinnie. He waited for the elevator along with two Herculean men, both shorter than him and twice as wide. A young girl came out of the elevator and looked at one man in a pouch that covered pretty much nothing. She scrunched up her nose and declared, "You're nasty," and skipped to the lobby.

In his room, Vinnie read the short note three times. "Book a seat on the hotel's excursion to the town of Tindari. No chauffeur. Go incognito. Trust no one."

Online information about Tindari did not suggest any possible connection to refugees. *Another fuckin' rendezvous for what?* Vinnie thought. *Another opportunity for someone to shoot me?*

130

He remembered Delgrado's admonishment: "Keep me informed about the next meeting and only call my private mobile."

Vinnie had second thoughts about the agreement. If he was right, the mystery shooter that saved him at the Museum was Paul's marksman waiter. If true, then he or Serafina was protecting him now. Why chance Delgrado being followed or his phone being tapped? Vinnie didn't know the Italian rules of wiretapping but was sure the Mafia could buy off the right people. He wasn't taking a chance. And he knew how to avoid Delgrado's surveillance team.

As he sat alone at the lunch table, Ben startled Vinnie.

"Look, we've got to fix this. I was worried about you. Your cryptic message. I know I'm to blame for most—" he said in a tumble of words.

"Yes, you are. What was that with Ciccio?"

"I don't know what you saw or think you saw—"

"Enough. I may not have actually seen him suck you off or you stick it up his ass, but I don't want to come back to the room for a live porno show with my husband the main feature."

Ben looked directly at Vinnie, his head shaking side to side. "Fuck you. That never happened."

Vinnie threw his napkin down on the table. "Yeah, then let's move on to the drugs and needles. I've been biting my tongue to keep harmony. Not anymore. I'm fuckin' done with this."

Ben's eyes shut and his brows came down like shutters.

"I've known a long time but these last two weeks you've really outdone yourself. I see the pimples and your ass looks sore. Did you also inject between your toes?"

Ben balled up his hands and jiggled a leg under the table. "I've got to prepare and you're not helping. And for the record, Ciccio did not suck me off and I didn't fuck him. Can you say the same about you and Paul?" The metal leg screeched across the tile floor as Ben pushed his chair back. He stood and started to walk out but was stopped in his tracks by Vinnie's words.

"Post cycle therapy can't wait," said Vinnie, who knew as much as Ben on the topic. "You could die if you take too long to detox. Get help. I'll help you."

Vinnie stopped at the competition registration desk and asked one of the clerks how many contestants were taking part.

"We have two hundred fifty. That's an incredible number of bodybuilders, fitness contestants, and martial arts specialists," said a smartly dressed woman.

Sounds like a woolly mammoth convention, Vinnie thought as he went backstage. He wasn't sure why he was doing this. Morbid curiosity?

Using his VIP pass, he entered the behind-stage men's pump room where the contestants prepped. For many, winning meant a pro card and that meant earning serious money, enough to support a family.

The room was a weightlifter's playground of barbells, kettle bells, and exercise bands. Mirrors everywhere. Men pumped weights, increasing blood flow to swell their muscles just before going on stage. Vinnie always found the special "paint" area erotic—the section for contestants to get oiled to highlight sculpted sinew with a dark grease color.

132

A lit match would ignite ten-thousand pounds of corrugated muscle.

He jumped with the bang of a dropped kettlebell. *Why didn't I hear the second shot? A silencer? I'd still have heard a gunshot even if it was suppressed.*

He saw Ciccio rolling tanning solvent along a man's back like pasting a highway billboard sign. He squeezed the man's ass and between his thighs, but a little too hard near his testicles produced a squeak of protest. *Very unprofessional,* Vinnie thought. *What did Ben see in him? He's good-looking but very immature.*

He'd had enough gawking and peeked into the main auditorium. He saw the standard drill: a panoply of photographers crowded the pit area taking pictures and videos of the onstage performance. Gianni Vaccaro was on the side and didn't aim his camera at the stage but focused on Vinnie. Gianni knew it was crazy but he was attracted to Vinnie with a crush he couldn't explain. That Vinnie had rejected him with diplomacy didn't matter. He'd prove himself worthy somehow.

Another set of eyes surveyed the room. Instead of focusing on Vinnie, they snapped Ciccio stroking Ben's arm while talking to him.

The Men's Lightweight group took the stage and Vinnie walked out.

Chapter 20

Having skipped the pre-judging, Vinnie saw no reason to return in the afternoon to watch the final five pose-off and the winner announced. He went out to a local trattoria for lunch, not wanting another confrontation with Ben in the hotel dining room. This was not the time to confide in Ben about Al, Paul, and the refugee camps.

He sat poolside with his iPad, learning more about Tindari. A great tourist location off the usual itinerary because it was relatively remote. *Why send me there to hand me some papers? It makes no sense.* His arms and face tensed, and his lips curled. *I'm going on a fuckin' scavenger hunt.*

A cheerful Gianni called out, "*Ciao*, Vinnie. Do you want anything from the bar? As you can see, you are the only client today so I can get you anything if you promise not to drown while I'm gone."

Gianni's words and broad smile stopped Vinnie frowning.

"*Frizzante. Grazie*," answered Vinnie. He closed his eyes until Gianni brought the sparkling water with ice and a slice of lime.

"Sit," Vinnie said. "You can save a drowning person from here. I'll help you keep a lookout."

They talked about nothing and everything. Vinnie smiled at Gianni's light-hearted attempt to quip in English. He studied Gianni's beautiful face, full lips poised to break into a wide smile. He mentally lusted after Gianni's hunky body.

A hotel guest walked past holding *La Repubblica*, a beach photo of the latest batch of dead refugees on the front page. Vinnie tapped the back of Gianni's hand.

"I went to a refugee camp the other day," he began, with no segue from their previous conversation. "It was depressing... it made me want to cry."

"Shh... that's okay," said Gianni, who had leaned forward as if to embrace him, but Vinnie moved back and Gianni did likewise.

"Can I tell you what's on my mind? You can't tell anyone," Vinnie said.

Gianni crossed his heart.

He started with Al Renato, and Gianni's head jerked back and his eyebrows shot up. He and every hotel employee in Giardini Naxos knew the dead American mobster's name.

"Wait," Gianni said, nodding toward the other deck chairs. "It's better we do not discuss serious topics here. I hear whispers from my lifeguard chair because the pool is like a... uh..." Gianni cupped his hand over his ear.

"An amplified sound system?" offered Vinnie, who knew that sound travels well over an expanse of water.

"*Si.* I must return to my lifeguard chair now," Gianni said, his chin gesturing to several more patrons arriving at the pool. Gianni stood and took a step backward. "Meet me tonight in Taormina."

"Huh? Why the secrecy?" asked Vinnie.

Gianni bent forward. "People are watching you. I heard the desk clerk talking to a big man but he was not a contestant," Gianni said with a finger on his lip. "Mafioso. And I saw a lion woman staring at you."

Vinnie's eyes grew large. *What's going on? Is Gianni a spy? An informant? For whom?*

"What else do you know?" Vinnie said, his voice accusatory. "Tell me everything."

"I know you identified Renato's body at the beach—"

Vinnie interrupted him. "How do you know that?"

Gianni shrugged. "I also know you are a good detective from New York—" and again Vinnie cut him off, asking him to explain his source.

"I googled you," Gianni said, grinning. "And I know you are a good person, and that's not from Google." Gianni touched his breast. "In here."

Praise and sweet talk had never worked with Vinnie but something about Gianni's authentic innocence touched him.

"Gianni, tell me straight up—are you spying on me? Why so nice? Are you trying to hurt me or Ben?"

Gianni closed his eyes, his hands prayer-like. He touched his lips and sat hunched.

"I'm sorry, I didn't mean to upset you. It's okay." Vinnie rubbed Gianni's shoulder then pulled his chin up and looked into his glossy eyes.

"I would never hurt you," Gianni said, whispering each word. "I like you so much. I know it's silly. I'm acting like a schoolboy. But there's something about you I noticed from the first time I saw you. *Sono proprio stupido.*"

"No, you're not stupid. And I like you too. Maybe not

in the way you want," Vinnie said and he touched Gianni's hand. "I can't. You know that, right?"

Gianni smiled. "*Si e grazie.*"

"Okay, what were you going to tell me before I overreacted?"

Gianni gave Vinnie the name of a small nightclub in Taormina outside the general tourist area and in the city's residential quarter.

Vinnie returned to his room, his investigative cynicism having kicked in. Had he been too gullible? Was Gianni in fact a spy for the mob? Or just another Ciccio, a gigolo among the gay bar set seeking to seduce?

His thoughts evolved looking out from the balcony to the pool below. He smiled watching a young woman looking up to Gianni in his lifeguard chair and for no reason he thought of Ben. *Can I talk to him? Will I make things worse between us?*

At the evening dinner, Vinnie was prepared to tell Ben everything, but his boisterous prattle about the day's winners and runners-up gave no opportunity for serious discussion.

"And number one hundred eighteen?" asked Vinnie with a slight yawn.

"Too bloated," pronounced Ben and Vinnie smiled.

Vinnie reached across the table at the end of the meal and touched Ben's hand.

"I want to talk about something that affects me and you," Vinnie said, and he decided it best to start with Commissario Delgrado.

"Sure," Ben said, head tilted.

"In our room."

Once in their suite with the door closed, Vinnie sat in a chair, his neck moist and throat restricted as if he was wearing a tightly knotted tie. "I saw Commissario Delgrado a few days ago," Vinnie said, "and, uh…"

Ben's forehead creased as he leaned forward.

"The thing is, well, did you hear about the two women found murdered in Catania?"

By the end of his summary Ben had turned a deep shade of purple, his eyebrows slamming down and obscuring his glare. He folded his arms, veins like snakes under paper-thin skin. His neck sinew stretched as he cursed and asked questions that turned into opinions on Vinnie's disregard for his warning years before: "Don't get involved with the mob."

He expected Ben to be upset, but he saw in the twist to his lips and the dark shade that hung over his eyes much more. He heard the growl as his fingers curled. This wasn't Ben but a man stoked with supercharged testosterone supplements.

"I know this is not what you want," Vinnie said, trying to sound conciliatory. "Me neither. But the thing is, if I don't help Paul then more young women will die."

"Why? I don't get it. How is Paul connected to this?" Ben asked, his voice steady yet an octave too low, sounding ready to explode at any moment. He asked Vinnie to explain the logic between the murder of two refugee women and Paul. How could Vinnie help?

"I can go places Paul can't now that he's in hiding. He has to wait until things settle down."

"And no one else is capable? Only you, the world's

greatest detective, can do this?"

"Yes. I mean no. It's that I have better cover. A local PI is too obvious, too exposed," Vinnie said, unconvinced by his own words.

"And why Messina?"

"I combined my interest in the Caravaggio paintings with a chance to talk to Delgrado."

Ben shook his head. So far what he heard made little sense. "You buy Paul's bullshit that he wasn't *really* part of the Aquafreddo operation? I'd expect better from you." He stood, face flushed, and both arms curling as if holding a barbell. "I've had enough. I've got to get in some toning," he said, and he went to the adjoining spare room to perform an insanely high number of push-ups and a series of floor calisthenics. He showered in the spare bathroom and then returned to the bedroom, his engorgement obvious. *He's injected something,* thought Vinnie.

"I'm tired. I think I'll have an early night," Ben said. "I'll be up early for more training. And I want you to stop this thing with Paul and Delgrado."

Vinnie looked out of the window. There was still a pink glow in the late evening sky and probably thirty minutes before darkness. He opened his wardrobe closet.

"Going out now?" Ben asked.

"I've slept most of the day. Maybe I'll stroll Taormina at night. They say it's beautiful when Etna is glowing."

Ben picked up his iPad and shot glances at Vinnie picking a shirt, replacing it, and choosing another.

"Vinnie, what's going on?" he asked.

"What do you mean?"

"You've picked out three shirts before choosing one. That's a lot of fuss for a casual stroll."

With a shrug, Vinnie continued to button his shirt.

"Enough," said Ben, throwing his iPad to the bottom of the bed. "Just tell me. Are you meeting Paul? Was all that stuff before just a fucking lie?" he demanded, pulling himself upright against the headboard. His gritted teeth suggested he was ready to pounce.

"No, I'm not. I told you—Paul is in hiding."

"Then what's going on?"

"Nothing. You do your thing and I'll do mine."

Vinnie marched out, even less confident he and Ben could repair their faltering marriage. It would take something very dramatic to turn things around and that seemed unlikely. "Be careful what you wish for, you might just get it" was an adage his mother had repeated many times, and for some reason it resonated tonight.

Chapter 21

A taxi dropped Vinnie at Gianni's chosen nightclub, a gay bar legacy to an obscure nineteenth-century German photographer, Wilhelm von Gloeden, who sought relief from tuberculosis in sunny Taormina. He photographed local, near-naked young men and teenage boys dressed in strategically placed loincloths and posed in seductive Greek and Roman motifs. And so von Gloeden helped to establish Taormina as a gay destination.

Vinnie needed a few seconds for his eyesight to adjust to the glare of a dozen shining disco balls reflecting flashing lights, a throwback to the clubs of the seventies. The rhythmic music pounded his ears.

The clientele included overdressed men dancing with others wearing next to nothing. *Essere alla moda*, meaning to be fashionable, took on a modern meaning. Vinnie was delighted, gazing around at the glorious sexual masculinity. Gianni crossed the room with a million-dollar smile.

"*Ciao, bello,*" he said, giving the obligatory *mwah mwah* on each of Vinnie's cheeks. "Let's drink and dance."

"Uh, yes, but I thought we could talk," Vinnie said.

"*Certo.* Of course we'll talk. But will your problem not

wait until we enjoy *la musica?*" Gianni hauled Vinnie to the bar and soon they were giddy with drink and danced for two hours.

During breaks and drink refills, they sat at a small round table. Gianni boasted of his childhood sleuthing prowess.

"Little things at first. As a young boy, maybe twelve, I helped people find their missing dog or cat. In high school I discovered who stole from Signor Schiavone's *tabaccheria*. I was a hero—well, to him and my mother. I read detective books—not only Camilleri's Commissario Montalbano novels but real crime stories as well."

Gianni explained as if it was a joke that his village didn't merit a Mafia presence. "We're too poor and too small. Our drug problem is old people's prescriptions. And then there's my sister's boyfriend..."

Vinnie nodded politely while recalling his own amateur beginnings. Gianni tapped Vinnie's shoulder.

"My big case. Is that what you call it?" asked Gianni, who didn't wait for an answer. "It was last year. I just started to work as the lifeguard and I arrived for work coming in a side entrance. I noticed a man pulling two cases. I don't know why, but it seemed odd."

Another nod from Vinnie, who had lost interest in Gianni's detective stories.

"Then," continued Gianni, "I followed him and saw him get into an old car. I ran behind and memorized *la targa*... uh, what do you say?"

"License plate."

"*Si, si.* And my memory is very good. I went into the hotel and there was a big noise among the guests and hotel staff. Someone had stolen a client's luggage while he checked out. Can you guess what happened next?"

Vinnie admitted he was impressed with Gianni's intuition and keen observation.

Before he added to the story, a man in his early twenties stood at their table. He was stylish but not overdressed. He had fine features and a profile that belonged on a Roman coin. He kissed Gianni on both cheeks and spoke for a few minutes with their mutual agreement to talk later. The young man looked Vinnie up and down and gave a not so discreet nod, pursing his lips, and turned to Gianni. *"Bello. Hai fatto bene."*

"What's he mean, 'You've done well?' You know this isn't a date, right?"

"Si."

While Gianni had been talking to his friend, Vinnie thought about how much he should reveal. That was his original intent but now he wasn't so sure. He had a good feeling about Gianni from the start and his detective stories, the interaction with an old friend, and his body language added to his impression. Gianni was a decent, intelligent person and that counted more than anything.

"There's something I want to tell you and I need a favor," Vinnie said, his voice slightly cracking. He rubbed his hands together and stared at Gianni for several seconds without speaking.

Gianni steered Vinnie to the club's outdoor courtyard and a table far from the others. Vinnie saw young men kissing and groping. *Is this a good idea? Maybe I'm wrong. He's a young lifeguard seeking thrills. I hardly know him but*

143

who else can I talk to? Vinnie thought of calling Blanca or Dan in New York but dismissed that idea. How could he explain long-distance? They'd have to be in Sicily to fully understand. And what harm could come from talking to Gianni? Who would he tell? He had already declared his village to be a Mafia-free zone.

I'll start with something personal, thought Vinnie. "It's about Ben's doping. We had a fight."

"He hit you? *O Dio,* are you hurt?" Gianni asked.

Vinnie realized Gianni took English words literally and clarified in Italian. "*Litigare.* We had a quarrel, not a fist fight." Vinnie took a second to add, "He flares up over little things."

"And this is a surprise? Everyone knows bodybuilders use steroids and it makes them a little crazy. They even punch people."

Vinnie frowned, wanting to dispel the myth that every bodybuilder has roid rage. *Is Gianni too judgmental without having all the facts?*

"I'm not talking about bodybuilders in general. This is about Ben," Vinnie said, knowing he sounded a little too harsh. He sipped his drink.

"The thing is, Ben supposedly gave up getting bigger, more muscular. He said it was over. I believed him." *Too much of our private life,* thought Vinnie. "Forget it. It doesn't matter. I'm worried about Ben and we argued, that's all really. I'll get over it."

Gianni sat intently focused on Vinnie, smiling at him.

Even if he lacks psychological insight he's a great listener. I want to tell him everything. "You know," Vinnie said with a hand across one eye, "I've just realized I can't talk to Ben about his drug stacking because he won't listen no matter what I say."

Gianni shrugged and sucked in his cheeks. He didn't understand the meaning of "stacking." Vinnie explained that it was an unrelenting regime of injections, pills that started with the As and ended in the Zs, suppository diuretics, and supplements.

Gianni whistled and said, "*Minghia,*" his eyes widening.

"Stopping is painful, both physically and emotionally. When a bodybuilder returns to normal size he's depressed that his former twenty-two-inch arms are now reduced to seventeen or less. Years of muscle vanished in months. It's a big adjustment and some have breakdowns." Vinnie's lips drew close. Was this Ben? Did he fear being normal?

The emotion swallowed Vinnie's energy and he wanted to return to his hotel room. He had more to say, but not now. Was Gianni the right person to confide in about Paul? Vinnie switched to small talk for a short time until fatigued.

"I'm tired and it's been a long day for me. I'm going back to the hotel."

"I'll come with you," said Gianni.

Vinnie shook his head. "See you at the pool tomorrow."

Gianni moved adroitly to the handsome man from before, now with shirt buttons opened to his bellybutton exposing small tufts of hair on an athletic torso. Vinnie waved goodbye and nodded his approval to Gianni.

It was after midnight when Vinnie returned to Hotel Mezzogiorno. He tossed and turned for ten minutes followed by intervals of sleep. His mind raced between thoughts of

Gianni and Paul, but Ben appeared the most. *What was he doing with Ciccio? And who I am to be suspicious when I'm hiding that I'm helping Paul? To deceive him, make him think I'm screwing Paul? A way to get back without actually having an affair? A false high road. Or am I searching too? I encourage Gianni's flirting to gain attention, not his help? And is Gianni seducing me?*

Then Vinnie briefly thought, *of course he's attracted to me*, then smothered his laugh to not wake Ben. *Am I really so fuckin' vain?* He propped his hands behind his pillow while staring at the ceiling. *I can trust him. He can't fake being that good.*

Vinnie managed another hour of on-again, off-again sleep and wrestled with the bed cover. He rose pre-dawn, moved to the spare room, and slightly raised the wooden blind covering the French doors to the balcony. Moonlight sparkled through the gaps between the separated slats. Vinnie tugged further and fully raised the blind. He stepped out onto the balcony, the moon bright in the sky. Below stretched the immaculate sandy beach. He remembered every detail of the night Al died.

Fatigue took over and Vinnie returned to bed, where he was awoken by Ben in the morning. As he left for breakfast Vinnie dressed quickly. He couldn't keep a secret from Ben, not this one. He had to tell him he was helping Paul to bring down the Aquafreddo mob. He'd be upset, very upset, but not as much if he heard about it later.

Taking the elevator, Vinnie wondered if Ben would create a scene. *Do I care anymore?* The time for full disclosure had arrived, come what may.

146

Chapter 22

Vinnie joined Ben in the hotel dining room as he finished his bran cereal and fruit. *If nothing else he knows the proper diet to make sure he looks good in front of an audience.* The fans want a supercut, five-percent body fat with no bloat and that's what Ben gives them.

"You were out late. Care to tell me where or with whom?" asked Ben, who was getting up from the table.

I can go out where, when, and with whom I like were the words Vinnie wanted to say as he pushed around the cereal in his bowl as if mixing cement. Maybe he wouldn't answer the "with whom" question. He wasn't up for a fight. He had something important to tell the bright-eyed Ben. *He's already juiced.* Vinnie shoveled more cereal into his mouth, preventing a private smile at his play on words. Most people in the room were juiced in one way or another.

"I'm going to the auditorium," Ben announced. "The pre-judging begins in an hour. I'll leave a backstage pass for you unless you're going out somewhere." He walked away with one arm twitching.

Yeah, he's juiced, thought Vinnie as he finished his cereal. He entered the half-full auditorium twenty-five minutes before the stage filled with the middleweight class contestants—the over 75kg or 165lb category. Vinnie flashed his badge to a guard and entered the pump room. He saw the identical tableau as the previous day, only these men had expanded to near double size. From all corners came grunting with men doing push-ups and clanging barbells together. The paint area with replenished tanning oil buckets guaranteed each man glistened, their skin a malt brown to highlight every sinew.

Ten minutes was enough for Vinnie. He walked into a three-quarters-full auditorium. Ben was conferring with the other judges on stage and Vinnie waited. *This isn't my thing,* he thought. *I've seen enough arid men with desert landscapes to last me the rest of my life.* He walked the corridor and didn't notice two bull-sized men following him. Although there were plenty of big men wandering about, these were not competitors.

Vinnie changed into his bathing suit and settled into his favorite poolside chair. He'd ordered a cappuccino at the pool café, hoping Gianni would serve him.

The only other clients were a young couple on chaise longues on the opposite side of the pool. A perfect setting to confide in Gianni if he showed up. A few minutes later he had his wish. Gianni crouched on his haunches and, eye-to-eye with Vinnie, asked if he had ordered at the bar.

"Please, sit a minute," Vinnie said.

Gianni adjusted his crouching stance and smiled.

Vinnie sketched what he was doing with Paul, making it sound like a stolen goods investigation. He glossed over details and ended by asking, "Can you come with me to tour the Catania warehouses, the ones that had the murders?"

Gianni's face blanched. "Murder? I don't know."

"I'm not looking to find the killers. I want to understand what happens at the docks. I'm sure they're like New York but I'd like to see for myself. I could use your help interpreting."

"*Va bene*," agreed Gianni. He walked away and returned with a tray of cappuccino, biscotti, and sugar, his lips spread impossibly wide.

* * *

"Keep a close eye," said Nino, speaking on his cell phone. He was talking to one of two walking blocks of beef at Hotel Mezzogiorno. He was pleased that on this occasion his men's size helped them blend in, more cattle among the herd of bodybuilders. He realized too late when he saw them that he should have suggested a wardrobe change.

The men had seen Vinnie enter the elevator, presumably to go to his room, which was confirmed with his return fifteen minutes later in a newly purchased, form-fitting bright purple bathing costume. Neither man knew the swimsuit was new, but their raised eyebrows suggested they knew their target's sexual preference.

The men followed Vinnie to the pool, taking no notice of the lifeguard talking to him.

"*Finocchio*," said one and the other agreed that the lifeguard was indeed a pansy. The young couple on the other side of the pool meant nothing for their purpose.

The bigger of the bulls, in a brown T-shirt silk screened with a well-known protein supplement logo, took out his phone from his pocket and signaled the other bull that he was going into the lobby. He speed-dialed before he was inside.

"Nino, *niente.*" Nothing happening. "The stooge is at the pool drinking a *capucch.*"

"Stick with him and keep your distance. Don't stay long at the pool. Without bathing suits you'll attract attention."

"Sure thing, boss."

"Better yet, go to the lobby. Anyone entering the pool will pass you. And he'll have to change clothes to leave the hotel. Don't lose him," said Nino, hanging up.

The man known as Brown T found his counterpart under an umbrella to avoid the heat of the noonday sun.

"Move inside," Brown T said and relayed Nino's message.

A female entered the lobby, whom they knew to be Serafina. The men were puzzled, then more so as they saw two of their associates, another pair of big men shaped like fireplugs. Although dressed in identical black outfits, the Plugs' wardrobes were classic gangster haberdashery.

"*Cos'*è successo?" asked Brown T, talking to his comrades outside. "Why are you here?"

"*Buh,*" they said together. "We're to follow Serafina and note who she meets."

Brown T hunched his shoulders. "What have you found?"

"Nothing. We followed *la stunata,*" said Plug One with a finger circling next to his head meaning bat-shit crazy in Sicilian, "...and she came here."

"Okay, we'll take over," said Brown T.

"Nino wants to know who Serafina meets because she

was with Renato the night he was killed. She says she saw and heard nothing but you know Nino doesn't like coincidences," Plug Two said.

"She doesn't know the boss is suspicious," said Plug One, clicking his tongue while baring his teeth.

A half-hour later Serafina marched past the two men without looking at them. But she had already noticed and knew she was being tailed from the moment she left the small café in Catania. These two were new, although she'd seen them with Nino. She chuckled softly passing them as they were still reading the same page of *La Sicilia's* Sports section, "Calcio Palermo Fires Manager." *How stupid can they be?* she thought. A man in a Catania football strip doesn't linger over an article about Palermo's football club manager. *Imbecille.*

* * *

Vinnie was passing through the lobby to his room to change when he noticed a woman he was sure he'd seen before. She left a room key fob at the hotel desk and swayed her hips like a car needing new rear suspension. "Serafina," Vinnie said under his breath. "Why the hell is she here?"

In his room he selected his Adidas sneakers instead of the Nikes. Putting them on, his right foot jammed. Tucked under the tongue was a note signed by Paul. *Serafina, no doubt about it,* thought Vinnie. She got the clerk to give her an extra fob key and that explained the extra ass wiggle she gave him as a reward. *But how did she know I'd choose the Adidas?*

The note confirmed Tindari as the meeting point but with a couple of amendments. The first was to delay a day until Friday. The second altered the specific location to the nearby Tindari Roman archeological site and not the Black Madonna Statue in the sanctuary. Nothing made sense to Vinnie. *Why the changes? Why send Serafina with the note and not have her just come and tell me?*

Vinnie consulted the hotel concierge when booking his trip.

"Only three seats available for the Friday excursion," he said, looking up from his computer screen.

"I guess it's popular, although I've never heard of it," Vinnie said.

"Do you want two tickets?"

Vinnie held up one finger. *"Uno."*

"The Pullman leaves at seven-thirty."

Vinnie purchased his ticket, returning to his room still puzzling over Tindari, a small hilltop tourist village. Its fame came from its spectacular views of the Aeolian Islands and a famously beautiful and atypical Black Madonna statue. Nothing suggested trafficking or refugees.

Should he tell Commissario Delgrado? Keep to their agreement or worry about a mole at the Questura? *Isn't that what happened last time?* Vinnie ruminated. Could he discover the Questura's mole with a trick? He shuddered. *I'd almost been gunned down at the museum except for my guardian marksman waiter.* Will he be there in Tindari or Serafina to stop the next assassination attempt?

He left a message on Commissario Delgrado's office phone to inform him the Tindari trip had changed to Friday. He didn't mention the Roman ruins and hoped this would expose the informant. Anyone other than the Commissario waiting at the Black Madonna statue instead of the Parco Romano entrance was the informant. Vinnie was confident Delgrado would spot the spy. He was sure this trap would work.

Chapter 23

With his Tindari excursion booked, Vinnie decided to closely observe Ben—calisthenics, gazing out from the balcony to the sandy beach, band exercises, and mirror flexing. He didn't stop moving and he was restless in ways Vinnie had never seen before, not even in competition.

Vinnie sat on the balcony and called Blanca in New York. He stood to update her, dashing through Paul LoBianco, Al Renato, John Margate, and the dead refugees. The call ended with Vinnie's ear tingling from Blanca's fury.

Ben returned from the morning pre-judging of the last Heavyweight class, men over 90 kg/198lbs to 102 kg/225lbs. He had two hours before his performance. The Super Heavyweight class came in the evening. Fifteen men with an official weight tally that averaged 265lbs. The heaviest man topped 310lbs and the lightest came in at 245lbs. The morning to evening transitioned from Davids to Goliaths and the latter all bigger than Ben.

Vinnie escorted Ben backstage and the pump room burst into loud applause. Yet Ben reacted with only a pint-size smile. He changed into a glimmering black satin posing suit speckled with gold. Vinnie nodded approval. Ciccio crouched behind Ben's redwood thighs to apply tanning oil.

"Hey, that's my job," yelled Vinnie, swaying in his furious queasiness.

"*Scusa*, I thought that… I just wanted to help."

"Yeah, *sure* you did. I'm here now so fuc—"

Ben turned. "Vinnie, cool it. Ciccio's only helping. Don't upset me, not now. I need to concentrate."

Vinnie nodded and kissed Ben's cheek. "You're right. I'm in a bad mood. Let's get you oiled up." Vinnie turned to Ciccio. "I'm sorry too. I'm on edge. Thanks for helping."

Ciccio gave Vinnie a thumbs up and went to oil another bodybuilder.

Sitting in his prime auditorium seat, Vinnie was caught off guard by Ben's music. He expected Puccini's "Nessun Dorma" to please the hosts and with a message to the contestants with the last line of the aria, "*vincerò*"—"I will win." Instead he heard Barbra Streisand belting out "Memory" from *Cats*.

Ben's relaxed, fluid motion qualified as modern dance, hard muscle popped from sinewy crevices. He bent to one knee into a Rodin's *Thinker*'s position and examined his single bulging bicep as if he'd never seen it before. A bizarre yet effective prelude to his panther leap into a full muscular pose.

Vinnie recognized the performance as a homage to Gunter. Ben's face hardened to a bluish tinge under the bright lights. His body had more angles than a Cubist painting. His back a stepping-stone of muscle tracing across one shoulder to the other. Ribboned veins ran the length of his forearms. He devolved into segments on every flex. As the

155

music climaxed, so too had every gay man with a muscle fetish in the audience. His standard finale was a double-bicep pose so big they'd eclipse the sun. Today he deviated, spreading his stanchion legs while Barbra belted out the final verse.

His massive thighs strained like a gymnast's, spreading one hundred eighty degrees and in this position he held his trademark double-bicep pose for ten seconds. Perfectly timed to the last note, he transitioned into a handstand press. No one could claim they didn't get their money's worth, in euros or dollars. He gifted them a cornucopia of muscle, which was exactly what the audience came to see.

His smile beamed across the galaxy while Vinnie's never made it to his lips. The song wasn't a tribute to Gunter or the split for Rita. It was Ben's signal he'd come out of retirement and returned to competition. It was a private message to Vinnie, delivered very publicly.

If Vinnie had any doubt, which he didn't, the confirmation came with Ben leaping off the stage into the crowd. He'd only done that twice in his career and for special circumstances. He walked down the aisle creating mayhem, flexing and letting anyone and everyone touch and caress him. *This isn't him*, thought Vinnie. He hated swarming hands running over his husband's body. He bent to allow the admirers to take hold of his shoulders and rub his pectorals or run their hands over his rippling abs. He circled the room encouraging a fray like a Black Friday sale riot. His smile stretched his face to the point of cracking.

Backstage Vinnie took several deep breaths standing at Ben's side.

156

"That was unbelievable. A fuckin' grand finale to end all grand finales," said Vinnie with a forced smile.

"Thanks," Ben beamed while wiping his face with a towel handed to him by a backstage assistant. "I think it went well."

They hugged and Ben lifted Vinnie like Nureyev hoisting Fontaine. He may have elevated Vinnie's body but not his spirit.

Ciccio pushed through the admirers and kissed Ben on both cheeks.

"*Bravissimo! Magnifico! Bellissimo*! I've never seen anything so beautiful. A wonderful performance." Ciccio turned to Vinnie. "He's magnificent, yes? Look at his muscles. I'm in love." Ciccio decided it was okay to touch Ben and his hands rubbed across his pectorals up to his shoulders and arms.

Vinnie clenched his jaw and his fingers curled into claws.

"It's okay, Vinnie. I invited this," said Ben, intervening.

"And the 'I'm in love' part?" asked Vinnie as his nostrils flared.

"It's just an expression. You know what Italians are like."

"Yeah, I do. And that was no expression. He wants to fuck you."

"No, no," said Ciccio. "I mean yes, but not so... how do you say... crude. But you two understand, yes? We are gay. We don't observe the formalities of straight people. Am I right?"

"No, you're not fuckin' right," answered Vinnie with his brows moving so low they crushed his eyes. He crossed his arms angrily.

A horde of photographers stampeded into the room to end the quarrel. Ben's sponsor pulled him aside to say they needed a few more poses and this was the best time with Ben still inflated and sweaty.

"Go on," Vinnie said. "They won't even need to do a touch-up and maybe Ciccio can kiss your backside to give you an incentive."

"Fuck you," Ben said over his shoulder as the sponsor guided him by his elbow to a posing room. He had a duty to promote the expo sponsor's protein mix.

After an hour, Ben returned to his head judge's seat, the auditorium packed. A burst of applause and chants of "Ben!" and "Mr. O!" filled his ears. A few spectators patted him on the back. He stood and flexed to wild cheers.

Ben announced the overall winner, a twenty-seven-year-old Ghanaian Super Heavyweight, a leviathan of obsidian blackness with razor-sharp angles. He praised him generously and told him privately that with the right trainer he'd claim the Mr. Olympia title. He remembered that Vinnie had predicted the Ghanaian would win.

Vinnie stood behind Ben hearing his private comment. But he also heard him telling the Ghanaian man to wait four or five years. Why? To avoid competing with him? Ben had told Vinnie he wasn't going to compete again but he shelved that promise when an admirer asked, "Will you return to compete?"

"I wouldn't say you're wrong," Ben said and popped a bicep.

"He fuckin' lied to me," Vinnie said, muttering to himself. "And this will kill him. I'm supposed to just stick around and watch this bullshit? Say nothing?"

Vinnie knew the stats. Anyone over thirty-five needs fierce growth-enhancement drugs and increased diuretics to stand a chance against the young bucks. Most sane body-builders know not to even try. He saw that the idolization galvanized Ben's irrational decision. He felt nauseous and decided to leave the competition.

On his way out of the auditorium Gianni intercepted him and took hold of his arm. Vinnie gave it a vigorous shake and Gianni released.

"Not now," he said, nostrils flared as he stormed past.

In the corridor Vinnie fumed. *Ciccio's a fuckin' scumbag. And Ben doesn't care about me, not like he used to.*

Ben walked into the same corridor twenty minutes after Vinnie. And he too was met by Ciccio, exclaiming, "*Magnifico! Bravo!* Best I've ever attended," repeating his backstage comments. He acted like a child getting an ice cream cone with his teammates after a soccer game.

"Your form was perfect. Look at these muscles," said Ciccio, squeezing Ben's arm, but he stumbled when the colossus shoved him away.

"Uh, sorry," said Ben, his voice flat. "I didn't mean to push so hard. I'm just tired. Have you seen Vinnie?"

"He left about twenty minutes ago," Ciccio answered with a shrug. "I don't know where he is."

Ben's lips partially opened to breathe through his mouth. *Why has Vinnie left and not told me?* "I've got to change before the final committee dinner," Ben said, coughing as he walked away.

Ciccio's phone chirped. "*Si, si. D'accordo*," he said. "I'll try but the committee dinner meeting is tonight. I'll wait in the bar. But he's tired. Tonight is not the best time to talk to him, I think."

Ciccio pulled the phone from his ear, hearing loud curses spewing out of his earpiece. He answered, "Si, I'll make sure I get him to come with me."

The call ended with Ciccio's face losing all its pallor. He went to the hotel bar to down his first beer, anticipating many more before the night ended. From his vantage point he would see Ben passing by after his committee dinner.

* * *

Gianni was at the hotel bar twenty minutes before Ciccio, sitting at a rear table so he didn't see him. His head was down, staring into his beer glass. It jerked up when Vinnie stood over him.

"*Ciao*, Vinnie. I didn't think you'd be here. I thought you'd be getting ready for the committee celebration dinner."

"Enough," said Vinnie and he shook his head. "I don't want to hear any more about the fuckin' expo in general or bodybuilding in particular. I've heard enough for a lifetime. Did you know Ciccio rubbed oil on Ben and it looked like a hand job? Fuck him. Everyone else wants to," Vinnie said with contempt.

"Not me. I like your body more. I would fuck you in a heartbeat."

"Never going to happen. I've just been fucked and fucked over. It's no fun."

Gianni's shoulders slumped, his face turning ashen as if about to cry.

"I'm sorry," Vinnie said, "I'm taking out my anger and frustration on you. Please forgive me." He surveyed the bar and saw no one suspicious.

"Gianni, I need to talk to someone about... uh... listen, can we get away from here?" he asked as he glanced around the room a second time. "A quiet place where we could find a good meal?"

"I know exactly where to go," Gianni said, his fist pumping the air. "Do you want to text the address to Ben?"

Vinnie shook his head. "He's at the farewell committee dinner. I'll text him later," and with that he switched his phone off.

Gianni walked to the employee parking with Vinnie trailing, and neither had noticed Ciccio waving to them from a table at the back.

Chapter 24

"You're kidding me. This is your ride?" Vinnie asked while his eyes moved from the front fender to the bright metallic blue tail fairing of an outsized Kawasaki Ninja 1000SX motorcycle.

Gianni mounted first followed by Vinnie behind. He shifted his weight forward to press against Gianni's butt. Vinnie didn't see it but he knew Gianni's face was on fire.

In a half-hour the motorcycle turned onto a secondary road toward the coastal town of Sant'Alessio Siculo, a medieval commune that predates the Magna Carta by one hundred years. Gianni parked in front of an old stone house, telling Vinnie that this was the ancestral Vaccaro home and his birthplace.

"My mother will be delighted to have an American visitor."

"Your mother? No, no, no."

Gianni placed his hands together wriggling at the wrist, the Italian sign for "don't even bother protesting."

Gianni's mother's enthusiastic greeting matched Gianni's prediction. "*Niente particolare*," she said apologetically, pointing to a feast.

Caterina, Gianni's sister, arrived in time to help her mother. She was even more beautiful than Gianni and her English more proficient. She talked about her courses in psychology at the University of Catania. She became more animated, smiling gleefully, and recounted her visit to New York. She loved it but was only there for a week and she missed it so much.

Gianni and Vinnie walked to the local bar for an after-dinner Campari. All heads turned as they entered and a chorus rang out. "*Salvo*, Gianni," "*Ciao*," "*Buona sera*, Gianni." Gianni beamed, his arm linked with Vinnie's.

"Do they know?" asked Vinnie, speaking softly as if anyone could hear or understand.

"Of course. This is a small village. And we are modern too. Ever since Gianni Versace, my namesake," he said with a laugh then rattled off prominent gay Italians. "One day they think I will become famous and bring many tourists here to see the house I was born in and make the town renowned and wealthy." Gianni finished with a guttural, heartwarming laugh and rubbed Vinnie's hand.

"Let's sit outside," he said, steering Vinnie to a small table with two wooden chairs. "We can talk without worry that anyone will be listening."

Across the patio were five old men playing cards. The indoor sounds percolated through the open doorway. Two teenagers had scored a goal against their opponents in a game of fusbol. An inane RAI Uno quiz filtered from the TV to the outdoor patio.

Vinnie relaxed yet nervously scratched the back of one hand with the other. Should he confide in a person he'd just met? And if he didn't, then who would he talk to? And he needed local knowledge, someone to speak the dialect and understand heavily accented Italian and Sicilian.

"Gianni, I've already told you about Ben—his steroid use and my concerns," Vinnie said, leaning slightly forward.

"*Si*," replied Gianni, who also edged closer to the table-top.

"But I haven't told you something… uh… that's a different problem."

In twenty minutes Vinnie covered his conflict with the Aquafreddo mob and the murders they committed, leading to an assassination contract on him but eventually rescinded—a story too long for him to explain in detail.

Gianni's face hardened on hearing his tale. "I'm so sorry for you. That's terrible."

"Yes, it was. But now I want to help Paul and hurt the Aquafreddo mob." Vinnie studied Gianni. He was a good listener. His PI skills lacked the fictional Sicilian Commissario Montalbano's prowess but at least Gianni was real.

I've said too much, thought Vinnie and rubbed his neck.

Gianni waited.

"Listen Gianni, to help Paul I must understand the Sicilian culture."

"Me," said Gianni, showing a set of bright white, cavity-free teeth that no doubt made his hygienist proud.

"What?" asked Vinnie.

"I know Sicily and Sicilians."

Vinnie's eyes widened. He didn't expect Gianni to make the leap so quickly. Or did he? Wasn't his question loaded? Was Gianni's eagerness too quick, a ruse to mask the expec-

164

tation of having hot sex? Was Gianni serious or was this a new seduction game?

"I have to ask, can I trust you?" Vinnie's question hung between them.

"Trust? I'm most trustworthy. Ask anyone. Shall I call those men playing cards over? Just ask, even at the hotel."

A smile crept around the edges of Vinnie's lips. *No one is this good at deception. But can he really help?*

Vinnie paused to phrase his words. "What I want is knowledge about the Mafia hiding locations and other stuff, although I don't exactly know what at this point." Vinnie closed his eyes. *Other stuff? I sound like an amateur.* He hummed while thinking. This was a big ask of a stranger, a happy young man who enjoyed his life.

Gianni spoke up. "I can help. I know who to ask. I can be your assistant."

"Huh," answered Vinnie, who thought he had concealed his concern. *He is good.* Vinnie took several sips of his Campari before saying, "When I work on a case in New York I bring my team together and we consider the options. They are usually corporate espionage or stealing by employees, nothing like this."

Gianni nodded. "Then I'm your team here in Sicily," he said with arms spread and cheeks puffed out. "Do I look like a team?" He laughed but Vinnie didn't join him.

"What do we do now?" Gianni asked.

The question seemed simple enough but Vinnie tilted his head and touched his nose. "I guess we review the client's needs."

"Then tell me about your client."

Vinnie's face sunk. He looked away, his eyes rotating as if searching for words. "At first I thought it was to help Commissario Delgrado solve Al Renato's murder." Vinnie puffed air. "Arrogant of me but I know who did it."

Gianni leaned forward, elbows on the table, eyes wide.

"Forget it, I'm not telling you." Vinnie put a hand over one eye as if squinting through a telescope. "Delgrado wants me to help Paul, and Paul wants my help in a different way."

An extremely loud cheer and cursing came from the fusbol table and Vinnie jumped. "Damn! They always this noisy?"

Gianni waved his hand as if circulating air.

"Let's look at the objectives," said Vinnie. "Delgrado wants Paul to come out of hiding and into FBI witness protection. I'm the intermediary." Vinnie saw Gianni's blank face. "*Mediatore.*"

"Okay, so now you know what to do."

"No, not so fast. Paul's goal is to expose the Aquafreddo mob's role in human trafficking." Vinnie stopped and saw Gianni's head tilted, his lips pursing. "I mean, what are the options? Do you understand?"

Gianni's fingers combed his hair.

Vinnie nodded as if understanding Gianni's gesture. "Am I working for Delgrado or Paul? Or are the refugees my client? And if so, how do I know what they want?"

"*Cosa?*" asked Gianni with an expressionless face except for the pursed lips.

Vinnie rubbed an earlobe between his thumb and index finger. "It's the refugees. And that means I have to help Paul."

Gianni said he only understood a little and Vinnie explained that Paul's interest in stopping Aquafreddo meant stopping the human trafficking, which helped the refugees.

"*Si, si*," Gianni said, smiling happily.

Sitting back in his chair, Vinnie looked at the dark night sky that seemed pitch black. "You know," he said with a sadness in his voice, "this is also about me."

Gianni's blank stare returned, although Vinnie sensed a smile was never far away.

"Okay, this is hard to explain," Vinnie said, lowering his voice, "but I need vindication. I want Aquafreddo to pay for the pain he caused me and my friends."

"*Va bene*. So, what do we do?" asked Gianni in a monotone.

"That's the problem. I'm following the orders of others. The Commissario, Paul, Maria Alba—I'm passive, a conduit for the will of others. Tomorrow I go to Tindari to get more instructions about something—God knows what. I'll go but that's the end of my taking orders."

"And me? I'm on your team," Gianni said, patting his chest as if he had won a prize.

The words struck Vinnie in a new way. He had to be sure Gianni understood his commitment.

"I told you, but I'll say it again. This may put your life at risk. Do you understand? I mean really understand? Is that okay with you?"

"*Si, si*."

"Gianni, these are truly evil men."

Gianni lifted Vinnie's hand to his lips and kissed it gently. "I know more about *La Cosa Nostra* than you do so don't think I'm ignorant. Don't worry about me."

For the first time Vinnie heard Gianni's adult voice. He wasn't a small-town gullible innocent or a gay playboy fool.

"No, I didn't mean it that way and I'll stop worrying," Vinnie said, knowing full well he had just lied.

* * *

Vinnie had called Ben twice while with Gianni and both times there was no answer. He didn't leave messages or send a text. *If he wants to behave like this then I'm not wasting my fuckin' time chasing him.* He switched off his cell. *Two can play this game.*

Vinnie didn't need his detective's sixth sense to tell him something wasn't kosher on entering the hotel bedroom around midnight and finding Ben wasn't there.

He had an early morning rise to get on the bus to Tindari. No time to sit up and confront Ben when he returned, if in fact he did. *He's probably out all night with his new fanboys,* Vinnie thought.

He needed to come up with ideas on how to get the information Paul wanted. The new location to assemble the hostages. The time and date of shipping. Paul had said he and Maria Alba were going over all shipping manifestos for the last three months, more than four hundred in total. *Is that what I'll learn tomorrow?*

Vinnie retired to the empty bed, saying a prayer. "Where the fuck is Ben? Amen."

Chapter 25

"I'm fucking hungry," Ben said as he turned his cell phone off while entering the hotel bar at happy hour. He had forty-five minutes to wait before the committee dinner. He spotted two of the organizers with their wives sitting at the bar with drinks in hand. *The others will be late. So typical.* He veered away and was surprised to meet Ciccio.

"*Ciao*, Ciccio."

"Sit with me," he said.

"I can't stay long. I have the committee celebration dinner in an hour. Have you seen Vinnie?"

Ciccio stuck out his chin. "I saw him leave with Gianni."

"Who?"

"The lifeguard."

"Fuck it. I'm not going to sit there next to Vinnie's empty chair. I'll grab a pizza in town."

With a smile too wide to fit on his face, Ciccio brightened. "Perfect. Come to my house for a home-cooked meal."

Ben thought this was a better option than a pizza joint where people gawked at him. The public didn't understand bodybuilding as a sport. He hated that ordinary folk half his size gave him surreptitious glances, not realizing he saw their mockery or pathetic sympathy for his intentional disfigurement.

"Why not? Let's go," answered Ben.

Ciccio nattered while driving. Ben pushed his seat back and closed his eyes. *If only he'd shut up.*

Ciccio reflected on Ben's performance then repeated that Vinnie had left with the lifeguard.

"Fuck him," said Ben out loud.

"*Cosa?*" asked Ciccio.

"Nothing, just talking to myself."

Ciccio turned to the right at a junction.

Ben knew Ciccio's house was near to his uncle Mario's home. After two weeks at Mario's gym, he knew the way by heart.

"Didn't you miss the turn?" Ben asked.

Ciccio lightly punched his shoulder and gave a short laugh. "We're going to my family's mountain cottage, which is close to Linguaglossa. Not far, maybe fifteen kilometers."

The talk turned to wine and Ciccio proudly extolled a fuzzy ruby red Mascalese grape. "Best *vino* in La Sicilia," he said with a sucking sound. "Wait until you taste it."

When they arrived Ben entered the stone cottage, admiring the granite architecture. The small living room was sparsely furnished, projecting an illusion of spaciousness. In contrast, the dining room seemed cramped by an eight-foot-long wooden table that was half as wide. A high cupboard dominated an entire wall. Ben walked sideways past the table into the kitchen.

The large size surprised Ben, who had anticipated it as having the same dimensions as the previous rooms. A small table occupied the center with four chairs tucked underneath. Closets lined every wall, and granite countertops covered base cabinets. Pots, dishes, two toasters, a microwave, ceramic serving plates, and sundry utensils lay on every surface.

Ciccio removed three covered pots from a large, American-style refrigerator.

"My mother stocks up for my father and uncle and their friends for unplanned visits," Ciccio chuckled. "Please, sit. I'll take care of the meal. Now that your show is over, you can drink *vino*."

Ciccio chattered while preparing the meal. Ben relaxed, absorbing the normalcy. Even Ciccio seemed different; solicitous and concerned for Ben's comfort. There was nothing overtly sexual, unlike his hovering in the expo pump room.

Ben drank the famous Nerello Mascalese wine that Ciccio poured from a homemade wicker-wrapped carafe into four-ounce glasses. The meal was excellent but Ben would have devoured it if it was dog food. He had starved himself of fats, carbs, and water for three days. With each bite and sip of wine he felt himself bloating. He didn't care.

Ciccio suggested they relax in the living room in front of the fireplace.

"But it's summer," Ben said.

"Yes, but even in July the night air descends Mount Etna after crossing the snow crown. The cool air comes down onto the villages." Ciccio lit the previously stacked kindling and tossed cushions on the floor for himself and Ben. They kicked off their shoes and socks then Ben asked for the bathroom.

He turned on his phone to dial Vinnie and again reached his voicemail, urging him to leave a message. *Why should I? He doesn't bother to call and leave me a message.* He turned off his phone and placed it on a counter next to the sink while he took a long pee.

The warm living room contrasted with the cool bathroom. He lay next to Ciccio, unsure why a small glass of wine should give him a buzz. "How strong is that wine?"

"This particular Nerello is fifteen to twenty percent alcohol, so higher than the typical thirteen to fourteen percent," Ciccio said, citing the statistics known to everyone in the region. He poured more wine into Ben's glass.

"That is high for wine."

"Yes, and makes it even better. Don't you agree?" asked Ciccio, his face flushed and not just from the wine.

Ben lay on his back, hands behind his head, meditating on his performance, the applause, and the cheers. The joy of the day returned. For once he relaxed unaided by Valium.

Ciccio turned sideways to rest his head on Ben's chest and Ben pushed him off.

"Your performance excited me. I got hard," he said. "You have no idea the influence you have on us gay men. I want to have all of you."

"What?! Look, Ciccio, I don't know what you expected but I didn't come here for sex. Sorry, but that's how it is."

Ciccio nodded and then continued to praise Ben's performance. His soft voice lulled Ben and the melodic Italian accent had a hypnotic effect. The fire radiated heat. Ciccio removed his shirt and encouraged Ben to do likewise.

"Look, I said no."

"Of course, but this will help you relax. I can see you're tense."

Ben agreed. He was tense from thinking about Vinnie going off with the lifeguard and why he didn't bother to send him a text.

The fire crackled, the light playing on the bronzing oil remnants as if firing his oven-ready clay muscles into fine porcelain. Flickering sparks accentuated his rippling sinew. Ciccio massaged Ben's large, swelled pectorals. Ben sighed. *It's only a massage and nothing more.*

"I've seen most of you but you've not seen me," said Ciccio, removing his pants.

Ciccio's erect stub throbbed.

"Ciccio, what the fuck? I said no! Get dressed."

"There is nothing wrong. Please don't be angry with me. We're alone and you'll see it helps relax to be naked by a hot fire."

Ben wasn't fooled but he also found Ciccio's words excited him. He thought of Vinnie and he became angry. *Why not undress?*

Ben arched his back and removed his clothes, his shaft rising.

"Show me again the leg extension. Let me see the quadriceps flare. The crowd went wild for it."

The leg pose was one of Ben's favorites. From his prone position he shook his bulldog quads, filling them with blood pulsing from heart to toe on a continental journey. Bam! His leg snapped muscles, an entire Latin anatomy dictionary from the *Vastus Lateralis* to *Rectus Femoris* to *Sartorius*. Ben held the pose while Ciccio ran his finger along each groove like a disc jockey playing the top twenty.

"What the fuck, man!" yelled Ben, pushing Ciccio on to his back.

"You don't like?"

"No, I don't like. You need to ask before doing anything like that."

Ciccio stuck his chin out and lifted his head while pulling himself upright to kneel. "I thought you might like it. Don't you have admirers that want to fuck you?"

"Not since Vinnie," Ben said, and saying his name out loud reminded him they'd not talked since the late afternoon. He closed his eyes. *He's doing whatever the fuck he wants. Having fun. And I know he fucked Paul and now he's with the lifeguard.*

With his imagination untethered, Ben's fury grew and his sexual arousal diminished. He sat up on his elbows and looked at Ciccio. He switched to contest-judging mode. *He's an amateur with some definition and a hint of bulk in his pickle biceps.* Ben stared at Ciccio's aquiline nose. His short-cropped black hair with doe-brown eyes made him desirable.

Ciccio walked out of the room and returned holding a pellet that resembled canary food.

"What is it?" Ben asked, watching Ciccio crush it into a powder and hold it under Ben's nose.

"A ticket to heaven," said Ciccio, raising his eyes to the ceiling. "Makes you float outside your body. You'll think you're expanding with the universe."

Lost in his temper and desperate to shake his negativity, Ben hesitated then took a snort and was reborn or reinvented or reincarnated. Re-something. He wasn't sure and had no interest in searching for the right word. He imagined his muscles pumped bigger than hot air balloons rising over the Rockies. His veins engorged. He was bigger than ever. He believed his cock extended across the room. An overwhelming, unstoppable desire took hold. He stroked himself until Ciccio took over.

Ben's penis howled. He was sweating, sucking air, throwing his arms overhead, then brandished a double-bicep pose. He was once again on stage. His vision slightly blurred as he saw Ciccio on the floor holding his knees to his chest, inviting Ben to enter. A grand sacrifice to a muscle god.

Enough fluid was exchanged to replenish a well run dry by the summer heat. Ben was spent, adding to the tiredness of a long and emotional day. He fell into a semiconscious state. Ciccio gave him more wine and added a sedative powder. Ben sneezed, and although groggy and confused he sensed his libido sagging. He went back into his half-slumber as Ciccio helped relieve Ben's tension.

Within the hour Ciccio heard the text messages ping his phone. Ben stirred but remained semiconscious.

"Who's that?" Ben said, mumbling his words. "Is it Vinnie?"

Before Ciccio answered he heard rapid tapping at the front door.

Chapter 26

Ciccio slipped from Ben's side, trying not to disturb him with no time to dress as the pounding increased. A van's headlights blinded him as he opened the door. Two men pushed past. They quickly and efficiently bound Ben's wrists behind his back.

"I don't think it necessary," Ciccio protested. "I thought you only wanted to talk. And as you can see I gave him too much so—"

"*Stai zitto*," said a squat, well-built young man dressed completely in black. "*E chi se ne frega?*" Shut up. Who gives a damn what you think?

His companion pushed Ciccio aside. He too was young and muscular. He wore white jeans with a Catania Calcio Club strip and a famous Italian soccer player's name on the back.

He shouted in Sicilian, "*A megghiu parola è chidda ca non si dici.*" Best to say nothing. He gave Ciccio a hard slap across the face.

Ben stirred, his eyes dull, his jaw slack, his throat burning. In a semiconscious stupor he saw the men. Did they want to feel his badass biceps or see him throw out his chest? He strained but couldn't move his arms. Had he overdone the diuretics, his muscles frozen stiff? Ben tried to stand and stumbled.

"Tie his ankles too," said the man in black, throwing another hank of nylon cord at Ciccio.

Calcio Man ordered Ciccio to help him and his partner carry the hog-tied Ben outside.

"Why? I was told you only wanted to…"

A grizzly look from the man in black stopped Ciccio's talking and he lifted Ben's head.

Ben blinked, looking at the ceiling. Had he finished his routine? Was he doing a handstand? He heard whispering, or was that tanning oil dripping in his ear?

"Wha… uh…aa… tt. Hello? Uh-oh… louder. Can't hear. My arm's stuck, muscle froze up or something."

"I'm so sorry. They only wanted to talk. If I had known I wouldn't have—" whispered Ciccio while laying Ben in the waiting van.

This second slap to Ciccio's face brought a redness to his cheek The man in black placed a hand over Ciccio's mouth.

"*Stai zitto*," he said. "Say nothing if you know what's good for you." The man in black entered the back of the van to ride with Ben. The other walked up to Ciccio.

"You going to be a problem?" he growled.

Ciccio shook his head. "No, I promise. Not a word to anyone."

Calcio Man shoved Ciccio toward the cabin and the van drove away. Ciccio stood naked and weeping in the darkness.

* * *

The dirty wooden floor matched the damp cinderblock walls permanently impregnated with mildew. Ben awoke groggy and disorientated, not knowing where he was or how long he'd been out. He knew it was no longer night as shafts of sunlight penetrated old, splintered, closed window shutters. He lay on the floor mattress without sheets and no pillow but with a lightweight cotton duvet over him. Sitting up slowly, Ben's head pounded from the wine and Ciccio's cocktail drug mix. He rested his back against the wall. He estimated the room to be about the size of his UltraFit office, making it twelve by fourteen feet. A small table and a wooden chair were positioned in the center with an oak door opposite him. Otherwise the room was bare. He rubbed his arms and neck. He had an urge to pee.

Rising slowly, he used the table's edge to steady himself to walk around and he stumbled as he neared the door. His head spun, he was disorientated in the unfamiliar surroundings. Sweat seeped out of pores he never knew he had. His throat constricted as he mispronounced Italian words then switched to English. His mind clouded and his body shook. He buttressed one hand on the wall beside him and the other turned the doorknob. He pulled but the forged hinges didn't budge. He pulled harder and heard the doorknob cracking. He'd break it off before the door opened. He banged and found his voice returned. He screamed, "Let me out. I gotta pee."

No reply. His hammering intensified. "Where am I? I've gotta pee." Another punch at the door and Ben sat on the floor to rest.

Using the doorknob for balance he struggled to stand. He repeated the pounding with less energy. He rested his elbows on the table. His head ached and he rubbed his temples. A metallic taste flushed his mouth along with increased spasmodic coughing. He had to start his post cycle therapy or it would get worse. He'd been on Trenbolone and Dianabol too long.

The early morning chilly mountain air cooled the room. A dampness penetrated his core. Being naked didn't help and then he noticed his clothes piled in a corner of the room. He dressed before pushing open the shutters, and the sunlight pierced his eyes and stabbed his brain. His eyelids thudded closed.

The oak door swung open, startling Ben. Two large young men about an inch shorter than him stepped through the threshold. Each carried a weapon, the barrel pointed at him and a strap at the tip that slung over their shoulders like handbags. Everything Ben knew about weapons came from watching action films with Vinnie. These were semi-automatic guns and that was the total extent of his knowledge.

A very thin man emerged from behind the gunmen as if he'd been hiding behind a barricade. He was their height but older. He was dressed in a sports shirt, fashionable jeans, and expensive Italian leather loafers and no socks. His deep voice was incongruous compared to his stature.

"Hello, Ben. I've wanted to meet you for such a long time," the man said in perfect English with a Brooklyn intonation.

"Yeah? And who the fuck are you and why am I locked

in this fucking shithole?" Ben's voice matched the baritone of the thin man but was louder.

"You're here because you serve a purpose. And as strong as you are, and I can see you've got muscles upon muscles, you're no match for these guns." The man gestured to the two men standing to his side. "And maybe even they could take you without their weapons."

The thin man turned and said something in Italian and the bodyguard in the Catania strip raised his arm and flexed one arm, creating a rising mound. The man in black did the same, his arm a cannonball.

"You see how big and strong they are?"

"Fuck you and fuck them. I don't care how big, I'll bet they're all steroids and they never lifted in their life. I ask again, who the fuck are you?"

"You know me, at least my name. I'm Frank Aquafreddo."

Ben held his breath, his eyes glued on Carmine Aquafreddo's eldest son. Vinnie had told him about the Gola nickname and Ben reflexively put a hand to his throat.

Aquafreddo moved closer. "Now you understand," he said with his pockmarked face sneering.

"And what do you want from me?" Ben asked while considering that if Aquafreddo came one step closer he'd be able to rip his head off.

"You? Nothing at all. It's Vinnie we want to help with a little matter and you're the incentive. If he cooperates, you two can return to your life of screwing each other until your assholes bleed."

180

Aquafreddo turned to the two men and spoke in Italian, and both gave false laughs to acknowledge their boss's wit. Aquafreddo didn't smile at his own joke.

"I've gotta piss," Ben said, which took Aquafreddo by surprise and he laughed.

"Sure, my men will escort you to the bathroom. We'll bring a pot in here too for the middle of the night. And just so you know, every door in this house is bolted shut." Aquafreddo looked to the open shutters. "It's a thirty-foot drop onto hard soil over a lava bed. You're welcome to try to jump but I'd guess with your weight you'd be lucky if all you broke were your legs."

"Fuck you."

"And, just to be clear, even should you beat these men," Aquafreddo said, gesturing to the guards, "which I doubt, I also have a gun." He pulled a revolver from his pocket.

"I just want to pee."

Aquafreddo's head tilted to the door and the two guards went to Ben, chained his legs prisoner style, and escorted him to the toilet.

Chapter 27

The hotel wakeup call came a minute before Vinnie's own cell phone alarm sounded as backup. He opened his eyes and saw there was no Ben. *Where the fuck is he?*

He had a massive headache and thought of staying in bed and missing the Tindari excursion tour and Sabrina. But then he thought of the refugees, staggered to rise, showered, dressed, and boarded the Pullman five minutes before the seven-thirty departure.

The bus zipped along the autostrada at one hundred twenty kilometers an hour while cars buzzed past. *Fuckin' crazy*, Vinnie thought. *They're doing at least ninety miles an hour.*

The Pullman's lush interior surprised Vinnie. It was nothing like a typical USA Greyhound bus. Soothing blue seats offset by light blue carpet and pastel blue walls. Tinted windows stretched from seat height to the roof, providing panoramic views. Electric shades blocked direct sunlight yet were translucent enough to enjoy the passing scenery. Small TVs recessed into each seat's rear showed views of the excursion with headset plug-in jacks giving commentary in seven languages. The other channels included weather, local and international news, and music videos. Two attendants served drinks and snacks.

Most of the passengers were retirees except for two families with children between ten and twelve years old. Two African bodybuilders with their girlfriends boarded, which surprised Vinnie. They were moved from their assigned seats midway along the aisle as their double-wide shoulders hindered the attendants' ability to serve. They swapped with four passengers in the rear bank's five seats, with one seat unoccupied due to a cancellation.

Vinnie sat next to a man from Canada in the window seat. To Vinnie's relief he wasn't interested in small talk. After ten minutes, he wished the Canadian was more talkative as the quiet had him ruminating about Ben. Four calls and two text messages with not a single reply. *What happened?* His anger melted into worry. *Is Ben okay?*

One of the attendants announced the spectacular view of the Straits of Messina with twenty-five minutes to their destination. Was this a mistake like Ben had warned? He stood to stretch, turning back to the bodybuilders, their girlfriends snuggling with smiling faces while the men wore chiseled frowns. He was sure the girlfriends had hounded them to take the trip with incredible sex promised on their return.

Approaching the high mountain village, one attendant stood in the aisle and over the intercom reviewed the tight itinerary. They'd be met by a local guide in the main piazza overlooking the Aeolian Islands. She would take them inside the Church of the Madonna Nera and to the statue of the Black Madonna. Vinnie's ears pricked—the original meeting point. Was the Commissario already there? The informant?

The attendant explained the importance of Tindari's Greek amphitheater and Roman ruins. "You'll stroll ancient streets before boarding for the second part of the tour, a visit to Patti on the coast with its famous ceramic laboratories."

Famous my ass, thought Vinnie. *Never heard of them and by laboratories she means discount outlet stores.*

"Our *pranzo* in a local restaurant is at one-thirty—all the details are on your itinerary. We return to Hotel Mezzogiorno by three." The attendant switched off the microphone and took her seat as the bus climbed up the curving mountain road.

The Pullman passed through Tindari's narrow ancient portal into the piazza but was stopped by two police cars. The passengers disembarked, with the local guide directing them to the far side of the piazza.

"I'm sorry," said the guide, "the Roman villa is closed and cannot be visited today. If anyone wishes to return another day, the tour company would be pleased to arrange a guide with advance notice."

Commissario Delgrado appeared from nowhere, took Vinnie by his arm and pulled him aside.

"Come with me," he said, his face unfriendly, his tone even less so. His hand squeezed Vinnie's arm to drag him away from the panoramic view.

"Hey, let go! What the fuck is going on?"

"Follow me," Delgrado said, releasing Vinnie's arm.

They walked along a passage following a sign for the Greek Theater and Roman Temples. Vinnie repeated his objection but Delgrado marched on in silence.

184

Three police cars with flashing blue lights were parked outside the villa ticket booth. Two Carabinieri blocked the entrance. On either side stood four Polizia di Stato. The two Carabinieri moved as the Commissario approached with Vinnie in tow.

The Commissario led Vinnie along a pebbled path built by the Romans and not repaired since. Vinnie recognized the scene unfolding before him. A dozen or so technicians in white garb, masks, and plastic bags covering their shoes—a forensic team. A collection relay formed with three technicians hunched over the back of a kneeling colleague who filled bags and returned them to be couriered to the unit's vehicle.

Delgrado asked the group to step aside.

"Take a look, Signor Briggs," Delgrado said.

Vinnie stepped forward to see a naked body on the ground with a purple-tinged face, bulging eyes, and black tongue extended from the mouth. A gaping wound lengthwise across the throat leaked congealed blood. Vinnie stumbled forward. Even with the disfigurement, the muscular body and facial disfigurement didn't hide the identity. Vinnie froze.

"I'm sure you recognize him."

"Ciccio."

"Correct. Want to take a closer look?" asked Delgrado, pushing Vinnie forward, and he pushed back. "Stop! This is..." Vinnie choked up. "Oh my god, what happened?"

"Safe to say his throat was cut, no? An earlier tour group found the body. We believe he was murdered here, maybe two or three hours ago."

Whether from the slit throat, the large puddle of blood, or the heat from the rising sun, Vinnie went into shock. His eyes welled up and he gave a barely perceptible cry. He blew his nose and sat on a nearby boulder before he fell.

"A friend?" asked the Commissario in a softened voice.

"We've met. He was Ben's friend more than mine. We weren't close but…" Vinnie gulped. "But this is…"

"Signor Briggs, it seems a lot of your friends turn up dead. This concerns me."

Vinnie realized Delgrado was speaking formally, not only in addressing him by his surname but he had abandoned *tu* for the formal *lei* third-person conjugation.

"And why are you so upset if this isn't a friend?" asked the Commissario.

Something like a smile briefly crossed Vinnie's face but it disappeared quickly. "I'm a bit of a crybaby."

The Commissario shook his head and Vinnie rubbed his eyes, emphasizing the movement.

"*Ah, un piagnone.* You call this 'crybaby.' I understand now. Don't worry, we Italians cry a lot too." And for a moment the Commissario seemed to return to his light-hearted demeanor until his next words. "This is your fault."

"What? That's fuckin' wrong. I would never have wanted anything like this!"

"But you didn't like him, did you?"

"No, but not this kind of dislike. We fought over Ben, I was a little jealous… but I'd never want him dead. I'd have told you."

"But you didn't," said the Commissario, sucking in his cheeks.

186

"Because I didn't know!"

"You knew about the change in the meeting location. You gave me the wrong information on my office machine—which I told you never to do. I had men posted before dawn at the Madonna Nera and not hiding among the ancient Roman ruins. Why is that?"

For the next hour Vinnie and the Commissario sat in a bar in the piazza below a blue sky dotted with puffy white clouds. The sunlight shimmered on the water surface that stretched to the end of the world. Vinnie's emotions drained him of tears, fears, then replaced them with anger.

"I made a bad decision. I killed Ciccio," Vinnie said, conjuring words he'd said in the past.

"No, you didn't kill him but as I said you're responsible. You didn't listen to me."

Tears flooded Vinnie's eyes and he blurted, "I don't know where Ben is. I haven't seen him since yesterday."

"Okay, we'll look into it. Check all the hospitals and talk to the hotel staff."

Vinnie recognized the police procedurals and knew they meant little if Ben had been taken hostage.

"Will they kill Ben?" he asked.

"We don't know he's been taken. Maybe he got drunk and is sleeping at someone's house."

"You don't know Ben. He's never been drunk, not like that." Vinnie didn't like the Commissario's quick and easy answer. "Here's my opinion," said Vinnie. "This is the mob and they've taken Ben to get at me and Paul."

Delgrado gave a quick nod and his eyes blazed.

"Maybe, but not necessarily. We know Ciccio helped

the mob with small jobs like kickbacks, collections, and transporting drugs between gyms. He wasn't actually part of the Cosa Nostra. More like what you call an extra, a bit player."

"Then why kill him if it's not a message to me?"

"Maybe he skimmed or he learned something he shouldn't know or he insulted or fucked—" Delgrado leaned over. "He's dead so this doesn't go anywhere. I'm not going to malign him or hurt his family with speculation at this stage. Do you understand?" he asked.

Vinnie promised not to tell anyone.

"We heard Ciccio had sex with a Mafia boss's sixteen-year-old son. It was all smoothed over as the son took the blame. Ciccio paid a large sum to the father to mitigate his, er, role in the transgression. We can't rule out that he didn't repeat the same thing with the same boy or another one. It might explain why he's naked."

Vinnie nodded. He easily believed Ciccio would be at-tracted to underage, developing teenagers. He looked at the Commissario. The open palm of one hand massaged the balled-up fist of the other. "Nice story but I doubt it's the reason he was killed here." Vinnie's chin pointed to the Parco Romano. "It's about me and Paul, trust me. And Ben is next, then it's my turn."

Vinnie's stomach clawed, wanting to retch its contents. If only he'd been open and truthful. He could fill a barrel with "ifs" and not one would atone for Ciccio Volpe.

"From now on," Delgrado said, "you tell me everything. And never use the Questura's phone line."

"Yes, I agree and this time I mean it," said Vinnie, who

thought the "I mean it" conveyed sincerity.

On the return journey the old-age pensioners slept. The kids listened to their music or fiddled with their iPads and the parents glued themselves to the TV screens or their phones. Vinnie stared out the window, grateful his Canadian companion snoozed. The African women snuggled deep into the arms of their boyfriends, who were smiling and anticipating the good time that awaited them.

Vinnie reviewed over and over the events leading to the trip. He recalled Ben's final words hours before departing JFK: "This won't end well."

Chapter 28

Vinnie returned to his hotel room and paced the spare room. This was an emergency by any criterion and he called Maria Alba.

"*Caro*, I have a friend in my bedroom with his pants around his ankles and I'm wearing a necklace and nothing more. This better be good."

Vinnie scoffed. He was sick of hearing about her sex life and wanted real information. He was surprised by her next comment.

"I heard about Ciccio. Don't worry."

"What!" screamed Vinnie. "Are you fuckin' crazy? I knew him. Ben knew him! And you say don't fuckin' worry?"

"Lots of people knew Ciccio."

"That's it? A fuckin' whoopie fuckin' boo-hoo, Ciccio's dead, move on. Not good enough, Maria Alba. I want answers."

"*Caro*—"

"And cut the *caro* shit."

"Vinnie, let me explain. Ciccio was indirectly involved with the mob. There were also rumors of him with teenage boys—"

"Yeah, yeah. Same bullshit I got from Delgrado."

"Leave it. Sabrina will find out the details. Give her time."

"And where was my guardian angel in Tindari?"

"She was there."

"A ghost?" Vinnie choked while talking.

"She called me to tell you but too late. You were already on the bus."

"Then why wasn't she there when I arrived?"

"Did you expect her to stick around surrounded by police? I thought you were smart."

Vinnie threw his mobile phone across the room, ranting. He looked around. *Where's Ben?* His eyes clouded over. He retrieved his phone and redialed Maria Alba.

"Vinnie, I'm sorry," she said in a calm voice.

"Fuck you and fuck your 'I'm sorry.' Ben's... uh..." Vinnie stopped speaking to catch his breath. "Ben's missing. Something's happened to him." And with the words out Vinnie broke down and cried.

Maria Alba repeated, "Vinnie, stop. Stop! Listen to me."

"Yeah?" asked Vinnie, wiping his nose.

"Ben's okay, I'm sure of it. We will find him, don't worry."

Vinnie slammed his fist on the desk. *I'd like to ring her fuckin' neck with her "I'm sure."*

"I want to talk to Paul. Ciccio wasn't murdered over skimming money or fucking a sixteen-year-old. Ben's next." Vinnie stopped talking, inhaling huge breaths and gulping half a bottle of water. "So?" he asked.

"Paul can't be reached," Maria Alba said, returning to

her usual cool indifference.

"Yes he can. And you do it or I'm out."

After a long pause, Maria Alba said, "Do one more thing."

"No. I'm done with this yanking me around by my chain."

"Vinnie, please. This will either solve it or you go home. Tomorrow go to the Museo della Ceramica in Patti at noon."

Vinnie thought he'd lost the connection as Maria Alba's voice became muffled. He heard in Italian, "In the bedroom and the blue gel in the side draw, *tesoro*. I'll be there in a minute." Then her voice returned to full volume. "There's usually no visitors. Come alone. *Buona notte*. Vinnie, I'm busy with someone. We'll talk tomorrow."

The line went dead. Vinnie's anger resurfaced. He'd had it with the one-way communication. He'd didn't need the condescending BS from a sex maniac. He finished his water before making the next call.

Gianni answered on the first ring. "*Ciao*, Vinnie. How was your trip?"

"Can you go to Patti tomorrow?"

"Huh?"

"I'll explain later. Can you take me to Patti?"

"*Si*, I'll tell the manager I'm sick. I've worked extra hours so he owes me."

"Can you get a car? If not I'll rent one. I'm not going on that death machine of yours."

"Okay, yes, I will use my sister's car."

"Great. I'll meet you at the hotel entrance." Vinnie paused. "No, park near the pizzeria across from Hotel Girasole and I'll find you. What kind of car does your sister have?"

"A Fiat Cinquecento."

Vinnie groaned. "Your motorcycle is bigger. Is that the best you can do?"

"No, you're thinking the *vecchio* Cinquecento from the sixties but this is the *Cinquecento Dolcevita*. It has the roof collapse."

"In an accident?"

"No, the car is new. I mean the roof opens."

"Ah, a convertible. And the color?"

"*Rossa*. A beautiful red like a ruby lipstick."

And no one will notice us, Vinnie thought after the call ended.

Vinnie thought the room was gloomier, the sky less blue. *How do I tell Ben about Ciccio?* Vinnie stopped to sit on the couch. *If I even find him? Is he dead like Ciccio?*

Vinnie began pacing the room, his eyes scooting across each wall. He made notes. With the expo finished, Ben had no obligations except for next year's planning meeting. He'd check with the committee to find out if he showed up. Maybe talk to Ciccio's uncle Mario. Vinnie scratched that off. *No, I can't face the grieving family. Better to let Delgrado do it.*

Vinnie recalled Ben's attitude over the last few days. He'd been erratic. He had a raging hard-on for days. He'd displayed the classic signs of roid rage, which he'd never had as long as they'd been together. Had he overdone his cycle? Was he cranked up and couldn't get down? He'd check with Delgrado for an update on hospital admissions.

He thought about the intended message with Ciccio's murder and the edges of his lips spread. It meant Ben was more valuable alive than dead or it'd have been his body in the Parco Romano.

Vinnie stood in the middle of the four free-standing mirrors in the spare room. Ben's spot. He mimicked a pose then checked his cell. No messages or text. Another attempted call to Ben that like before went straight to voicemail. If he hadn't gone off with Ciccio, then with whom? Was he bored with Ciccio? Did he hook up with one of the contest winners? The South African would have been to Ben's liking, even if he didn't place. He was intelligent and funny. *Where the fuck is Ben? He has to be alive.*

Chapter 29

Gianni's sister's red Fiat convertible was more spacious than Maria Alba's classic Cinquecento. Comfy but conspicuous.

Vinnie wasted no time babbling his thoughts to Gianni as they flew along the autostrada. He spilt his guts and fears over Ben. "That scumbag Ciccio did something, I'm sure of it," he said and he sucked in air. He shouldn't have said that of the dead. Vinnie hands fidgeted and his eyes swiveled like an owl searching for prey from the front windshield to the side window.

"Gianni, I've been thinking. I've asked too much of you. This is more dangerous than I thought. Drop me off and you go home."

"But I accept the danger. I like you too much for anything bad to happen."

Whatever Gianni intended, the words didn't soothe Vinnie's nerves. His eyes rested on Gianni's profile, his high cheekbones and deep tan. He belonged in a movie, his handsome face projected onto a big screen.

Gianni parked his sister's car in a postage stamp space kissing the front and rear bumpers of neighboring cars. Vinnie stepped onto the sidewalk and imagined every mafioso snapping photos of him and Gianni and the red convertible. He thought everyone was a spy. Was that old lady looking in their direction? Did the barista stare too long?

"Where's the museum?" asked Vinnie.

"You said *mezzogiorno* and it's only eleven-thirty. We have time for an espresso." Gianni pointed to the small café bar with two vacant outdoor tables in front.

Vinnie shook his head. Gianni had no concept of an early arrival to scope out the museum's surroundings.

"What do you mean 'scope?' You want to visit the museum?"

"No. I mean... ah, forget it. We're here to get information from Serafina. If nothing happens then I'm done helping Paul and I'll concentrate on finding Ben."

Vinnie was sure Gianni misunderstood the directions to the museum as he turned into a parking lot in the *Zona Industriale.* A sign over an abandoned convent pointed to the Museo Ceramico di Patti. There wasn't much to scope out. Vinnie's watch showed it to be a few minutes past noon.

A diminutive woman met them as they entered the museum's foyer and introduced herself as the custodian. Her bright yellow shirt, white pants, and sneakers contrasted with her soulful face replete with sorrow that Vinnie guessed hid a misfortune.

Gianni explained who they were and her demeanor brightened.

"*Buon giorno. Per piacere,*" she said in a soft voice. Seeing Vinnie take out his wallet she wagged her finger saying, "*L'ingresso gratis.*"

Vinnie thought he should leave something given the

meager state of the room, so typical in Italy with insufficient funds given to maintain local historical treasures. The woman guided them with her hands as if backing a truck onto a loading dock.

They entered a small room with glass cabinets. A treasure of ceramic pottery jammed every case. In the center was a table with a vase five or six feet high decorated in typical Sicilian bright reds and oranges.

Maria Alba entered from a rear door, which surprised Vinnie. She came within a foot and spoke sharply. "I said come alone. Who's he?" She lifted her chin, aiming it at Gianni.

"A friend and my guide."

"He can't be here."

Vinnie's nostrils flared. "He stays or I go. From now on I give the orders and ask the questions and you answer. *Capisce!*"

The last thing Vinnie expected was Maria Alba's horsey laugh and the patting of Vinnie's cheek. He was also surprised she didn't ask Gianni questions.

"*Va bene.* Come with me," said Maria Alba.

"Wait. Where's Serafina? Has something happened?"

"No. Just a change of plans. Now follow me, we don't have time to waste."

She took Vinnie and Gianni into a large room with many shelves packed with ceramics of all shapes and sizes.

"Too many to display," explained Maria Alba, and she pointed to a small table with four chairs. She went into detail about the trafficking and gave a summary to Gianni in Italian. Her words chilled the air in the un-air-conditioned building.

"This is too cruel," Gianni said. "It's okay when they kill each other but not these poor innocent people."

"Not everyone is innocent," she said. "Ciccio may have brought about his own death from what Serafina can piece together. We don't know what he did but his death is a message for Paul."

"Thanks for the great insight, Sherlock," said Vinnie.

Gianni shrugged—he didn't understand and Mari Alba brushed past the insult.

"Let's get to it. What do I do to help?" Vinnie asked and Gianni tapped his hand. "*We* do," Vinnie corrected himself.

Maria Alba gave an overview, repeating it in Italian to be sure Gianni understood. The assignment was to catch the mob in the act of loading young girls and boys into crates.

"Real proof, not hearsay or circumstantial, that's the point."

"I know this. But how do I… I mean *we* help?"

"They know Paul worked out the original location and date. They made a big mistake murdering the woman refugees at the Catania warehouse and putting the entire Catania province police force on high alert. They'll move to another province and our guess is Messina. That'll mean another shipping date too."

"So?" Vinnie asked, chewing his lip.

"Listen, stop interrupting," she said, an eyebrow arching.

She gave more overview of how trafficking depended on large containers, the kind used in wine or ceramics exportation. The key was to have the hostages at one location prior to being loaded into containers.

"I get it. Big stuff sent in large containers," huffed Vinnie. "So?"

"And the payment is also coordinated. Everything at the time of shipment. Paul worked on this for months to figure out how and it's not straightforward."

Vinnie thought he was going down a rabbit hole. He'd exposed corporate embezzlement before but nothing this complicated because it usually involved the movement of money electronically, nothing large or tangible. Nothing like humans.

For fifteen minutes Maria Alba lectured him on Mafia commodity economics, with the commodities heroin, diamonds, and trafficked hostages, notwithstanding that the latter were people rather than goods. "Think of each traded for the other like Mafia bitcoins," she said, "because the amount in real money—dollars—is too large to wire transfer, even to offshore accounts."

"Why?" asked Vinnie.

"Terrorists."

"Huh. How?" asked Vinnie. Gianni's head shake also showed he too didn't understand.

"Because governments increased their monitoring of large bank transfers to uncover the next terrorist plot. In a way, the terrorists have interfered in the affairs of organized criminals."

Vinnie knew about cryptocurrency, something that he learned for a client to reveal embezzlement. He stood and paced the room.

"So, you're saying they trade one object for the other. Heroin for diamonds for hostages?"

"*Cento punti,*" said Maria Alba. "You get an A+."

Vinnie sat then realized he had no idea on how to exchange real commodities.

"Paul's on this," said Maria Alba. "He thinks it might be related to the salt shaker."

"Why?"

"Because Serafina took it from Al and he wasn't the kind of guy to collect souvenirs. A salt shaker is perfect to transfer heroin or diamonds," answered Maria Alba.

"You're kidding me. There's cocaine or diamonds in my shaker?"

Maria Alba gave a wry smile before answering. "No. And it's not clear Al's shakers are the exact items. It's a subtle clue and may mean nothing." She paused to examine her nails.

"Yeah, a little too subtle. I'm supposed to look in all of Sicily for salt shakers?" Vinnie shook his head slowly. "And why not tell me this from the start?"

The smile reappeared on Maria Alba's face, only wider. "Because we think your room might be bugged."

"The Mafia bugs hotel rooms?"

"No, the anti-Mafia division bugs hotel rooms. Remember their inside Mafia informant? And we couldn't be sure you wouldn't tell Ben, who in turn might tell someone at the gym."

"Ben can keep a secret as well as me. He wouldn't tell anyone. I didn't."

Maria Alba and Gianni laughed simultaneously.

"You're both fuckin' idiots," Vinnie said, red-faced. "Of course I told him," he said while pointing at Gianni. "I needed to talk out my ideas, it's what I do." Then he added, "Uh-oh."

"What?" asked Maria Alba.

"Ben complained about Paul and his Mafia connection to me in front of Ciccio."

No one spoke for ten seconds, all processing the same thought. Ciccio linked Ben to Vinnie to Paul.

Maria Alba examined her nails one last time before looking up.

"Paul's narrowed the possible locations to six *laboratorio di ceramiche*, what you might call a ceramic factory. Tourist call them showrooms. Paul believes a workshop in Patti is the most likely location to gather the people in one place. That's the reason for the Tindari setup. A perfectly good reason for you to visit the historic mountain village. Serafina was to give you a list of ceramic showrooms in Patti to visit on the second part of your tour and allow your famous detective intuition to kick in."

Vinnie was soaking up the new information. He again stood to pace.

"How's this for a start? Gianni and I will visit each showroom like we're looking for presents to give friends."

Gianni jumped up waving his hand. "Why not as *promessi sposi*." He looked at Maria Alba, who translated for Vinnie. "He means 'betrothed' but I think you Americans prefer 'engaged.'"

"Yes," Gianni said, "and we're are looking to buy the *bomboniere matrimonio*." He again turned to Maria Alba for clarification.

"Wedding favors."

Gianni's face glowed. "*Grandissimo*. I will be married to Vinnie."

Hearing the words, Vinnie tapped his wedding ring and immediately realized a problem. If he removed it he'd have a white band on a tanned finger.

"I'll need a bandage to cover this. Maybe two, as if I cut myself," Vinnie said, looking at Maria Alba, who nodded but pointed out it was not necessary to actually cut his fingers.

Vinnie wanted to know how many factories/showrooms Patti had. Maria Alba handed him Paul's shortlist with six addresses.

"*Va bene*. You two are the perfect couple, *belli, giovani e persone di classe*. Now go find the *laboratorio*," commanded Maria.

"And if we locate the factory, then what?" asked Vinnie.

"We tell Commissario Delgrado to setup a stakeout and be ready for the loading. We'll have to estimate the shipping date."

"And this will bring down the Aquafreddo mob, right? But what about Ben? How does this help him?"

"Yes, Ben too. But we don't know for sure he's been kidnapped."

Vinnie stormed around the museum room cursing and came close to smashing a ceramic vase.

"Of course he's been fuckin' kidnapped."

"Let's be sure, then we can make a plan for his release," Maria Alba said using her measured, courtroom tone.

Vinnie threw up his arms. "Not good enough."

Gianni gently massaged Vinnie's shoulders.

"Let's try one thing first," Maria Alba said, softening her voice "Then you can come up with an alternative plan for Ben."

"Yeah, sure. Let's look at your brilliant idea," said Vinnie with a stern look in Maria Alba's eyes. "Based on wishful thinking, isn't it?" he asked.

"How?" asked Maria Alba.

"Because Delgrado will seize low-level foot soldiers, the ceramic store owners, and van drivers. Big fuckin' deal. Someone will have to name names. That's called wishful thinking."

"*Caro mio*—no wishing involved. We'll convince a handful of what you call low-level Mafiosi to name names and testify."

"You've heard of *omertà*, right? It was invented here," Vinnie said with his lips twisted.

Maria Alba gave her now familiar raucous laugh. "*Caro*, do you know what will be offered to the *pentiti?* You say penitents or canaries, yes? Each one and their families will become US citizens and be put into the Witness Protection Program. Every poor Sicilian wants to go to America, and this is even better because it's all expenses paid and a job waiting. Enrico Bianco becomes Henry White."

In the car, Vinnie told Gianni, "I don't think we should involve Delgrado at this point."

"But didn't you promise him?"

"I know what I promised but I don't trust him to include Ben as part of his job. I think we need to learn about the Questura's informant. And we can't involve Delgrado."

Chapter 30

By the third *Laboratorio Artigianale* Vinnie knew the setup as each showroom was a variation of the one before: a large sign in the window reminding customers that all items were hand-painted, *"Dipinto da mano."* Inside, an even bigger wall-mounted sign in English proclaimed, "Worldwide Shipping. All Credit Cards Accepted."

Gianni enjoyed holding Vinnie's hand or looping his arm through his. Emboldened after the last stop, he cheek-pecked Vinnie, who was examining a ceramic vase.

"Cut it out. You don't need to overplay the role," Vinnie said, wiping his cheek.

"But I like it."

"I don't. Stop it."

They'd been to three showrooms and not one had made an impression. Showroom No.4 was next door to No.3 and shared a parking lot. Vinnie dragged himself into the store and faced the identical and indistinguishable setup as in the neighboring store. The difference was in the pottery patterns and colors.

Gianni spoke to the owner explaining they—meaning him and his betrothed in the far corner of the showroom—were looking for something special as their wedding favor. The proprietor smiled and called his young daughter, who replicated his enthusiastic cheer. She showed Gianni their very popular wedding cups filled with five sugar-coated white almonds and the names of the wedding party printed in gold or silver. Vinnie joined Gianni and the young woman as she was explaining that the five almonds symbolized five wishes granted to the married couple: health, wealth, happiness, longevity, and fertility. With a little giggle she realized her mistake in mentioning the last one.

The shop had a large display of ceramic kitchen utensils and Vinnie mentioned to the young woman that he'd seen a lovely salt and pepper set at a friend's house. Would this be a good wedding favor? The young woman's pupils widened.

"Our specialty," she said with delight as she moved to another corner of the showroom.

Blinking several times to be sure his eyes were focused, Vinnie recognized the shakers as identical to the one Paul had given him. He turned one over to see the inscription, CERAMICHE SICILIANE BELLANI. He turned to Gianni and said, "Yes, this is perfect."

Gianni understood and asked the assistant for the price. He thought her quote outrageous, especially for the eighty guests invited to the wedding. Gianni entered into noisy negotiation over a lower price until Vinnie pulled him aside.

"What are you doing?"

"Didn't you understand? She is charging too much because she knows you're an *Americano*."

Vinnie reminded Gianni that there was no wedding, but Gianni said he didn't care because it was the principle.

Walking back to the car, Vinnie recognized Maria Alba's white Fiat Cinquecento driving past. He told Gianni to hurry up and follow her. She might lead them to Paul.

With only a single main road they were able to keep their distance yet not lose sight of the vintage Cinquecento. A few sharp bends brought moments of blindness, but unless there was a side turnoff Maria Alba had to keep going straight. A kilometer outside Patti, two African women stood on opposite sides of the road separated by fifty feet. The scantily dressed women waved.

"*Battona*," said Gianni in Sicilian which Vinnie didn't understand.

"*Prostituta*," said Gianni.

"Oh," said Vinnie, and he paused before adding, "They're forced to do it. Let's stop a second and see if we can help." Vinnie recalled his visit to the refugee camp and the Nigerian family. He'd been disgusted learning young women were forced into prostitution.

"È davvero una minchiata pazzesca, bello!" Gianni said.

"No, it's not a stupid idea. And stop with the sweetheart."

Vinnie opened his window and the young woman leaned in, exposing her breasts. She spoke a broken Italian that was hard to understand. Vinnie explained in his own flawed Italian he wanted to help her and her friend.

The woman stood back, waving him to move on. "*Niente. Vai*. Go away," she managed in English.

"No, really," Vinnie said, holding out a fifty-euro bill. "Just for you. *Gratis*."

At that moment a small white van came crawling along.

The woman stepped back onto the verge. Gianni pressed hard on the pedal, causing the car to jolt forward.

"What did you do that for!" Vinnie asked angrily.

Gianni braked hard after two hundred feet, giving Vinnie's vertebrae another violent jerk.

"Turn around," Gianni said.

Vinnie saw a man get out of the van and drag the woman inside.

"Go back! We've got to help her!"

Gianni again floored the pedal and the car shot forward, the van and women no longer visible once the Fiat rounded the curve.

"You've only caused her a problem. That was a big mistake."

They had a clear view to the winding road below and Maria Alba's Cinquecento. Gianni accelerated, the tires squealing on the bends. Vinnie covered his mouth with his hand. In no time Gianni closed the gap between them and Maria Alba.

After a half-hour following her, Gianni pointed to the mountains of Parco dei Nebrodi, proclaiming it to be one of Sicily's grand parks that tourists ignored and the government didn't promote. In his opinion, that was a good thing since it put a stop to overdevelopment by resort hotels.

They entered a small village, a former citadel outpost during the Norman period. The main piazza reminded Vinnie of the scene in *Cinema Paradiso* with the townspeople's summer entertainment a movie projected on a church wall in the main piazza. Maria Alba's Cinquecento was nowhere to be seen even though they had trailed it into this village. Vinnie was sure this was important. A hunch and nothing specific.

Gianni circled the village, unable to identify anywhere to hide a car. Vinnie saw a small *pensione* near the church, a three-story building wedged between two smaller houses of only two stories. The height gave the *pensione*'s top floor an unobstructed view of Etna's billowing smoke.

"Gianni, stop here. Let's go inside. The top floor might be a perfect place to spot Maria Alba's car."

Signor Cucuzza and his wife Signora Cucuzza were the proud owners of Pensione al Bosco. They had started this small B&B forty-five years ago when it was bequeathed by Signora Cucuzza's childless uncle.

Vinnie gave the pretext that he and Gianni were looking for a place with a view to stay the night. They were in luck, beamed Signor Cucuzza, as the last available room was the top-floor penthouse. The lower floors were fully booked for the rest of the summer by nature enthusiasts and avid hikers seeking cheap accommodation. The top-floor room cost more—"*Camera con vista*," Signor Cucuzza said proudly and hastened to add, "*bagno privato*." The cheaper lower rooms shared a single bathroom.

Climbing the narrow staircase up three flights, Vinnie went to the window. As described by Signor Cucuzza, it gave an unobstructed and spectacular view of Etna, the Nebrodi Parco Nazionale, and most of the village. But not Maria Alba's Cinquecento.

Gazing over the village, Vinnie decided a stay might be worthwhile. He didn't want to return to the hotel and spend another night without Ben.

Gianni clapped his hands at the idea with a smile that stretched his face into clownish proportions.

Chapter 31

Gianni spoke in Sicilian to Signor and Signora Cucuzza about taking the top-floor room for the night. They responded with glee, adding they had no problem with two men in a *matrimoniale* without luggage. "*Non preoccupare, avere tatto.*"

Vinnie got the message. The Cucuzzas were discreet. They also explained that over the last ten years they had hosted many gay and lesbian couples who all tipped generously and were always courteous.

"*Beh,*" was Signor Cucuzza's comment. Apparently there were more problems with the traditional married couples who stayed.

Gianni translated and Vinnie was puzzled. Why had they explained at all? Gianni shook his head. "They can't help themselves. They weren't explaining as much as talking. A Sicilian throwback that means speaking was more polite than silence."

Gianni continued to talk in Sicilian to the proprietors but it didn't fool Vinnie. He was bargaining. Vinnie pulled him back and stepped in front. He handed Signor Cucuzza the asking price in cash, earning a pout from Gianni and profuse thanks from Signor and Signora Cucuzza. They said the cash avoided credit card surcharges but apparently their Sicilian instinct to talk didn't extend to explaining that cash payment also avoided provincial room tax. Breakfast was served between six-thirty and eight-thirty. Cereal, sandwich meats, and fruit were available on self-service to accommodate the early birders who required a five am start for optimal sightings.

Signor Cucuzza directed Gianni to an alley to reach the *pensione's* designated parking lot behind the building. *Even better,* thought Vinnie. *It'll keep the ostentatious blood-red car from view, especially from Maria Alba who no doubt saw it when we tailed her.*

The room's one drawback was the *letto matrimoniale,* a double bed. Gianni tested the firmness by bouncing on it. Vinnie scowled and pointed to a divan in the corner, causing Gianni to frown.

If luggage was unnecessary, Vinnie didn't feel the same about toiletries. Following Signora Cucuzza's directions he went to a mini-market at the end of the street. He purchased toothbrushes, toothpaste, and deodorant for both of them. He decided against a razor, thinking a day's growth wouldn't hurt and a little fuzz on Gianni's face might make him look older, maybe more handsome if that were possible.

While Vinnie shopped, Gianni did a reconnoiter of the main piazza. He read the local church's sign announcing daily Mass at seven am. Too late for serious hikers, but the service was for locals and not tourists.

Vinnie joined him and scoffed. "Nobody but a few elderly widows and the odd villager will attend Mass at seven in the morning. I'll bet a total of three and that's including the priest."

"We should go," insisted Gianni.

Vinnie vigorously shook his head almost to the point of decapitation. He wasn't attending Mass even for his own funeral.

Gianni whined, "But Vinnie, it's important. I know these small villages."

"Not important to me. I haven't set foot in a Catholic church since I was fourteen," snapped Vinnie.

Vinnie's cell was dead so he couldn't call Ben or indeed anyone. He asked to borrow Gianni's but it wouldn't allow international calls to the American carrier that he and Ben used, so he couldn't contact Blanca or anyone in the office.

Signor Cucuzza offered to charge Vinnie's phone but they had a discount brand that was incompatible with Vinnie's handset. Signor Cucuzza said he would ask his neighbor, who was away but returned in the morning.

"He never shuts up about his iPhone. He has money to throw away on expensive gadgets," grumbled Signor Cucuzza, unaware that the same snarky comment also applied to Vinnie.

* * *

The next day Gianni woke Vinnie with just enough time to make the morning Mass if they hurried. A dozen people filled the pews, which meant Gianni won Vinnie's hypothetical bet. Vinnie was surprised that four African women sat on the front pew. He was shocked when he recognized the one who was on the road when they drove into Patti.

"We have to talk to her," Vinnie whispered.

"Why? We've already caused her enough problems."

Vinnie disagreed, explaining that it was best to spread a wide net when the unknowns are properly unknown. If these women were refugees forced into prostitution then there was a slight connection to Ben, although more of a supposition than from concrete facts. It didn't matter. "We have to try every avenue."

At the end of the Mass the four women exited via the sacristy. Vinnie and Gianni ran outside, scouring the street for them or a white van. They saw nothing and returned to the church, where Vinnie marched onto the altar through the side door leading to the sacristy. Gianni protested as he trailed behind.

The priest looked at Vinnie as if being visited by Jesus himself, although he didn't think Jesus would wear Levi's.

"Can I help you?" he asked, figuring that was the least he could do for the Lord Savior.

Vinnie stumbled with his Italian so Gianni took over, translating. He introduced himself and Vinnie. The priest relaxed, relieved he wasn't talking to Jesus in jeans. He explained he was Don Carnivale, the church pastor. Gianni explained that they were curious about the African women. "Can you tell us about them?" he asked.

"*Boh*," answered Don Carnivale, meaning either he didn't know or wasn't telling.

Gianni pressed, with Vinnie nudging him. The priest explained the women came in a van with permission to attend Mass under the condition they enter and exit via the sacristy. They came every day, prayed, took communion, and left. On Saturday he heard their confession.

On the walk back to the hotel, Vinnie was proud he'd chosen Gianni to be on his Sicilian team. He suggested Gianni switch careers from lifeguard to private investigator.

Gianni laughed. "Private investigators don't last long in Sicily."

At the Pensione al Bosco for breakfast, Vinnie asked Signora Cucuzza if their room was available for another two nights.

"*Certo,*" she said, full of delight. The room was not taken until September when the price dropped.

"Good. We'd like to stay, please."

"*Certo.*"

Gianni drove at normal speed to Giardini Naxos, leaving Vinnie at Hotel Mezzogiorno to pack a small suitcase with a change of clothing, a razor, and his iPhone charger.

Vinnie looked around and saw that nothing had changed except that housekeeping had made the bed. Ben's gym bag was still missing. Vinnie plugged in his cell and used the room phone to call the front desk for messages.

"Nothing, Signor Briggs."

"And for Ben Hausen?"

"Nothing."

"Have you seen him?"

"No."

Vinnie's cell showed 12 percent battery, enough to turn on. He checked for messages but there was again nothing from Ben and only a few from Blanca in New York asking why he had not checked in. She sounded pissed. He dialed Ben's number and his call went straight to voicemail.

Sweat crossed Vinnie's brow. He knew Ben had been kidnapped or murdered. He knew that from the moment he saw Ciccio's body. He had intended to call Blanca on his return from Tindari but it was three in the morning New York time. And he had an irrational superstitious belief that if he didn't call then Ben would show up.

He'd abandoned his stupid delusion and called Blanca. Before she uttered a word, he asked if she's heard from Ben.

"And why would he call me? What's up? Where is he?" she asked.

"It's too long to explain," Vinnie answered in a subdued voice.

"*Tonto. Besa mi culo*," said Blanca in her Puerto Rican Spanish. Vinnie replied he had no intention to kiss her ass.

"Then start explaining," she said.

Vinnie gave an abridged rundown of events that brought on even more Puerto Rican invectives way beyond his high school Spanish. Before she hung up she told Vinnie to call her every day or she'd be going to the police. He begged her not to but the line went dead.

His next New York call went to Ginny and Dan Livorno to preempt Blanca, since he knew she would call them. He and Ben were godfathers to the Livorno children.

Ginny answered.

"Hey, Vinnie. How's Sicily? Are you and Ben having a great time? I can't wait to hear all about it. And you'll have to tell me what the women are wearing."

"Uh, Ginny…" Vinnie's words stuck in his mouth. "… Ben's missing."

There was complete silence for several seconds.

214

"Hello? Ginny? Hello! You still there?"

"I don't understand," she answered in staccato, her breath short. "What do you mean 'missing'?"

Vinnie gave the version he told Blanca. Ben went out after his performance with a group of admirers. "I didn't join him because I'm helping the police with their investigation about an American."

"What investigation? You're on vacation."

"Too much to explain. I'm worried… I… I don't know where Ben is. Something's wrong." Vinnie's voice finally cracked.

Dan joined the conversation on speaker phone and went through possible scenarios. Had he checked the hospitals, called the Bodybuilding Federation Committee members? Vinnie said he had, which was almost true as it was Commissario Delgrado who did the checking. No one knew anything and there were no matching hospital admissions.

Like Blanca, Ginny made him promise to call as soon as he had any information. Dan went further, saying he was flying over to help.

"No!" snapped Vinnie. "That's the last thing you should do. It's too dangerous."

"What the fuck is going on?" Ginny said, her voice leaping skyward. She couldn't speak and walked away, leaving Dan to continue the conversation.

"What the fuck is going on?" Dan said, repeating Ginny's words but with greater force. It was only the fourth time in as many years that Vinnie had heard Dan say "fuck."

Vinnie had no choice but to explain about Paul LoBianco and the Aquafreddo mob. He told him everything. He heard Ginny crying in the background. Dan kept saying, "Unbelievable. How could you be so stupid?"

The emotion got to Vinnie and his sobs grew into full-blown hysteria. He couldn't speak. Dan said he was taking the next flight over. Vinnie panicked and found the energy to plead.

"I'm begging you—don't come. Please. It won't help and it may do more harm. And you have children." Vinnie coughed and took a deep breath. "Promise! I need to know or you'll only add to my worries."

Dan said, "If you miss calling once I'm on the next flight."

Vinnie ended the call but the conversation repeated inside his head on a never-ending loop. With sweating palms, he dialed Commissario Delgrado's personal cell and left a message.

Chapter 32

Commissario Delgrado returned Vinnie's call and barraged him with complaints for his lack of communication.

"I've been trying to reach Paul through Maria Alba. We met in Patti," explained Vinnie.

"What?" asked Delgrado. "You went to Patti with inside information and didn't tell me? I'm disappointed in you."

Vinnie cut the Commissario off, reminding him that Ben was still missing. As soon as he ended the call with Delgrado his phone squealed. A New York number.

Last thing I need is a sales call for a discount on a magazine subscription, thought Vinnie. He let the phone ring out. A minute later the phone buzzed a second time with the same number. This wasn't a sales call, but something about the delay from the time he answered to hearing a voice made Vinnie realize the call had a New York area code but didn't originate in the States.

"Ah, Vinnie, old family friend here. Haven't seen you in years, not since you were a little snot-nosed kid running around the neighborhood. My favorite neighborhood fag as I recall. How much lunch money did I take from you?"

If nothing else, Vinnie knew the identity from the voice

of years and years ago. The same scratchy violin screech of a ten-year-old bully who extorted local kids' lunch money. "Fuckin' Frank Aquafreddo, you piece of shit."

"Hey, Vinnie, that's no way to talk. I have something of yours and I'd like to make an exchange."

Vinnie's jaw slackened and his hand shook so much he almost dropped his cell. His mind froze, coming as close to an apoplectic fit as possible without dropping dead. He heard Aquafreddo's labored breathing. Vinnie fumbled for his phone. *He'll kill Ben without blinking an eye,* he thought.

"You see, Vinnie," rasped Aquafreddo, "you have someone we want. We get LoBianco and you get your husband back in one piece, every one of his pumped-up muscles unharmed. We don't hear and maybe he loses one or two pieces of meat. Let's just say he won't be giving any more exhibition performances."

Vinnie had no doubt Frank Aquafreddo meant it and thought back to his school days. *We used to say Frank made the Devil shit his pants.* After a few inhales he stuttered, "I... uh... I don't know where Paul is."

"Then find him and be quick about it. And Vinnie, don't bother with the anti-Mafia commission or calling the FBI. We'll know about it and then you won't see Mr. Olympia in one piece again. No one will."

The line went dead and Vinnie stared at his luggage. He sat on the bed, fixated on the floor. His trance was broken by a strange ringing sound. It took him a few seconds to realize it was the room phone.

"*Ciao*, Vinnie, I'm in the lobby. I'll be outside by the car."

Gianni stood beside a Ford Fiesta after dumping his sister's "sex car."

"It's my uncle's. A few years older than Caterina's and lots of miles but it runs well. It's not good on curves and it's a bit slower than Caterina's," Gianni said, tapping the car's roof.

On the drive to Pensione al Bosco, Vinnie told Gianni about the call from Frank Aquafreddo. He didn't see a need to keep secrets from his investigative assistant and this was as good a time as any to talk.

"I should call Delgrado. He must have negotiated lots of kidnappings," Vinnie said.

Gianni stuck out an index finger and wagged it. "No, don't do that. The Italian State doesn't negotiate with kidnappers. I mean of course they do, but it's not usually successful. Even with famous people like our prime minister Aldo Moro back in 78. They failed, although some believe the failure was intentional on the government's part."

Vinnie wasn't in any mood to learn about Italian politics or the inner workings of their police procedures. He just wanted Ben's safe return.

"And even if Delgrado agreed, I have a problem. I don't know where Paul is, and even if I did, could I trade his life for Ben's?"

"Hmm." Gianni tapped the car's steering wheel. "Why not call Maria Alba to ask Paul? Let him decide," Gianni said, letting go with one hand on the wheel to tap Vinnie's shoulder.

"They'll kill Paul once they have him," Vinnie said, a hand covering his mouth to stop a scream.

"And Ben," Gianni added.

The rest of the drive was silent until the arrival at Pensione al Bosco. Gianni carried the luggage to their top-floor room and Vinnie remained in the car.

He dialed Commissario Delgrado's number and told him everything that had happened since they last spoke. Delgrado's advice was not to tell anyone. Vinnie's nose wrinkled hearing the last words as if a foul miasma had entered the car.

He called Maria Alba and she didn't raise the "no communication" protocol, showing more empathy.

"Tell no one," she said as if she had eavesdropped on the Commissario's phone call.

"Of course," Vinnie replied and decided not to tell her about calling Delgrado just as he wouldn't tell Delgrado he had called Maria Alba.

"I'll talk to Paul," she said, softening her voice, "but I'll be honest. I'll advise him against it. There's no guarantee they'll release Ben once they have Paul. Or that he's even still alive."

Her conclusion went further than Gianni's, and she raised the possibility that Ben was already dead. Vinnie swiped at his eyes. Was he too late? He sat in the car for a half-hour until Gianni opened the driver's door and sat down.

"You okay?" asked Gianni.

"Not if you think fate just gave you the middle finger," said Vinnie, illustrating the gesture with both hands. "I've no plan. I just need to walk."

"Sure. Let's go."

"No, I mean alone."

Vinnie didn't know why or if there was a why but he walked to the parish church. He convinced himself this was as good a starting point as any to find Ben or get evidence against the Aquafreddo mob. One or the other. He knew this was an irrational thought based on seeing the African women praying and then the quirky priest.

He sat a few minutes in a church pew and didn't expect any revelation and didn't get one. Returning to Pensione al Bosco, he received a call from Commissario Delgrado.

"We'll meet tomorrow morning. Where are you staying, because I know you're not at Hotel Mezzogiorno?"

Vinnie hesitated.

"Stop this nonsense. Tell me," said Delgrado angrily.

Vine gave the *pensione* name with directions to the village.

"I'm from around there. I know the village. I'm the rare exception of a cop with more brains than a donkey," said the Commissario with a chuckle.

Vinnie and Gianni strolled around the village after supper then checked emails and messages in their room. By ten pm Vinnie had put on his silk pajamas and crawled into bed. He yielded half the *matrimoniale* to Gianni, feeling sorry he'd made him sleep on the lumpy couch the night before. "Stay on your side and keep your hands under your pillow or you're back on the couch," he warned.

Gianni entered the bed nude, which Vinnie quickly vetoed. "Put something on or get back to the goddamn divan."

Vinnie was mentally exhausted yet lay awake. He slept for ten minutes, awoke, then another brief period of sleep followed. The pattern repeated.

After an hour Gianni sat up. "What's a matter?" he asked with half-open eyes.

"I made a mistake and it may cost Ben, Paul, me... all of us our lives. I shouldn't have told Delgrado about this *pensione*. Everyone, even you, says the Questura leaks like a sieve."

"Stop worrying," pleaded Gianni. "You called his mobile."

"Yeah, right. I forgot," said Vinnie, yawning. About two hours after he managed sleep his phone rang to wake him.

"Hello," said Vinnie, groggy, and then his eyes snapped open. It was his father calling.

Chapter 33

Vinnie recognized the number before he answered and heard his voice. He moved from the bed to the couch before he answered.

"Hello, Vinnie? Can you hear me? It's your father in New York."

"Yeah, I know where you live, Pop. Do you know what the time difference is?" Vinnie asked, then slapped himself for slipping out an unimportant question. A call from his father meant something was wrong. "Is Mom okay? Tell me."

"I don't know what you're doing over there and I don't want to. But whatever it is, just stop."

"Huh? What's up?"

"What the fuck is up is that your mother received a message saying if you contact the Italian police again she will have difficulty walking for the rest of her life. That's what the fuck is up."

Vinnie couldn't believe it. How had they gotten to his mother so quickly? How did they know he'd talked to Delgrado?

"Uh, yes. I don't know what it's about. Can I talk to Mom?"

"Not a fucking chance. She didn't want me to speak to you. You say one word to her and I'll... well, just fucking don't." The line went dead.

Vinnie's heart raced. He eyes moistened. He sat on the couch. *What have I done?* "I'm fucking stupid," he said loudly, pounding a fist against the side of his head.

"*Cosa?* What's a matter?" Gianni asked, moving to the couch to be next to him.

Vinnie shook his head, saying he didn't want to talk, and returned to the bed joined by Gianni, who rubbed his shoulder. "Do you want me to make you some tea? We have a kettle. Or maybe a neck massage? You're so tense. What can I do to help?"

"Nothing, Gianni, just nothing. Stay on your side of the bed," said Vinnie, disturbed but not angry.

"*Va bene.* But sometimes a hug helps. It's only touching, nothing else. We learned this in my yoga meditation class," Gianni said, his hand continuing to rub Vinnie's shoulder.

"I appreciate the offer but I'm vulnerable. I'm... just don't."

"Okay. But you know I would never try to seduce you, especially if you're... uh... I'm not that kind of person. You understand."

"I do," Vinnie said, feeling drowsy yet knowing he wouldn't sleep. He needed peace and quiet.

* * *

The next day Vinnie rose early and tired. Gianni was on the sofa with a pillow and a light cover over him. *I must have tossed and turned all night,* Vinnie thought, looking the disheveled bed sheets. He shook Gianni awake.

"Get into the bed. You'll sleep better. I'm going downstairs."

Gianni removed the covers and was nude, a few used tissues beside him. *Poor man,* thought Vinnie. The frustration must have been too much to bear. Rays of sunlight danced over Gianni's naked body enough to bring a smile to Vinnie as he looked him over. *Somebody someday is going to be fortunate to have him.*

Vinnie pulled the covers over Gianni as the cool night air had descended from Etna's snow caps to lower the room temperature. He attended the morning Mass convincing himself it was as a PI and not a zealous religious devotee. He saw the four African women as he had hoped. He left the church before the Mass ended and walked to the parking lot behind the sacristy. Standing by a construction dumpster he snapped photos of the women, the driver, the van, and the license plate. He waited before returning to the *pensione* for the eight am breakfast.

Most of the other guests had finished and gone to hike or fish. Vinnie pushed his *cornetto* around on the plate. He'd give Gianni until nine before waking him. *What a beautiful body,* he thought. *If only I could satisfy him,* and then he quickly rebuked himself for such lecherous thoughts.

Vinnie nursed his morning coffee while he read his office emails. He'd taken advantage of the *pensione*'s high-speed broadband and Wi-Fi, which Signora Cucuzza explained was their lifeline to book new and returning clientele. Vinnie was searching for clues about human trafficking when Commissario Delgrado sat down at the table. A minute later Signora Cucuzza brought him a coffee and brioche.

"Grazie, mille. Molto gentile," he said, looking at Signora Cucuzza as if she was his mother. He turned to Vinnie. "These country folks are kind and generous. Best people on Earth. We should all move to the countryside."

"Wouldn't that turn it into cities?" Vinnie asked.

Delgrado laughed, his humor restored until he inched closer to Vinnie.

"This matter of your husband is delicate and complicated. The decision is yours but officially we don't negotiate with kidnappers."

The same crapola given by Maria Alba and Gianni. Delgrado didn't mention the failed attempts to negotiate. Vinnie bit his tongue.

"Just tell me, what are Ben's chances?" he asked.

"I'm going to be blunt. The prospects are never good."

Vinnie shook his head.

"Now wait, there are some positives in this case—" Delgrado added.

Vinnie interrupted. "Commissario, I'm not in the mood for bullshit. Whenever I hear police say there are positives I know that it means there's nothing."

Delgrado sat back, brushing his chin with his hand. "You're correct but I'm not bullshitting, as you say. The positives are that your husband is an American and a world-famous champion bodybuilder."

"Yeah, and the Mafia don't kill famous people?"

A wry smile crossed Delgrado's face. "They do, but it also interrupts their operations for several months. They are businesspeople. Yes, a dirty business but like all businesses they do a cost-benefit analysis. Cost sometimes paid in lives but benefits always in euros."

Vinnie shivered and his head jerked back. He didn't need higher math to know the balance was against Ben. If Paul testified then it was the equivalent of bankruptcy for the Aquafreddo mob.

"Let's work on a way to find Ben, save Paul, and get the trafficking evidence," Delgrado said.

"Not possible," said Vinnie, shaking his head. "A trifecta is always a long shot."

Delgrado rose to leave and as he did he rested his hands on Vinnie's shoulders. "Let me work on a few ideas and I'll call you later."

Vinnie agreed without telling Delgrado about the phone call from his father. Even their breakfast might compromise his mother's safety if anyone at the Questura had learned of the Commissario's visit or the mob was already watching the Pensione al Bosco.

Vinnie tiptoed into the bedroom with Gianni still fast asleep. He reached the en suite bathroom to wash the tears from his face. He wasn't going to wake Gianni and instead sat in a chair next to the couch, his legs outstretched. He continued surfing the web on his cell to learn about shipping regulations and companies that specialized in ceramic ware. He wrote notes on a *quaderno*, an Italian schoolchild's exercise book gifted him by Signora Cucuzza.

Gianni startled Vinnie by pecking his forehead. Gianni showered and dressed then noticed Vinnie tapping the cover of the *quaderno*.

"Something's come up and I don't know where to start," Vinnie said.

Gianni peered over Vinnie's shoulder to read the notes and the first line caused him to gasp.

MOM THREATENED

"*O Dio!*" said Gianni. "How? When?" Gianni delivered non-stop questions that seemed random and irrelevant to Vinnie. He waved his hand for him to stop.

"The call last night that I didn't want to talk about was my father. Aquafreddo knows I've been talking to Commissario Delgrado."

Gianni sat on the couch, lifted Vinnie's bare feet to his lap and rubbed them.

"How can I help?" he asked.

Vinnie glanced at his notebook then read out the few points, too meager given he'd been working on ideas for an hour.

1. Don't tell Delgrado about threat to Mom

2. Stakeout Ceramiche Siciliane Bellani

3. Identify van driver

4. Talk to Paul

5. Follow African woman from the church

6. Talk to parish priest again

Gianni nodded as Vinnie read each bullet point. He made one suggestion. He'd ask his sister to talk to her boyfriend, the police officer with the anti-Mafia division, and get his opinion of Commissario Delgrado.

"What? No, that's crazy."

"No, don't worry. He's been dating my sister for a while. He's a good person. My parents like him. And it won't be about what we're doing, just a casual comment. I'll explain to her."

"I don't like it but I'll think it over," said Vinnie. "In the meantime, we can find a good place for our stakeout of the ceramic store."

Gianni found an inconspicuous parking location on a bend across the road from the Ceramiche Siciliane Bellani. From there they had unobstructed views of the vehicles at the front and could see them if they drove to the rear loading dock, although that wasn't visible.

Using an estimated time for when they had stopped to speak to the prostitutes on the road as five or five-thirty, they came up with ideas on possible opportunities for loading dates and times that Vinnie marked in his *quaderno*.

"And the van is the same one I saw at the church this morning," said Vinnie, showing Gianni a photo on his cell phone. Gianni nodded in agreement.

"We can't say for sure there is connection between the van, the prostitutes, and the trafficking, but it's all we have so far," Vinnie said, teaching Gianni his investigative deduction methods. Gianni continued to nod.

"You know," continued Vinnie with more energy than he had had all day, "maybe your sister's boyfriend can help without connecting me to Delgrado."

Gianni's nodding seemed to increase in speed.

"What if you ask this policeman to trace a license plate for the van? You could say you accidentally scratched it and you want to contact the driver."

Gianni agreed but would change the reason.

"No Italian would admit to causing accidental damage. They'd say the other vehicle parked illegally or at a bad angle. No Sicilian volunteers to pay for damages. I'll think of a better excuse."

Vinnie agreed and it confirmed his view that Gianni would made a good investigator at the Briggs Investigative Group, Sicilian Branch.

They returned to their *pensione*, asking Signora Cucuzza for advice on where to get a takeout sandwich for lunch.

"Right here," she said, smiling. "I prepare small picnic basket for hikers. Only nine euros. Is that okay?" Both men nodded, knowing the lunch would be better than anything they could buy from a corner grocery store.

While waiting for their lunch, Gianni called his sister.

"*Tutto bene*, all's okay," he relayed to Vinnie, telling him his reason was to ask Caterina to get Enzo, her boyfriend, to help.

"You'll like this," said Gianni, all teeth on display. "I said someone told you of a van driver that added small, private deliveries at a reduced cost by hiding them in large business shipments to Rome."

Vinnie thought this reasoning was okay so far, but reserved judgment until he had heard the rest.

"I told Caterina that before you could reach the van the driver pulled away and all you had was a photo of the license plate." Gianni continued to show his sparkling teeth. "And I asked if Enzo could find out the name of the driver. Wasn't I good?"

Vinnie answered with a non-committal tongue clucking.

"She'll ask Enzo today and you will know by tomorrow."

They arrived at one of Gianni's favorite Parco dei Nebrodi picnic sites. From the Fiesta's trunk he retrieved a blanket, two folding chairs, a portable butane campfire, a two-cup Moka coffee pot, plastic mugs, coffee, and sugar stored in tins. After their espresso, Gianni cleaned the blanket of crumbs then spread it over a bed of soft pine needles.

Vinnie reviewed his list. The next bullet point was a talk with Paul but this part of the Nebrodi Park had no cellular signal so he moved to the next two bullet points on the list: "Follow the African women" and "talk to the parish priest."

Gianni liked the second option. "We'll have to wait until the siesta period is over so let's relax and take our own nap."

They lay on their backs, each lost in contemplation until Gianni turned on his side, gazing at Vinnie.

"No, Gianni," Vinnie said.

"I know. I'm not going to touch you. I just want to watch how you think."

Vinnie burst into a huge laugh. "Gianni, you know you can't actually see someone thinking, right?"

Gianni lit up, his face bright and eyes sparkling.

"No, but you can get someone to think you can."

Vinnie laughed again. "You know, you're a good person. If only we'd met years ago." He sighed and didn't want to admit that it felt good being next to someone. Within a few minutes Vinnie slipped into a deep sleep.

"*Ciao, bello.* Time to wake up," said Gianni, gently nudging Vinnie.

"What? Uh, how long was I asleep?"

"One hour."

"Jesus! Why didn't you wake me sooner?" Vinnie asked with an irritation he didn't mean and saw Gianni crumble. "I'm sorry, I didn't mean it that way. You were right to let me sleep. I'm just worried because we have so much to do."

"And nothing from two until five gets done in Sicily. How do you feel?"

Vinnie had to admit he felt invigorated, relaxed, and clear-headed. Maybe there was something to the afternoon siesta.

"Let's go talk to the priest," Vinnie said, hoping the parish priest's afternoon nap had put him in a cooperative mood.

Chapter 34

Gianni parked outside the *pensione* for the short walk to the rectory. Vinnie leaped up the steps and knocked rapidly on the front door. An elderly housekeeper peeked out from the partially opened rectory door, suspicious because few parishioners arrived in the afternoon without an appointment to see Don Carnivale. The exception was an urgent request for the sacrament of Extreme Unction, the housekeeper preferring the old term, overruling the Second Vatican Council's rename to *The Anointing of the Sick*.

She didn't recognize Vinnie or Gianni so buttressed her foot against the door's bottom edge.

Gianni enunciated his Italian, introducing himself and Signore Vinnie Briggs. His angelic face beamed charm. The door cracked open another inch. He explained that they had already met Don Carnivale after morning Mass, that it was not an incursion.

"*Con permesso. Solo due parole,*" pleaded Gianni for permission to have a few words. He put his hands together in prayer.

The housekeeper didn't believe short prayers were answered—this wasn't Twitter and God needed more than two hundred and eighty characters. What could they possibly say to Don Carnivale in a few words? Gianni flashed his sparkling teeth like family jewels, supplicated, and batted his sensual eyelashes that bewitched men and women alike—including grandmothers.

"*Un attimo. Aspettate,*" said the housekeeper with a barely perceptible grin as she opened the door wide and ushered them into a reception area.

After a few minutes she escorted Vinnie and Gianni to a large office. Don Carnivale stood and held out his hand.

"Ah, my sacristy intruders. Well, no harm done. I understand you are an American," he said, shaking Vinnie's hand, and he sounded like he was delighted. He greeted Gianni in Italian with the same vigor and a rehearsed devout smile.

"I suppose you prefer we speak in English. If you accept that mine is not so good, I will try," said the priest, beatification emanating from his entire body.

"English is better for me," said Vinnie, "and thank you for seeing us without an appointment." Vinnie could ooze graciousness as well as anyone when required.

The priest nodded and gestured for him to continue.

"I expected you'd recognize us and I apologize for that intrusion," Vinnie said, coming closer to crossing the barrier of ingratiating himself. "We noticed the women leaving from the rear of the sacristy. I know the matter's delicate but I want to help. I'm prepared to offer them shelter to get them out of their, uh… situation."

"If only it was that easy," said Don Carnivale as if explaining to a young boy entering puberty and fearful his nightly emissions would lead to his eternal damnation. "The women are not free like you. They are refugees bound by certain... uh, regulations and other constraints. You cannot change one part of their life and expect no consequences in the other."

Vinnie wondered if it was the priest's poor English or intentional obfuscation.

Don Carnivale pulled Gianni aside and spoke in Italian too rapid for Vinnie to understand. The housekeeper escorted them from the church with the drill of an exterminator cleaning out pests.

Vinnie grabbed Gianni's arm as they walked along the narrow street to their *pensione*. "What'd he say?"

"You're going to make it worse for them," answered Gianni, stepping off the curb to let an old man and his dog pass. "He knows they are forced to do things that are wrong but if he, you, or anyone interferes their lives will become even more miserable."

"So his fuckin' excuse is do nothing because it will make things worse? A chickenshit answer."

"No, it's not. You don't understand. He says Mass slowly in the week to add five minutes and gives longer homilies on Sunday by as much as fifteen minutes. Parishioners have complained they've burnt midday meals or missed the opening of a *calcio* match. And he slips the women small change from the collection basket."

"That's it? We got a fuckin' donut hole for our effort."

"No, not entirely. He saw a van in the piazza during the early evening, maybe eighteen-thirty ... I mean six-thirty or seven."

"So?" asked Vinnie, turning the corner onto a large street and wider sidewalk.

"He didn't say," answered Gianni, who was holding Vinnie's arm, "but I think it's to pick up the woman on the road or to drop off more *turno di notte*... uh..."

"Night shift?" offered Vinnie, and Gianni nodded.

After rolling his eyes, Gianni added, "That can't be true. The road has no traffic late at night. Business would be bad." Gianni put a hand to his mouth. "I shouldn't have said that. Besides, the women should be in their camp to prepare the meal and later give relief to the driver and the crew." Gianni pumped his fist.

Vinnie lightly tapped Gianni's shoulder. "We'll start our surveillance at six-thirty."

"One more thing," said Gianni, who seemed afraid to speak.

"Yeah, go on."

"Don Carnivale said one of the women whispered to him that a few days ago at the camp she saw a second white van." Gianni stopped. "He may not have heard correctly."

Vinnie gestured for Gianni to continue.

"He thinks she said the cargo doors were open and inside was a large man who was unconscious as he lay without moving. She didn't see much but knew he wasn't a refugee as his body was covered by a blanket."

"What!" Vinnie stopped walking. "That's Ben. When was this?"

Gianni shrugged. "Don Carnivale said that was all she told him. Maybe she's confused." With a hitch of his eyebrows, Gianni added, "There is more. He said the woman was trembling after she told him and pleaded for him not to tell anyone. She even asked if she could confess it so he could never tell."

"Is Don Carnivale holding back? He doesn't want us to question the woman about the white man?" said Vinnie. "Too fuckin' bad."

For a moment Gianni shook his head and closed his eyes.

"Why did Don Carnivale tell me?" asked Gianni.

"Uh... good point," replied Vinnie. He bounced the five fingers on one hand off those of the other. His eyes narrowed and he kicked a stone beneath his foot. "Maybe he's worried we'll talk to the women and they'll repeat what they told him. This way he confides and tells us not to talk to them, saying they are afraid. But he knows something, I'm certain, and that's why he doesn't want us to talk to the women."

"*Potrebbe essere*—it could be," Gianni said, but he didn't sound like he believed his own words.

"Doesn't matter, we have to talk to them," said Vinnie.

"If we do it'll put them in danger. And they won't know any more than they already told us," Gianni grumbled.

Entering the Pensione al Bosco, Vinnie said, "Ben's somewhere in the Nebrodi National Park, I'm sure of it. We'll have to stay longer."

Vinnie asked Signora Cucuzza about extending their visit for another five days. She kissed both his cheeks and did the same for Gianni. Vinnie promised to pay in cash as soon as he found a Bancomat to withdraw the funds. Signora Cucuzza flung her hand around. "Don't worry. I trust you."

On the ride to the stakeout, Vinnie called Dan Livorno in New York and gave him the update of "no change." He didn't tell him about the threat to his mother. He followed with a call to Maria Alba using the phone's speaker so that

Gianni could hear. She repeated that Paul had no phone reception.

Vinnie raged and cursed like a high school juvenile delinquent. Maria Alba waited for him to exhaust himself then told him to grow up or get laid. She added that she would be pleased to oblige but only if it included the gorgeous Gianni and she made kissing sounds. Vinnie hung up cursing. Gianni was smiling.

"What's so fuckin' funny?"

"I'm gorgeous according to Maria Alba. Doesn't that make you want me?"

Vinnie ranted with more curses but was calm by the time they reached the stakeout location. They waited an hour across the road from Ceramiche Siciliane Bellani but the white van was a no-show.

"Maybe this is the driver's day off. Like me." Gianni paused. "And…"

"What?" asked Vinnie.

"When you were outside peeing in the bushes," said Gianni with a grin, "I called the hotel for more time off. They gave me lots because… uh, I am, how do you say, *sono licenziato*," Gianni said with a sad face.

Vinnie didn't understand and Gianni made a gesture of throwing something out the window. "*Buttato fuori*."

"Fired from your job? Oh God, Gianni, I'm so sorry."

"Don't worry, I can get another."

"I'll hire you and pay better than the hotel."

Gianni kissed Vinnie on the mouth.

"Do that again and I'll fire your ass," Vinnie said, but his voice was too gentle to be angry.

Gianni couldn't stop grinning. "Rule *numero uno*. No kissing the boss."

Vinnie laughed then suddenly went silent, covering his face with his hand. Gianni parked the Ford Fiesta in the Pensione al Bosco's parking lot.

Signor Cucuzza called Vinnie as he and Gianni were climbing the stairs to their room.

"Gianni, you have a message." He spoke in Italian relaying a message from Gianni's *cognato*.

"*Grazie*," replied Gianni, who translated for Vinnie that his future brother-in-law, Vice-Ispettore Enzo Mancuso, would arrive in the morning.

Vinnie didn't understand. Did Gianni tell his sister the name of the *pensione*? He was about to ask when he was interrupted by his ringing cell phone.

Without a greeting, the caller spoke and Vinnie recognized the voice—Maria Alba. "Paul has an idea on the possible date of transfer. I've checked it out and it seems plausible."

Vinnie rolled his eyes at her confident, spirited tone. In his past investigations he had learned that if he became cocky he was often let down.

"And how does this help find Ben?" asked Vinnie.

"Vinnie, you ask too much. Be patient. We'll find a way to save Ben."

Maria Alba hung up before hearing Vinnie tell her where to shove her patience.

The next morning a tall, handsome, olive-skinned man— bulky but not fat—entered the Pensione al Bosco's breakfast room and sat opposite Vinnie.

Chapter 35

Vinnie stared at the stranger sitting across from him at the breakfast table.

"*Buon giorno*," said the man in a pleasant, soft-spoken voice. "I'm Vice-Ispettore Mancuso, but please call me Enzo."

"*Ciao*," said Vinnie, about to dip his brioche into his cappuccino. "You're early. Please join me. Gianni is still asleep."

Vinnie waved to Signora Cucuzza, who brought the vice-ispettore a cappuccino and placed the sugar bowl in front of him. Vinnie thought Enzo's suit looked tailored to fit his broad shoulders, then remembered that in Italy even off-the-rack suits can be tailored on request.

"Has Gianni taken you around the beautiful sites? I'm sure you enjoyed Tindari," Mancuso said, then stopped. "Too bad about the unfortunate event at the Roman ruins. But I'm sure you saw the Madonna Nera and the panoramic view of the Aeolian Islands." He spoke as if delivering a ballad, nothing like the typical staccato police chatter. His English was better than Gianni's. "Not many tourists go there but it really is spectacular."

"Yes, lovely," said Vinnie, and he turned his attention to finishing his brioche. "But you're not here to listen to my tourist itinerary, are you?"

Mancuso beamed and wagged his finger. "You Americans, always in a rush to do business. Please, finish your cappuccino and relax. Nothing will happen in the next ten minutes."

Whether Vinnie wanted to hear them or not, Vice-Ispettore Mancuso revealed his favorite Sicilian attractions, each worth the effort to visit. He talked about the island's interior with its wild, desert-like landscape that many tourists miss. Vinnie thought Mancuso acted more like a travel agent than an *ispettore* in the Italian anti-Mafia division.

Yet innocent questions slipped in, nothing substantial but it was still an interrogation of sorts. He asked about the Bodybuilding Expo that led to questions about Ben. He wanted Vinnie's opinion of the Messina Museum.

"Caravaggio requires two sets of eyes to understand," said Mancuso.

He didn't skirt the "unfortunate" museum shooting incident, the second time he used the same word. He asked if Ben or a companion went with him.

"No, just me. He's been too busy."

"*Grazie a Dio* you weren't hurt."

Mancuso's words swirled, lulling Vinnie. Then he leaned back, his face growing stern.

"Vinnie, tell me what you want. I know it's not a shipment to Rome."

The abrupt transition caught Vinnie by surprise. Should he be open with Mancuso? He'd obviously looked over logs and notes at the Questura and anti-Mafia directives. Vinnie also realized he should have known Gianni's excuse to Caterina was nonsensical.

"Yes Enzo, you're right. I need help with Paul LoBianco," Vinnie said, still reticent on how much to reveal. He'd not say more than he gave Delgrado.

"You are in contact?" asked Mancuso.

"I work through an intermediary."

"A woman? Who?"

Vinnie was caught by surprise. How did Enzo know it was a woman?

"I don't know her name. She calls me." Vinnie stared hard into Vice-Ispettore Mancuso's face but only saw a handsome man with a friendly demeanor.

"Do you trust her?"

Vinnie's jaw slackened. He was being interviewed, not the other way around. And in a way it made sense. Why would a vice-ispettore in the anti-Mafia division blab the inner workings of the Questura to a stranger? That's what he had told Gianni and he was right.

"I do. She's been reliable so far," said Vinnie, nearly gagging on his words.

"Good. That helps."

"Helps? How?" asked Vinnie.

"To make arrangements for LoBianco to come to the Questura. We'll have the FBI ready too."

"I see," Vinnie said. "The idea is to get Paul to voluntarily expose himself by coming to the Questura. The problem is he doesn't know who to trust."

"You mean the leaks. Yes, the popular opinion is that

the Questura leaks like a colander and would be more useful to drain pasta than prosecute criminals. That way lawyers get information to help set their guilty clients free."

Mancuso sat back and took another sip of his cappuccino and somehow avoided foam settling on his upper lip. Vinnie wondered how Italians managed to do that and made a mental note to ask Gianni.

"Do the leaks worry you? Is that why you won't tell me the woman's name?"

"No. Like I said, I don't know it," answered Vinnie, firming up his decision to keep Maria Alba his secret. And he had a feeling Mancuso had read some report at the Questura about Vinnie's outside assistance. Would Commissario Delgrado be careless and reveal Maria Alba's name? *Or did I make a mistake and say it on the Questura answering machine? What did I say?*

Something else nagged Vinnie. How did Mancuso know he was staying at the Pensione al Bosco? Did Gianni tell his sister? He'd ask him as soon as Mancuso left. Vinnie rubbed his face.

"Let me be frank with you, Enzo. I wanted to talk to you about a delicate matter," Vinnie said.

"Yes, what's that?"

"Can I trust Commissario Delgrado? Is he the leak in the anti-Mafia division?" asked Vinnie, shifting the conversation away from him and Maria Alba.

With a wagging finger, Mancuso answered, "I'm not going to reveal the inner workings of the ant-Mafia division." He rubbed his chin, then continued. "I will say that sometimes the Commissario goes outside the official boundaries so we don't know everything he does. Probably legitimate pursuits but possibly also stretching the law." Mancuso's eyes narrowed. "A few of his solid investigations were dismissed by the prosecutor and judge. There can be many reasons so it means nothing by itself. Everyone believes Delgrado is an honest man as far as we can tell."

Vinnie stared stone-faced. That wasn't a compliment or high praise. Was Mancuso advising him to be wary of Delgrado? If so, had he already told Delgrado too much? And should he tell Mancuso about Ben?

"So, Ispettore," began Vinnie, who saw Mancuso shaking his head, "I mean Enzo, out of curiosity did you try to find the name of the van driver? Not that I need it to send anything to Rome. It's about a private matter, nothing to do with Paul LoBianco. I'm a little embarrassed. Let's say it's a gay thing. I haven't told Gianni."

Vinnie watched the creases on Mancuso's forehead as if thinking how to evade the question.

"There's not much," answered Mancuso after a few seconds. "The van is licensed to a small commercial transport company. They are like FedEx or DHL but restricted to regional consignments and deliveries mostly from one part of Sicily to another. They have around twenty employees. Nothing extraordinary other than a few parking fines but no legal entanglements. As for the specific driver, I couldn't say from the license plate alone. I'd have to go to through the company logs to check schedules and I have no reason to do that. I've already stretched the regulations to give you this information. I suppose I'm a little like the Commissario, willing to help a friend." Mancuso winked.

Vinnie pretended to be disappointed but became wary. *What friend? I'm just the fiancée's brother's boyfriend.*

"Well, it's not important. Forget it," said Vinnie, glad he didn't mention the van or local church or African women to Delgrado so there was no way anything about them could be leaked.

Mancuso stood and looked down on Vinnie. "Does Gianni know about your work with Delgrado?"

"No, nothing. We're here for other reasons. To be honest, Ben and I found the expo and the traveling hard on our relationship. We're taking a few days apart. I don't know if it's permanent but we thought a small adventure outside of marriage might be good for us—we both have an itch that needs scratching."

Now Vinnie knew the time had come to make a tactical decision. Should he tell Mancuso about Ben's kidnapping? Assume he knew from Delgrado's investigation at the Questura? Or was this one of the times the Commissario went out of bounds? If so, was he looking for Ben?

Vinnie gave a crooked smile. He avoided mentioning Ben, instead committing to the promiscuous gay marriage excuse. Mancuso put his forearms on the table.

"You know," said Vinnie, trying to give a coy smile, "this is what gay couples do that straights don't unless they're in an 'open marriage.'" Vinnie air-fingered quotation marks. "We're liberated. You'd be surprised what we do to spice up our sex lives."

Vinnie almost broke out laughing at the sound of this cow manure. Had he overplayed the last part to fire Mancuso's imagination? He was thinking of the very acts he believed

Ben had engaged in with Ciccio. Poor Ciccio. He was straining to remain faithful. He'd kept Gianni at bay—the very desirable Gianni. Vinnie smiled but didn't laugh.

Mancuso stuck out his lower lip. "I don't think Caterina would go for it," he said, puffing out a chuckle. "But to be clear," he said with a stern look, "I recommend you to not tell Gianni anything. As you said, he's not a trained investigator and probably wouldn't understand. Best to keep this conversation private, just between you and me."

He thanked Enzo, who handed over his card with a private number printed on it. "Call me anytime, and especially if it can help bring LoBianco to safety."

Why didn't Mancuso find it odd that he and Gianni were in a remote *pensione* at the Nebrodi National Park and not in Taormina or Palermo where they'd have access to hot gay clubs? Unless Mancuso thought they spent all day and night screwing each other.

Vinnie stared into his empty cup. Was Mancuso a decoy for Delgrado?

Something's weird, he thought, mounting the stairs to wake Gianni for breakfast.

Chapter 36

Vinnie lightly touched Gianni's shoulder, causing his eyes to flutter open. Smiling, he gave Vinnie a big yawn and stretched his arms as wide as the bed. Gianni showered leaving the bathroom door open and it steamed up the room. He entered toweling his dripping wet body. He showed no signs he was in a hurry to dress and dropped his towel, and more than an after-shower smile greeted Vinnie.

"Gianni, put on some fuckin' clothes. We're not doing that..." Vinnie pointed at Gianni's fully erect member.

"Don't you like?" Gianni asked twisting his lips, his pout competing with a smile.

"Not the point," said Vinnie, who stared despite himself, which for no reason triggered thoughts of him and Ben lacking *passionate* sex for weeks. Or was it months?

"I have to ask you serious questions and I can't do it with... that exposed," said Vinnie, turning his head away.

Gianni put on skinny jeans, a Valentino polo shirt but no footwear. He sat on the divan with hands together positioned over his lips as if waiting patiently for a surprise.

"Did you tell your sister or Enzo that a woman is helping me?" asked Vinnie.

"No. Why?"

"Because Enzo didn't buy the story that I wanted to send a shipment to Rome. Yet he knew all about me, including that I identified Al Renato's body and my trip to Tindari where I saw Ciccio's body."

"Is that bad?" Gianni asked.

"Not necessarily. Maybe he read the notes on the two murders and I'd be on the witness register."

Gianni folded his feet under his legs and rested his elbows on his thighs, bending slightly forward to match Vinnie's leaning closer as if sharing secrets.

Vinnie chewed his lower lip. "The bigger dilemma is how did Enzo know there's a woman helping me? I'll ask again and would like you to think hard. Did you tell your sister?"

Gianni tugged at his ear. "I don't understand. Why would I tell Caterina? I only learned about Maria Alba a few days ago."

"Gianni," said Vinnie in his PI interview mode, "it's okay if you did. I just need to know. Are you certain?"

"*Si, si. Senza dubbio.* I swear on my mother's life, I never told Caterina. If I didn't know, how could I?" Gianni's head bowed as if examining his toes protruding from under his legs.

"You never mentioned a woman at all? Never!"

Gianni trembled, water filling his eyes. "Vinnie, I swear, not a word. I... I don't understand. Did I do something wrong? *O Dio*, please tell me. What did I do?"

Vinnie found Gianni's reaction evoked his own emotional response. He lost his train of thought. *How did Mancuso*

248

know to ask about the woman? The only remaining possibility was that the question was unprompted and came from
nowhere.

Gianni softly rubbed the corner of his eye as if flicking
dirt from it. Vinnie moved from the chair to the couch,
placing his arm around Gianni's shoulders. He pulled him
closer and rested Gianni's head on his chest.

"It's okay. You didn't do anything wrong. There's no
need to be upset."

They sat for a few minutes listening to their lungs fill
with air as if background noise for a suspense drama. Vinnie
heard Gianni's breathing become less labored and he pecked
his forehead.

"What happened to 'no kissing the boss?' " asked Gianni,
a smile creeping out from under his nose.

"That wasn't a real kiss, and the boss can grant an exception," said Vinnie, soaking up Gianni's glow.

Vinnie leaned back on the divan, crossing one leg over
the opposite thigh. He missed the flush of carefree love that
he and Ben had in their first years together. Their unabashed
joy of exploring each other's bodies. Just then a noise from
the street below broke Vinnie's trance.

"Gianni, I have to go back to the question I asked, so
don't get upset. If you didn't mention Maria Alba to your
sister then how did Mancuso know?"

Before Gianni repeated his protest, Vinnie signaled him
to stop. "Now listen. I'm not saying you did, I'm just trying
to work out how Enzo knew. He could have asked if 'a man'
was helping me or even the more neutral 'someone.' And
why does he think I'm getting help?"

Vinnie fidgeted with the buttons on his shirt and mumbled. Gianni gave him a quizzical look.

"How long has your sister known Mancuso?" Vinnie asked.

Gianni's fingers ticked off months and did a second round. "Sixteen months."

"And did Enzo do anything unusual in that time?"

"*Cosa?* Like what?" asked Gianni.

"I don't know. Maybe an expensive gift or new car or something unusual."

Gianni pursed his lips and swayed his torso. "He gave Caterina a big trip."

"You mean the New York trip that she talked about? That was his idea?" asked Vinnie, looking out the window. "Birthday or Christmas gift?"

Gianni shook his head, clucking his tongue.

"When was this?"

"Maybe three months ago for *primo Maggio*. You know the first of May is a big holiday to celebrate solidarity among workers, right?"

Vinnie rubbed his chin. "And was Enzo with Caterina all the time?"

"*Buh*," said Gianni, using the Italian expression for "who knows?"

"What do you mean?"

"Was Caterina ever alone?" asked Vinnie.

The question puzzled Gianni and Vinnie explained, "Not 'alone' as in being solitary but to shop or tour by herself."

"Ah, yes. She told me she went to the Museum of Modern Art by herself because Enzo had official business with the

FBI's anti-Mafia branch. He gave her two hundred dollars to shop after the museum at big-name stores. She bought—"

Vinnie whistled, one hand held high. "Two hundred dollars! Didn't this seem strange to Caterina or you or your parents?"

"Strange? How?"

Vinnie re-evaluated Gianni as PI material.

"I mean he paid for two airline tickets to New York, the hotel, and then he gives Caterina two hundred bucks for a spending spree. Doesn't that seem too much?"

Gianni shrugged. "He said he got a big bonus from a wealthy family for saving their son from doing something stupid. He didn't tell us the name because the *polizia* cannot accept gifts for doing their job or people think it's a bribe. He refused the money until the young man's father took it as an insult. And Sicilians don't like to be insulted!" Gianni said with his hands slashing through the air.

Vinnie scrimped a smile. "We have a saying, I don't know how to translate. 'If something is too good to be true then it usually is.'"

"Why do you accuse him of being bad?" asked Gianni with an index and middle finger waving "no."

"I'm not saying he is," said Vinnie, realizing that it wasn't cool to cast aspersions on a person Gianni thought of as a family friend.

Gianni walked to the window. He stared out, searching for truth among the clouds. "We all like Enzo."

"I'm sorry, but in my line of work you have to be cautious and distrustful."

"Just because he's generous?"

"Yes. Expensive gifts raise a red flag." Vinnie watched Gianni lean against the window and go quiet.

"Look," he called out, "I'm not saying Enzo is corrupt. Maybe he did get a bonus from a grateful parent and he could hide the gift by saying Caterina paid her share of the New York trip."

"Yes, in fact my parents asked her not to tell anyone. My father was embarrassed."

This explanation may have merit, thought Vinnie. *But it's a little too neat and it bothers me.*

He cleared his throat. "Now, Gianni, here's where a little cynicism helps me do good detective work."

Gianni's lips protruded and he shrugged.

"We'll use the same facts but reverse the explanation. Imagine Enzo used Caterina to conceal his New York trip from the anti-Mafia commission. He'd tell them it was Caterina's surprise for him. No one would imagine he'd abandon his beautiful *fidanzata* for a half-day to meet the ugly old man Aquafreddo."

Gianni backed away from the window to face Vinnie. "Enzo's a good person."

We won't resolve this now, Vinnie thought. "Let's try another approach," he said to Gianni. "Come sit next to me." Vinnie tapped the divan's cushion. "I'm going to ask you more questions. Think carefully before you answer. Okay?"

"*Si*," said Gianni, who pretended to zip his lips as he resumed his couch position of legs folded under him.

Vinnie wrote the questions in his *quaderno*. "Always keep notes, Gianni. Remember this is part of your detective work."

Gianni nodded but the funny face he made gave away his not taking the lesson seriously. Vinnie lightly punched his shoulder.

"Okay, smart ass. Now, question one. Did you tell your sister or Enzo that we were here at Pensione al Bosco?"

"*Buh*," grunted Gianni. "Probably not. I thought Enzo would call me with the name of the van driver. Why would he take time to meet you?"

Vinnie tapped one finger over his lips as if mulling over Gianni's response. "Question two. Did you mention my trip to Tindari?"

"Why would I? Caterina has no interest in your tourist itinerary."

"Question three. Same as the last only about my visit to the Messina museum."

Gianni rolled his eyes and waved three fingers like he was giving a Papal blessing.

"Again that's a no," said Vinnie. He chewed his tongue. Gianni's answers were definitive yet the interpretation relating to Enzo's prior knowledge was inconclusive. "It's a fuckin' conundrum. We need Enzo's help. This isn't good," he said. "I think we have no choice but to trust Enzo."

Gianni clapped his approval.

"But I won't tell him about Maria Alba or tell Delgrado about Enzo."

Vinnie moved to the bed with a pillow behind his neck. "Let's work on getting Paul's evidence." Vinnie adjusted the pillow to move his head higher. "What do we know about trafficking logistics?"

Gianni signaled that he knew nothing.

"Me neither. But think about it. The refugees are not going on a cruise ship. They don't have reservations or a check-in time and departure lounge. They'll be gathered hours or days ahead and locked into a secure room that allows for quick loading into containers."

"*Si*, that's true," said Gianni, who sounded more like he wanted to please than he understood Vinnie's deduction.

Vinnie's stomach tightened. He rose from the couch to slowly pace the room. His logic had messed up before and people had got hurt or died. Ciccio died. Two women refugees died. He didn't want Ben to die.

Chapter 37

In the early evening Signor Cucuzza knocked on Vinnie's door. Vinnie peered out with a towel wrapped around him from his shower. He'd been desperate to wash away his sweat after sitting in a hot car all afternoon staking out Ceramiche Siciliana Bellani. Gianni preferred to take a stroll around the village. Signor Cucuzza announced the man from breakfast was waiting in reception.

"*Ciao*, Enzo," Vinnie said, hand extended as he crossed the reception area.

"*Ciao*, Vinnie. I hope this is not inconvenient. I had an investigation nearby and thought we should talk some more. I know a very good pizzeria in Barcellona Pozzo di Gotto. Locals just say Barcellona and no one thinks they're in Spain. I'd like you to join me."

"Sure, but Gianni isn't back yet."

"That's okay. He doesn't need to hear what I have to say. You haven't told him about our conversation this morning, have you?"

"No. Like I said, I don't want him involved because that's not the reason we're here. I prefer to keep it that way. Besides, he's not a licensed investigator, not that my license is valid in Sicily but I have training."

"Good. Call Gianni and make an excuse. Tell him I found the van driver but we had to hurry to catch him."

Vinnie said he'd left his phone in the room, which was untrue but he wanted to call Gianni away from Enzo Mancuso's prying ears. He went upstairs to make the call in private.

"*Ciao*, Gianni, I'm with Enzo—" Vinnie said but Gianni interrupted him.

"Hold on. Let me explain. Enzo just showed up. He's waiting for me in the *pensione* reception and I'm calling you from our room. I've got to be quick."

"*Va bene*. I'm listening," said Gianni.

"Enzo has something to tell me and doesn't want you to know," said Vinnie and he rushed through the pizzeria plan. "Enzo's using the van driver as an excuse so remember this if he asks you later."

At the end of the call, Vinnie rushed down the stairs to find Enzo standing in the doorway.

The Pizzeria Nebrodi was larger than Vinnie had imagined but near empty at five-thirty except for a few teenagers and a family, probably tourists. Red and blue checkered tablecloths covered each table. On one sidewall was a hand-painted mural of Etna erupting. The opposite wall had a panorama of Parco di Nebrodi. A large printed menu hung on the rear half-wall behind the pickup counter.

An aroma of roasted garlic assaulted Vinnie's nostrils on entering the pizzeria. A glowing wood-burning oven added to the ambience.

Mancuso selected a rear table away from the teenagers

and family and he signaled to the counter. A boy no older than ten brought a carafe of house wine and two small glasses to the table.

"The best Pizza Margherita from the highest quality *mozzarella di bufala* and homegrown *basilico*," boasted Mancuso as if was going to make it himself.

"*Salute*," he said, lifting his glass to clink Vinnie's.

"*Salute*," responded Vinnie, wondering if the toast to good health extended to the refugees trafficked for sex and to Ben, whose life was in danger.

The boy-waiter served Vinnie and Enzo Pizza Margherita with oregano and *peperoncino rosso* as extra topping. Flavors erupted in Vinnie's mouth, the kind of excitation Don Carnivale would probably classify as a cardinal sin. *Whatever might be said of Enzo Mancuso*, thought Vinnie, *no one can doubt his ability to choose a pizza joint.*

On the second refill of wine, Mancuso began with a question. "What's the news from your female liaison?"

"Nothing."

"Can't you contact her?"

"Unfortunately I can't. She uses a different burner phone for every call," Vinnie said, prepared for this question.

Mancuso sloshed a slug of wine in his mouth, swallowed, and said, "What is she waiting for?"

Another question Vinnie had anticipated. He stayed close to the truth, hoping it might force Mancuso into revealing whose side he was on. "She and Paul have worked out a timetable for the shipment. I'm not sure what she means or where but she'll let me know soon. She hopes no more than one or two days," explained Vinnie.

Now came the time for Vinnie to talk about Ben. He'd act as if confiding in Mancuso, who would have known about Ben being a hostage if he was with the Aquafreddo mob and would not if Delgrado had kept his promise to keep it out of the Questura manifest.

"Can I tell you something in confidence?" asked Vinnie, bowing his head. "The Commissario knows but he promised to wait before telling your anti-Mafia group." Vinnie waited for Mancuso to nod.

"My husband, Ben Hausen, was taken hostage. It happened while he was having an affair with Ciccio Volpe, the man found murdered in Tindari. Not to speak ill of the dead but Ciccio lusted after bodybuilders and Ben was a prize as a former Mr. Olympia." Vinnie hoped the last sentence gave more weight to his revelation and added credence to the pretext he was having an affair with Gianni.

Mancuso nodded with a short, low whistle.

Vinnie let his next words slip out slowly, marshaling them to emphasize their significance. "Commissario Delgrado says the official Italian position is not to negotiate with kidnappers."

"That's true," said Mancuso, effecting an official, solemn tone.

"But I will."

"Money? How much?"

"Not money but an exchange. My husband for Paul LoBianco," answered Vinnie, reaching across the table for a paper napkin and pretending to wipe his chin but needing to dry his sweating palms. "As far as I'm concerned, it's worth it. I like Paul but I love Ben. Paul chose to be involved with the Mafia and I'm not going to risk my husband for his poor decision."

Mancuso nodded, empathy seeping out of every pore. For an instant Vinnie believed Enzo to be an ally.

"The problem is that I don't know where Paul is hiding. I'll ask my contact to bring me to him if that helps him feel secure," Vinnie said with a stark stare into Mancuso's eyes.

"Won't she refuse?" Enzo asked.

"Possibly. But if she does I'll tell her I'm finished. I'm sure she and Paul won't risk me quitting."

Mancuso gave a confirmatory nod. With a crooked grin he added, "I can help. I'll put a tracker on Gianni's car and follow you to Paul's hiding location."

This was one possibility Vinnie had not anticipated. He didn't want Mancuso to follow him since he might try to meet Paul, but not for the reason he gave. Vinnie's mind raced. He sipped his wine and slowly chewed the remaining pizza slice to buy some time. He recalled Gianni's excitement at driving his uncle's car so Vinnie wouldn't have to rent one.

Vinnie swallowed the last slice then said, "That won't work. Gianni will return his uncle's car tomorrow or the next day, so I'll rent one." Vinnie paused. "What if I call you once I set up the meeting location? You'll have a few hours' notice and can tail me."

Mancuso rubbed his chin. "*Si.* That works but you must call me as soon as you know. Any delay and I might not make it in time."

"Absolutely. And even if something goes wrong I can call you from the location. I'll make up an excuse. You can track my cell phone."

This was untrue since his US carrier made international calls via VoIP, the Voice Over Internet Protocol that was hard to trace without sophisticated tracking equipment.

Mancuso said he needed to use the toilet, but Vinnie suspected he was making a call to inform his boss—not Commissario Delgrado but the *capo* of the Catania mob or even Aquafreddo himself.

With Mancuso gone, Vinnie studied the table setup. He examined the glass salt and pepper shakers and held one high to the light. There was something familiar about it. He'd seen the exact same shakers in a pizza parlor on Lexington Avenue in New York. If not for them being perfect replicas he would not have noticed. This seemed an odd coincidence. He carried a salt shaker to the takeout counter.

"Can I speak to the owner please?" he asked the boy behind the counter, who called out in Sicilian. A short, stocky man in his mid-forties with the beginnings of a paunch appeared from the kitchen. He rested on the counter, his large forearms earned from decades of kneading dough. He looked at Vinnie as if he was a talking dog.

"*Scusi*," said Vinnie politely and in a singsong voice, "I'm curious about these shakers. They seem familiar. Where did you get them?"

"Oh," replied the pizza maker with more cheer than his glare and hulking body had suggested. "Believe it or not, they come from New York every few months and pre-filled with salt and pepper."

"Isn't that expensive?" asked Vinnie, and he pointed to the ceramic plates. "I've seen ceramic salt and pepper shakers here in Patti that match your plates. Wouldn't it be cheaper to use them?"

"You're right. But my partner says we get a much better price on salt in filled shakers and we save time filling them. He has four pizzerias in Sicily and two in New York so he buys in bulk and ships most of them to us, *credici o no*."

Of the pizza maker's two choices—believe it or not—Vinnie chose to believe.

"And how often? I mean that's gotta be a lot of shipments," said Vinnie.

"Oh, three or four times a year. The next one arrives in two days. The long delay comes from waiting for container ships to dock in Sicily. But we're in no rush," said the jolly pizza man.

"What do you do with the empties?" asked Vinnie, turning the salt shaker around in his hand.

"*Boh*," said the man, shrugging his shoulders as if trying to scratch his ears. "Whatever isn't lost, broken, or stolen my partner handles. I just make pizza."

"And it's a great pizza..." said Vinnie, pushing an index finger into one cheek and rotating it to prove he knew Italian sign language.

The return to Pensione al Bosco was pleasant. Mancuso's charm lulled Vinnie into thinking maybe he wasn't Mafioso after all. *I'd introduce him to my sister if she wasn't already married.*

Vinnie entered the bedroom to see Gianni on the divan examining a brochure.

"What's that?" asked Vinnie.

Gianni looked up smiling. "A Parco dei Nebrodi map of roads and hiking trails from Signor Cucuzza. There are many more trails than I knew of."

Gianni's words sparked Vinnie's imagination. Nudging his shoulder to make room for him, Vinnie sat on the couch.

"I have an idea," Vinnie said, leaning in for a closer view of the map. "Can I see it?"

Vinnie caught Gianni's high-beam smile as he handed him the map. He understood how Gianni bewitched people. It wasn't his good looks, which helped, but the friendliness he exuded and the pleasure he took in doing favors for others. Vinnie understood too well; he'd been like that at one time. Gianni had yet to cross over into grownup land so retained a childlike joy of life. Vinnie envied Gianni and felt closer to him, like the brother he wished he had.

"Okay, let's start," said Vinnie, leaning over the map on his lap.

Gianni rubbed his hands as if washing them.

Vinnie's first idea was to use his off-the-cuff lie to Vice-Ispettore Mancuso and make it true. He'd rent an off-road 4x4 at Catania Airport.

"You know, if Enzo is a good *ispettore* he'll assign someone to follow the Ford Fiesta. He might even put a tracking device on it."

Vinnie called Blanca and requested she reserve a car at Catania Airport using their special corporate credit card, not from the Briggs Investigative Group but registered to a Delaware shell corporation established for their corporate espionage investigations. Only big governmental agencies could trace it back to the Briggs Investigative Group. It had never happened so far.

He also asked Blanca to call Dan and Ginny and let them

know he would cut off communication for the next few days for security. He figured it coming from her would convince Dan against jumping on a flight to Italy.

Vinnie needed to retrieve the shell credit card that he had left in his Hotel Mezzogiorno room safe. Gianni laughed at Vinnie for taking all his credit cards when he traveled.

"Hey, I never have to worry about being stranded with no money."

He extended his stay at the Mezzogiorno for another week, which wasn't a problem as it was still two weeks before Italy's August *Ferragosto* high season.

Back at the Mezzogiorno Gianni waited in the hotel parking lot for Vinnie and was shocked by the sharp rapping on his window from the hotel manager. He offered Gianni his former lifeguard job, but on the condition he had to start now.

"Did you do this?" asked Gianni, his head tilted as Vinnie entered the car.

"Just a recommendation on my part," said Vinnie. He didn't mention Gianni's rehire had come at considerable expense for him. Vinnie didn't know that the manager also wanted Gianni to return as his replacement disappointed the guests in his attitude, spoken English, and mediocre looks. If nothing else, Gianni hawked his marvelous curved ass, rippling abs, bulging bikini pouch, and Adonis smile to please female guests of all ages.

For Vinnie, the re-employment was for show in case they'd been followed. This was Gianni's reason to remain at the hotel while Vinnie went to Catania Airport for the car hire.

His second idea needed a few more hours to carry out.

Chapter 38

Vinnie drove the 4x4 Jeep like a timid teenager who had just got his license. He returned to Giardini Naxos five hours after he set off for the airport in a taxi. During the slow return drive he ruminated on his second idea, a concoction of hopes and wishes. He explained to a preoccupied Gianni at the pool, who was staring at some attractive young men sun tanning.

"Most I've ever taken at one time," said a gleeful Gianni counting his tip jar.

"Great," replied Vinnie unenthusiastically as he pulled Gianni inside the pool café. "Listen carefully for both our sakes. A misstep can ruin everything."

The plan was simple to explain but not easy to execute if Mancuso had people watching them. "We'll follow the white van from the Laboratorio Ceramiche in Patti after the afternoon pickup. We'll need the Jeep and the Ford to avoid anyone noticing us."

Gianni nodded as if this was common sense.

"I'll park at a Nebrodi Park picnic site that I've marked on Signor Cucuzza's map. It's near to a campsite where you'll be with the Ford Fiesta. Can you make a copy of the map in the hotel office?"

"No need. I know both places very well from camping trips with a friend," Gianni said with a slight blush.

Vinnie left Hotel Mezzogiorno an hour before Gianni to allow extra time for his slow passage on the autostrada. Gianni arrived soon after Vinnie in the last minutes of the passing twilight. As arranged, Gianni drove past Vinnie's parking lay-by to the nearby campsite. Vinnie waited to watch if a car followed him. Ten minutes passed then Vinnie used a bright LED flashlight to guide him along a trail to Gianni's campsite. As he passed the Fiesta he checked underneath the chassis for a tracking device but came up empty.

"Mancuso may have stationed someone at the Pensione al Bosco." Vinnie knew this might be all for naught. He had not one iota of evidence to suggest Enzo Mancuso was the inside informant or working with the Mafia. It could well be Commissario Delgrado.

They left Vinnie's Jeep in the Nebrodi Park and returned to the Pensione al Bosco in Gianni's Fiesta. With the car parked in the lot behind the building, Vinnie linked his arm through Gianni's and pulled him to the front door rather than use the rear entrance. At the doorstep he pulled Gianni closer.

"Give me a kiss."

"What? I thought you—"

"Don't argue, just do it," commanded Vinnie.

Gianni dove into Vinnie's mouth like a treasure hunter. After the brief but passionate kiss, Vinnie broke away.

"Enough already."

"Huh? Are you angry? You asked me to."

Vinnie grinned. "No, I'm not angry. The kiss was for show for anyone spying on us. I want to reinforce this as a gay getaway."

Gianni whispered in Vinnie's ear, "*Amore*, I wish this was real and you felt what I felt."

The words were like a sharp slap to Vinnie. The kiss stirred him as much as he denied it. They'd been inseparable for days and Vinnie couldn't help but notice Gianni's good looks, fashionable clothing, great body—*really* great body—and he was the sweetest person he'd ever known.

"Gianni, I can't do this with you. I'm not going to deny that under other circumstances I'd be jumping all over you. You'll find someone someday soon and they'll be very fortunate."

Gianni blushed from cheek to neck. He rubbed his eye then turned away hoping Vinnie wouldn't notice, but he had.

In the morning, Vinnie and Gianni returned to the Nebrodi Park campsite. The trail was easy to follow in daylight to Vinnie's Jeep. He hauled Signora Cucuzza's picnic feast. "*Un panino farcitura al prosciutto, pecorino stagionato, e pomodoro fresco e al fine burrata,*" she had explained. Vinnie smiled, missing most of her rattling ingredients, but it all clarified on his first bite of the fresh homemade bread filled with a local ham, aged pecorino, fresh tomato, and spread with a traditional Sicilian mozzarella-like cheese filled with cream. Signora Cucuzza also included a bottle of local wine. Vinnie was sure this was the number one decoy of all time.

The plan itself required that they return to the *pensione*

during the *mezzogiorno* siesta, not before and not after.

"We'll move the Jeep to the village's municipal parking lot."

Gianni went ahead in the Fiesta, circled the lot, and parked next to a row of cars. Vinnie parked two rows behind and duck-walked to partially hide beneath the cars and reach the Fiesta. He slid down in the passenger seat. This maneuver was their most exposed point if someone had been following the Fiesta.

"Don't worry," Gianni said smugly, "even Mafia hit men observe the afternoon siesta."

And as Gianni predicted, not a single car or pedestrian went past them as they drove back to their *pensione.*

Entering the bedroom, Vinnie declared himself exhausted emotionally, and Signora Cucuzza's picnic feast in his stomach didn't help. He hopped into the bed and was asleep before Gianni came out of the bathroom, himself yawning with fatigue.

A four-thirty alarm woke them for part two of Vinnie's plan.

"We'll stroll around the town center holding hands," explained Vinnie and he looked at Gianni. "Stop grinning. It's just for show."

He explained they'd retrieve the Jeep, only this time Gianni would duck-walk between the cars, whose numbers had increased by half a dozen. Gianni drove the Jeep two blocks and retrieved Vinnie concealed behind a covered bus stop. They drove to Patti on the main road.

After a few miles, Gianni veered onto a small secondary road to spot anyone following them. He continued until reaching a dirt path that looped to a small local road and returned them back to the state road SS116 heading to Naso which ended at SS113, the old main road before the A20 autostrada. They arrived in Patti ahead of the pickup time that they estimated from Don Carnivale's observation.

"We'll follow the van and not worry about the cargo if it shows up."

At six-forty-five a white van pulled into the Ceramiche Siciliane Bellani's parking lot and proceeded to the rear loading dock. With a pair of auto-focus binoculars Vinnie had purchased in a high-end optical store in Messina, he watched with a steady vision no matter how shaky his hands.

"How much did you pay for them?" asked Gianni.

"Enough."

"Over one hundred euros for a pair of binoculars?" pressed Gianni.

"Much more, and the store salesman called them 'Individual focus binoculars with two diopter adjusters,' so you can imagine the price."

Gianni asked Vinnie if he was rich.

"I do okay," said Vinnie, too embarrassed to reveal his net worth was higher than an average wage earner took home in fifteen years, all from winning a compensation lawsuit. Vinnie never had imagined he'd have more money than he needed. He felt dirty yet on occasions like this he appreciated the value of a near-unlimited cash reserve.

Twenty minutes passed and the driver emerged without the women. Gianni and Vinnie exited the Jeep to gain a direct line-of-sight view. Vinnie discovered the binoculars did not auto-focus while he walked. "That fuckin' sales rep can kiss my ass."

"Is that offer open to me as well?" asked Gianni.

"Sure, as soon as you sell me some binoculars that work."

Back in the Jeep, they continued their surveillance but nothing interesting happened. As the van left the Laboratorio, they followed with Gianni driving.

The white van entered the Nebrodi Park. This presented a problem, with fading daylight made worse by the dense forest filtering the remnants of the sun. The compensation was that the van's glowing rear lights helped. But to see the road Gianni needed headlights, which made them easy to notice if the van driver checked his rear-view mirror. Gianni extinguished the main beams to rely on the dim running lights and he cut his speed by half.

After twenty miles, the van turned onto a side road. Gianni stopped the car and took out Signor Cucuzza's map.

"I think we're here," said Gianni, pointing to the map. "This road goes no farther than two kilometers and then ends."

Driving on the minor road risked them being seen. At a normal walking pace they could cover a half-mile in ten minutes so Vinnie calculated half that time if they went at a slow jog.

Gianni pulled the Jeep off-road to park behind a clump of bushes using the four-wheel drive to cross the rough terrain. They jogged until Vinnie had a clear view and used his binoculars to see the white van five hundred yards ahead.

They slowed their pace and with sailboat tacking moved from one tree to another until they got to within three hundred feet of the van. Vinnie stopped and Gianni crouched down on his haunches.

Two men with automatic weapons guarded the van. One seemed tethered to a mythical beast until Vinnie observed through his binoculars the man held a leash attached to a huge Rottweiler.

"A fuckin' douche pooch," said Vinnie.

Gianni didn't understand so Vinnie explained, "A bad dog to meet at night... or day."

Vinnie focused his binoculars on an upstairs curtainless open window. He counted fifteen young girls but he might have missed a few as they flittered around like moths.

"We've got them," said Gianni with a nervous laugh.

"We have and we haven't. They could explain this as providing the women with respite from the refugee camp."

On the return journey the normally chatty Gianni said no more than a handful of words and Vinnie didn't respond to any of them.

They crawled into bed. Vinnie allowed Gianni to cuddle him and admitted to himself he also needed the comfort. Vinnie's tossing caused Gianni to turn over and cling to his side of the bed. Sweat rolled down Vinnie's brow, which he wiped using his pajama sleeve. He couldn't shake an image of Ben chained up in the bowels of a stone farmhouse with his throat slit from one ear to the other.

Vinnie tossed from one side onto his back and then the other side. *Will Ben be dead by morning?*

Chapter 39

The early morning cloudy day was made worse by a cold wind descending from the snowcaps of Mount Etna that chilled Ben. He found the shirt he'd discarded yesterday due to the unbearable heat. Now he covered his bare chest to stop shivering. He oscillated from hot to cold to hot, from sweating to dry skin. He flung open the shutters of the single window, dislodging them from rusty hinges. At the second-story height he saw secondary-growth forest stretching beyond his view.

He'd been captive for four days, not counting the night with Ciccio. The biggest goddamn mistake of his life. And what would Vinnie think? What was he doing? Would he descend into a hysterical panic? He wasn't far from that himself.

Lacking gym weights, he performed Marine-style exercises—variations of push-ups, handstands, crunches, and isometrics for his arms and chest. He lacked concentration and enthusiasm, the workout resembling a beginner's first trip to a gym.

Where is Vinnie? Is he held somewhere else? Tortured? Dead? His questions came faster than he could conjure answers, or at least those he wanted to be true.

On his fifth set of forty push-ups the door opened. Frank Aquafreddo and Sandro Grattinato entered, chatting in Sicilian. Behind them stood two granite-sized lunkheads with weapons hanging off their shoulders. Ben didn't know them but recognized their type—shitbags. He glared at Aquafreddo's putrid grin.

"You're quite the specimen even if I say so myself," chuckled Frank. "Don't you agree, Sandro?"

"We've given him enough sausage, roast pork, and local cheeses so he should be. And Zuppa," said Grattinato, pointing to the Catania Calcio Man, "shared his protein shake, Mr. O's brand. He's a big fan." Grattinato finished with a bizarre laugh. "You appreciate our good food, right, Mr. Olympia?" he said with a cruel laugh.

Ben ran his hands over his face and kept them there a second to cover his eyes.

"Not in the mood for conversation?" asked Frank, his scattered facial pockmarks constricting the extent his lips could spread. "At least show us your muscles."

"Fuck you," said Ben.

Frank's veneer smile slid off his face. Grattinato's head moved from side to side to show he knew Ben Hausen had just made a grave error by talking back to the dyspeptic Frank Aquafreddo.

The bodyguards raised their automatic weapons.

"It's not a request," said Frank, taking out his cell. "We need a picture of you to send to your pal, that scumbag Vinnie Briggs. He'll want proof you're alive and in good shape, so take off the shirt and show us your fucking muscles."

272

Aquafreddo's information pleased him and answered one of his questions about Vinnie—he was alive and safe.

"Okay," said Aquafreddo with his hands forming into fists, "we can take your picture in a different position and you won't like it. Nor will Vinnie."

And more confirmation, thought Ben.

Ben took off his shirt as one guard stepped forward. He straightened his back and flexed his half-moon biceps. Aquafreddo's phone camera clicked several times.

"Hey, Frank, where's the newspaper?" asked Grattinato.

Aquafreddo cursed. He'd forgotten they needed to show the date. He barked at a guard to fetch today's *La Sicilia* and then handed it to Ben to flex one arm and hold the paper in the other. He put his hands on Ben's arm to raise the paper higher, next to his face.

"Christ, they're like rocks. Now hold this in front of your chest and flex again," Aquafreddo ordered.

"And smile," added Grattinato with a leer.

Aquafreddo snapped more photos and showed the pictures on his phone to Grattinato. "Will these do, Sandro?"

Grattinato nodded and Frank Aquafreddo's face contorted as he moved closer to Ben. Without a word he pistol-whipped him twice across the face. "Don't you ever disrespect me again, you son of a bitch."

"*Basta,*" said Grattinato. "We're done here," and he looked at Ben's bloody face. "You can go back to making more muscles or jerking off. Whatever you like. Today is spaghetti carbonara. I'm sure you'll enjoy," Grattinato grunted.

The welts rose on Ben's face, blood trickling down his

chin and his busted lips. He splashed water on his face from the basin on the table. His head rattled with what seemed a precursor to thrombosis. He tried to stretch his arms, a trick he used to counter nausea after a steroid injection and ingesting Benzedrine tablets. It didn't work, not this time. His dizziness increased and he lay on the mattress. His throat gummed up. *I have a concussion.*

He worried about Vinnie. *I've been inconsiderate... acting like a fucking idiot. Why did I have to become jealous of Paul? Maybe Vinnie was telling the truth and he wasn't having an affair. What have I done?*

A few minutes later, Zuppa the Catania Calcio Man entered the room and threw an envelope onto Ben's chest. *"Un regalo da Frank,"* repeated in broken English, "A gift."

Ben pulled out a grainy A4-sized photograph from the package. It took him several seconds to realize he was staring into Ciccio's vacant eyes, his throat a congealed mass of blood, his eyes black and blue, and his cheekbones crushed.

Ben's stomach churned and acid reflux rose up his esophagus. His tightened throat holding back his vomit prevented him from screaming. Furrowed lines plowed his forehead, casting shadows on his already dark gray face. The welts on his injured face turned purple and blood caked his cheeks. He temples throbbed, one eye closed completely and the other remained only half-open.

He spoke to the photo. "Ciccio, I don't blame you. I'm so sorry," Ben whispered in prayer, setting aside his non-religious belief and hoping Ciccio heard him.

Blood dripped from his broken nose. *For fuck's sake,*

I didn't know what I wanted or didn't want. I should have never gone with Ciccio. Never doubted Vinnie.

In the early evening a guard brought Ben his supper and a fresh basin of water, soda, and a face cloth to wash the dried blood off. Grattinato stood behind and placed a pen, paper, and instructions on the table next to the food.

"Write a note that we'll include with your photo. Tell Briggs to cooperate and you'll be released unharmed. All he has to do is give us LoBianco."

A lie, thought Ben, touching his aching jaw. *I'm a dead man no matter what Vinnie does and whether or not he turns over Paul LoBianco.*

Grattinato gnashed his teeth attempting to smile before he spoke. "And make it personal so he knows you wrote it. Say nothing about us or your condition."

Ben's note talked of their summer on Martha's Vineyard. *Remember the strange woman and her weird philosophy that made us laugh?*

He meant Dr. Anna Swinburne, Ginny Livorno's psychologist mother, but he kept her identity from Aquafreddo. He smiled, thinking about Dr. Anna's weird therapy methods. "My patients are crazy so I never believe anything they tell me. I interpolate the truth." He omitted writing this in the note, hoping Vinnie understood the hidden message.

Frank approved the note, attached it to Ben's photo, then dispatched it to Hotel Mezzogiorno.

Chapter 40

Vinnie rose before sunrise after another sleepless night at Pensione al Bosco. He nudged open the window blinds two inches so as not to wake Gianni, who was still fast asleep with his face buried in his pillow and the covers pulled up to his neck to hide his semi-nude body from the chill night air.

What should we do next? He was out of ideas. For a diversion he composed an email to Blanca with an update and reminded her to contact Dan and Ginny. He recalled that his first break came from Don Carnivale. Maybe an epiphany was due, or perhaps a full-on miracle.

At six-thirty he pulled off the light bed sheet from Gianni, revealing an enormous tumescent penis peeking through his underwear like a spokesperson for all gay men.

"Looks like someone had a nice dream," said Vinnie.

Holding his penis, Gianni said, "And guess who was in it?"

"Get dressed."

Gianni looked down. "And what am I going to do about this?"

"We're going to Mass, so you'll confess."

"The dream wasn't that bad," pouted Gianni. "It's not

mortal until I fire it off."

"Drop it and hurry," said Vinnie, not wanting to waste time bantering over venial versus mortal sins. If jerking off was a mortal sin, then he'd be joining Gianni in Hell.

Gianni dressed quickly with Vinnie snapping at him to hurry. They arrived in church as Don Carnivale stood on the altar greeting the congregants. The four African women sat in their usual front pew.

During communion Vinnie went around the outside of the church. The white van had not returned, so he entered the sacristy. Gianni remained inside to watch the women.

With the final blessing, the four women followed the priest into the sacristy. All five were shocked to find Vinnie grinning and wiggling his fingers in a friendly greeting.

"*Buon giorno,*" he said, and the women responded likewise. Don Carnivale wasn't as welcoming.

"*Cosa fai?*" he said, wanting to know what Vinnie was up to.

"I'd like to ask your parishioners a few questions, especially her," he said, pointing to the woman he had spoken to on the road a few days earlier.

"I told you not to interfere," Don Carnivale said, motioning for the women to leave.

Vinnie blocked the exit. "I just want to know about the large white man she'd seen."

The woman looked puzzled then turned to Don Carnivale, who spluttered phlegm trying to answer.

"It's an easy question," said Vinnie, his Italian failing to think of another way to ask. "Yes or no, did you see a big man?"

The woman sobbed and begged to leave. One of them tried to rush past Vinnie but he didn't budge. Then the vestibule door flew open, hitting him in the back, followed by a man wider than the door with a neck like a telephone pole that supported an enormous head. He ordered the women to get into the van. Vinnie stood in front of the women. The driver shoved Vinnie, pushing him into Don Carnivale, and they were both knocked to the floor. The man's face was red, his tongue roaming around inside his mouth. He spat out his words to Don Carnivale. "What the fuck did you do? This will have repercussions. I should cut off your balls and jam them down your throat, you stupid asshole."

Instead of his anger dissipating it seemed to grow. He took hold of Don Carnivale's vestment and with one hand lifted him off the floor to a standing position.

"I didn't know about this. He just barged in," squeaked the priest, begging with bowed head.

"*Non me ne frega un cazzo.*" He shook the priest like a baby's rattle then released him and he again fell to the floor. He didn't give a fuck.

The driver continued to curse in Sicilian, kicking Vinnie and knocking the wind out of him. The priest rose unsteadily and the angry driver pushed him once more and knocked him on top of Vinnie.

Gianni entered the altar as the monolithic caveman slammed the sacristy door behind him. Gianni pulled it open and went outside to hear the driver screaming at the women to get into the van. He returned to the sacristy, taking the priest's hand, and brought him upright.

Vinnie righted himself and saw Gianni motion to him, which he didn't understand.

The priest removed his chasuble, folded it lengthwise, and placed it in a bureau. Closing the draw, he turned to Vinnie.

"*Che cazzo?!*" which Vinnie took to mean, "What the fuck?"

Vinnie began to explain his reason for trying to talk to the women but Don Carnivale muttered, "*Buh,*" which in this case he translated into the more extensive, "I don't give a fuck about your excuse."

The priest turned to Gianni and spoke in rapid Sicilian for a few minutes, his hands flying overhead, to his side, and at one point Don Carnivale was crouching like a woman about to give birth.

On their return to the *pensione* Gianni summarized the priest's sentiments as "We royally fucked up," only the Sicilian version involved donkey balls and Vinnie's mouth.

"He's sure the women will not be back and will probably be punished," said Gianni.

Vinnie's face took on several hues of red, the flush reaching his neck.

He and Gianni sat at the breakfast table in silence until the ever-cheerful Signora Cucuzza entered and poured *due cappuccini* then placed a basket of fresh pastry, *cornetti*, and brioche in front of them. She had prepared soft-boiled eggs fresh from the chicken coop.

Gianni took Vinnie's hand.

"Not now, Gianni, I'm too upset. I miscalculated."

"No, not that—I have something for you. One of the

African women dropped this on her way out." Gianni placed the object into Vinnie's palm. It was a small cloth pouch, stitched closed.

Nothing registered as Vinnie turned the pouch over several times. He took out his pocketknife, cut open the stitching and put his fingers inside to fondle small, coarse pebbles. Turning the pouch over, a dozen little rocks the size of match heads fell onto the table. Vinnie picked up one white stone amongst the browns and yellows.

Gianni chose a brown one and held it up to the light. Vinnie pulled his arm down. "Do you know what they are?"

"Diamonds?"

"Yes, uncut diamonds."

Vinnie put the pouch in his pocket and they finished their breakfast in a hurry.

In their room, Vinnie mulled over this new evidence, if that was what it was. He had to tell Delgrado about it, or was that also a mistake? Or maybe Mancuso? Should he reveal it came from one of the women? If it leaked, then Ben's captors would know from the van driver of Vinnie's location.

A mid-morning knock interrupted his thoughts. Signor Cucuzza spoke through the closed door.

"*Si*," answered Gianni.

"*Mi scusa*," said Signor Cucuzza. "A very big man is at the desk wanting to talk to Signor Vinnie."

Gianni thanked Signor Cucuzza and said they'd be down in a minute.

"We can go out the window," said Gianni.

"It's a forty-five-foot drop to a hard sidewalk."

"He'll assassinate us in front of Cucuzza and maybe kill him too."

Vinnie thought for a minute and shook his head. "That's not what a hit man does. A professional assassin avoids being identified as much as possible. He isolates the victim unless a difficult target like a politician or an international celebrity forces his hand."

"How can you be so sure?" asked Gianni.

"Because I have insurance: Paul. They need me alive or they can't find him," said Vinnie.

For all his bravado, Vinnie wasn't sure who to expect and how a stranger knew where to find him.

Chapter 41

On entering the lobby, Vinnie saw Signor Cucuzza's "big man."

"Ah," he said to Gianni, "he means tall."

Vinnie held out his hand and said, "I know you. You served the meal I had with Paul."

The man's oversized hand covered Vinnie's like wrapping paper. He gave a short nod as an answer.

"How did you know where to find me?" asked Vinnie.

The tall waiter tapped his nose and said, "Her."

Vinnie guessed he meant one of the two women who knew he was helping Paul. He'd put money on Serafina and said as much.

The waiter again gave a nod.

"And why are you here and not her?" asked Vinnie.

The waiter's expression didn't change. He handed Vinnie an envelope that had been left at the Hotel Mezzogiorno. "For you."

"How did you get this?" asked Vinnie, frustrated that again the waiter said nothing. "Look, stop fucking around."

The reply came in a deep baritone, "She has her ways."

Before Vinnie examined the envelope's contents the tall

waiter had gone. Back upstairs in the third-floor bedroom Vinnie opened the package to pull out a photo and note. His face drained to a bleached white.

Gianni grabbed the photo from Vinnie and repeated several times, "*O Dio,*" then fetched water for both of them.

Vinnie reread the note, his eyes running over the page to look for words in a secret ink or something he had overlooked. He again examined Ben's photo.

Gianni peered over Vinnie's shoulder. "He looks okay. What does 'strange person' mean and who is Martha and her vineyard?"

Gianni's words helped reduce Vinnie's worst fears. Ben did look okay. He was alive as of the time of the newspaper printing. Vinnie concentrated despite his upset. He paced the room with the note then sat to reread it out loud. He turned to Gianni. "Martha's Vineyard is an island on the southern shore of Cape Cod in Massachusetts."

"Uh-huh," said Gianni with no great curiosity. "And the strange woman?"

"That's Dr. Anna Swinburne, a well-respected psychiatrist and a friend of ours. I think I understand Ben's meaning and repeated the same thoughts Ben had while writing the note. Ben is saying that if I trade him for Paul..." Vinnie's face hardened, his eyes sunk deep into their sockets with skin a shade of gray. "...Aquafreddo will kill him anyway."

Tears flushed Vinnie's eyes and he cursed his crybaby reaction, but if he was honest this was the time to cry if ever there was one.

Gianni brought tissues from the bathroom.

Vinnie said he was going out for a walk.

"Wait," said Gianni, "I'll put on some shoes."

"Thanks, but I want to be alone."

He slowly ambled around the village until he was at the fountain in the main piazza. He sat on a bench and phoned Maria Alba.

"I need to talk to Paul."

Maria Alba reminded Vinnie that Paul had no cell reception. Vinnie cursed loudly, attracting attention. He lowered his voice and begged. She refused and Vinnie stood to find a secluded location.

"Let me put it this way. You fuckin' find a way to get Paul to a fuckin' phone or I'm on the next flight to New York. You fuckin' *capisce*?!"

Maria Alba laughed. "*Va bene.* I'll do it but you need to tell me the reason. What's changed?"

Vinnie told her about Ben's photo, note, the threat to his mother, and him meeting Mancuso.

"And I know Frank Aquafreddo. He's a deranged psychopath. Paul will tell you the same. He'll torture Ben then slice him to death. Worse than Ciccio."

After a short silence, Maria Alba asked, "How does talking to Paul help?"

Vinnie was no longer yelling yet his voice was still shaky. "I have a plan and I need Paul to participate. Only he can agree and I need to hear him say so. I don't want it coming through you."

Maria Alba blasted Vinnie's eardrum in Italian, Sicilian, and English. She finished with a promise she'd talk to Paul and if he agreed then he'd call Vinnie.

"It has to be now," said Vinnie. "I'm not waiting around

all fuckin' day. Do it or I'm gone."

"Give me at least two hours."

"Can't you people do anything quickly?" Vinnie said, exasperated.

"Vinnie, *vaffanculo!*" shouted Maria Alba. "Never insult an entire race and certainly not my heritage. Can't you Americans show respect for other cultures? You know what, go to hell and go back to America, which is pretty much the same thing."

Vinnie knew he'd become the ugly American. He had gone too far with his insult and Maria Alba was testing this tough truth. She'd let him return to New York, which abandoned Ben as much as Paul. He apologized.

"Then you wait and do nothing until you hear from Paul," and the line went dead.

Chapter 42

Vinnie called himself an asshole on nearly every step as he returned to the Pensione al Bosco. He asked Gianni for privacy while he called New York. Gianni said he'd be at the local bar for a *spremuta d'arancia*. He believed drinking freshly squeezed orange juice every day kept him fit and healthy. Vinnie pointed out that his daily two-hour swims were probably the more likely reason.

Blanca answered her cell at six am.

"At this hour, it better be important, *cabrón*," Blanca said with a frog in her throat that Vinnie thought made her Puerto Rican accent sound even sexier. He shuffled across the room, now accustomed to women cursing him in foreign languages.

The call didn't help. He had hoped that hearing her voice would alleviate his loneliness and give him clarity. But Blanca was too far away for that, which he subconsciously knew all along. He had Gianni but he couldn't replace Blanca's many years of friendship. His depression returned.

Gianni entered the room displaying all his teeth like he had found a few extra. He opened the palm of his hand, holding the cloth pouch. "I washed it. Take a look."

Vinnie examined the bag and shrugged.

Gianni moved to the balcony. "It's better in full light. Without the dirt you can see the bright green and yellow colors. *Bella*. Look at the wiggly pattern."

"Yeah?"

"Caterina has a scarf exactly like this. A friend of Enzo's brought it to him from South Africa and he gave it to her."

With his eyes wide and jaw dropping onto his chest, Vinnie gasped, "You're fuckin' kidding me?"

"I called Caterina to ask where she got it, pretending that I saw something similar at the local market. She read the scarf label and now we know the place."

Vinnie felt the midday sun's warmth high in a sky the shade of blue found in a kindergartner's crayon box.

"Let's take a walk," Vinnie said.

Vinnie explained an idea and changed his mind every few steps. "No, that won't work." "Better still…" "We could try to…" "How about…"

Gianni asked a few questions, his arm looped through Vinnie's as a gesture of friendship and a traditional Sicilian custom among men. He chuckled, repeating to Vinnie his own logic that this helped keep their cover should anyone be watching.

At the *pensione*, Signora Cucuzza had their picnic lunch prepared. This time they went to the Patti coast and not the Nebrodi National Park.

They stretched a picnic blanket under a large palm tree to enjoy their *panini*. Gianni said he liked to watch the horizon where sea and sky met. Vinnie told him he was poetic.

Vinnie reclined on his back, his hands behind his head as if he were a botanist surveying the overhanging palm leaves. Gianni rested on his side, studying Vinnie as if he was a new and exotic species of man. They soon drifted into sleep then were awoken by Vinnie's cell phone buzzing.

"*Pronto*," answered Vinnie, anticipating the caller would be Maria Alba.

"Vinnie, it's Paul."

Vinnie jumped up and walked away from Gianni onto the pebble beach. He didn't waste time with pleasantries. "Paul, there's a chance to save Ben but at a big risk to yourself," Vinnie said anxiously.

"Tell me," said Paul with no concern in his voice.

"You'll have to show yourself before we get the evidence to entrap Aquafreddo. There's a chance we'll not get it and all this will have been for nothing."

Paul waited and Vinnie continued.

"Tell me when's the next shipment of salt and pepper shakers from New York?"

"What? I don't get it. Are you still talking about helping Ben?" asked Paul, sounding annoyed. "This has nothing to do with Ben or trafficking."

"It does. Can you find out the arrival date for a pizzeria in Barcellona?"

"Why should I care about a pizzeria in Spain?"

"No, not Spain. Ask Maria Alba to explain."

The phone went silent except for faint murmurs in the background. Paul returned, his voice calmer.

"Maria Alba knows about it. She says we get small shipments for the pizzeria every few months. The salt and

288

pepper shakers are shipped with other specialty items to make it cost-effective. Why does this matter?"

"Find me the exact date of the next shipment," Vinnie said, the urgency of his speech increasing. He made a point about how they'd have to include Commissario Delgrado.

Paul interrupted. "Vinnie, it's too much. A real long shot, don't you think?"

Kicking small pebbles, Vinnie cursed and stomped his feet.

Paul repeated, "Hello? Vinnie? Can you hear me?"

"No plan is perfect," answered Vinnie. "Everything with the mob is a long shot. If it was without risk then the result wouldn't be worth the effort."

Vinnie overheard Maria Alba. "You're outside the safe location and exposed. We must return now."

"I've got to go. I'm sorry," said Paul.

Vinnie knew Paul was right. *Just one more screwed-up idea of mine.*

"No, wait," said Vinnie, panicking. "Give me a second."

"Vinnie, be realistic."

"And what? Lose Ben?"

"I'm sorry."

"Then you tell me why you needed my help. You'd said it wasn't dangerous."

Vinnie sat on the pebbled beach. He wanted to smash his phone.

"Paul, level with me. What's going on? I've made a big request of you but you did the same of me. I trusted you. Have I been wrong? Has this all been a joke or scam?"

Vinnie heard Paul arguing with Maria Alba then shouting

for her to go away. He wanted his conversation to be private.

"She's gone to the car," said Paul. "Now I'll tell you about me." He waited a few seconds. "The thing I've not wanted to admit to anyone, not even to myself, is that I arrange the shipments, all of them. The ceramics, wines, and olive oil transported in cargo ship containers. I knew they carried drugs. I never understood the salt shakers but what you said makes sense. The empties are refilled with uncut diamonds and sent to India."

Paul stopped to blow his nose. He sniveled his words. "I swear I never knew about the human trafficking."

Paul metered out his thoughts. "I never wanted this life. But it came so easy... the money, the women... yeah, I still enjoy the special sensation only a woman can give, but I prefer men. I live in luxury yet I'm unhappy. That's why John and I broke up."

Paul inhaled, the kind that sucks in a universe. "I've made lives miserable and people died." He paused, blowing his nose again. "I'm so sorry."

Vinnie's anger dissipated but he wanted to hear more. "Then why?"

"I don't know. Easy? Too hard not to go along with it? You tell me why people do bad things."

Vinnie thought the silence that followed was too long.

"Paul, you there? Paul? Hello, Paul?"

Vinnie thought the line had gone dead or Paul had hung up.

"Yeah, I'm here... for fuck's sake, Vinnie, say something."

"You want forgiveness?"

"No. Okay, yes, but what's that dumb expression? 'Closure.'"

Vinnie agreed the expression was dumb but not the concept. Paul wanted to belong to the tribe of commodities, a life of comfort, so he forfeited integrity and his true self. He embraced the Mafia honor code, narrowly construed.

Vinnie wasn't sure he believed Paul once the call ended. Had he really changed? Wouldn't he soon miss the glamour, the riches, the men and women at his beck and call?

Walking along the beach, Vinnie made two decisions. The first was to provisionally forgive Paul. In a way, he had no choice. Paul had agreed to help save Ben. The second decision was to call Commissario Delgrado.

"*Ciao*, Vinnie, you're on my list of people to call. Not today but definitely someday soon," Delgrado said, chuckling.

"Are you fuckin' kidding me?" Vinnie said. "My spouse is a hostage and you haven't called once with an update, and now I'm on your 'someday' scheduled?"

Delgrado clicked his tongue. "Why call when I have nothing to report? As much as I enjoy our chats there are crimes to solve."

"The last time I checked kidnapping was also a crime," Vinnie said while knowing this wasn't the way he wanted this conversation to go.

"I'll make a note. *Kidnapping is a crime*," said Delgrado in a sarcastic voice.

"Fuck you. I know where Paul will be in two days and I know where the trafficking takes place," said Vinnie with vindication's superiority.

"I'll prepare a team," said Delgrado with more authority.

"We can guard Paul to bring him into custody safely."

"That's not my plan. I'll get Paul to the loading location to meet me. No cops in sight."

"Then why call me?"

"Because after I get Paul, I'll signal to you so your men can save the refugees."

"And Paul?" asked Delgrado.

"He's Ben's insurance. Aquafreddo wants Paul for Ben and that's what he'll get."

"That's not our agreement. I'm not going along with this."

"Then you lose the women and the trafficking. I still have Paul."

"And will Paul agree?"

"He has to." Vinnie hesitated then added, "And there's someone else that could get hurt."

"Who? This is new."

"I'm not telling you, but Paul knows this person very well," said Vinnie. He had told Paul about the threat to Vinnie's mother, which was the final thing that convinced Paul to go along with the exchange plan. He had been to the Briggs home many times. He had spent nearly every weekday at Vinnie's house having supper in front of the TV.

"Even if I agree, to make this work how do you let the Aquafreddo mob know you have Paul?" asked the Commissario.

"They'll know because after this call I'll make one to your Questura number and leave a message. I trust the mole will hear and pass it along to Ben's captors."

"And my men?"

"They'll be between Tindari and Capo d'Orlando."

"They're forty kilometers apart and one is up a mountain. How can they respond quickly to your call?"

"Get faster police cars. Try Amazon Prime." Vinnie thought maybe he should not have jibed Delgrado with his joke. He'd apologize later.

As promised, Vinnie dialed the Questura office and left a misleading message, hoping the informant was listening. This version gave a different time than the real one. He also added irrelevant items for credibility.

Vinnie wiped his brow. Was the machine working? Would the informant listen? Was Mancuso the informant? He'd soon learn using the next part of his trap, which he didn't tell Commissario Delgrado about. And the most important thing above all was if the fuckin' turd Frank Aquafreddo brought Ben to Patti for the exchange.

Chapter 43

Gianni called his sister an hour after Vinnie spoke to Commissario Delgrado.

"*Ciao, Caterina, com'*è stai? Tutto a posto?" Gianni tried to sound normal, asking his sister the usual "how are you?" and "is everything okay?" questions. He often called his sister daily for general gossip but rarely twice in twenty-four hours.

"Gianni, what's the matter?"

Vinnie was rolling his eyes and motioned with his hand as if eating.

"Yeah. *Tutto okay*," began Gianni, trying to recuperate from his stumble. "I'm with Vinnie and... uh... he wants to meet you and Enzo for a pizza. He said Enzo showed him a great place and he'd like us to go on a double date."

"*Come mai?*" asked Caterina.

Gianni answered, "*Fare un'uscita a quattro.*"

Caterina giggled at Gianni's suggestion they go on a double date. He'd never suggested this before and she assumed he now did so for a good reason, but what it was she couldn't guess.

"Okay, I'll ask Enzo. *Ciao.*"

Twenty minutes later Caterina confirmed the double date at Pizzeria Nebrodi for eight o'clock.

During the afternoon siesta, Vinnie insisted he and Gianni remain awake to review the plan. Gianni closed the window blinds to avoid the afternoon sun heating the room to blast-furnace temperature. Vinnie didn't appreciate that for Gianni the siesta was imprinted on his biological rhythm and to remove it would require invasive surgery. Gianni was asleep in fifteen minutes.

Vinnie moved to the downstairs parlor. To his surprise, Signor Cucuzza sat at the dining table reading *La Gazzetta dello Sport.*

"Siesta?"

"*Venti minuti,*" answered Signor Cucuzza, flashing ten fingers twice. "I don't need as much as I used to."

Vinnie looked at the newspaper, folded on the horse racing page.

"Hobby. A few *scudi.*" Signor Cucuzza rubbed his thumb against his index and pointed upward, lips pursed.

Money and the never-ending pursuit, thought Vinnie, *even for the rich.* Not that he thought the Cucuzzas were rich. He was sure no one in the village was wealthy and asked Signor Cucuzza about the local economy, which led to a discussion about how a poor village maintained the parish.

Vinnie decided to be blunt. "Mass attendance is low and I'd guess the collection plate isn't much to shout about."

Signor Cucuzza explained with a series of dramatic gestures and eye squinting that the church may be poor but Don Carnivale wasn't.

"How so?" asked Vinnie.

"*Busticedda.*"

Vinnie shrugged. He didn't understand the Sicilian word.

Signor Cucuzza pushed his hand into his pocket, turned his head the other way and pretended to put something in Vinnie's hand.

Bribe or payoff or something like it. Vinnie wasn't sure which but it didn't matter because whatever the meaning, it was illegal, not to mention immoral. *That has to be a sin of one kind or another,* thought Vinnie. But what kind?

* * *

Vinnie and Gianni arrived in Barcellona just before eight. From all the cars and people walking the street Vinnie was sure they'd have a long wait at the pizzeria. It was packed yet Caterina and Mancuso were already at a prime outside table.

"How early did you arrive?" asked Vinnie.

"Oh," Caterina said, broadcasting a smile to a nearby galaxy, "Enzo knows the owner and asked him to reserve us a table. Wasn't that sweet of him?"

"Yeah, very," said Vinnie, wishing he could tell Enzo where to shove his sweetness.

Vinnie noticed Gianni's and Caterina's mutual affection—no sibling rivalry. Mancuso's charming words matched Pablo Neruda's poems in the movie *Il Postino.* Yet he and Enzo knew they didn't come for the wood-fired pizza oven.

Vinnie waited until the conversation waned in the way conversations do and he gave Gianni their pre-arranged signal. Gianni stood and asked Caterina for a word in private.

Caterina's surprise was anticipated and Gianni had a prepared response.

"*Cosa di famiglia*," he said. "I don't want to talk about family in front of others."

"Has something bad happened?" asked Caterina in a frenzy.

"No," Gianni quickly added, having not anticipated his sister's fearful reaction. "Follow me," and he walked away from the table. Caterina reluctantly tailed him. Gianni wished he smoked to calm himself. He had never lied to his sister in his life.

Vinnie said nothing, but patiently waited to see brother and sister reach the street corner. Just as he was about to speak Mancuso preempted him.

"Why couldn't we do this over the phone?" he asked, no longer friendly.

"I think mine is tapped."

"*Cazzate!* Bullshit."

"No, it's not. And I think Delgrado has a tail on me. Gianni and I have managed to avoid them coming here tonight and that's the reason we were late. And I thought if we were followed, then Caterina's presence makes this appear normal. Even if I'm paranoid—and I'm not—I wanted to talk in person. I'm arranging an exchange of Paul for Ben."

Mancuso sat back rubbing his chin. Vinnie knew this was the point he either convinced Mancuso or the entire plan went down the tubes. Everything depended on one crucial event—that Enzo Mancuso had listened to the recording Vinnie left on the Questura answering machine.

"I've spoken to Delgrado. Because of my... you want

to call it paranoia…? I gave him false information. He thinks the exchange of Paul for Ben happens in two days. It doesn't. It's tomorrow. That's why we had to meet tonight. My intermediary will bring Paul to Patti. I'll call you with the time as soon as I know. Can you be ready at short notice?"

Vinnie examined every inch of Mancuso's face. Did he accept the lie? Had he heard the Questura recording?

Mancuso stuck his chin out, his head tilted slightly back, a good impression of mulling over the idea. But it was also possible he was refining the plan. That he wasn't the mole Vinnie had thought he was. Maybe it was Delgrado, the one person above suspicion. Vinnie's eyebrows buckled. Had he picked the wrong horse like Signor Cucuzza? Only his stake was a lot more than a few *scudi*.

"*Va bene*," said Enzo. "I can be ready. I'll need one person with me and I know just the man I can trust. I'll call him after I take Caterina home."

Vinnie expanded on the exchange location and Mancuso made small modifications of no significance yet worthy of a police officer. *He could be legit*, thought Vinnie, *and I have this all wrong.*

By the time Gianni and Caterina returned, the waiter was presenting *il conto* of sixty-five euros and change including wine and *il servizio*. Vinnie grabbed for the receipt but Enzo snatched it. "You're the guest. This is my treat."

Vinnie mustered his most gracious "*Grazie mille*."

Kisses landed on everyone's cheeks, a four-way smooch fest.

Gianni drove at a moderate speed on the return to Pensione al Bosco while Vinnie called Maria Alba.

"Paul's ready," she said.

"Good, I knew he would be."

"And everything is ready to go on our side. The ship is on schedule with no expected delays."

"What delays might be expected?" asked Vinnie.

"Sometimes a berth is unavailable at the last minute because a docked ship doesn't depart, usually vessel malfunctions or loading or unloading issues or missing paperwork, et cetera. Then our ship can't dock and sits in the harbor for hours if not days."

Vinnie groaned. "How likely?"

"*Boh!*"

Yeah, of course you don't know. You're a lawyer. "Okay, so we're all set," said Vinnie.

The conversation ended confirming Paul's arrival in Patti would coincide with the van driver's schedule. He'd call Mancuso in the morning to create a sense of last-minute timing.

Vinnie's stomach cramped. Sweat seeped through his shirt. He'd learned that when a plan seemed perfect there was always something unexpected that thwarted it. For his corporate espionage cases it didn't matter other than delays in the end result. No lives were at risk. He couldn't bear thinking that Ben or Paul might die—or him. He preferred it to be himself, not that he had a death wish.

His mind went over the events leading up to tomorrow. Why did he get involved? If he had arrived on the first day ten minutes later or earlier he'd have missed meeting Paul and Al. And if he had not met Joseph, Ezine, and little

Ibironke at the refugee camp he'd have stepped away from helping Paul.

Before arriving at the *pensione*, Vinnie turned to Gianni. "Let's get the Jeep now and not wait until morning. We'll park it in the municipal lot."

"*Va bene*," came Gianni's carefree response.

And Vinnie recognized in Gianni's voice his own five years earlier, his arrogant self-confidence that nothing bad could happen, that no one gets hurt and no one dies.

With the Jeep parked in the municipal lot, Vinnie walked down a narrow alley to enter the waiting Ford Fiesta. Gianni drove to their designated spot at the rear of Pensione al Bosco.

Sleep did not come easy for either of them. Gianni worried about lying to Caterina. Vinnie worried he'd never see Ben again.

Chapter 44

Even though the exchange was in the evening, Vinnie rose early for breakfast at six am. An English couple greeted him with god-awful cheeriness. They were about to go on a birding—or, as they called it, "twitching"—excursion and were concerned they were already too late to have the best sightings. A German couple across from Vinnie asked his recommendation on trails.

"They're all..." Vinnie caught himself before saying they were all the same, one tree after another. "...special. I couldn't possibly select one."

The English couple ate quickly, followed by the Germans. Two empty tables, one soon filled by four Italian men around forty. They greeted Vinnie, told him they were from Verona and asked about his home country. They applauded New York for no apparent reason. They had hiked all the major Italian National Parks with Sicily being the last to conquer. They held each other's hands, revealing their excitement over their achievements, which Vinnie understood was more than tramping around forests.

When the men left, Vinnie finished his third cup of cappuccino.

"*Troppo. Si fa male,*" said Signora Cucuzza, worried about Vinnie's health drinking so much coffee yet dutifully pouring his fourth cup.

Gianni sat woozily at the table. "What time is it?" he asked, yawning.

"Nearly eight. You slept a long time."

"Didn't really sleep until after two. I should never have told Caterina I thought our mother is very ill... it's like tempting fate. What a terrible thing to say."

Vinnie half-closed his eyes as he recalled lying to his best friend Dan Livorno on his first case. He had hated himself and felt awful about it. And each lie on every case thereafter dredged up the same feeling of disgust at himself. He justified his deception to save lives but that didn't always work out.

Gianni finished his brioche in two bites. With breakfast completed they told Signora Cucuzza that no lunch box was required today. They planned to have their midday meal at a restaurant by the sea.

"*Bello il mare,*" she said, but Vinnie detected Signora Cucuzza's disappointment they didn't want her to prepare their meal.

Vinnie drove the Jeep and followed Gianni driving the Fiesta to Marina di Patti, a seaside district noted for its excellent fish restaurants. After lunch they ambled to the nearby beach. Gianni removed a few large stones from the coarse, sandy beach to spread out the same blanket they had used in the Nebrodi Park.

Despite growing anxiety, Vinnie quickly fell asleep. After some time Gianni nudged him awake.

"Did I sleep long?" he asked, disorientated.

"Not so much."

Vinnie checked his watch. "An hour. Why didn't you wake me? We'll be late."

Gianni covered his smile with his hand. "It's a ten-minute drive, maybe less."

Gianni drove the Ford Fiesta to their lookout location while Vinnie parked the Jeep a block away. He walked quickly to reach Gianni in under four minutes. Inside the Fiesta, he adjusted his binoculars to scan the horizon and saw nothing of note.

Gianni opened his door and began to step outside until Vinnie took hold of his arm. "Someone may be watching."

"I don't see anyone," Gianni said.

Vinnie shook his head and tapped his binoculars.

"Ah, they may have binoculars?"

Vinnie nodded. For the next half-hour they observed typical human activity. Teenage girls walked past chatting, with occasional carefree laughter. A squad of ten-year-old boys kicked a soccer ball along the street. Tourists entered Ceramiche Siciliane Bellani and a few came out carrying bags.

The sun was low in the sky. As six-thirty approached, the white van pulled up, which Vinnie thought was too small for the anticipated twenty or so refugees. His concern grew as the time he gave Mancuso and Delgrado approached.

Six-forty and still no truck. Vinnie despaired. Had he miscalculated? Another fifteen minutes went by and there were no more vehicles to be seen.

"We'll wait until seven and then call it quits. I blew this big time."

A minute before seven Gianni choked, spitting out his words. "Look over there," he said, nervously pointing out the window. "A *camion*... uh...?"

Vinnie focused his binoculars on the large vehicle to confirm Gianni's observation that a heavy-duty truck had rounded the coastal road. Five minutes later the truck was backing into the loading dock of Ceramiche Siciliane Bellani. The driver climbed out of the cab. A few seconds later a man exited the passenger side door. Vinnie thought he recognized him and focused his binoculars on the man's face. "Gianni, it's the guy at the sacristy—the one with the big neck who knocked me and Don Carnivale to the floor."

The driver and the neck man looked down the street opposite the direction they'd arrived. Vinnie thought they were searching for him. He trained his binoculars from man to man. "They're not looking for me but someone else."

"How do you know?" asked Gianni.

"Because they are staring at a specific part of the road. If they were looking for me they'd be scanning in both directions." Vinnie put down his binoculars and his entire face tightened as he thought about what he'd seen. "Something's wrong. I've got to warn Paul." Vinnie was about to call Maria Alba on the burner.

"Stop," said Gianni, pulling Vinnie's arm away from the phone. "Look, they're moving onto the loading dock. Maybe they were just checking for *la polizia*."

Vinnie wanted this to be true. Adjusting the high-power binoculars he caught sight of the owner of the shop.

"The proprietor," he said to Gianni in an unnecessary whisper.

Neck man lumbered to the rear of the truck and waited for the owner and the van driver. He then opened the roll-up cargo door and the van driver signaled for the cargo to come out.

Vinnie gasped, seeing at least thirty people inside, mostly young girls but also a few boys. They huddled, handcuffed in sets of three or four. Vinnie pulled the binoculars away from his eyes. Gianni asked to see but Vinnie held tight. He wiped away his tears before continuing his surveillance.

"No! No, no, no."

"What?"

"Oh my God, it's her."

"Tell me. What is it?"

"The woman I offered money on the road and in the church. She's in the truck."

"*O Dio!*" yelled Gianni.

Vinnie didn't know what to do. He lowered the binoculars, his body trembling. Gianni gave him a hug.

"*Forza*, Vinnie," said Gianni. "Don't stumble now. Ben needs you."

Yes, thought Vinnie, *time to do something*. He began to walk to his parked Jeep, leaving Gianni the binoculars to evaluate the situation, and he reminded him that if anything looked wrong he should call the Commissario and then dial the Polizia di Stato. Vinnie was almost certain it was Mancuso informing the Mafia and not Delgrado.

Vinnie parked the Jeep in the Ceramiche Siciliane Bellani's empty visitors' parking lot. He came out of the car wearing Paul's white straw fedora straight out of an old Cuban cigar advertisement, the hat being a signal for Paul.

He mounted the three front steps and stood next to a ceramic vase half his height and twice as wide containing a potted seven-foot palm.

Maria Alba's Cinquecento rounded the bend and slowed as it approached the ceramic store.

Paul walked across the parking lot when a horn blared. Vinnie looked up the hill to see the Ford Fiesta's flashing high beams with horn still blasting.

"Paul, get down!" yelled Vinnie.

Paul dropped to the ground. A burst of shots sounded, bullets hitting the wall of the storefront and shattering pots. Vinnie ducked behind the large palm. Bullets hit the ceramic vase but the densely packed soil slowed and deflected them from their target.

Vinnie knew he had very little time before the gunman would approach him. He saw the Fiat Cinquecento drive by at high speed. The gunman took shots but was too unbalanced to hit the fast-moving, zigzagging car.

"Fuck you, Briggs!" said a voice that Vinnie instantly recognized as Mancuso's.

Vinnie didn't answer and lowered himself to the ground, remaining hidden by the huge ceramic vase.

"You think you're so clever. I knew you were warning Paul the minute I saw that fucking fedora! It's his, isn't it? Now you'll die wearing it instead of him."

Vinnie remained on the ground but looked up to see Mancuso's snarling, chestnut-tanned face staring down at him.

"You're the mole."

Mancuso aimed his gun point-blank at Vinnie's head. The shot sounded like a cannon, followed by silence.

306

Chapter 45

The Laboratorio's marble statutes reverberated and amplified the gunshot. A second later Vinnie was surprised to open his eyes. Gianni and Commissario Delgrado were staring at him.

"You're wounded," Gianni said with a teary face, kneeling and pointing to the blood on Vinnie's shirt.

"Huh," said Vinnie, looking at the stain. "Not mine," he replied and touched himself to be sure he wasn't shot.

Commissario Delgrado stood behind Gianni with his Beretta 93R service weapon drawn.

"What fuckin' happened?" asked Vinnie.

"You fainted as best as I can tell," said Delgrado with a small grin emerging, "but I'm no physician. I'd have thought you were used to gunshots all the time in the Bronx."

"Brooklyn. And we don't have gunshots all the time."

"*Basta!*" cried Gianni. "I nearly pissed my pants. What took you so long?" he asked, pointing at Commissario Delgrado.

"I got here in time. Okay, a minute or two sooner might have been better."

"You shot Mancuso?" asked Vinnie, knowing the question was unneeded as he saw a body a few feet from him.

"*Beh*," shrugged Delgrado. "Not me. I thought you did, or Maria Alba, but she's not here."

"There's no one around," said Gianni. "The only person I saw was a woman in jeans with a large bag at the bus stop and she was running away. Who wouldn't on hearing gunshots?"

Vinnie turned back, taking a glance at Mancuso's head blown open, blood covering the ceramic-tiled steps. He turned away, blowing air through his lips. A policeman gave Vinnie a bottle of water. The Ceramiche Siciliane Bellani parking lot resembled a scrum of police cars, each with flashing blue domes.

"And the hostages?" asked Vinnie.

"Safe. We also have the *laboratorio* owner, his daughter, and the truck driver. The van driver and the bodyguard got away."

No one's mentioned Paul, thought Vinnie. *He's gone and the exchange for Ben failed*. Vinnie's jaw dropped.

"And did they bring Ben?!" he yelled.

The Commissario clucked a "no."

"Mancuso knew this was a setup. How?" Vinnie asked.

Delgrado suggested Mancuso heard something wrong in Vinnie's message at the Questura. A slip-up or hesitation in Vinnie's voice.

"He was a damn good detective," said Delgrado, wetting his lips with his tongue. "As well as a very bad man. In my opinion, they didn't bring Ben because they never planned on an exchange in the first place and not because they knew it was a sting."

"Then why try to kill me? Why not just run?" Vinnie pitched to one side as he walked. Gianni extended his arm but Vinnie waved it away. He doubled over. "Ben's dead. They killed him before the meeting or will as soon as Aquafreddo hears about the shootout and Paul's escape."

Delgrado took hold of Vinnie's arm and straightened him up. With his chin Vinnie motioned to Mancuso's body. "How was he going to explain to you my being shot?"

"He'd have an answer ready. If it were me, I'd say an assassin gunned down Paul from a passing van and I'd shot back and you were caught in the crossfire."

Vinnie agreed. "And why did he not shoot at Paul as soon as he was on the steps?"

"Maybe he didn't have a clear shot and thought he had time to wait, not knowing Gianni would blast a warning."

Vinnie lost his concentration. He'd screwed up. "Ben's dead, isn't he?"

Commissario Delgrado put his hand on Vinnie's shoulder. "It was always a long shot, remember?"

Gianni added, "It's like prayers. Some get answered and some don't but not even a priest can tell you which one is which."

Vinnie's eyelids fluttered as if he was about to go into shock. He didn't move and his breathing became so shallow it was imperceptible.

"You okay? *Tutto bene?*" Gianni asked.

Vinnie stumbled down into the parking lot with Delgrado extending a hand to steady him.

"If Ben's alive we might still save him," Vinnie said almost to himself.

"How? And assuming he is alive, we don't know where they are holding him," replied Delgrado, his forehead crushing his brows.

Gianni agreed with Delgrado's conclusion but kept it to himself.

Vinnie didn't behave like most people when faced with life-and-death situations. His mind boiled over with ideas. He evaluated each, rejected most, and one or two eventually emerged as plausible. He looked at the Commissario and asked, "Did you get the salt and pepper shakers in the truck?"

Delgrado's blank expression was the answer. He asked a policeman to check the truck's cargo. The officer brought him a large box and Vinnie opened it.

Inside were smaller cartons containing a dozen salt and pepper shakers amounting to four hundred. On Delgrado's signal, the policeman opened one. A pile of salt poured into his hand along with a dozen uncut diamonds.

Vinnie raised his arms like a sprinter breaking the tape at the finish line.

"What?" asked Gianni.

"They didn't finish their delivery. These were for another destination."

"*Buh*," replied Gianni and the Commissario agreed.

"Don't you see?" Vinnie said, excited. "Until that delivery takes place, Frank Aquafreddo doesn't know his men were captured. That buys us some time."

"Time for what?" asked the Commissario, pointing to an empty parking space. "He got away. He'll call Aquafreddo."

"Maybe, or if my hunch is right, he has Ben somewhere in the Nebrodi Park with no cell phone service."

"Even if true, we don't know where he's keeping him," Delgrado said, trying to be sympathetic, but he could not conceal his frustration with Vinnie's false hope.

"*We* don't, but I know who does," said Vinnie with a tone of self-satisfaction. He turned to Gianni.

"You just said even a priest doesn't know which prayers will be answered. That made me think of Don Carnivale. I think he knows, not about prayers but about Ben's location."

"I don't understand. Why?" asked Delgrado.

Gianni repeated the question and added, "How? He's the parish priest."

"You mean priests don't do bad things?" Vinnie asked with an edge to his voice. "Because I can tell you they do and everyone knows it."

A short silence passed to let Vinnie's comment soak in.

"Look, we're wasting time," Vinnie said, upset and near shouting. "This may be a stretch but the woman Gianni and I met on the road saw a large white man. She told Don Carnivale and I'm sure this was for a reason related to their lodging location."

"And where's that?" asked Delgrado.

"I don't know exactly, but somewhere in the Nebrodi Park."

"Why?" asked Gianni.

Delgrado answered for Vinnie. "Because transporting the women to daily Mass had to be efficient."

The Commissario asked more questions to understand Vinnie's conclusion and found himself being shouted at.

"We're fuckin' wasting time! Let's get to the priest and

311

as fast as possible. You're the Commissario, arrange a police escort," Vinnie demanded, walking randomly with constant changes in direction.

"Okay. Calm down," said Delgrado. He followed a police cruiser to the church rectory and two cruisers trailed him. Vinnie sat in Delgrado's front passenger seat and Gianni in the back.

"Don't get your hopes up. We don't know where the van driver or the bodyguard went," Delgrado said.

Vinnie stiffened and he screwed up his face. "Don't you fuckin' say that."

Gianni leaned into the back of Vinnie's headrest. "I saw the van go toward the autostrada and not the provincial road to the Nebrodi Park," Gianni said.

Delgrado talked into his police radio. "Stop all cars leaving the A20 at Vigliatore." He turned to Vinnie. "That's the nearest exit for the Strada Statale, the state road. All other exits lead to small provincial roads that add an hour to reach the Nebrodi Park entrances."

"I know it," said Vinnie. "It was the road Mancuso used to go to the pizzeria in Barcellona, and even that road has a lot of sharp curves. It's not good for high speed, especially in a van." Vinnie's voice had a little more spring to it.

Delgrado glanced at the clock on the dash. "It'll take them an hour to reach the nearest Nebrodi Park entrance and another thirty minutes to get anywhere with cabins or abandoned farmhouses," Delgrado said.

"We can do this," Vinnie said with the enthusiasm of a coach pushing his team.

"Yes, it improves our chances but we still have to assume

they've phoned ahead. Aquafreddo either already knows or will very soon once he gets the call."

Vinnie sternly wagged his index finger at the Commissario. "Not necessarily. Gianni and I know there's no mobile reception in the Nebrodi Park anywhere near our hotel. We tried and failed," said Vinnie.

Gianni called out, "*Si, si,* and Signor Cucuzza told me that most of the northeast is without service."

"Assuming that's the zone where they're keeping Ben," cautioned the Commissario.

Vinnie kept quiet and lowered his eyes.

The Commissario pressed the pedal to keep up with the lead police car that had picked up speed. All sirens were blaring and dome lights flashing. They were five minutes from the village church.

Chapter 46

Commissario Delgrado's car tires screeched rounding the last corner at high speed. Vinnie chewed his nails. Everything rested on his assumption that the parish priest knew about the refugee women's housing, and maybe Ben's location.

The rectory caretaker cracked opened the door with her customary hesitation. The police cars' flashing blue lights reflected in her dark eyes. She recognized the rude *Americano* who had barged in the other day. She put on reading glasses to study Commissario's identification card—*Commissario Lello Delgrado.*

"No need to announce us," said the Commissario, "just take us to Don Carnivale."

Out of habit, she squared her body to protest but stopped as the Commissario bent down to put his nose close to that of the diminutive woman.

"*Subito. Non fai la brutta figura,*" said the Commissario—don't look foolish.

She nodded.

Don Carnivale sat at his desk and was surprised to hear his housekeeper tell him three men were asking to see him.

"*Permesso?*" asked the Commissario, extending the courtesy to the priest to ask first before entering his room.

The priest waved him in with Vinnie and Gianni following. Don Carnivale began with pleasantries but Vinnie abruptly stopped him.

"We don't have time for this. You need to answer a few questions truthfully," he said, waving aside the priest's invitation for him to sit. "Let's start with the refugee women. Where are they housed?"

"I'm... what is this about?" the priest asked, sitting upright in his high-back leather desk chair.

"Don Carnivale, with all respect please answer Signor Briggs' question. Or, if you prefer, I can take you to the police station to hear your answers there."

"I don't know what you want, I'm a simple parish priest. I know nothing of these things," Don Carnivale said as he stiffened and sat a little more upright.

"So simple that I heard you had a week's vacation in Israel in March," Vinnie said, leaving out that he heard this from Signora Cucuzza passing on village gossip.

"Not a holiday. A religious excursion to the holy sites," the priest said with a hint of indignity.

"Then what about the week in June you went to Paris? I heard about that trip too. Was that also a religious experience?" asked Vinnie chewing on his lips, his face getting red.

"What has this got to do with the women?" Don Carnivale asked, sticking his chin out. "Don't come in my house, my office, and ask me to explain my travels."

Vinnie shifted his feet, his hands curling into fists.

"Stop the bullshit. You know more than you're saying

315

and the expensive trips are proof—" Vinnie was interrupted by Don Carnivale.

"Proof? Of what? This is outrageous," said Don Carnivale, looking at the Commissario.

Delgrado stepped in front of Vinnie and leaned over to be closer to Don Carnivale's face.

"You either start talking now or we go to the Questura with you in handcuffs. You know we'll get to the bottom of this sooner or later and there are lives at stake. Where's your compassion man? Fidelity to God to do good?" asked Delgrado with his lips thinning and face puffing.

Don Carnivale closed his eyes, his hands folded together. He let out a sigh and looked up.

"I'm not sure if this helps, but the... uh... the parish owns a large cottage in the Parco di Nebrodi that is no longer used," Don Carnivale said but he was interrupted by Gianni.

"I know it. We went there with our Catholic Youth Organization for weekend camping and prayer. We always had a great time but the trips stopped after I turned twelve," he said.

I can guess why, thought Vinnie but stifled his lingering anger with the Church.

"Yes," said the priest, staring at Gianni, "it was a loss to the CYO. When not used by the youth clubs it was rented to outsiders as a bed-and-breakfast. After a few years the cost of upkeep didn't justify continuing to rent it and the property fell into disrepair."

Vinnie turned to the Commissario and said, "Signor Cucuzza complained about guests he lost because of the retreat house's ideal in-the-park location. Room tariffs were subsidized by the dioceses. The parish is poor, but not Don Carnivale."

"Care to explain?" asked the Commissario, looking at the priest.

"Explain what?" he answered.

"Enough evasion." Delgrado walked around to the back of the desk and took hold of Don Carnivale's arm.

"No, no," complained the priest. "Okay, I'll tell you but I didn't know at the time."

"Plenty of opportunity for excuses later. Start talking," said Delgrado, his face becoming a charcoal gray with knitted eyebrows. He let go of the priest's arm and rejoined Vinnie at the front of the desk. He positioned his arms to leave no doubt he could reach across to grab the pastor by the throat if he wanted to.

Don Carnivale spoke slowly and softly. "A Catania transport company showed up one day and told me they worked in the refugee camps. They wanted a place to bring the migrants for respite. They paid the competitive room rates, made repairs, and upgraded the kitchen and toilet facilities at their expense."

"And what did you get?" asked Vinnie.

"Me?" asked the priest as if he'd been asleep.

"Yes, you. How much?"

"Nothing... very little," said Don Carnivale.

"That new car in your driveway doesn't seem like very little to me," Vinnie said with teeth bared.

"I... well, I received a commission for making the arrangements with the dioceses."

Vinnie's eyes narrowed and he leaned across the desk

mimicking Delgrado. The priest pushed his chair back to the wall behind the desk.

"When did you realize this was the Mafia and the cabin was used for prostitutes to work the highway? And don't tell me you never thought about it."

"No... not at first. The man who came to me was well-spoken in a tailored suit. Good leather shoes too. He introduced himself as Sandro Grattinato, a lawyer for the transport company. I met with the caretakers a few days later for the usual turning over the keys and examining the cabin for problems that might affect the insurance. As soon as I saw them I knew they were Mafiosi. You could smell violence on their breath. You met the van driver..."

The Commissario pulled Vinnie back by his shoulder as he saw his raised fist about to swing at the priest.

Don Carnivale bowed his head to whimper, "I tried to help the women. I insisted that part of the arrangement was for the Catholics among them to be allowed to hear Mass. I heard their confessions, which I will not repeat, but it confirmed everything you think is happening. I gave them money from the collection box."

Vinnie wanted to curse and scream but knew he had no time to vent his rage.

"And tell us about the man in the back of the van, what the woman told you."

"I don't know any more than what I said before. I'm telling the truth." Don Carnivale rubbed his arms to stop himself shaking.

"Why did you tell us about the man in the first place?" asked Gianni in Italian. "You didn't need to say a word."

The priest looked up. "I don't know. No reason. I prattle when I'm upset or to release tension."

"So no fuckin' reason, is that it?" asked Vinnie.

"Yes," whispered the priest with head bowed as if he'd just disclosed a dark secret about himself.

Vinnie and Gianni shook their heads. All their speculation leading to this interview was because Don Carnivale blathered when nervous.

"So where did they take this man? Or is he at the retreat house?"

"I don't think so... but... well, there's a smaller diocese house that's intended for clergy on silent retreats. Usually four priests, five maximum. It's for novitiates to contemplate in silence before taking their final vows. It doesn't get used as much these days with novices being so low."

Vinnie shook his head thinking, *Yeah, right? A handful of young, robust novitiates in a remote wooded cabin contemplating their celibacy vow. They may not speak but I doubt the nights are silent.* He almost burst out laughing.

"And this cabin, did you rent it to the same transport company?" asked Delgrado, stepping in for Vinnie.

"Uh... yes, but only in the last month. They were using it for management bonding or something like that. It meant nothing to me and the house isn't booked until the next monastic retreat in October. This rental is a bonus, a way to increase alms for the poor."

The Commissario leaned across Don Carnivale's desk. "And where is this house?"

The priest said the place didn't have an address but he could describe the road and turnoff marker, about a thirty-minute drive along narrow mountain tracks.

"I know it," said Delgrado.

"Me too," added Gianni.

All three left the rectory with Delgrado telling Don Carnivale he'd deal with him later. Outside the building, Delgrado barked at his officers to get rid of their cigarettes and put their asses into their cars.

"We'll have to hurry," Delgrado said, abandoning his own car. "Better to go in an official car," he added, then pointed to a policeman. "He drives faster and safer than me. We've lost the time advantage over the van—we may already be too late."

Vinnie climbed into the back seat of the police car. Gianni started to follow but Delgrado pulled him back. To Vinnie's surprise, Gianni threw a tantrum like an eight-year-old only with more vigor, disregarding his *bella figura* image. Delgrado relented and Gianni sat next to Vinnie, who couldn't believe the tantrum tactic had worked. That would never happen in New York City.

The Commissario motioned to one of the policemen from another vehicle to use his car to take Don Carnivale to the Messina Questura headquarters.

"And send more backup."

Vinnie cursed himself for not thinking about Don Carnivale sooner when Signor Cucuzza complained about him doing so well. He'd attributed the comment to a disgruntled hotel owner unable to compete with the church's subsidized retreat house. His body shook. Was it too late? Was Ben dead and they'd not even find whatever was left of his body?

Vinnie's remaining hope was that the retreat house had

no cell reception. If true, then the race between them and the van began at the ceramic store. The van had a head start, taking the autostrada to avoid capture, but the extra distance increased their time to reach the cabin.

The police Alfa Romeo had neared the Nebrodi Park entrance when Vinnie's burner rang.

"*Pronto*," he said, trying to sound calm.

"Vinnie, thank God. I thought for sure…" Paul LoBianco spoke haltingly. "…I don't know how… I can live with myself—"

Paul's soft sobbing replaced his words. Vinnie also choked up but said nothing.

"How? Where are you?" asked Vinnie. "I don't know what to do about Ben." The crying increased on both ends of the call.

A female voice came over. "Vinnie, it's Maria Alba."

"*Ciao*, Maria Alba, nice to hear your voice," said Delgrado with resolve and calm. Just as Maria Alba had done with Paul, he had yanked the phone from the hands of the speechless and emotional Vinnie Briggs.

"*Ciao*, Lello. We are with people who can't stop crying so it's up to us grownups to work this out."

Delgrado switched the phone to speaker, broadcasting the conversation to everyone. Vinnie didn't follow the rapid Italian and turned to Gianni for explanation but Delgrado shushed him.

To everyone's surprise, Maria Alba knew the priest's cabin location, having grown up in one of the small villages in Etna's shadow. Ironically it wasn't far from Paul's hiding place. She and LoBianco would meet them, and Delgrado cautioned them to wait for their arrival.

"Lello, I never proceed without you, otherwise why would I need you?" Maria Alba said, keeping her informal intimacy.

"Do they have cell phone reception?" yelled Vinnie into the phone in the Commissario's hand.

"Could do. It's a bit hit and miss in that area," Maria Alba replied.

Vinnie's face elongated, his eyes looking upward. Gianni shrugged and said, "*Buh*," with a nervous smile. Delgrado made no comment.

The setting sun illuminated Etna's fiery eruption, the smoke plume turning into a battleground of colors. Vinnie's mind pitted fear against hope.

Chapter 47

Ben stared at his sparse food tray with only a *primo piatto* of spaghetti alla Norma and no *secondo* main course. He knew this was his last meal.

The guards had abandoned their former semi-courteous attitude. Ben consumed his meal in minutes then shoved his plate across the table toward the oversized goons. One pointed his gun at Ben while the other tossed him a bed pan, his hand lowered to his zipper gesturing him holding his penis. "*Fare la pipì. La cacca,*" he shrugged and pointed to a corner of the room. Ben got it—piss in the pot, shit in the corner. Humiliation for his last day on Earth.

With the guards gone, Ben lamented his mistakes, his bodybuilding obsession, his treatment of Vinnie. The list went back years to his wife and son that died; then his first true boyfriend and lover died and bequeathed Ben his fortune—fat lot of good it would do him now, and no heirs except Vinnie and the Livorno godchildren. He'd let them all down for muscle that by the end of the day would be dumped in a hole in an unmarked grave. Etna at some future date would belch fresh lava to encapsulate him for eternity.

Ben fell asleep from depression more than fatigue.

He awoke with the door slamming into the wall. Frank Aquafreddo and Sandro Grattinato stood inside, flanked by the two bulldog guards with their weapons at the ready.

"We're waiting for the exchange. You'll be released when we have Paul," Aquafreddo said. "You'll want to clean up." One guard carried in a half-full water basin, soap, wash cloth, and towel.

"A shower would be easier and faster," said Ben, knowing this was all for show. There was no exchange. The lie was easy to expose but why bother? It wouldn't change the outcome. "Shall I take the plates as souvenirs?"

Sandro laughed and Frank's Sicilian curse brought smiles to the guards. Ben asked if they wanted to watch. He flexed his pectorals, tightened his abdominal muscles, and rubbed a hand across his crotch. Another short laugh came from Sandro while Frank's scowl stretched wider. A third man arrived with Ben's clothes ironed and neatly folded. Ben thought there'd be no end to this Goldoni comedy.

"You still have it," said Frank, flexing his own arm. "I'm sure Vinnie will appreciate the effort you've made to stay in shape."

Ben's eyes rolled into his eyelids. "I'll finish here in a few minutes. If you don't intend to stay and watch and get off on seeing me naked, then just fuck off and leave me alone."

Aquafreddo glowered. He stepped forward, his jutting neck forcing his head forward. "You're a fool," he said, grabbing for his belt knife. Grattinato's arm pulled him back and turned him to the door.

"Get ready. It won't be long," Frank Aquafreddo said as the door slammed shut.

324

* * *

Darkness seeped into the dense forest canopy. Maria Alba's Cinquecento flew around the last bend on two wheels and Paul gave a sharp scream.

"We're fine," said Maria Alba, turning to Paul. "I know these roads and I can see oncoming cars by their headlights."

"Keep your eyes on the road for fuck's sake!"

The next few bends were not as sharp and Paul's tension released for few seconds, which was like the brief relief as the dentist changed drill bits.

"What happens when we arrive? Have you and Delgrado worked this out?" asked Paul.

The engine roared as Maria Alba downshifted to negotiate a hairpin bend. Three more curves came in quick succession followed by a steep climb and then a short descent around another hairpin with Maria Alba braking hard.

"Almost there. It's down this dirt path about a kilometer." Maria Alba tucked the Cinquecento between two trees in a space not wide enough for a large dog to wag its tail. "I'll go ahead and you wait here for Delgrado and his troop of uniformed buffoons."

Paul protested as she grabbed her purse from the back seat.

"You afraid I'll steal it?"

She unlatched the top to remove a revolver then handed the bag to Paul. "Spend whatever you like. And stay in the car to keep from becoming a meal for the feral dogs." She marched off like a Marine on parade.

"And try reaching Delgrado," she called over her shoulder as she jogged to the stone house.

Maria Alba knocked on the cabin door to be confronted by a *portiere* gatekeeper whose size was measured in cubic yards. He was six inches taller than her and sneered with an acne-riddled face, his cube-like head squatted on a bollard neck. He blocked the entryway as Maria Alba craned her neck to look up at the gargoyle looming over her. Through his semi-closed eyelids he stared at her as if she were the weirdo. She demanded to enter with a self-assurance that took him by surprise.

He escorted her along a single corridor with all rooms on one side as if replicating the old-style Italian Ferrovie dello Stato railroad carriages. He nudged Maria Alba's back, thrusting her into a kitchen, and if not for his tight grip around her upper arm she would have sailed across the room. Frank Aquafreddo and Sandro Grattinato looked at Maria Alba as if their takeout pizza had just arrived.

"Well, the elusive female contact," said Frank.

"I know her," said Grattinato. "She's the bitch-lawyer Maria Alba Vitale. She handles the Italian side of our contracts with that *faccia di stronzo* turd LoBianco."

"Better than the sheep snout next to you," said Maria Alba, her chin tilting toward Aquafreddo.

Aquafreddo withdrew his gun and aimed it at Maria Alba's forehead, but Grattinato pushed the barrel down toward the floor.

"You've got our attention," said Grattinato, signaling Frank to put away his weapon then tapping the tips of his opposing fingers as if he'd been waiting a long time. "You're here, so I assume you think you have something that will stop us from killing you and the muscle freak?" Grattinato said, then unconsciously looked up to the ceiling.

"Go ahead, pull the trigger," said Maria Alba as if turning down a date. "Then you'll never find Paul and I don't think your boss Mimi Ragno or Frankie's father Carmine will be happy. On the other hand, I can make them very happy."

"How? Paul's dead," Grattinato said.

"I guess you haven't heard. He's alive and I can give him to you."

Chapter 48

Paul stood outside the cabin as instructed by Maria Alba. He checked his phone. Zero reception. Could it be different at the house?

Five minutes later he saw the glare of headlights on the main road that then suddenly vanished. The beams had been switched off and only the dimmer running lights were on as the vehicle moved down the dirt lane. He concealed himself behind a tree at least fifteen feet from the verge and recognized the white van from the ceramic *laboratorio* in Patti. The driver didn't slow, which meant he or she was familiar with the uneven road.

Paul followed along the verge using the shrubs and bushes as cover but turned to step out onto the road and caught the glare of more headlights on the main access route. Like the van moments earlier, the car lights dimmed as it traveled down the dirt road. He walked back and with his cell phone's bright LED flashlight signaled to the police entourage.

The Commissario was first out to meet Paul.

"What are you doing standing exposed?" he asked. "Where's Maria Alba?"

Paul shook his head and rolled his eyes. "She's gone to the house."

"You're fuckin' kidding me," said Vinnie, pushing Paul and nearly causing him to fall. "She was supposed to wait."

"Let's not waste time," said Delgrado, who began to walk at speed down the path.

"Stop," Paul said. "A white van passed here only a minute ago."

Vinnie's hands covered his face and he doubled over. *We're too late.* He swayed and Gianni clasped his hand around Vinnie's forearm to steady him.

"*Basta!* Enough!" called out Delgrado in full police commander mode. "We're wasting time. No need to go in on foot—I'll drive us closer."

He turned to Vinnie, Paul, and Gianni. "You wait for the other cars and tell them to park here and run to the house— they'll be our surprise element," Delgrado said, knowing the fit young graduate cadets would cover the one kilometer in under five minutes.

Delgrado sat at the Alfa's steering wheel with four passengers but only one policeman, the other standing outside.

"What are you doing?" Delgrado said to Vinnie in the front passenger seat with Paul, Gianni, and the former police driver in the back.

"I'm coming," said Vinnie, and Paul and Gianni echoed his words.

Delgrado told the second policeman to get in the back seat and for Gianni to get out.

"No problem," said Gianni. "I'll run behind. I swim three kilometers every day so this will be nothing."

The Alfa moved slowly along the dark path without headlights and Gianni jogged along behind.

"Hurry up," said Vinnie, sitting impatiently in the passenger seat.

The Commissario gave Vinnie a quick glance as if to say he was welcome to get out of the car at any time. He then slowed the car to walking speed as the white van's taillights came into view about fifty yards ahead. The air within the Alfa Romeo stagnated.

Within a hundred feet of the house the car slowed to a crawl and then stopped. All got out to stand next to the Commissario, including Gianni who arrived a few seconds later as if he'd been on a leisurely stroll.

"Follow my instructions exactly. *Capite!*" Delgrado barked and then threatened to shoot anyone that didn't comply.

He turned to Gianni, giving him instructions in Sicilian. "Use all your strength to stop him," he said, pointing to Vinnie, "and keep him from following me and my police officers. His life and everyone else's depends on you. I don't care how you do it but make sure you do."

Gianni answered in Sicilian more or less guaranteeing he'd restrain Vinnie if necessary.

"Me and my men will go ahead and you wait…" but before he could finish Vinnie was already running down the road with Paul and Gianni following. The Commissario caught hold of Gianni's hand as he was passing.

"You fucked up already. Now wait here. You're the last witness if we don't return."

"*Si, si,*" answered Gianni, his eyes listless and his body

bent over as if having a stomachache.

The van's brake lights blazed red in the pitch-black wood, appearing like a small forest fire. The van was parked in a small bay to the side of the retreat house a hundred feet from the front door. Delgrado pointed to two men walking to the other side of the van, presumably to retrieve something. The cabin's front door momentarily opened and the vestibule light spilled around a large man who called out for the new arrivals to hurry up.

One van man told the *portiere* to mind his fucking business and they'd be with him in a minute. They entered carrying guns.

"They'll tell them what happened," said Paul, crouching with hands on his knees to steady himself. "Maria Alba's as good as dead. She has nothing to bargain with at this point. We have failed."

Vinnie knew all about plans unraveling at the crucial last moment. His mind raced. "We have three or four minutes max before they explain." Vinnie stood. "Paul and I are going in," he said, imagining this to be like a TV cop show.

Delgrado looked at Vinnie as if he'd turned into a goose. "That's crazy."

"Now twenty seconds have passed," said Vinnie. He ran forward toward the cabin. Paul followed and the Commissario began to chase but caught Gianni in his peripheral vision.

"*Che cazzo?*" he growled. "What the fuck happened to following orders?" He blocked Gianni's path and told him to take his car and drive back and tell the recruits to forget jogging and drive at full speed.

"And don't forget to tell them there are four of us good guys inside so not to shoot everything that moves."

Delgrado gave up on any kind of stealth approach. He turned back to Gianni with one more order.

"And they should pack extra ammunition."

Vinnie reached the front door estimating they had two minutes or so before everything went south. He pounded on the front door, putting as much strength as he could behind each blow without breaking his wrist.

The lunk opened the door, looking down at two more little people on his doorstep. His pitted face turned purple. He was more menacing and uglier close up. Vinnie thought he and Paul were like children lost in the woods facing a monster. The *portiere* didn't notice that fifty feet behind stood Commissario Delgrado, crouching with gun drawn.

"Yeah, what you want?" asked the beast in Sicilian so thick neither man understood and only guessed his question from his intonation.

"We're here to talk to Frank Aquafreddo," said Paul, replying in Italian.

"And why would he want to talk to you?" asked the man, switching to Italian, but his heavy southern accent didn't improve their comprehension by much.

"Because I'm Paul LoBianco."

Vinnie calculated at best they had a minute before the van driver revealed the raid at the Ceramiche Siciliane Bellani. No time to waste talking to the Phantom of the Opera. Vinnie crouched down the way a shorter basketball player dribbles around freakishly taller players. He barged across the threshold, taking the beast by surprise. The man swiveled to grab Vinnie by his shirt collar. Paul took advantage and slipped past on the other side. The big man didn't have the flexibility or coordination to swing around to catch Paul while holding Vinnie, who kicked him hard in his knee.

The *portiere*'s momentary indecision and pain caused his grip to loosen. Vinnie wriggled free and sprinted down the hallway past Paul, who stumbled. They dashed forward with the lumbering doorman in pursuit. Vinnie quickened his pace but rather than turn into a room with voices he continued to the end of the hallway, his hand signaling Paul to go into the room. Paul understood the divide-and-conquer maneuver, seeing Vinnie mount a staircase at the end of the hall.

Paul entered the kitchen to hear the end of a conversation.

"...you're telling us they have our women and our diamonds?" asked Grattinato, talking to the van driver.

Frank Aquafreddo reach behind his belt, not for his gun but for a large hunting knife.

"You fucking stupid bitch," growled Aquafreddo. "You'll pay—"

Before he finished his sentence he had the knife angled at Maria Alba's throat, just as Paul entered the room followed by the giant *portiere*, setting off a domino effect. Paul stopped but the enormous *portiere*'s body obeyed Newton's Laws of Motion and he bowled into Paul, who knocked Frank Aquafreddo into the kitchen table, his knife dropping to the floor. The two guards pulled out their guns but were unsure if they should aim at Paul or the doorkeeper.

Aquafreddo pushed away from the table and turned to Paul. "Good, now we have the fucker, the lawyer bitch, and the balloon bodybuilder! *Finito*," said Aquafreddo. He ordered the driver and his assistant to shoot them but leave Paul unhurt.

"I'll take care of this fucking traitor myself," Frank said, bending to pick up the blade from under the kitchen table.

The men froze, unsure if they had heard correctly, and looked to Sandro Grattinato.

"No! Stop. Not here. The mess will be too much to clean up. We'll leave evidence." He turned to the van men while swinging his arm in an arc from the driver and his assistant to Maria Alba and Paul.

"Tie them up and put them in the van," he ordered. "And dispose of them far from here."

Maria Alba realized she'd been granted an extension on her life, the second in minutes.

The doorman headed to a corner cabinet to bring out a length of rope. He tied Maria Alba and Paul up while the driver's and his assistant's guns pointed at their heads.

"And what about the other guy?" asked the *portiere*.

"The bodybuilder?" asked Grattinato, whose words told Paul that Ben was still alive. For now.

"No, the little one. He must have gone upstairs."

Frank Aquafreddo darted out of the kitchen's back door to find Ben's bodyguards smoking.

"Hey, you two—get the fuck inside and upstairs and shoot the guy running around!"

The guards tossed their cigarettes and entered the kitchen, guns drawn. One waited for Frank Aquafreddo, who waved him to go on. He heard cars on the lane and wanted to check it out.

The guards entered, slamming the door with Grattinato barking at them, "Get the hostage and the little *finocchio* faggot with him!"

Frank walked to the cabin's front and stepped into a rut from a broken water drain spout. He fell over, spraining his ankle. He rubbed his injury and twice stumbled trying to stand. "Fucking goddamn shithole of a place! Can't even keep up the repairs!" On the third attempt he was upright yet faltered moving forward. He gained an unobstructed view of the curved gravel driveway to see police cars rounding the bend. He had no time to warn the van driver and bodyguard so he returned to the kitchen.

* * *

Vinnie was midway along the hallway when he heard a commotion downstairs. He stood at a large oak door with a heavy bolt across it. *This is Ben's room,* he thought. He pounded on the door with his fists. *I'll need a sledgehammer to break in.*

More fist pounding. "Ben! It's Vinnie. Can you hear me? Are you okay? Ben! Ben!"

Vinnie waited and heard a muffled sound.

"Ben! Is that you!" he yelled.

With his ear pressed against the door he heard, "Hmph-mruph." Then came loud footsteps mounting the stairs and entering the hall. Vinnie ran to the end of the corridor to the last room. He slammed the door shut. The sparsely furnished room had a single bed, a small night table with a candle on it, a large wooden wardrobe, and a worn leather high-backed chair with a lamp next to it. A small wooden desk with a single solid wood chair was in another corner. A crucifix hung over the bed and a picture of Pope Francis over the desk. All the other walls were bare.

Vinnie wedged the wooden chair under the doorknob as a temporary restraint that might buy him a few minutes before the guards burst in.

Gunshots sounded. "Oh no, not Ben. Please not Ben."

Chapter 49

The *portiere* pushed his two captives to the front door trailed by the van driver and his bodyguard. The thug shoved Maria Alba and Paul to one side while he opened the van's sliding door. A cold barrel pressed against the *portiere's* temple.

"Stop!" Commissario Delgrado demanded. Two policemen emerged from behind the Alfa to reach the van and handcuffed the giant. The *portiere's* size and the night had prevented the van driver and the bodyguard seeing Delgrado until too late. Two policemen and the Commissario flanked the van driver and bodyguard with guns drawn. Delgrado cut Paul and Maria Alba loose.

Four policemen drove at speed down the wooded path but without the lights and sirens.

"Vinnie's inside," Paul said, his voice quivering. "I don't know where he is exactly but he went to the staircase in the back." Paul's body shook and he was waving his hands in frantic gestures.

Delgrado and three police officers ran into the stone house. They turned into the kitchen and saw Grattinato take a step out of the back door looking for Frank Aquafreddo. He squinted into the darkness, saw nothing, and returned to the kitchen.

"What the fuck!" yelled Grattinato, startled to see guns aimed at him. He gently lowered his own onto the floor and raised his arms.

"Where's Vinnie?" asked Commissario Delgrado.

Grattinato smirked with lips sealed tight as if smiling might cause his teeth to fall out. Two more officers entered the room and handcuffed him.

Delgrado mounted the staircase two at a time followed by a policeman and policewoman, guns drawn.

The policewoman moved ahead of the Commissario. She crouched, advancing slowly down the hallway while peering into open bedrooms. An addition to the original farmhouse created an odd shape upstairs with an S-curve hallway to align new with old. The curve prevented seeing the entire hallway but did not block out sound. The policewoman heard a voice.

"Not in here," called out a guard.

She signaled to the Commissario that the voice was on the left and she continued moving forward followed by Delgrado and the second policeman.

"Not here. He's in the last room," called out a second voice.

The policewoman signaled Delgrado that the noise came from a room on the right.

The guard on the left-hand side entered the hallway. Whether he heard a sound or out of habit, he looked toward the policewoman. Before he could say anything, the guard from the right was in the hallway but proceeded down the hall to the end.

The first guard had his semi-automatic gun pointed at the policewoman and she had her weapon aimed at him. Commissario Delgrado yelled to the policewoman to drop to her knees. She did and he shot the guard through his shoulder and he dropped his weapon.

The second guard turned around upon hearing the gun-shot.

"Put down your gun!" yelled Delgrado.

The guard fired his semi-automatic, the hail of bullets forcing Delgrado and the two police officers to duck into rooms.

The shots reverberated down the hall of the old retreat house. Vinnie was frantic and said out loud, "Please not Ben!" Then added, "And not Paul either."

He had no choice but flee or be killed. Vinnie opened a window to peer down at the ground. The second-story bedroom was too high for him to jump without risking a broken leg.

With more rapid gunfire, Vinnie reasoned that jumping would cause less damage than a bullet in the back of his head.

Beneath the window was a flat and narrow overhang that ran the length of the rear porch to a rain downspout at the end. Vinnie gingerly moved sideways along the slippery wooden board covered with moss. He stopped twice and each time the flimsy wood edge creaked and flexed.

At the end he slipped as a piece of the overhang snapped off. Vinnie took baby steps to reach the gutter. He knelt then lay flat on his stomach to inch backward over the edge. His foot hit the downspout and he wrapped his legs around it.

He shimmied down until halfway when the masonry

pipe snapped, dropping him onto his side. A searing pain ran up his groin and his ankle throbbed. His knee hit a large boulder, adding to his injuries. He didn't think he had broken bones but that didn't lessen his agony.

After several shallow breaths and one large inhale, Vinnie staggered into the forest unable to run. The tree line was thirty feet from the house. He had to reach it for cover to avoid anyone having a clear shot. Then he'd put as much distance between himself and the retreat house.

Is Ben dead? Paul? The questions prevented him from devising a strategy. He continued limping to the first tree despite knowing the answers to his questions were back at the house. From behind the tree he looked at the building. A large man peered out of the upstairs window into the darkness—one of the guards.

He didn't take long to smash in the door, thought Vinnie, breathing through the pain.

The guard stepped onto the flat ledge and moved along to the end. He'd spotted Vinnie, pulled his gun, and took aim.

Vinnie ducked as the guard shot. He waited until there was no more gunfire, then peeked out from behind a tree. He saw the bulky guard writhing on the ground. He'd fallen. *I knew that roof edge would snap.* Did the guard break a leg? Vinnie didn't wait to find out and resumed limping into the forest and away from Ben.

* * *

With the cop cars approaching the house and the van holding three of the Mafia team, Frank Aquafreddo retraced his steps

340

to the kitchen to find a guard on the ground clutching his leg and moaning.

"The cops are here. Help me up, my fuckin' leg's broken," said the injured man.

"What happened upstairs?" Aquafreddo said, jerking his head upward.

"They caught us by surprise. The guy escaped out the window and I saw him going into the woods." The guard pointed in the direction of Vinnie's tree. "The bodybuilder is locked in the room."

Aquafreddo spat at the guard. "Vinnie Briggs got away! You goddamn piece of shit!" He stood behind the guard's head, pulled a long knife from its sheath, and causally slit the man's throat. He wiped the blade on the dead man's shirt as he coughed and spluttered blood all over the floorboards, then returned it to the sheath on his belt and hobbled into the woods.

* * *

Delgrado knelt next to the guard he'd shot.

"Where's the bodybuilder and his friend!" he shouted.

The wounded guard remained mute, his face a mask of agony.

The policewoman stepped over the man, nudging past Delgrado. They walked further along the hallway to the last room, passing a wide, solid oak door locked with a nine-inch bolt screwed into the wall and secured with a large metal padlock. The policewoman called to Ben advising him to move back and she fired her gun. The lock fractured on the first shot. She entered with her gun held in front followed by Delgrado.

"Anyone?" asked Delgrado.

The woman moved her head upward while clicking her tongue, Sicilian for "no."

A banging came from behind an overturned table. "Don't shoot," came a low voice with a slight tremor.

"This is Commissario Delgrado. You can come out now."

Ben stood, his shirt ripped at the sleeves, his face a glossy red.

"Where's Vinnie? Is he okay? I heard shots. What happened?"

"He's somewhere in the woods. I'm going after him," Delgrado said and he turned to run down the hall.

Ben pushed past the policewoman, overtook the Commissario, and charged down the staircase. On the bottom step he gasped for air, taking deep breaths, then stormed out of the front door.

Delgrado stopped to instruct the armed police to enter the woods on opposite sides and find Signor Briggs. By now he was fifty feet behind Ben.

Although there was a cloudless sky, the thick forest canopy diminished the harvest moon's usual brilliance. Visibility was about fifty feet. Ben stopped to get his bearings and saw the Commissario dart behind the stone cottage.

I've got to keep going. He'll cover a different section, thought Ben. He listened for sounds, a noise, crackling twigs, anything to signify Vinnie's location. He saw movement but a brief shimmer of light proved it to be a swooping owl.

Ben slowed to orientate himself. He had lost sight of the Commissario's cell flashlight. His lungs demanded more air and his heart rate pumped at turbine speed. Without a proper flashlight he stumbled easily until he happened across a trail. He saw nothing trekking through the woods.

Where's Vinnie? Is he alive? I have to find him! That he could lose Vinnie and yet still survive became a new torment. Another loss in his life. Another person he had let down.

"Don't you dare get killed," he said to a Mediterranean pine.

He began to hyperventilate, became dizzy, and his vision blurred. His walked to regulate his breathing and his eyesight improved. After a short distance he came to a field, which he crossed hearing a cacophony of baaing from a disturbed flock of sheep. He used the bleating as a beacon. He marched across the short stubby grass then saw the noise epicenter—the sheep corralled in a pen. He struggled with his breathing yet picked up his pace. He made the enclosure his goal.

Chapter 50

The deeper Vinnie advanced into the forest the greater his disorientation became. A dull pain throbbed in his leg each time he climbed over a fallen branch or stubbed his foot against a rock. *Am I moving in circles?* He caught glimpses of the moon through fragmentary forest canopy openings. After ten minutes he came upon a footpath, neglected but at one time a route to somewhere. And even if overgrown it was easier to navigate with a leg injury.

He continued for what seemed forever until the path led onto a mosaic of heather, gorse, and scrubby grass. Crossing the open land exposed him but the harvest moon in a cloudless sky gave increased visibility, meaning faster movement. At the far end of the field stood an enclosure that he thought to be some kind of corral. If correct, then a farmhouse would be close by.

Halfway across the field he stopped to rub his knee. In bending over his peripheral vision noticed movement to his right. *A deer? A person to assist him?* He grimaced as he crouched and stared. A slim, stick-like figure was on the perimeter. The angle of walk and swinging arm reminded Vinnie of that same purposeful stride of the neighborhood bully in his Brooklyn school years. The only difference was this person had a noticeable limp.

On turning to run away, Vinnie stepped into a rut, reigniting his knee and groin injuries. He flinched and reflexive movement placed both hands on the searing pain shooting from his leg up his spine.

"Fuckin' leg," he said to himself, rubbing his inner thigh. The inflammation spread to his hip. He stood upright while grimacing and dragged the injured leg behind him, slowing his approach to the farmhouse.

The sight of Frank Aquafreddo sent Vinnie's mind racing. *Did Aquafreddo shoot Ben? No, it can't be. He has to be alive.* Another glance behind and he saw Frank gaining on him. Vinnie's heart pounded. He saw the farmhouse roof that was towards the bottom of a hill. Probably the distance of a football field from the corral, which he determined to be a sheep paddock from the sound of occasional bleating.

Aquafreddo limped along but was still faster than Vinnie, who knew the gap between them was narrowing. *I'll never make it to the farmhouse. He'll shoot once in range.* Vinnie's leg ached. *No, Frank won't use a gun. He'll want revenge. He'll slash open my throat and smile as I bleed out.*

He had no hope of reaching the farmhouse or any assurance someone was home and able to help. He changed destination for the sheep pen. He wanted to sit for momentary relief from the excruciating pain but kept going. Approaching the pen, the sheep jostled and increased their nervous bleating. He wasn't concerned about the noise revealing his location as Aquafreddo had already spotted him.

Sitting with legs extended, Vinnie nestled at the pen's gate, bringing the sheep toward him. *Should I go inside and try to hide among them?* He decided against this idea because it would only give Aquafreddo more of an advantage in the same way years ago that he had cornered Vinnie in a dead-end alley.

My best chance is to open the gate to release the sheep. I should have done it sooner.

Vinnie peeked beneath the sheeps' legs and saw Aquafreddo's slow, laboring walk and a grim look upon on his face. Taking advantage by holding onto the pen's frame, Vinnie lifted himself upright and released the gate's catch.

The flock bolted out in an exodus to freedom and knocked Vinnie on his ass. He crawled away from the gate as the pen emptied. He had an unobstructed view. The sheep surrounded Aquafreddo, who became disoriented. He momentarily stopped walking before continuing his march toward Vinnie.

"Hey, Briggs, I'm coming for you and I'm going to enjoy watching you cry, you little pissant."

A half-dozen nervous sheep surrounded Aquafreddo and one bumped into him and he fell.

"Fucking sheep!" he said. He pulled his gun and shot the two nearest him. He was getting closer to Vinnie.

"Feel at home, *Pecora*," blurted Vinnie. He had wanted to call Frank by his childhood nickname for years and was always too afraid, but it didn't matter now.

Vinnie raised one arm to cover his face seeing Aquafreddo withdraw his eight-inch blade from its sheath.

"You fucking little cunt," yelled Aquafreddo, slashing

wildly, enraged by Vinnie's insult. He was unsteady with the pain in his foot and cut into Vinnie's forearm but not at the angle he wanted.

Vinnie screamed, pulling his arm to his chest and holding it with his other hand to stop the bleeding.

"You're fucking dead meat, Briggs," said Aquafreddo as his raised his knife.

Chapter 51

Frank Aquafreddo swung his knife, this time having a clear aim at Vinnie's throat. He was unaware that behind him stood Ben, taking deep breaths as he lifted a sheep and threw it. The sheep hit Aquafreddo square in the lower back. He instinctively let go of the knife to place his hands in front of his face as he fell forward. The scurrying sheep stomped the knife into the soil. Aquafreddo lay flat on his chest, an emaciated man who resembled a refugee.

Ben placed a foot on Aquafreddo's chest and pulled on his arm until he heard the pop of a dislocated shoulder. He then stamped Aquafreddo's kneecap with the power he used to push a quarter-ton weight and was rewarded with the sound of crunching bone. Frank Aquafreddo's screams clogged his throat just before he passed out.

Vinnie picked up Aquafreddo's gun and aimed it at him, his shaking hand causing the gun barrel to bob and weave.

"Better give that to me before you kill one of us," Ben said, holding out his hand.

"Is anyone with you?" Vinnie asked, his heart bursting at seeing Ben alive and well.

"I was following Delgrado but we got separated."

"Maybe shoot the gun in the air? Get their attention?"

Ben's eyes brightened and he fired off a round then said to Vinnie, "You really are a smart detective, aren't you?"

"And you really are fuckin' strong."

Three groups descended from different directions onto the field, all running with weapons drawn. Gianni arrived first thanks to his youthful vigor. Without hesitation he hugged and kissed Vinnie, who pushed him back while introducing him to Ben.

Gianni threw his arms around Ben's neck and kissed him on the lips. "You have a wonderful spouse. I envy you."

Ben's stare was as blank as the sheep around him, forgetting he was clutching an automatic weapon until a policeman pried it loose from his grip.

"You're lucky you're still alive," Delgrado said to Vinnie.

"I don't think he's going to harm me now," said Vinnie, pointing to the handcuffed Frank Aquafreddo doubled up in agony on the ground.

"Not him," said Delgrado with his lips tight and thin. "I mean me. I'm debating whether to shoot you myself."

Vinnie and Ben kissed and held each other's hands. Vinnie didn't manage more than two steps before his knee gave way. Ben picked him up and turned to the Commissario.

"He needs to get to an emergency room right now."

* * *

Vinnie sat upright in the hospital bed, propped by a large pillow behind his head. He listened to the doctor explain the seriousness of his wound. Frank Aquafreddo's knife had cut deep into his forearm and it required fourteen stitches and a splint to immobilize it.

The distinguished-looking surgeon wore an official white coat with a stethoscope hung around his neck and held a clipboard in one hand. He stroked his thin mustache with the back of a pen while making facial gestures as he surveyed Vinnie's injuries. He lightly touched his wounded arm. Ben, on the other side of the bed, winced for Vinnie.

"You were very lucky," the doctor said in a surprisingly deep voice. "The wound is deep but it has not severed tendons or blood vessels. I cleaned it during surgery but you'll need to keep it spotless. Don't get it wet for at least two days, so no bathing."

"Yeah, yeah," Vinnie said, pulling back the bed sheets with his good hand as he started to rise. "I'll feel even better once I get back to my room."

The doctor pouted and shook his head. "Yes, of course, but Signor Briggs, I've admitted you and if all goes well you'll be discharged tomorrow afternoon or early evening."

"What?! No way," said Vinnie, scrunching up his face. "In New York it'd be stitches, Band-Aid, and out the door. No fuc... fudgin' overnight admission."

The doctor stared and tapped his pen on the clipboard.

"C'mon, Doc, is this really necessary?" asked Vinnie.

"Yes, if you want to use your fingers and hold a glass of wine again," answered the doctor. "The knife may have injured your ulnar nerve. It could be worse than a bad case of carpal tunnel syndrome. You might have no finger movement in a month. I've ordered blood tests, an MRI, X-rays, and nerve conduction tests."

Before Vinnie protested further, Ben approached the bed

to place a hand on his chest and push him back onto his pillow.

"Don't worry, Doc, he's staying even if I have to hold him down all night."

"A good idea, except you can't stay when visiting hours are over," said a petite nurse behind the doctor.

"What? No, I'll sleep in the chair," Ben said and his arms tensed, pressing hard on Vinnie's chest until he squealed and Ben relaxed the pressure.

"Sorry, Signor Hausen, it's against hospital policy unless the patient is a child or near death."

Commissario Delgrado entered the room, overhearing the nurse, and suggested the child status might apply to Vinnie. He waved his badge, which the staff disregarded.

Delgrado stood next to Ben and looked down on Vinnie.

"We'll need your help with the police paperwork and we'd like to record your testimony at the Questura. Can you stay a few days after you're discharged?" he asked with a flickering smile.

"You know," said Vinnie, "you could do the paperwork for the filing cabinet in one day if you didn't take a fuckin' nap every afternoon."

Commissario Delgrado looked at Vinnie's bandaged ankle. "Would it help your decision if I shot you in your other fucking foot?" he said, touching Vinnie's good leg.

The Commissario moved closer to Vinnie once the medical staff had retreated. "I've brought someone to see you even though it is strictly against protocol."

Paul LoBianco entered, limping from a sprain to his ankle he had sustained while running across the field.

Ben looked at Paul then Vinnie. "I'll leave you two alone. I'm going downstairs to get a coffee. Want one?" asked Ben.

Vinnie shook his head. Ben looked at Paul. "You?"

"Uh, no thanks."

"We're not enemies, you know," said Ben with a faint smile. "I heard from Vinnie that you... well, that you didn't... I won't say I'm happy you got him involved but we both know Vinnie." With that Ben left abruptly.

Paul rested one hand on the bed but avoided touching Vinnie. "You going to be okay?"

"Yeah, just a nick, nothing serious."

"Fucking liar, Vinnie Briggs. You were never any good at it."

After more banter, Paul's face blanched. "I don't have much time. Delgrado wasn't happy about me coming here. He wants me in a safe house ASAP. He posted two Carabinieri in the hallway and another two at the hospital entrance."

"What's next for you? I mean after you leave here?" Vinnie asked.

"I testify before an Italian anti-Mafia tribunal then go to a secret New York address waiting to testify before a Grand Jury. After that, who knows?" Paul shrugged. "Assuming I survive."

Vinnie's eyebrows raised. *Survive? Does anyone survive? And what kind of survival, separated from family and friends? And for how long? Does an assassination order have a sell-by date?* He couldn't shake the image of Aquafreddo's evil, pockmarked face, thin lips, pinched nose, and dirty face. The long-bladed knife glinting in the bright harvest moon.

Vinnie shuddered. He'd have nightmares once he finished the sedative medication. He'd been here before.

"What about me and Ben?" asked Vinnie, quietly pleading for the answer to be "yes."

With his head cocked, Paul answered, "You've survived so far."

Vinnie touched the bandage covering his stitches. He chewed his tongue a little before he said, "A skilled marksman shot Mancuso, not Delgrado." He paused. "Or should I say sharpshooter because it was a woman?"

Paul's eyebrows lifted but he said nothing.

"If I can't lie, you can't keep a straight face when trying to act dumb. We both know it was Serafina." Vinnie stopped and pointed his finger at Paul. "Don't plead ignorance."

Paul shrugged.

"And she killed Al Renato as well."

Another shrug.

"Why does she endanger her own life?"

"A tragic personal story," said Paul with a slight shake of his head. "This stays between us."

Vinnie nodded.

"It's a long and sorry tale but the upshot is the mob killed her family for their refusal to continue paying protection money on their vineyard," Paul explained. He told him about Serafina's life as an orphan when she was taken in by her aunt and uncle, who were Maria Alba's parents.

Vinnie's words tumbled out. "I get her killing for revenge, but… uh…how do I say this? Why the prostitution?"

"Everyone's pleaded with her to stop. Her aunt, uncle, Maria Alba, and me but she wouldn't listen," said Paul, showing his teeth. "It's her choice. She wants to inform on the highest level of power, which she can easily access given her extraordinary beauty. She gets to choose and she does—the top bosses, judges, and politicians. Al was an exception, but that was at the request of the anti-Mafia squad and their interest in the Aquafreddo connection."

For a few moments neither spoke.

"I want to tell you something I should have said a long time ago," Paul said as he touched Vinnie's hand. Vinnie started to retract then took hold of Paul's fingers.

"Go ahead, tell me."

"It goes all the way back to high school. My mistake. I've no one to blame. Call it cowardliness. I couldn't accept who I am. My biggest regret is that we are not together."

Vinnie withdrew his hand from Paul's and held it up.

"No, it's not like that," said Paul wistfully, looking at his palm devoid of Vinnie's. "I'm not asking you to leave Ben. I wouldn't and... well, you know the isolation of exile. I won't see you again once I'm in the Witness Protection Program. This is our last time together. I wanted to tell you that I've always had a deep affection..."

Paul stopped and laughed. "What a goddamn corny expression! Here's what I want to say. I love you. I've loved every minute we were together in our childhood and through our immature adolescence in high school. I loved every meal your mother prepared for us... well, I loved everything before it all went bad."

Vinnie shook his head. "Me too, yet here we are. Different life paths. I wish you had found courage, not just to come out, but that you'd rejected your uncle's lure of money, luxurious lifestyle, and the sex—both, right?"

Paul's head rotated from side to side.

Their conversation petered out with nothing left to say but goodbye. Vinnie motioned for Paul to lean over and gave him a kiss on his forehead. "To what might have been."

"Goodbye, Vinnie," Paul said, making his best effort to prevent his shiny smile from crumbling. He walked away then stopped to turn around. "And thanks for everything."

Paul's back heaved, loaded down by the forever farewell.

Chapter 52

The hospital discharged Vinnie the next day in the late afternoon with all test results negative for nerve damage. He hobbled into Hotel Mezzogiorno on crutches, complaining as Ben held his arm.

"I can do this. I've had a broken leg before so I know how to use these fuckin' things." Vinnie shook one crutch.

"Sure. Just want to help... and not only with the walking. I've been thinking about us, what happened to our life together." Ben touched Vinnie's shoulder and gave it a squeeze.

"Wait until we're in our room," said Vinnie.

Ben pulled his hand back but Vinnie reached out and took his arm. "Maybe a little help wouldn't be a bad idea."

The hotel staff had removed the mirrors, making the spare room emptier and less imposing. Vinnie sat on the couch waiting for Ben to bring him a bottle of water from the minibar. When he did he tested his injured hand on the lid and winced. Ben took the bottle from him and twisted the cap off.

"I'd have gotten it off," said Vinnie.

"I know, but why risk further injury? Wait a day or two until you're stronger."

Hearing the last word caused Vinnie to unconsciously look at the desk that once contained Ben's drugstore supply of enhancement supplements and needles.

"I discarded everything," said Ben with a nervous intonation. "Even the painkillers, which now seems like a bad idea," he added with a wistful smile.

"Ben, it's time we talked."

"Uh-huh, I guess so." Ben sat with the timidity of a child caught with his hand in the cookie jar. He nodded, his face grim. "This isn't easy for me... it's still raw. And I don't just mean the shootings. I mean—"

"Yeah, me too," said Vinnie, hearing fear in Ben's voice that sounded like his own. Was this the beginning of the end?

Vinnie continued, his voice shaky as if a wrong word would ignite old emotions, the bad ones. "It's hard for both of us," he said and hated his irrational fear of talking to his husband. If they couldn't talk freely then what kind of marriage was it?

"Yes, it is," said Ben. "You know when I think about what might have happened—" He shook his head and closed his eyes.

Vinnie shuddered, believing he had the same thought as Ben. This could be a graveside eulogy.

Ben opened his eyes, touched his breast, and let the words trickle out.

"Vinnie, we risked our own lives to save each other. To me that's proof of something. Is it love? If not, then why are we shaking like rabbits afraid to say the wrong thing?"

Vinnie sniffled, then rubbed his eye as if wiping away dust.

"You know I love you, Ben," he said after a few seconds, "I love you so much…"

"Me too," Ben said, slowly shaking his head and pursing his lips, the furrows in his brow a deep trench as he blurted out, "Damn it, Vinnie, I had sex with Ciccio. Only once… no, that's a stupid thing to say. I did it and how many times doesn't matter. I'm so sorry."

"I figured as much," answered Vinnie, "although I thought it was more than that."

"And where does that leave us?" asked Ben, his words halting.

Vinnie had never seen Ben, the strong alpha male, so nervous. His voice had always been steady, his words confident. This new personality didn't suit him and Vinnie didn't like it.

"I don't know," said Vinnie as he partially covered his eyes with his good hand. "A few days ago I'd have bolted out of here. I was mad. I wanted to spit in your eye." Vinnie stopped and bit his lower lip. "I wished Ciccio dead but not in the real sense." He paused again then whimpered, "I am so sorry what happened to him."

Ben inhaled as if sucking in all his mistakes but said nothing.

"You're alive and that's what matters more than anything. I… I just don't know what…" said Vinnie, choking on his words.

Ben put his arm around Vinnie's shoulder. "I feel the same."

The silence absorbed their thoughts, untangled emotions. Vinnie knew what he had to say yet feared going forward.

358

He had no choice. He had to know.

"Do you want an open marriage?" Vinnie asked Ben with more force than he'd intended. He saw Ben's forearm tighten. "Do you want a sex free-for-all? That's not what you said when we first dated. If you've changed your mind...uh...well, I don't know if I can go along with it."

"We didn't really date, not in the traditional way," said Ben with a little smile. "And no, I don't want to cruise bars or gyms for sex. I shouldn't have—"

"Then why'd you do it?" asked Vinnie.

"Why? I don't know," replied Ben.

"Sure you do. Just say it. Let's begin with why Ciccio?"

"Ciccio?" Ben looked at the palms of his hands seeking the truth, the cleft of his breast visible through his stretched shirt.

"I never got it," said Vinnie. "I mean I'll admit Ciccio is... was... a good-looking guy, easy-going, eager to please. But he didn't want a relationship. Let's be honest, he was a vagabond lover. He'd do anything to rub muscle. So why him? He was immature and nothing like you."

"He was there. Available." Ben stopped. "And someone to hook up with fast. I couldn't stand the thought of you fucking Paul."

"I didn't! I tried to tell you! I didn't have sex with Paul, or anyone for that matter. I've been faithful to you."

Ben's eyes were a portrait of sadness, his words crackling. "I didn't believe you. I was certain you had. A mistake, like everything else I've done." He looked at the spot previously surrounded by four mirrors for his posing.

"I wasn't sure I'd be good enough. I overloaded and the

stacking didn't help my emotion or thinking. I guess I don't like being older, where gains are harder. I need two weeks now for what used to take one. And then the dieting, losing the fat, water retention... everything is harder."

"So drugs and revenge were your motivation?" Vinnie's neck muscles ratcheted tight.

Ben nodded and he leaned forward, resting his elbows on his thighs and with his head up.

Vinnie stared into his eyes. "You subscribed to death on the pay-as-you-go plan for more muscle and glory. And it begs the question, why did you need to do it?" asked Vinnie, straining his jaw. He didn't want to repeat his mantra of long-term therapy to strip away the self-imposed shame. Remorse wasn't a solution. Vinnie knew this was not the time to remind Ben of people he'd lost but he couldn't stop himself as his anger rose. "It's your past, isn't it?" he said, his face flushed.

Ben's chest expanded with the hissing sound of air entering his nostrils. A moment later came a long exhale and no words.

Vinnie waited until impatience got the better of him. "We can't resolve this here. You know that as well as I do." He wanted to lecture him, tell Ben to forgo his muscular armor and being a bodybuilding god. "When are you going to discover the humility of being human?"

"I hate that expression, the so-called muscle-god syndrome. That's not what I want or ever wanted. I got caught up in the attention and I wanted to help Gunter reach the top. So I became what I'm not. You knew that all along or you would never have been with me."

Vinnie sighed and rubbed his face.

"You don't believe I can stop the stacking? That I can't change?" asked Ben.

"Not on your own. You're not omnipotent. No one is."

Vinnie strained to stop from saying more and paused to watch Ben's blinking eyes. He opened his mouth to break the silence as Ben began to talk.

"Can you ever trust me again? After Ciccio? After what I was doing?" Ben pointed at the desk and went quiet.

"What is your goal now?" asked Vinnie.

Ben's gaze swallowed Vinnie's eyes. "I'll wean off the test and... see a shrink," said Ben, puffing out small, laugh-like breaths. "I'll bet you never thought you'd hear me say that." His next words tumbled out from barely moving lips. "Can you forgive me?"

Can I? Vinnie asked himself, taking time to compose an answer.

"Right now, I want to." He looked at his injured arm. "Your near death, mine, everything... it's all changed. I don't know what I'll feel in a month when this is all behind us. I honestly don't."

"Me neither," Ben said.

Vinnie managed a small smile. "You know I forgave Paul, which was hard, and I still have moments of anger at him. And at this moment I want us to be together. And I know that no matter what, if we stay or separate, you'll always be in my life."

If Vinnie expected a reply, he got none and stared into Ben's eyes as if it were a window on his mind. *Did Ben not want it? Why the hesitation? What would I do without him? I thought him different from all the other guys I dated. He wasn't always all about strength and getting big. We talked about articles in the* New Yorker *and books, good ones and fun trash with homoerotic sex scenes. That stopped. Could we start again?*

Vinnie didn't know if he was about to cry or get angry. He needed to know Ben's thoughts and damn the answer. "What do you want to happen for us?"

"I want us to be together," Ben said and he knelt, pressing his lips to Vinnie's chin, then kissed him.

With that gentle touch Vinnie stirred. His skin tingled and his mouth dried. He opened his mouth and his tongue sought Ben's. He'd forgotten the sweetness of their kisses. For months they'd merely jousted, their perfunctory scripted acts. This was desire, not just sexual lust but love for something deep inside.

Vinnie's jaw ached and his forearm throbbed with the pulsing of his heart. He grew large. He moved his tongue faster and Ben did the same. Vinnie's good hand shot up to hold on to Ben's shoulder and he moaned.

"You okay?" asked Ben.

"Better than okay. I need you. I want to have sex with you," Vinnie said as his hand brushed over Ben's lips. "And you?"

"Me too, but..." Ben said and he pointed to Vinnie's injured forearm and his head tilted to the bandaged leg.

"If you're careful..." Vinnie would have leaped off the couch and risked more injury if only to appease the swell in his pants. He grabbed Ben's stiff crotch and knew him ready. *I missed this passion. We've been slaves to his artificial desires brought on by his roid urges. I miss his arms wrapped around me, squeezing to crush then release and do it again to make me feel safe. And I want to turn him on like never before.*

With an unruly noise outside, Ben turned to the window although it was too high to see below. "Sounds like kids playing soccer."

Vinnie thought about their first ballgame at Yankee Stadium, then Ben's surprise with tickets to *Madam Butterfly* at the Met and return home for great sex on the couch or floor and once on the kitchen table, which was a bit uncomfortable.

More noise outside. A definite cheer. Someone had scored.

Vinnie took hold of Ben's chin and forced his head back. "Let's try."

"Okay," he said, and he lifted Vinnie from the couch without straining.

The weightlessness excited Vinnie. This was not the first time Ben had hoisted him into the air. He often combined strength and agility for incredible acrobatic sex. *I've missed this so much, the lightness of being carried.*

Ben laid Vinnie carefully on the bed, checking his arm and leg positions were not tangled. He unbuttoned Vinnie's shirt but was afraid to pull it over the injured arm so he shredded it at the seams. Vinnie smiled, surprised he was not more upset that one of his favorite shirts had been ruined.

Ben lowered his head to unbuckle Vinnie's pants and Vinnie tapped his skull.

"Don't you dare split them," he said with a growl, "they're brand new."

Ben's head lifted to broadcast a wide grin before he returned to unzipping the pants. He pulled the waist wide open and slipped his hand inside to deftly lift Vinnie's buttocks while his other hand pulled the pants around his thighs to below the knees. He stared at Vinnie's boxers, gave a snorting laugh and ripped them in two pieces. Vinnie's penis sailed out. Ben gave it a light stroke on the underside and Vinnie shivered. Ben took less care with his disrobing but as a solidarity gesture he ripped open his shirt and flung it on the floor.

"Show-off," said Vinnie with a laugh.

"And what about this," said Ben, showing all his teeth and standing in naked glory, his Corinthian legs framing his manhood. He flexed a double-bicep pose.

Vinnie grinned and rolled his eyes. "Seen it before. What can you do with it?"

Ben propped himself next to Vinnie on the bed and lay on his side, his head jacked on one arm to let his eyes survey Vinnie's naked body. He moved closer until he rubbed against Vinnie's hardness, then hand massaged both as one.

Vinnie thought his skin would scorch from Ben's body heat. He groaned deliciously as Ben gently stroked him. All nerve synapses fully ignited and firing to amplify every movement. The smallest of breezes sent an electric shock up his spine. He ached.

He was in a reverie rubbing Ben's chest as he thought, *I love the way the tanning oil darkens his skin, makes it soft and silky, and I adore feeling the hard muscle underneath. Even the ropey veins that once revolted me are a turn-on.*

"I want this so much," Vinnie said softly.

Ben's hand gently stroked the back of Vinnie's neck,

exciting the small hairs on his nape. With a gentle roll he moved Vinnie onto his good side to run his hand inside his thigh and up to his ass, squeezing each cheek, and then massaged between the cleft of his legs from underneath. Vinnie yelped.

"You okay?" asked Ben.

"Don't stop," replied Vinnie as he lifted his buttocks back toward Ben. He shivered with anticipation. His toes curled and his limbs trembled. He begged Ben to go all the way, his words bubbling out.

"I want to but it's too risky," Ben said, turning Vinnie onto his back.

Ben's head rested on Vinnie's breast, listening to Vinnie's rolling sighs. Ben's massage started below Vinnie's sternum then moved down to gently twirl Vinnie's erection between his skilled fingers. His strong thumb pressed along the length from root to tip. Vinnie's mouth gaped. He thought he saw sparkles in the ceiling. He crumpled the sheets between the fingers of his good hand and worried he'd couldn't last much longer. He couldn't wait for Ben. His head filled with starbursts and flashing lights.

This was true love, not cheap, fast sex. He had never been this big and hard before. And inexplicably he recalled that he once told Ben, "I'm not just an Italian calzone after a hard night in the wood-fired oven." And they had both laughed so hard they fell on the floor.

Vinnie stopped grinning and repeatedly begged Ben to go further or at least try, but Ben refused.

"You'll enjoy what I've got planned, believe me," he said.

The refusal disappointed yet Vinnie was proud that Ben commanded action rather than reaction. This was the person he had fallen in love with. A man that planned rather than let raging artificial hormones dictate his desires.

Vinnie's arm moved along Ben's, digging his fingers into elongated sinew and every hard line of muscle. *This is my man, the one I want.*

"Get as close as you can against me," urged Vinnie, his throat dry.

They caressed and kissed each other's bodies. Ben's tongue rounded Vinnie's chest, who watched every move. Vinnie's face broke into a glowing smile as if he'd never seen their joint masculinity beating against each other.

Restricted to hands and mouth, Ben's lovemaking inspired ingenuity, not that he hadn't done it before. Nothing new, yet somehow all novel.

Ben whispered, "Leave the moving around to me."

He straddled Vinnie's torso and hovered inches above, push-up style, one leg on either side of Vinnie's and a hand next to each shoulder. Ben lowered, kissed Vinnie from forehead to lips to throat and then down along the chest. He scuttled down to continue kissing all the way past Vinnie's navel to the pulsing big prize.

This was the magic Vinnie had wanted for this Italian adventure. The excited, unbearable rapture like their first time. He wanted this moment to last forever and a day, and he hoped this was a prelude to their long and happy future together.

They held out for as long as possible then erupted, crying out the pain of the past and the pleasure of the present. They were spent and spirited.

They held each other as if shackled. Vinnie thought he couldn't be happier.

"Do you love me?" Ben asked.

Vinnie touched Ben's lips with two fingers. "As high as the moon and around the Earth and down to the bottom of the ocean."

"You better, because I love you even more," replied Ben.

Author's Note

A huge thank you to everyone who has taken the time to read *Salt & Pepper Man*. Readers help writers improve and sustain them, so I am grateful for your encouragement.

If you enjoyed *Salt & Pepper Man*, then please remember to leave a review. I listen to comments and use them to understand what works best for readers. I can't do much on the characters base personalities, because they are who they are.

You can learn more about the series and find more content by joining my mailing list. Be the first to learn of new releases in the Vinnie Briggs Mystery series by visiting the official website:

http://www.charlespuccia.com/

My experiences inspire my stories although the characters are fictional. Tell me your thoughts. What captures your interest in a mystery or romance novel? Describe a memorable event: outrageous, moral dilemma, unusual, or funny. If something similar has happened to me, then this may be Vinnie's next case. You can send comments to carlo60@charlespuccia.com

Share your opinions with others on Vinnie and his crew. And, please, if you enjoyed reading *Salt & Pepper Man*, leave a rating or review—one or two sentences are enough.

Review of *Detour Man*

"If you enjoy a 'thoughtful' mystery, the sort of story that keeps you guessing, a story populated with well-constructed characters, then this is for you."

—A 'Wishing Shelf' Book Review

Review of *Outlier Man*

"Reminded me a little of the old *Death Wish* films with the vigilante killer. Cleanly written with solid punctuation and grammar, I could imagine anybody who enjoys a sexy thriller would like this."

—Female reader, aged 56

Reviews of *Ice Cream Man*

"… feast of a book, Ice Cream Man! In his first novel, author Charles Puccia spins quite a tale, a believable story, filled with intrigue and, yet, fascinating to the point of amusement. Clearly a page turner!"

—P. Fontana, Amazon verified.

"A rollicking, raunchy read of corporate shenanigans with mafia overtones. Great characters, fun read."

—Andra, Amazon verified.

Reviews of *Baseball Man*

"From the start, Puccia won me with a Boston terrier named Ralph. I've got a weakness for dogs. Puccia crafts ordinary situations into eloquent prose like a fine artist. His use of strong verbs and gripping dialogue entertain and keep you engaged."

—R. Levinthal, Amazon verified.

"A wonderful romp of a novel, as Vinnie continues to lurch through a world inhabited by some rather unusual types. An engaging read, well-conceived and well-executed."

—Steve, Amazon verified.

Other books in the Vinnie Briggs series:
Ice Cream Man (No 1)
Baseball Man (No 2)
Outlier Man (No 3)
Detour Man (No 4)

Also available as audiobooks:
Salt & Pepper Man (narration by Austin Rising)
Detour Man (narration by Austin Rising)
Ice Cream Man (narration by Derick McClain)